"I'm not sure I lik[...] Riker said.

"I'm not sure I do, either." Admiral de la Fuego's tone had become stiff and bracing, discouraging dissent. *"The simple fact is that during the months since Typhon Pact–allied Breen agents made off with Federation slip-stream technology, Starfleet Command has been more concerned about internal security than at any time since the parasite infestation eighteen years ago. Ever since Andor's government announced its secession from the Federation, Command has become wary of Starfleet's Andorian personnel."*

Riker's stomach had begun to tie itself into a knot of disgust. "Admiral, I hope you're not saying that Starfleet Command intends to push its Andorian officers into accepting . . . forced repatriation."

The admiral shook her head slowly. *"No, Captain."* A look of thoughtful sadness crossed face as she trailed off, as though weighing her next words with the utmost care before delivering them. *"But Starfleet Command has decided it would be best for everyone concerned if all nonrepatriated Andorian personnel were to accept redeployment to some of Starfleet's less sensitive posi-tions, at least temporarily."*

Riker felt his frown deepen; he knew how easy it was for temporary measures to ossify into permanent fixtures.

"How soon?" he asked.

"In Titan*'s case? As soon as the* Capitoline *arrives to begin crew rotations."*

Don't miss all of the thrilling novels in the bestselling *Titan* series!

Fallen Gods
Michael A. Martin

Synthesis
James Swallow

Over a Torrent Sea
Christopher L. Bennett

Sword of Damocles
Geoffrey Thorne

Orion's Hounds
Christopher L. Bennett

The Red King
Andy Mangels & Michael A. Martin

Taking Wing
Michael A. Martin & Andy Mangels

STAR TREK
TITAN™

FALLEN GODS
MICHAEL A. MARTIN

Based upon *Star Trek*® and
Star Trek: The Next Generation®
created by Gene Roddenberry

POCKET BOOKS
New York   London   Toronto   Sydney   New Delhi   Ta'ith

Pocket Books
A Division of Simon & Schuster, Inc.
1230 Avenue of the Americas
New York, NY 10020

This book is a work of fiction. Names, characters, places, and incidents either are products of the author's imagination or are used fictitiously. Any resemblance to actual events or locales or persons, living or dead, is entirely coincidental.

First Pocket Books paperback edition August 2012

POCKET and colophon are registered trademarks of Simon & Schuster, Inc.

For information about special discounts for bulk purchases, please contact Simon & Schuster Special Sales at 1-866-506-1949 or business@simonandschuster.com.

The Simon & Schuster Speakers Bureau can bring authors to your live event. For more information or to book an event, contact the Simon & Schuster Speakers Bureau at 1-866-248-3049 or visit our website at www.simonspeakers.com.

Manufactured in the United States of America

10 9 8 7 6 5 4 3 2 1

ISBN 978-1-4516-6062-3
ISBN 978-1-4516-6063-0 (ebook)

*This book is dedicated to those who showed the courage
to put everything on the line
for fairness, for justice, and for basic decency,
from the shores of Tripoli
to the boardroom bunkers of Wall Street.*

HISTORIAN'S NOTE

The story begins about two months after the conclusion of *Seize the Fire*, or approximately two weeks after the finish of Dayton Ward's *Paths of Disharmony* (roughly stardate 59833.8, or November 1, 2382).

Trust not in princes—in a son of man,
For he hath no deliverance.

—*The Book of Psalms*, chapter 146, verse 3

If I have seen a little further it is by standing
on the shoulders of giants.

—Isaac Newton (1643–1727)

Prologue

TA'ITH

With the Thousand standing behind hir in reverent silence, Eid'dyl watched as the Heart of the Cosmos sank ever lower in the purpling sky, its baleful glow throwing long shadows across the ruined minarets and spires of the Sacred City's expanse.

Like any able-bodied member of hir tribe, Eid'dyl had ventured from the relative safety of the subsurface Preservationist Arcologies to make the same arduous journey during several bygone Pilgrimage Seasons, mostly during hir youth. Now, as then, skeletal remains of the architectural wonders left behind by the Whetu'irawaru Progenitors stood in broken, snaggled ranks amid eons of accumulated detritus, endlessly repeating a pattern of inevitably encroaching chaos that stretched out to the edge of the long-abandoned necropolis and past the limits of Eid'dyl's vision.

But the tableau that Eid'dyl now faced was freighted with neither the stillness nor the silence of those earlier

visits. Today the Sacred City's broad streets and boulevards reverberated with the murmurs and clamor
of life and hope. The throng that had begun gathering
here today was comprised entirely of Arava'whetu, to
be sure, rather than the extinct Whetu'irawaru who had
birthed them in the same misty antiquity that shrouded
the Sacred City's founding. Nevertheless, Eid'dyl could
almost make hirself believe that the approaching people
belonged to the former race rather than the latter.

"The Deconstructors come, Sachem Eid'dyl," Garym
said unnecessarily, punctuating hir words by gesturing
toward the gathering multitude with hir batonlike frontmost pair of forelimbs. Garym had served for many
Heartlaps as Eid'dyl's subsachem, hir steady hindlimb in
overseeing the business of the Preservationist Council,
the body that organized and perpetuated the ceaseless
labor of maintaining the tribe's frustratingly incomplete
store of extant Whetu'irawaru knowledge. Despite hir
lengthy experience, Garym had never lost hir proclivity
for uttering the obvious.

Deconstructors, Eid'dyl thought with no small
amount of distaste. S/he twirled hir midlimbs in a gesture that denoted both acknowledgment and impatience.
Trashers.

"I see them, Garym," the Preservationist leader said
aloud. "Let us hope their new sachem will understand
the benefit of leading hir people onto a path they have
yet to try." Eid'dyl had good reason for maintaining this
hope. The old leader of the Deconstructor faction had
been too full of superstitious fear to so much as consider
attending an intertribal summit like the one that was
about to begin here today.

The late-afternoon sky abruptly brightened, giving

Eid'dyl a graphic reminder of why such a fundamental change was so critically important for the survival of all who dwelled beneath the Heart of the Cosmos, the dispassionate Giver of Life and Death. The sudden brilliance caused hir to flinch involuntarily, and a collective groan of dismay passed among the Thousand who stood behind hir, and through the ranks of the approaching Deconstructors. In the scant pulsebeat before instinct pulled all four of hir forward sensory stalks beneath their wrinkled dermal hoods—thereby protecting the sensitive vision patches at each stalk's tip—Eid'dyl noted that the lightgeysers that marked the top and bottom of the Heart of the Cosmos had brightened tremendously, and had grown both thicker and longer. As if that change hadn't been dramatic enough, the sides of the Heart had swelled noticeably as well, the poles flattening as though the great orb were nothing more than a lump of moist clay set in the center of a crazily accelerating potter's wheel. Without any conscious volition, Eid'dyl raised a pair of multijointed forelimbs and spread their manipulative petals protectively across hir field of view, even though each of hir sensory stalks had already contracted more than tenfold. Pale orange light rushed in regardless.

"The Heart grows ever more restive," Eid'dyl heard Garym observe, hir words carrying a discomfiting air of portentousness.

Eid'dyl understood as well as anyone on Ta'ith that the Heart of the Cosmos knew all and encompassed all. But interpreting the specific content of the Heart's innermost thoughts and motivations was another matter entirely. Unwilling to pretend to understand that which might well remain forever beyond Ta'ithan comprehension, Eid'dyl could only wonder.

But presumptuous though Garym's words might have been, Eid'dyl found hirself unable to dismiss them outright. Could it be that the Heart's copious patience had at long last run out? Despite the risk of sacrilege, Eid'dyl couldn't resist speculating: Had the mighty fireglobe decided to render a final, irrevocable judgment against the Arava'whetu for having fallen so far short of the achievements of their long-dead Whetu'irawaru betters?

But like hir parents and their forebears, Eid'dyl had always believed that the Heart's judgment, when it finally came, would be both inescapable and permanent, bearing scant resemblance to the bizarre, fading afterimages that now raced across hir overloaded retinal tissues; though Eid'dyl had glimpsed but a literal eyeblink's worth of the Heart's latest eruption, hir visual cortex reeled from a slowly receding onslaught of dark, pyroclastic shapes and splotches of brilliant firecolor.

"The Heart becomes ever more ferocious as well," Garym said with a rattling shudder. "Perhaps because the passage of time has diminished its overall size."

Eid'dyl vibrated hir metal-rich organic carapace in affirmation until hir shell sang out in several distinct overtone pitches. Thanks to the Old Records, Eid'dyl knew well that the Heart was now but a pale remnant of the Great Daystar that had illuminated the firmament during Ta'ith's ancient Whetu'irawaru epoch. According to the eons-old Whetu'irawaru records, the Heart had once been both considerably larger than its present size as well as a far more stable source of life-sustaining illumination.

"You speak true, Garym," Eid'dyl said quietly. "Sadly, that truth has only grown deeper over the past quarterlap. All Arava'whetu now living upon the face of Ta'ith must credit the Heart not only for their lives—but also for the present sad brevity of those lives."

We cannot continue to live with the Heart for much longer, Eid'dyl thought, interlacing hir limbs, a gesture of determination commingled with desperation. *And yet we cannot live* without *it for any length of time either.*

Though Garym's tertiary thoracic stridulators quavered with audible sadness, the tone and timbre of hir speech—made audible by hir primary and secondary soundlimbs—were free of any evident fear. "And now we stand directly in the path of the Heart's full fury, without the roofs and walls of the Arcologies to protect us. I wonder if that means we are soon to join our ancestors beyond the Veil."

Eid'dyl experimentally relaxed the dermal hood on one of hir sensory stalks, tentatively exposing one of hir vision patches to the western horizon. The Heart of the Cosmos appeared to have set and forgotten its tantrum, at least for the moment. Though the reddening orb remained visibly flattened, its east-west axis and polar lightgeysers still distended as it continued its descent, the angry brilliance of the Heart's outburst had already declined to a far more pedestrian level of fury. Because the setting Heart had drawn so very near to the horizon, its radiance had to penetrate far more of Ta'ith's atmosphere than would have been the case a mere quarter-dayturn earlier.

"For good or ill, Subsachem," Eid'dyl said, working hard to keep hir speech stridulations calm and even, "I suspect your curiosity will soon be satisfied."

Eid'dyl watched silently as the foremost Deconstructor echelons came to a stop a mere dozen bodylengths away, their sensory stalks and forelimbs bent forward at aggressive right angles. Eid'dyl could feel the silent fear and tension of the Thousand who stood resolutely behind hir. Positioning hir own sensory stalks as nonprovocatively as possible, Eid'dyl took a cursory head count of hir approaching adversaries and determined quickly that the Trasher phalanx and hir own Thousand were a fairly even match, at least in terms of numbers.

"Where are the new Deconstructor leaders?" Garym said quietly—quietly enough, Eid'dyl hoped, so as not to provoke any ill-advised action from the Trashers' front ranks.

Eid'dyl watched in silence as Garym's query began to answer itself. To murmurs of surprise from the Preservationist Thousand, a gap opened up in the middle of the first row of Deconstructors, as though an invisible wedge had driven two of the nearest Trashers apart, forcing those on either side to make way. A moment later the second row behaved similarly, as did the next several, each in their turn. It was as though the massed Deconstructor ranks had parted down the center in a manner that made Eid'dyl think of the fault-riven magmalands of Ta'ith's geologically active equatorial region.

A pair of Arava'whetu, their exoskeletons adorned with numerous multicolored badges of office, emerged from the gap and strode directly toward Eid'dyl. Though their carapaces were pitted and rough in texture, looking more careworn and bowed than those of any but the most ill-fortuned Preservationist, Eid'dyl immediately recognized the new arrivals.

"Sachem Fy'ahn," Eid'dyl said by way of greeting after the pair had come to a stop at an uncomfortably close proximity. Taking great care to avoid reacting to the unpleasantly moist nearness of hir adversaries' respiration plates, Eid'dyl extended one of hir sensory stalks in a gesture of peace aimed at the older and more colorfully decorated of the two Deconstructor leaders.

Deconstructor Sachem Fy'ahn took no evident notice of Eid'dyl's formal somatic diplomacy as s/he stridulated a perfunctory greeting-response that might well have been calculated to give offense. "My subsachem, Yrsil," Fy'ahn said as s/he gestured absently toward hir lieutenant, using several upper right-side limbs. "We come with more than a thousand of our most accomplished weaponwielders so that we might bring the rumbles in the sky to a decisive end."

Fy'ahn's sentiment struck Eid'dyl as risible. Did the Trasher sachem intend to challenge the Heart of the Cosmos to combat? Eid'dyl held hir stridulators quietly rigid for a moment, allowing the temptation to sound an unresolved tritone of ridicule to pass by harmlessly. After all, this was no laughing matter. S/he knew in the deepest meat beneath hir carapace that hir own Thousand, specialized as they were to practice the Preservationist arts, could never stand against a like number of Trashers. Provoking the new Deconstructor sachem in any manner would be unwise in the extreme—especially with the fate of the entire world literally at stake.

But Eid'dyl also understood that lying to hir Trasher counterpart would be every bit as foolish.

"I am uncertain that such a thing is even possible," Eid'dyl said at length. "But if either of our tribes is to survive the furies that the Heart of the Cosmos still has in store for us, it will be because we have carefully preserved and attended to the wisdom of our Whetu'irawaru forebears."

"We crave that wisdom as well," Fy'ahn said. The

Deconstructor leader turned toward hir lieutenant as though seeking affirmation.

"That is so, Sachem Fy'ahn," Yrsil said, hir posture and limb position arranged to suggest carefully schooled neutrality. "That is why we have continued to live on Ta'ith's surface, as our mutual ancestors did. That is why we have not retreated to the deep places, as *your* tribe has done, Sachem Eid'dyl."

Despite the obvious distaste that colored Yrsil's last remark, Eid'dyl felt encouraged. In confident yet carefully composed stridulations, s/he said, "Our tribe and yours would appear to hold a common reverence for our mutual forebears."

"Of course we do," Fy'ahn said.

Eid'dyl's hopes soared higher still, though hir instincts counseled caution. "Then you can help us expedite bringing resolution to whatever ails the Heart. To that end, you can assist us in ascertaining the correct interpretation of all that we have archived about Whetu'irawaru technology."

Fy'ahn's forelimbs began moving in sharp, sawing motions, generating a harsh series of staccato phonemes. "Interpretation? What need have we of interpretation? The only possible course of action is self-evident."

"One must understand one's knowledge thoroughly in order to use it correctly," Garym said.

Eid'dyl feared for a moment that Fy'ahn might strike Garym for having spoken out of turn. Instead, the Trasher leader merely allowed hir own Yrsil to respond in hir stead.

"There can be no use for the knowledge of the Whetu'irawaru," said the Trasher subsachem. "Other than, perhaps, as fuel for our cookfires."

"I do not understand," Eid'dyl said, wondering if the Deconstructor worldview might be impervious to the change s/he had hoped its new leadership would bring. "I had been told that your agenda would differ from that of your predecessor."

"That is indeed so," Fy'ahn said. "I believe my tribe's previous sachem to have been inadequately dedicated to the central Deconstructor precept—the complete and utter extirpation of the Old Knowledge, before it destroys all of *us*."

As Eid'dyl considered Fy'ahn's words, a sick, vertiginous feeling began to gather in hir mid-gut. S/he knew Ta'ith's post-Whetu'irawaru history better even than most Preservationists, and certainly better than any Trasher. Because Arava'whetu tended to be peaceful by nature, no serious fighting had occurred among the tribes for tens of hundreds of season-cycles. There had been occasional exceptions, but these were almost always confined to relatively brief disruptions of Ta'ith's uneasy intertribal geopolitical equilibrium. Skirmishes between the tribes occurred predominantly during times of extreme environmental stress, such as when the climate shifted and forced mass relocations, or when food supplies grew scarce during unanticipated migrations of Ta'ith's agricultural zones.

Eid'dyl had to acknowledge that the latest such fundamental disruption—perhaps an unprecedentedly violent one, as befitted what was likely to be an extinction-level challenge for all Ta'ithan life—might be about to begin on hir watch. Irreconcilable, mutually destructive intertribal war now seemed a distinct possibility, unless s/he was extraordinarily careful—not to mention fortunate.

"You cannot be serious, Sachem Fy'ahn," Eid'dyl said, hir primary stridulators quivering despite hir best efforts at maintaining hir composure.

"Destroying that which our forebears left here," Fy'ahn said, gesturing with half hir stridulators toward the necropolis's forbidding skyline, "is the only way."

"The knowledge of the Whetu'irawaru represents our only hope of surviving the Heart's furies," Eid'dyl said. "If we are to save ourselves, we must relearn what our forebears knew. Otherwise, we face certain extinct—"

"Frass!" Yrsil interrupted, hir stridulators sawing to produce dark intervals of contempt. "Our ancestors vanished because they offended the gods with their sorceries."

"Sorceries?" said Garym. "The Whetu'irawaru who spawned both our tribes practiced no sorcery. But they did create an abundance of texts and diagrams, which we are pledged to preserve."

"Witchery," Fy'ahn said with a dismissive motion of hir eyestalks. "All of it is an offense to the natural order of the cosmos. Its continued existence is the reason the Heart rages against us."

Eid'dyl fought to keep hir tone steady and emotionless. "We are the heirs of miracles, not sorcery. Blessings, not witchery. Ancient texts, some of which describe machines that can control the very climate, perhaps even to the extent of soothing the rage of the Heart itself. Mathematical disciplines whose meaning and significance the passing eons have rendered obscure, but which hold the potential of banishing death itself."

Fy'ahn approached menacingly, bowing hir topmost stridulators in a blunt gesture of negation as s/he moved. "The knowledge your people preserve will bring down upon both our tribes the very oblivion that took the Whetu'irawaru."

In defiance of hir every instinct, Eid'dyl stood fast, refusing to give ground either literally or rhetorically. "That knowledge that could be indispensable to the survival of every living thing on Ta'ith. It may be all that can save us."

Four limbs seized Eid'dyl in an iron grip before s/he even realized it. "You are wrong, Sachem Eid'dyl," Fy'ahn said, hir stridulators all but drowned out by the clacking of hir carapace and a swelling roar that was coming from the Trasher horde. "Only a thorough cleansing with fire can do that."

Eid'dyl stumbled as the limbs that pinned hir dragged hir away from Garym, who swiftly vanished in the tumult and confusion that followed. No one reacted to Eid'dyl's keening pleas as the Deconstructors turned as one away from the obviously confused, aimlessly milling crowd of Preservationists. Dragged along with hir captors, Eid'dyl watched helplessly as the Heart of the Cosmos, the Giver of Life and Death, retreated beneath the distant horizon.

Undeterred by the relentless advance of night, the Trasher horde moved purposefully toward the Sacred City's debris-strewn core.

One

U.S.S. TITAN

Lieutenant Commander Melora Pazlar reached across the light-years and cupped the rapidly spinning neutron star in her outstretched palm. She held it gently, carefully rotating the bright, oblate body's south pole until the energetic prominence that originated there pointed almost directly toward her face, while its northern counterpart pointed almost directly away. The vast, star-flecked cloud of gas and dust that a supernova explosion had left in its wake millennia ago—nestled deep inside the Gum Nebula, an even more expansive cloud of gas and dust generated by a still more ancient supernova—mirrored the change in the pulsar's orientation, turning obediently on the gravitational tethers that subtly linked every particle of matter in the universe.

Known in the Federation's astronomical catalogs as the Vela Pulsar, the intensely bright object that lay in Pazlar's open hand was now positioned so that the nearest of its polar jets had become the electromagnetic equivalent of a fire hose; the pulsar's immense gravity had so accelerated its outer shell of infalling matter that its poles emitted powerful streams of energy that encompassed every wavelength from gamma rays and X-rays to visible light to radio waves to the subspace bands. She flinched involuntarily, releasing the pulsar as the stream of false-color brilliance geysered into her face. She knew that the resulting light show was entirely harmless, a holographic representation of the real thing, even though she noted with a turn of her head that it extended through and past the space she occupied; it formed a long tail beyond her head, as though she wasn't even there. And yet she had flinched, her reaction fueled by some primal instinct she was incapable of taming. Her senses found the illusion all too convincing, despite her certain knowledge of its unreality. If the holographic object before her possessed any of the Vela Pulsar's characteristics other than its fierce appearance, she would have been utterly fried long before she had come anywhere near the object's seething photosphere.

As she drifted like a dust mote in the expansive variable-gravity imaging chamber that comprised the bulk of the stellar cartography lab's volume, she silently upbraided herself. *Melora, you'd think by now the fact that you routinely soar through interstellar space wearing nothing but an ordinary duty uniform would keep you from forgetting that you're safe, toiling in your cozy personal workspace.*

A familiar Efrosian lilt rose from the combadge attached to Pazlar's uniform tunic, interrupting her reverie. *"Are you busy at the moment, Melora?"*

She gave the combadge a desultory tap. "You might say that, Xin," she told *Titan*'s chief engineer. "I'm about to start a long-range analysis of our next destination. The captain wants to know as much as possible about the Vela Pulsar before we arrive and start the actual survey mission."

"Do you think you might put that task aside for a few minutes?" Commander Xin Ra-Havreii said. *"I could use your assistance here in engineering."*

Pazlar listened carefully for any sign of flirtation or double entendre, but found neither. Although she knew that Xin took his job as seriously as she did her own, she had learned very early in their still-evolving relationship that he wasn't past suggesting a midday tryst occasionally.

"Why?" she said, unable to keep a slight edge out of her tone.

"It's almost time for Captain Riker's conference with Admiral de la Fuego, and he's expecting to tie it in to the shipwide holoimaging system. The system has developed a few glitches that I can resolve more quickly with your help."

She frowned. "Troubleshooting holoimagers sounds a lot more like your department than mine, Xin."

"Running the stellar cartography lab the past couple of years has made you more of a holography expert than you realize, Melora," he said. *"Besides, you're easily the shipwide holosystem's heaviest user."*

His words struck her with the force of a mild slap, reminding her that she had once allowed herself to become entirely too dependent upon *Titan's* integrated network of internal holoemitters for her own good. *How could it have been otherwise?* The system allowed her to visit essentially any section of the ship without risking bone breakage via exposure to the crushing artificial gravity levels that prevailed nearly everywhere aboard *Titan*. It obviated any need for either a bulky contragravity suit or an antigrav exoskeleton, not to mention the necessity of leaving the safety of either the stellar cartography lab or her quarters, both of which faithfully recreated the microgravity environment of her homeworld.

But over the course of the past year Pazlar had gone out of her way to avoid using the shipwide holosystem. On the advice of Counselor Huilan Sen'kara and others—advice that she had rejected at first—Pazlar had come to recognize that she was overusing telepresence technology, and had turned it into an unhealthy form of self-imposed social isolation.

She scowled and pushed the Vela Pulsar hologram away, allowing it to recede several virtual light-years into the simulated distance. *If Xin really is looking for a nooner,* she thought, *then he's doing a damned poor job of pouring on the charm.*

"What exactly are you saying, Xin?"

Pazlar knew that her ability to concentrate on matters astronomical would depend upon what Xin Ra-Havreii said next.

"I'm saying you've had more experience fixing the system on the fly than anybody else aboard Titan, *with the possible exception of myself. The captain needs the holosystem running glitch-free—now—and I don't want to disappoint him. A second pair of trained eyes could go a long way toward making sure I won't have to. Please come down to engineering, Melora. I won't need you for very long."*

Adrift in microgravity like a piece of cosmic flotsam, she considered his request. At length, she said, "All right, Xin. Give me a minute."

She could visualize the satisfied grin behind his reply, and imagined his snow-white mustachios going gently aloft like the delicate underlimbs of a telepathic Gemworld Lipul. *"Thank you, Melora. Ra-Havreii out."*

Pazlar activated one of the several small compressed-air maneuvering thrusters she had incorporated into her uniform tunic. In obeisance to basic Newtonian physics, her body began moving in the direction opposite the gentle thrust, toward the lab's central consoles and the network of catwalks and railings that surrounded them.

Once she reached "ground level," she headed for the locker where she kept her contragravity suit. Thinking better of it while en route, she turned in mid-motion, used her thrusters to arrest her momentum, and then launched herself at the nearest console capable of accessing the holosystem.

Just in case he really *did* have a hidden agenda that he couldn't carry out unless she came to him in the flesh.

Captain Will Riker noted that he'd reached his destination nearly two minutes early, and decided to take that as a good omen.

Standing alone in the dimly illuminated main observation lounge, he paused to gaze out the panoramic window and take in the breathtaking vista it displayed. He looked outward across *Titan*'s broad bow into the mysterious, tantalizingly luminescent depths of the Gum Nebula that lay in the starship's path.

What are we accomplishing out here, really? he thought. Lately his dreams had been plagued by images gathered from a dozen or more worlds—Federation members and allies—that had been hit hardest during the Last

Borg Invasion. Deneva, Vulcan, Andor, Tellar, Qo'noS, none of these planets were done picking up the pieces yet. Could they ever recover fully, considering how much wholesale death the Borg Collective had dealt?

Riker turned and glanced around the observation lounge's interior. He had ordered that the room be made available exclusively to him at fifteen hundred hours, the scheduled time of his conference with Admiral de la Fuego. He would have preferred to have Deanna at his side, considering one of the topics to be discussed. However, this was a command-level affair, for the captain's eyes and ears only. Some of the ground to be covered would be sensitive, which was why he wanted the meeting conducted in full three-dimensional holography. If Admiral de la Fuego expected to ram an unpalatable policy down his throat, she'd damned well better be prepared to look him straight in the eye when she did it.

At the broad, round conference table that dominated the room's center, Riker sat with his back to the observation windows. He sighed, then said, "Computer, open secure holographic subspace channel Starfleet Seventeen-Tau-Alpha-Epsilon. Authorization: Riker-Beta-One-Zero-Two. Increase lighting to point-seven-five of standard."

The illumination level rose instantaneously. Within the space of a few heartbeats, a hologram began to coalesce in a chair across the table from Riker. The image shimmered, gradually gaining solidity before it began to fade away behind a curtain of static. It was almost as though the admiral were being beamed aboard *Titan* with a faulty transporter, which was losing her pattern.

The captain scowled and whispered a pungent curse. Just as he was reaching for his combadge, the holographic image in the chair suddenly acquired clarity, depth, and resolution. It was as though the admiral were sitting in the room with him rather than watching him from across a gulf of thousands of light-years.

Riker had chosen to conduct his end of the briefing in a room that would prominently display Beta Quadrant space behind him, thereby quietly emphasizing *Titan*'s unique position and the special weight and gravitas that her CO deserved.

Admiral Alita de la Fuego, her graying black hair pulled back into a severe bun, the light-brown skin on her forehead striated by new worry lines, was the first to speak.

"Captain Riker. I regret I've had to let so much time pass since the last time we spoke. What's it been? Nine weeks?"

"Ten and a half, Admiral," he said, offering what he hoped was an ingratiating smile. "Not that I'm keeping score. I know how full your plate has been lately."

The admiral nodded curtly, then said, *"I've just reviewed the report you filed after the Hranrar affair. I see that Commander Tuvok was injured rather severely at that time."*

Riker understood her motivation. When he'd been assembling *Titan*'s crew, he'd become aware that his tactical officer had mentored de la Fuego, and remained one of her oldest friends.

"Tuvok sustained a serious neural trauma when he tried to establish a telepathic link with the artificial intelligence we discovered aboard the ecosculptor." In response to her blank look, he appended, "The Brahma-Shiva device." The now-defunct terraforming machine, which *Titan*'s science specialists had dubbed

Brahma-Shiva, had been constructed by a long-vanished alien species. It would have wiped out the biosphere of the planet Hranrar—including that world's high-order civilization—had the crew of *Titan* not intervened.

The admiral leaned forward, her anxiousness apparent as she spread her virtual but solid-looking hands across the conference table. *"How's he doing now?"*

"Better than anybody expected," Riker said, delighted to have some upbeat news to report. "We did a *Suus Mahna* workout together before breakfast this morning. He's been working a full duty schedule for the past six weeks."

"I didn't realize you were such a stern taskmaster, Captain."

He raised both hands in a placating gesture. "Putting Tuvok back on the active duty roster wasn't my idea. It was against Doctor Ree's recommendation, too. But you're probably familiar with how . . . determined the commander can be."

She flashed a small grin. *"The adjective I would have chosen is 'stubborn,' Captain."*

"I tend to agree," he said, matching her smile. "But he's performing his job brilliantly. Ree reports he can't find any significant lingering aftereffects." *At least*, Riker thought, *not so far.*

"Glad to hear it," she said. *"But there's one particular 'lingering aftereffect' that Starfleet Command is interested in more than any other."*

"I don't follow you, Admiral."

Her smile imploded. *"The terraforming machine you discovered at Hranrar, Captain. And then blew up."*

The admiral's last words sounded to Riker like an ugly accusation. "Brahma-Shiva," he said evenly.

"Brahma-Shiva, exactly. The source of the AI your crew discovered, according to your report. Our science divisions and the Corps of Engineers have been champing at the bit to get even a glimpse into that thing's inner workings. The mind-meld that Commander Tuvok performed with the Brahma-Shiva AI might represent our only opportunity to discover what made it tick. Now that Tuvok has made a full recovery, has he succeeded in recalling any of the particulars about that meld?"

Riker felt his throat tighten involuntarily. He willed himself to relax. Wherever de la Fuego might stand on his decision to destroy Brahma-Shiva, the captain knew that he had done the right thing. The terraforming technology stored within the artifact might have alleviated a great deal of the Federation's suffering—not to mention enhancing its position vis-à-vis the Typhon Pact—but blowing up Brahma-Shiva had been the only way to avert the extinction of an entire civilization.

"Unfortunately, no," he said. "So far, Tuvok hasn't been able to recall any of the details."

Looking thoughtful, the admiral twirled an errant lock of hair. *"You don't suppose he might be withholding anything, do you, Captain?"*

Riker heard that tone of accusation again; it was subtle, but definitely present. There was only one answer he could give, and he tried to keep his tone even as he supplied it. "I trust my senior staff implicitly, Admiral. Tuvok was lucky to survive that encounter. Another member of my crew tried to link with the Brahma-Shiva AI, but he wasn't quite as fortunate as Tuvok was."

The admiral frowned for a moment, her confusion evident. Then a look of understanding smoothed some of the lines from her face. *"Ah. You're referring to the artificial life-form you brought aboard some months ago, according to your reports. Blue-White."*

"SecondGen White-Blue," Riker said, gently correcting her.

"Of course, Captain."

Riker was willing to admit that his long friendship with the late Lieutenant Commander Data might have heightened his sensitivities regarding inorganic colleagues. But since there was no point in belaboring the issue, he set the matter aside and continued with his report.

"We were hoping that White-Blue's linkup with the Brahma-Shiva AI would have yielded teraquads of information to guide us in duplicating Brahma-Shiva's terraforming capabilities. Ensign Torvig Bu-kar-nguv has been working nearly nonstop over the past two months to reactivate him, or at least to extract any readable files. But I'm afraid he's had no success so far. The damage was evidently too extensive."

"You're not giving up, Captain," she said, once again employing an accusatory tone. Or was he simply imagining it, projecting his own doubts onto her?

"No, Admiral," he said, once again feeling a surge of doubt about Starfleet's wisdom in dedicating two of its most advanced ships of the line—*Titan* and her *Luna*-class sister vessel the *Ganymede*—to pure exploration in the face of everything that was going on in the Federation. Perhaps the *Luna*-class ships might be better used in watching the Federation's back in case of aggression on the part of the Gorn Hegemony or one of the other Typhon Pact powers that laid claim to large swaths of deep Beta Quadrant space. The upheaval created by Andor's recent secession from the United Federation of

Planets—not to mention that world's internal struggles—wasn't making life in the Federation any easier.

As Riker pushed aside these nagging issues, he wondered if the Federation Council would even stop to consider the ramifications of using the Brahma-Shiva artifact. Perhaps it was for the best that the ecosculptor technology was, for all intents and purposes, lost.

The captain noticed that the admiral seemed to be looking through him. He realized a moment later that she was staring deeply into the reaches of the Gum Nebula framed in the observation window behind him. She leaned forward and fixed him with an expectant stare that made him believe she envied him his mission.

"Tell me about Titan*'s next destination, Captain,"* she said.

"The Vela Pulsar," Riker said as he finished keying a command into the padd that lay atop the table. A false-color image of a flattened star that emitted twin jets of golden fire from both top and bottom through an orange halo of radiation materialized in the air between them. Though the image appeared static, Riker knew better; according to Dr. Cethente, not only was the incredibly dense, Manhattan Island–sized object spinning so quickly that the human eye couldn't detect the motion, the extremities of the pulsar's energy streamers were oscillating madly, twin runaway whipcords of hard radiation that lashed back and forth at better than half the speed of light.

"Spectacular," de la Fuego said. *"Looks pretty violent."*

"It is. It's an eighty-nine-millisecond-period pulsar, the remnant of a supernova explosion that happened here several thousand years ago. It's the brightest object of its kind in the entire Gum Nebula, and one of the most potent sources of X-rays, gamma rays, and graviton waves in the entire Beta Quadrant. Our astrophysics department thinks it could give us some fundamental insights into how matter and energy interchange, down to the quark level or maybe even further."

"Outstanding, Captain. The science divisions have been ecstatic over the astrometric data Titan *has supplied so far from the Beta Quadrant's rimward side."*

Riker grinned. "I think they might be about to get giddy. *If* we can get close enough to take precise measurements, that is."

"How close can Titan *get to the pulsar and maintain a margin of safety?"*

"Astrophysics is still putting together a detailed gravitational map. We'll know a lot more once we get closer to it. I'm expecting *Titan* to enter a conservative standard parking orbit in less than a day. Close enough to make the pulsar accessible to our sensor arrays, but far enough out so that our shields will still be able to protect us from the object's output of hard radiation. During the survey, we'll be giving priority to our long-term maintenance and repair objectives."

The Gorn affair two months ago had significantly lengthened *Titan*'s repair-and-maintenance list. Riker was grateful that the next eight weeks would afford *Titan* an opportunity to catch up.

"Then you should be pleased to hear that Starfleet Command is in a position to help Titan *expedite her repair schedule,"* de la Fuego said with a broad smile. *"One of our new* Vesta-*class starships is already en route to your present position: the* Capitoline, *with her slipstream drive, should rendezvous with* Titan *in three days."*

Riker found this news unexpected, and wondered if diverting the *Capitoline* was entirely necessary. He knew that *Titan* wasn't in dire need, although the ship was short on certain nonreplicable components. Complicating his misgivings were his proprietary feelings toward his ship, sentiments that he knew he had in common with his engineering staff—most notably Xin Ra-Havreii. The last thing either Riker or his chief engineer needed was a new team of specialists. "What will the *Capitoline* be assisting us with?"

"Mostly, she'll be hauling components," de la Fuego continued. *"The parts you'll need to build replacements for the four shuttlecraft that have been destroyed since* Titan*'s initial deployment. The* Capitoline *will be outfitted to take care of everything on* Titan*'s wish list. You should be receiving a detailed manifest within the hour. The* Capitoline *will also provide some necessary crew rotations."*

"Thank you, Admiral," Riker said, almost at a loss for words. It all sounded almost too good to be true.

There has *to be something wrong with this.*

She leaned forward over the table, her gaze gaining intensity as she studied him. *"You seem troubled, Captain. What's on your mind?"*

After pausing to chide himself silently for failing to bring his bluffing skills to bear, he said, "'Troubled' might be a bit of an overstatement, Admiral. I'm simply wondering why you've given this meeting a 'captain only' classification. So far we haven't covered anything that exceeds the security clearances of any member of my senior staff."

"This briefing isn't finished, Captain," said the admiral, withdrawing behind a stony façade. *"We haven't discussed the Andor situation yet."*

Riker gave her a somber nod. "I can hardly believe it. One of the five founding worlds of the Federation leaving."

"I feel exactly the same way. I never thought anything like this would happen during my lifetime."

"Maybe the damage isn't permanent. The Andorians have always had a reputation for shooting from the hip before thinking things through. Is it possible they might reconsider after they've cooled down a little?"

"Ever since Andor announced its secession, the diplomatic corps has been holding out at least some hope for that possibility—not to mention any number of olive branches." She paused, shaking her head sadly. *"But they've had no luck. In fact, Andor has remained so intransigent that the Federation Council officially stepped down its diplomatic efforts as of yesterday evening."*

"What about Andor's Repatriation Act?" Riker asked. The Andorian government had issued what it had termed a "formal request" that all Andorian nationals residing anywhere in Federation space be returned immediately to their homeworld. Riker interpreted it as less a formal request than a nonnegotiable demand.

"The Council will make an announcement later today that it intends to honor Andor's wishes—but only up to a certain point."

Riker could feel his forehead crumpling involuntarily into a frown. "Admiral, they've 'requested' that every reproductive-age Andorian national be returned immediately to Andor. By force if necessary."

"And that is the line the Council will not cross, Captain."

"I'm relieved to hear that, Admiral," Riker said.

"In light of that stipulation, the Council has authorized

*a measure that will furnish 'assistance and transporta-
tion' for all 'willing, reproductive-age Andorians.'"*

Riker nodded. Though he was unhappy with the entire situation, he had to admit that the Council's decision
was a measured one and even made a certain amount
of sense. Nobody was being forced to leave Federation
space, nor was anyone being coerced into staying. If a
sovereign planet could change its Federation member-
ship status unilaterally, it followed that individuals could
do so as well.

"Because of security considerations, however," de la
Fuego continued, *"Starfleet has more leeway to act than
the civilian government does."*

Realizing that this particular point had to be the rea-
son de la Fuego had wanted to confer with him alone,
Riker said, "I'm not sure I like the sound of that,
Admiral."

"I'm not sure I do, either." Her tone had become stiff
and bracing, discouraging dissent. *"But whatever either of us might like or dislike is neither here nor there.
The simple fact is that during the months since Typhon
Pact–allied Breen agents made off with Federation slip-
stream technology, Starfleet Command has been more
concerned about internal security than at any time since
the parasite infestation eighteen years ago. Ever since
Andor's government announced its secession, Command
has been scrambling to shut down and extract every
Starfleet facility in the Procyon system, from our repair
base at Laibok to the Starfleet Academy annex at Lai-
kan. Command has become wary of Starfleet's Andorian
personnel."*

Riker's stomach had begun to tie itself into a knot of
disgust. "Admiral, I hope you're not saying that Starfleet

Command intends to push its Andorian officers into accepting . . . forced repatriation."

She shook her head slowly. *"No, Captain. I'd be lying if I said it wouldn't greatly simplify my job if every Andorian in the service were to accept repatriation tomorrow. But I'm not going to assume guilt by association and insist on it. However . . ."* A look of thoughtful sadness crossed her face as her voice trailed off, as though she were weighing her next words with the utmost care before delivering them. *"But Starfleet Command has decided it would be best for everyone concerned if all nonrepatriated Andorian personnel were to accept redeployment to alternate postings, at least temporarily."*

Riker felt his frown deepen; he knew how easy it was for temporary measures to ossify into permanent fixtures.

"How soon?" he asked.

"In Titan*'s case? As soon as the* Capitoline *arrives to begin crew rotations."*

He could scarcely have been more stunned had the admiral's holographic image suddenly brandished a phaser and shot him with it. "Admiral, I have seven Andorian crewmembers serving under me at the moment."

"I am aware of that fact, Captain. It's the reason we're having this briefing. I'm not proposing that any of your Andorian personnel be cashiered or discharged. Unless your Andorian crewmembers wish to accede to the Andorian government's repatriation request, Starfleet Command will transfer them to less sensitive positions."

"How do you define 'sensitive' when it comes to *Titan?*"

The admiral leaned further forward, favoring him with a hard glower as she steepled her fingers before her.

"Captain, you have to admit that there are few places more sensitive than the cutting edge of the Federation's deep Beta Quadrant exploration efforts."

"I trust each and every one of my Andorian officers implicitly, Admiral. All of them, without exception, have always upheld their oaths as Starfleet officers."

"I understand that only too well, Captain. And that's why I regret having to do what circumstances have forced me to do. All of your Andorian personnel will have to accept passage aboard the Capitoline, *and reassignment."*

Riker seethed in silence for a long, unmeasured interval, during which he never broke contact with the admiral's dark, resolute gaze. At length, he said, "I'll . . . ask them how they feel about this."

She leaned back, softening her steely intensity only a little. *"This is* not *a request."*

Riker considered the situation. Deanna had already told him that Lieutenant Pava and the other half-dozen unbonded Andorians who now served aboard *Titan*— each of them young enough to satisfy Andor's "reproductive age" criterion—were already extremely unhappy at the prospect of being forced out of their current posts for purely political reasons.

The captain knew he was in a far better position than any of them were to challenge Starfleet's hierarchy—or perhaps even to shame it into doing the right thing.

"Permission to speak freely, Admiral?"

Admiral de la Fuego's face took on a long-suffering aspect. *"Granted, Captain."*

He leaned forward, hoping to demonstrate that he wasn't in any way intimidated by the admiral's rank or authority. "In my opinion," he said, "this new Andorian policy is a mistake—especially when we're talking about a crew as diverse as *Titan*'s. This ship runs on mutual trust and respect, and Command is about to destroy that. I can't believe that Starfleet would seriously consider sacrificing good, reliable officers on the altar of politics."

After Riker finished, de la Fuego sat still and regarded him in protracted silence.

"I can't disagree with anything you've said, Will," she said at length, her tone gentler. *"And there was a time, before I started flying this desk, when I might have made the same kind of statement."*

The admiral paused, straightened up, and added, *"The* Capitoline *will be picking up the Andorians serving on* Titan. *Whether they accept repatriation or reassignment will be up to each of them individually."*

Riker leaned back in his chair and folded his arms across his chest. "Suppose some of them reject either choice. What happens then?"

The admiral's eyes narrowed, her entire visage growing hard and flinty. *"Captain, you are to make it crystal clear to them that that isn't an option. Is that underst—"*

The hologram abruptly winked out of existence.

What the hell? Riker thought as he got to his feet. He slapped the combadge on his chest. "Riker to engineering."

"Ra-Havreii."

"My holographic subspace channel to Starbase 185 just collapsed. Any idea why?"

"My apologies, Captain. I've been having trouble with the system all morning. I suspect it may have something to do with that pulsar we're approaching. Regardless, I'll do everything I can to get the channel back up and running as quickly as possible."

"Thanks, Xin." He paused to tap his combadge again. "Riker to stellar cartography."

"Pazlar here. What can I do for you, Captain?"

"I need to pick your brain, Melora. I just lost contact with Admiral de la Fuego. How much is the Vela Pulsar interfering with our subspace channels?"

"Well, the pulsar's energy releases did *begin to intensify significantly at roughly the same time* Titan *entered the sector."*

"Coincidence?" Riker asked.

"I think we've got to call it that. At least until I can find some physical mechanism that would allow Titan*'s presence to affect the output of a pulsar across more than two parsecs of interstellar space."*

"Could our warp field be interacting with the pulsar somehow?"

"I suppose it's possible. But those sorts of effects generally only manifest themselves at much closer range. A thing like that shouldn't be scrambling our subspace traffic yet, even on the high-bandwidth channels."

"Keep a close eye on it. I'll send Commander Vale down to help troubleshoot it. Riker out."

He looked down at the table, where the holographic image of the enigmatic Vela Pulsar still hovered. Riker studied the swiftly rotating image in silence, paying special attention to the ominously glowing object's twin cattails of angry, twisted magnetic force lines and braided jets of unimaginably intense charged-particle showers.

As impressive as these forces of nature were, he doubted they'd prove as dangerous as the fallout that Starfleet's new Andorian policy was sure to generate.

Two

IOTA LEONIS II
STARBASE 185

Staring at the blank wall in her office that had formerly provided a backdrop for the image of Captain Riker and the depths of the Gum Nebula, Alita de la Fuego slapped at her combadge in annoyance.

"Jenny, what the hell just happened?"

A young woman entered the office at a trot, her long, strawberry blond ponytail coiled over the shoulder of her dark uniform tunic. She pulled a standard-issue Starfleet padd out from under her left arm and began studying its display.

"Sorry, Admiral. Our subspace connection to *Titan* just collapsed. I don't see any hardware glitches on this end, and since the twins aren't misbehaving at the moment"—she gestured toward the broad polarized window behind de la Fuego, through which both Iota Leonis

A and B were clearly visible—"I'm thinking the problem must be on Captain Riker's end."

"Try to reopen the channel," de la Fuego said.

The fingers of the young woman's right hand moved swiftly over the padd's touch-sensitive surface. She shook her head in frustration, and then her eyebrows rose in surprise.

"What is it?" de la Fuego said, rising from behind her immaculate desk.

"I'm unable to open a subspace connection," said de la Fuego's aide. "But the starbase comm system is working correctly."

"How can you tell that?" de la Fuego said, frowning.

"We're receiving an incoming transmission from the fleet admiral's office in San Francisco."

"Put it through, Jenny," she said with a nod. "Security scramble. And give us some privacy."

The lieutenant acknowledged the admiral with a nod and wasted no time entering the appropriate commands into her padd. Once done, she vanished through the door that led to the outer office.

A broad, towering holographic shape began coalescing into existence in the space that Riker had occupied. Fleet Admiral Leonard James Akaar stood before her, appearing as solid as a mountain and nearly as large. The thick mane of steel-colored hair that framed his craggy countenance only served to reinforce his air of authority.

"Have you explained the new Andorian policy to Captain Riker?" the Capellan asked, his voice a low, tightly controlled rumble.

Though she was standing, de la Fuego had to crane her neck upward almost painfully to look him in the eye.

*"Our briefing was interrupted, probably by local inter-
ference. But I managed to cover the key points before I
got cut off from Titan."*

She wondered idly why Akaar hadn't contacted Riker
himself. The fleet admiral had always taken a keen interest in the explorations being undertaken by *Titan* and
her *Luna*-class sister ships; Akaar had even been aboard
Titan on her inaugural mission. *Maybe he's channeling
his communications with* Titan *through her command
base so as not to step on my toes*, she thought.

"I doubt that he showed much enthusiasm for it,"
Akaar pointed out.

Since she was familiar with Akaar's aversion to beating around the bush, de le Fuego spoke plainly. "Captain Riker made it clear that he doesn't like it. Frankly,
sir, *I* don't like it either—any more than I like having to
keep Riker in the dark about the bigger picture. When
it all comes to a head, *Titan* will be one of the first to
deal with the consequences. Riker and his people are in
harm's way."

*"I know, Alita. I know. But until the current diplo-
matic crisis is settled—until all the remaining security
holes are plugged—my orders regarding the disposition
of Starfleet's Andorian personnel must stand as written."*
Akaar paused as though grappling with his words before
continuing, his tone colored by regret.

*"And we will deal with whatever consequences may
come as they arise."*

Three

U.S.S. TITAN

Deanna Troi took a seat at one end of the low sofa that ran along the wall facing the captain's desk. On the other end of the sofa sat Christine Vale, *Titan*'s first officer and second-in-command.

The first thing Troi noticed was the captain's conspicuous absence from his own ready room. This didn't surprise her, given how troubled and distracted he'd seemed to her when he'd asked his two most senior officers to meet with him. The interior storm of emotion she'd felt in Will Riker was buried deeply enough beneath his studied façade of equanimity to have escaped the notice of anyone not married to him—or those lacking the empathic gifts that were Troi's Betazoid birthright.

Troi then noticed that Vale, who sat with her chin resting on her hand, seemed to be in an emotional state not unlike that of her husband.

"You know something I don't, Chris," Troi said, "and you don't like it."

A small grin tugged crookedly at the edges of Vale's mouth. "There seems to be a *lot* not to like about what's been going on today."

"So I've gathered. I assume it's why Will called this meeting. So, what's at the top of *your* list of things not to like?"

"Our balky subspace link to Starbase 185 gets the number one spot," Vale said. "And number two would have to be whatever Admiral de la Fuego thought was so sensitive that she could only share it with the captain."

Just beyond Troi's end of the sofa, the ready-room doors parted with a pneumatic hiss. Will stood framed in the open doorway, a low-key chorus of bridge instruments filtering in quietly behind him.

"If I had to take a wild guess, I'd say there's been a new development in the Andorian situation," Troi said as the captain stepped into the room. Vale got to her feet instinctively.

As the doors closed behind him, Will pulled a face somewhere between a grimace and a smile. After making a silent "as you were" gesture to his first officer, he turned to Troi and said, "I hope Starfleet Intelligence never discovers how often your 'wild guesses' turn out to be right, Deanna. They'll start sending headhunters."

"Don't worry, Will," Troi said, grinning. "I've never been very friendly to poachers." *Except*, she thought once the irony of her words had become apparent to her, *when* we're *the ones doing the poaching*. Christine Vale had served under Jean-Luc Picard as the *Enterprise*-E's security chief until Will had convinced her to accept her current post aboard *Titan*.

"Anything new happening on the Andorian front?"

Chris asked, retaking her seat a moment after Will had occupied the chair behind his ready-room desk.

"Enough to give your CO a splitting headache," he said. He was obviously trying his best to gloss over something that was a good deal more dire than his tone was letting on. "But at the moment I'm more concerned about whatever interrupted Admiral de la Fuego's transmission."

"You haven't been able to reestablish contact?" said Troi, frowning.

Vale shook her head. "Melora and I have been trying. No luck."

"And until *Titan* reconnects with the relay network, it'll take five days for our subspace messages to reach Starbase 185 at this distance," Will said.

"Which means we're facing a wait of at least ten days for a reply," Vale said.

"Any idea why we can't contact the relay network?" said Troi.

"We've narrowed it down to two possibilities," Vale said. "One: there's been a spontaneous failure in a subspace relay node that's critical in keeping *Titan* linked to the long-range comm network."

"How likely is that?" Troi asked.

Riker shrugged. "Can't absolutely rule it out. Even the most reliable components will break down, given enough time. But Starfleet always plans for that. The subspace relay network is so important to commerce and security all across the Federation that the Corps of Engineers maintains an aggressively proactive maintenance schedule."

Vale nodded. "On top of that, the network has scads of built-in redundancies and failsafes—all designed specifically to keep the subspace relays up and running, no matter what."

"Then there's possibility number two," Riker said over his steepled fingers, "that some critical part of the network has fallen victim to deliberate sabotage."

"The Gorn have already shown us that they're willing to waste entire planets to replace their lost warrior-hatchery world," Vale said with a nod. "I don't think they would have any qualms about disabling our long-range communications grid."

"The Gorn aren't the only suspects," Riker said. "There's the rest of the Typhon Pact to consider. The sabotage could just as easily be the work of the Romulans, the Breen, or the Kinshaya."

"Or the Tzenkethi," Vale said. "There could even be disaffected Andorians involved."

Troi's spine stiffened involuntarily in response to the flare of tightly reined ire she felt radiating from her husband. When Riker spoke, she noted what a superlative job he was doing keeping that anger out of his voice.

"There's no evidence pointing to that yet," Riker said. "And I'm not about to start lobbing unsupported, knee-jerk accusations at Federation citizens who happen to be Andorian."

"I'm not suggesting we do that either, Captain," Vale said, her earlier air of informality falling away. "But I wouldn't put sabotage past the Andorian splinter groups."

"*Leaving* the Federation is one thing," Will said. "Actively working *against* the Federation is something else entirely."

Vale offered up a wan smile. "I wouldn't have believed it either. But three weeks ago nobody could have persuaded me that one of the Federation's original founding members would have even *considered* secession—much less brought it to a vote domestically and actually carried it out."

Though Riker was outwardly impassive, Troi could feel the intensity of his disappointment burning like a persistent flame. "I still can't quite believe it myself. And then there's Starfleet Command's reaction."

"Which must have been the highlight of your conversation with Admiral de la Fuego," Vale said.

The captain nodded. "I assume you're both familiar with the details of the Repatriation Act that Andor's government passed last week."

"Please don't tell me that Starfleet actually plans to help Andor *enforce* it," Troi said with a nod of her own.

"Not exactly. But Andor's new status makes Starfleet Command see every Andorian who chooses to remain in the service as a potential security risk. When the *Capitoline* catches up to us, Admiral de la Fuego expects me to hand over *Titan*'s entire complement of Andorian crewmembers as part of a 'routine crew rotation.'"

Vale regarded the captain with a puzzled frown. "That doesn't exactly sound 'routine.' A ship's command staff is supposed to make the crew rotation decisions."

"That *is* standard operating procedure," Will said, the muscles in his jaw quietly clenching and unclenching in a rhythmic manner. "But not this time."

The first officer brushed several stray strands of her shoulder-length brown hair away from her eyes. "There has to be a good reason. Has Command leveled any specific accusations against our Andorian personnel?"

"No." He shook his head again. "Not that I know of." The captain stroked his beard thoughtfully. "But if the crewmembers in question decide to protest . . ." His voice trailed off.

Vale's brow crumpled in apparent confusion. "Admiral de la Fuego and Starfleet Command have cut official personnel transfer orders, Captain. Those orders won't leave you a whole lot of wiggle room."

Troi saw a tiny wry smile begin to tug at Will's lips as he gazed out the ready-room window into the depths of the Beta Quadrant. "Practically speaking, I have more 'wiggle room' than you might think, Chris. Mainly because of the fact that the subspace relay network has malfunctioned."

"Admiral de la Fuego is *not* going to be happy about us taking advantage of that," said Vale.

"Fortunately, we can count on up to ten days of 'subspace grace' before I get dressed down over it," Riker said. "And it'll take about as long for Starbase 185's JAG office to weigh in on the formal protest I've already transmitted."

"Assuming, of course, that we don't fix our comm problems in the meantime," Vale said.

"I'm not *assuming* anything, Commander," Riker said as he turned away from the port and faced her. "Understood?"

The XO nodded. "Understood, Captain. At least ten days of guaranteed wiggle room, coming right up. I'll explain it to Commander Ra-Havreii." She appeared to want to say more, but instead fell silent. Troi sensed that something was gnawing at her.

"Chris, I know you're not a big fan of getting sideways with Starfleet Command. If I thought I had any other option . . ." His voice trailed off again.

"It's not that," she said, shaking her head. "Hell, we've served together on two different starships; it isn't as though I've never seen you bend the rules before."

"Then what's bothering you?"

"It's the Andorians. I mean *our* Andorians. I find it awfully . . . *convenient* that this communications snafu happened just as Admiral de la Fuego gave you those orders."

He frowned. "If anybody on board could have interrupted our link to the relay network, then why wouldn't they have done it *before* the admiral gave me those orders?"

"Maybe they were only *monitoring* the comm system up to that point. But once they learned about the reassignments, they disrupted the subspace relay connection—"

Riker interrupted her. "And counted on their captain to act like an offended civil libertarian and start stalling on their behalf."

"I didn't exactly say *that*," Vale said, spreading her hands before her. "Look, *somebody* needs to play devil's advocate for Command right now. Maybe those reassignment orders make sense in terms of the bigger interstellar political picture. Maybe we shouldn't be standing in the way of that."

"Maybe. But that's not what my gut is telling me right now. I'm not faulting you for exhibiting a healthy sense of paranoia, Chris. I know you can't be a good first officer without it. But I don't expect to get that same type of paranoia from Command. That never turns out well. And that's *another* thing I know from personal experience."

Troi saw that Will's simmering anger was apparent even to Vale. Holding up a hand in a placating gesture, the exec said, "All I'm saying is that since we've both admitted that we'd rather not believe the worst about Andor, you and I share a potential vulnerability, and that's a blind spot that a saboteur aboard *Titan* might exploit."

"When you say 'saboteur,' you really mean '*Andorian* saboteur,' " Riker said very quietly. "Don't you?"

Vale rose from the couch, a resolute expression on her face. "If I learned one thing when I was serving as a cop on Izar, it's that ruling out any possibility prematurely makes for sloppy police work. And I'd be a piss-poor first officer if I were to do that here."

Riker's electric blue eyes flashed at his exec, momentarily reminding Troi of a pair of phaser banks. "Chris, have you ever heard Ensign Vallah sing the Federation anthem?"

"Once, on the holodeck," Vale said. "Right before a baseball-game simulation three or four months ago. I get it. You weren't the only one who got misty-eyed when Vallah stretched out that last high note. But putting on a patriotic show shouldn't earn anybody a 'get out of jail free' card."

The captain's eyes narrowed. "*No one* serving on this ship has ever shown any disloyalty to the Federation."

"Until recently, nobody serving on this ship was from a homeworld that's just summarily decided to withdraw from the Federation," Vale said, precisely matching the steel in Riker's tone.

"You have the bridge, Commander," Riker said, his intense gaze locked with the defiant stare of his XO. "Dismissed."

Christine Vale stood. Troi knew she wanted to say more as she watched the muscles in Chris's face grow taut. But then the XO's expression relaxed as she thought better of continuing the argument. "Aye, aye, sir," Vale said at length, and headed for the bridge.

Once Troi and her husband were alone in the ready room, Will said, "Deanna, I want you to talk to Lieutenant Pava, Ensign Vallah, Lieutenant Aris, and the rest of our Andorian contingent. Make sure they receive the full text of the reassignment order right away."

"I'll get started now," Troi said as she rose from the sofa. "With the *Capitoline* on her way, our people won't have long to process what's about to happen. They're bound to feel singled out."

"That's because they *are* being singled out," Will said, speaking in a near growl. "I want you to find out how each of them wants to respond to de la Fuego's orders. Who knows, maybe one or two of them will be content to go along and beam right over to the *Capitoline*."

An uncomfortable feeling was settling over Deanna's gut. "Will, they've all been reassigned. Starfleet isn't giving them any choice in the matter."

"No," he said. "But *I* am."

"Are you sure you really want to do this, Will?"

"I have to, Deanna." His voice sounded calmer now, but it was filled with resolve. "I'm not going to let this . . . witch hunt derail the careers of seven good people. If I don't take a stand for any crewmember who wants to fight this, then the Federation Charter isn't worth a damn."

"That may be true. But Admiral de la Fuego could have you court-martialed."

With a wry half-smile, he said, "That looks like a distinct possibility."

"This is *serious*, Will," she said with a scowl. Deanna knew that he sometimes used a lighthearted manner as a coping mechanism, but she was in no mood for it now. "This could land you in a penal colony." She paused when her voice caught in her throat. She noticed then that his bearded face had taken on a softer cast. "You might be separated from Natasha and me for years."

Will's eyes shone with moisture at the mention of

their sixteen-month-old daughter. "I know that, Deanna. But it doesn't change what I have to do."

She needed to reason with him, to help him find a workable alternative—because there *had* to be a workable alternative. *You don't have the authority to just ignore Admiral de la Fuego's orders*, she told him wordlessly, using their special empathic connection. *Right or wrong, this isn't your decision to make.*

Deanna, it's an unjust order. Besides, we're way out in the wilderness, and cut off from Starbase 185 on top of that. That makes me the highest Federation authority within a hundred parsecs of this ready room.

His bold yet plaintive declaration reminded her of the ancient Western stories her late father had told her during her childhood. *Titan* was the equivalent of a little pioneer community perched on the ragged edge of a perilous frontier. And Will Riker was the town sheriff.

But you can't make life-changing decisions on behalf of our Andorian crewmembers, she asked him in thought-speech.

"No," he said, speaking aloud. "But I *will* protect the Federation citizens I'm responsible for from a witch hunt—even if the hunter is Starfleet Command."

Troi reached out with her mind and gently caressed his worried, fevered thoughts. She felt his intense sense of concern for everyone subject to his command, and drew some comfort from that. But there was no escaping the less-than-pleasant emotional subtext that shadowed him, the backdrop that subtly colored his entire psyche.

It was a profound, aching sense of loneliness that Troi knew even his wife and daughter could not assuage.

Four

TA'ITH

As hir captors continued to drag hir ever deeper into Ta'ith's stony bowels, Preservationist Sachem Eid'dyl kept doing what s/he could to keep the movements of hir four strongest walking limbs coordinated. Unfortunately, even hir most diligent efforts to avoid landing in a painful, limb-entangled heap on the unyielding cavern floor did little to prevent the many cuts and scrapes that scored hir body as the crowd shoved and pulled hir inexorably forward.

Eid'dyl felt moist warmth flowing slowly from the countless small abrasions and cuts s/he'd received from innumerable inadvertent brushes of limbs and carapace against rough stone. Those injuries, invisible to hir in the near darkness, along with the coppery scent of hir own blood and the enraged, fearful stridulations that echoed menacingly from every direction, fed Eid'dyl's rising sense of dread and incipient panic. The constant effort to maintain hir balance while being dragged along with the mob kept all seven of hir remaining functional limbs engaged in a prolonged, almost comic stumble. Eid'dyl could only hope that the Deconstructor mob would soon call a halt to its pitiless march.

A sudden small upsurge in the ambient light level caught the attention of the vision patches located at the end of Eid'dyl's cranial sensory stalks, startling hir nearly enough to bring hir bleeding, stumbling body down in a tangled heap. Illuminated by the biolumi-nescent lichens that adorned the stone passages and the Trashers' crackling torches, the Eternal Undercity—the miraculously surviving remains of the long-vanished Whetu'irawaru's mostly inexplicable machineries—had begun to reveal itself. The irregularities of the surround-ing mineral formations and the lattices of dark-adapted climbing vegetation were now giving way to the regular planes, sharp angles, and hard corners of objects created untold eons ago by the manipulation limbs of Eid'dyl's Whetu'irawaru forebears.

The arms that were holding fast to Eid'dyl's upper carapace abruptly released their grip. The Preservation-ist sachem immediately pitched forward onto the hard stone surface; only two of hir ambulation limbs had suc-ceeded in reacting quickly enough to get between hir carapace and the slimy rock to avoid a serious—perhaps even lethal—breach of hir already distressed thoracic chitin layers.

Just above hir, Eid'dyl heard the angry stridulations of Sachem Fy'ahn, the supreme leader of the Decon-structor sect. "This place should have turned to dust ages ago," said the Trasher leader, hir every somatic phoneme dripping with disgust and outrage.

"No doubt it would have, Sachem," said Yrsil,

Fy'ahn's faithful Second, "but for the powerful sorceries that linger here."

"The legacy, no doubt, of the Whetu'irawaru," Fy'ahn said. The Trasher sachem reached down simultaneously with four grasping limbs and unceremoniously hauled Eid'dyl to a wobbly standing position. "You and your people consider yourselves the keepers of the fell magicks of our ancestors."

"I lead the sect that would preserve the knowledge that could save us all from the frenzies of the Heart of the Cosmos," Eid'dyl said guardedly.

Fy'ahn scoffed, stroking hir mouthparts together in a chittering cacophony. "You have taken upon yourself the task of protecting that which our dead forebears left here," s/he said. "That implies that you know of a way to bring about its destruction."

The very notion filled Eid'dyl with horror, making hir forelimbs tremble visibly. "Why would we even consider such an act?"

Fy'ahn's grip on Eid'dyl's upper thorax tightened painfully, and the Trasher sachem hauled hir upward by nearly half a resting bodylength with little effort. The crowd that milled about stridulated a chorus of hostile cheers until Yrsil angrily called for silence.

"You regard us Deconstructors as your intellectual inferiors," Fy'ahn said, hir mouthparts sawing at one another in a naked display of aggression. "We understand that you would not want the sorceries of our mutual forebears to fall under the control of a sect such as ours."

Eid'dyl found this confusing. Dark spots were beginning to dance in the center of hir narrowing visual field, and several of hir walking limbs churned uselessly in the stale cavern air. "But you and your people have always rejected Whetu'irawaru technology," Eid'dyl said.

"Irrelevant," Fy'ahn said, a forelimb squeezing hard against Eid'dyl's upper breathpassage. "I believe you possess the means to destroy all of this." The Trasher leader paused, using the silence to point two of hir midlimbs at the heart of the underground necropolis. "You will divulge that knowledge, so that the Deconstructor sect can save Ta'ith from the Great Daystar's wrath—by annihilating every last vestige of Whetu'irawaru sacrilege."

"I possess no such knowledge." Eid'dyl knew instantly that hir words convinced no one, since s/he could have said nothing else. Even if s/he had possessed the knowledge that Fy'ahn sought, s/he would have been obliged to keep it concealed.

Though Eid'dyl's vision was fading, s/he could still see Fy'ahn's maxilla clearly. The Trasher sachem's mouthparts and the forbidding ring of clawlike chelicerae that surrounded them had spread out in a hostile grin that reminded Eid'dyl of a carnivorous flowering plant.

"I pass this one into your care, Yrsil," said Sachem Fy'ahn. "You will persuade hir to tell us what we need to know."

"I will begin at once," Yrsil said.

Eid'dyl felt Fy'ahn's grip suddenly slacken, and s/he landed painfully on the hard ground. Blood flowed hot from a crack in hir carapace.

"And until we discover how to rid Ta'ith of this blight quickly," Fy'ahn continued, "tell the people to set about destroying the old machines directly, any way they can."

No, Eid'dyl thought. Waves of despair threatened to engulf hir. *No, no, no.*

"It will be done, Sachem," Yrsil said. Though hir visual patches had again retreated to the interior of her sensory stalks, Eid'dyl knew that the limbs that were gathering hir up from the cavern floor belonged to Fy'ahn's loyal Second.

"Even if all they have at their disposal," Yrsil added, "are rocks and the limbs to hurl them."

Five

U.S.S. TITAN

Hovering like a disembodied spirit, Will Riker stared in fascination at the false-color rendering of the ancient, rapidly revolving celestial ember that floated before him. The yellow-orange plumes of hyperaccelerated particles that jetted from both sides of the pulsar's spin axis appeared to be almost within arm's reach. Understanding that this almost disconcertingly realistic image was the reason Lieutenant Commander Melora Pazlar had requested the briefing be held in the stellar cartography lab, the captain gestured toward the nearer of the object's two matching fiery polar tails.

Momentarily turning his gaze away from the holographic inferno that dominated the lab's expansive three-dimensional viewing space, Riker looked back to the platform some six or seven meters below, where Troi and Vale stood. Both women seemed content to remain in the one section of the lab that offered Earth-normal gravity.

Deanna called out from the platform, "Looks like the Vela Pulsar's started stepping up its energy output."

Thanks to the microgravity that prevailed across most of the lab's extensive upper volume, Pazlar hung suspended only a few meters away from Riker; her body was inverted relative to the captain's, her shoulder-length hair forming a pale, lazily drifting halo about her face.

With a nod, Pazlar said, "It's become more active, and not just in the visible spectrum. The pulsar's emissions of X-rays, gamma rays, gravitons, and berthold rays are all nearly off the scale, and there's been a huge increase in subspace noise and EM-radio static all across the spectrum. I've never seen anything quite like it."

"Which is why Ensign Evesh and Ensign Dakal will have to perform their full systemwide sensor survey from our present distance," Vale said.

Riker looked back toward the pulsar and the multi-layered torus of infalling debris that swaddled its swiftly spinning interior with an angry cloak of reds and yellows, producing a seething, gravity-fueled conflagration. Despite the ever-present spur of his curiosity, he had no regrets about maintaining the extraordinarily wide orbit *Titan* had just entered, keeping approximately 32,000 AUs between his ship and the object. There simply wasn't any need to challenge one of space's deadliest phenomena, however fascinating any of *Titan*'s science specialists might find it.

"We're already as close to the pulsar as I care to get, under the circumstances," he said, nodding in agreement with his first officer.

"I'll break the bad news to the sensor jockeys, Captain," Pazlar said. "I'm sure Dakal will find a way to make it work. But Evesh is bound to be unhappy, not to mention

vocal about it. I can almost hear the complaints already."
The stellar cartographer released an audible sigh.

"I'm sure you can handle it," Riker said with a chuckle.
On Evesh's native Tellar, complaining had long ago become a universal cultural pastime, at times even rivaling
the crafting of insults, a practice that had been the planet's
dominant folk art since antiquity. During the early phase
of his Starfleet career, Riker had found these Tellarite ten-
dencies off-putting. Once he'd learned that most Tellarites
could take complaints and insults as well as they could
dish them out, the captain had come to regard the species'
querulousness as an endearing characteristic.

"Evesh can always set up an appointment to see me
if she needs a shoulder to, ah, growl at," Deanna dead-
panned.

The first officer made a face. "If you're smart, you'll
refer her to Counselor Haaj," she said. "Of course, that's
just a layperson's opinion."

Vale's idea struck Riker as a damned fine one. Being
a Tellarite himself, Pral glasch Haaj could easily side-
step whatever cultural mine fields might sabotage the efforts of even the most accomplished and conscientious
non-Tellarite counselor. Besides, Haaj had built a considerable professional reputation by employing a unique
brand of "insult therapy," an unorthodox treatment re-
gime that seemed to work quite well across lines of species and culture.

Riker noticed that a small, globular shadow was beginning to make a leisurely transit across the simulated
pulsar's blazing, oblate face. He reached out toward the
simulation of the planet—*Titan*'s initial long-range scans
showed that it was the only local world to have survived
the ancient supernova that had created the pulsar—so

that his index finger just grazed the atmosphere's murky, umber-colored cloud tops. Responding to his gesture, the stellar cartography computer swiftly reversed the relative sizes of pulsar and planet, allowing the latter to dwarf the former.

"I don't envy anybody who has to live there," said the captain. As though punctuating his words, a dazzling pink-and-gold aurora—a visible manifestation of the otherwise invisible ongoing collision of the pulsar's relentless particle flux with the planet's magnetic field—blazed across the planet's north pole, generating a swath of atmospheric pyrotechnics.

"My thoughts exactly," Pazlar said. "Which is why I've assigned a high priority to finding out if anybody *is* living there."

Riker frowned. "Doesn't look very likely."

Pazlar reached for a control on her belt and fired a small air-thruster that immediately began changing her spatial orientation. A second firing in the opposite direction quickly halted the motion, leaving her body at a relative stop, and more or less aligned with Riker in terms of up and down. She reached out to touch the beach ball–sized holographic planet; in response to her gestures, the image expanded again by about a factor of four.

"In spite of appearances, Captain, life as we understand it isn't an impossibility on this world," she said. "At least not if you take the planet's magnetic field into account."

Riker wanted to share the stellar cartographer's optimism. But he knew he had to weigh it against the assessments of others whose expertise he valued every bit as much as he did hers. However, the planet's hostile appearance seemed to negate Pazlar's thesis a priori.

Riker shook his head. "Most of *Titan*'s bioscience specialists seem to disagree."

"So far," Pazlar said with a shrug.

Riker heard confidence in her voice, and found it admirable.

"I just spoke with Doctor Ree," the captain said. "He says he has trouble envisioning any kind of complex life capable of withstanding a radiation bombardment, the planetary magnetic field notwithstanding."

"That view is becoming a consensus, Melora," said Deanna, speaking from the lab's lower section. "Lieutenant Commander Shrat in astrobiology has sided with Ree. Doctor Cethente from astrophysics says he wouldn't care to bet much on any unprotected life surviving for very long on that planet's surface."

If the contrary opinions of her fellow scientist had shaken Pazlar's confidence, she betrayed no sign of it. *I wonder how she'd do playing poker*, Riker thought.

"Maybe I've interpreted the available data differently than a biosciences specialist like Ree might," Pazlar said. "Or even a radiation-proof Syrath like Cethente. But that's only because I've taken the planetary magnetic field more fully into account."

"All right, Commander. Tell us what everybody else has missed," Riker said.

"First off, there's clear evidence that this planet is— or was at some point during its history—home to a high-order civilization."

Riker said, frowning, "What are you basing that on?"

Pazlar pointed at the auroral display over the planet's north pole, which reminded Riker of the Northern Lights that he'd seen so often during his childhood in Alaska. The planet's extraordinarily active magnetosphere was pulling and braiding the aurora's bands of brilliance, twisting them like so many strands of multihued taffy. The glowing magnetic field lines seemed to be slowly tightening around the planet right before his eyes, like a boa constrictor preparing to squeeze the life from its prey.

"The planetary magnetic field," she said. "It doesn't fit any of the standard models. I know of no natural process capable of generating such an intense field in a body of this one's size and composition."

"What's so unusual about the magnetic field?" Riker said, genuinely curious.

In response to Pazlar's touch, the image of the planet grew larger and more detailed. "First, consider the fact that the planet's not much bigger, more massive, or denser than Sol I, the first planet in your own home system."

"Mercury," Riker said with a gentle smile; no one from Earth ever referred to that barren, airless, alternately sun-baked and freezing world as "Sol I."

"Mercury, right. Other than your own Earth, it's the only rocky planet in the Sol system that generates a significant unified magnetic field."

"Because of its large iron core," Riker said with a nod, pausing to gesture toward the holographic world and its gradually tightening straightjacket of shimmering magnetic field lines. "But Mercury's magnetic field is nowhere near as powerful as *this* planet's field. The one Mercury generates is only a fraction as strong as Earth's half-gauss field."

"Exactly," Pazlar said as she made a circuit of the planet by means of small, nearly silent bursts of the small thrusters she wore over her uniform tunic. "And while it's true that the planet we're studying has more mass and is denser than Mercury, it's still neither massive nor dense enough to generate a field like the one we're measuring. I think even Cethente would agree that the field is far too intense to have developed naturally."

The captain was still skeptical, but Pazlar's notion had piqued his interest nevertheless.

"Melora, are you saying that this planet has an artificially constructed geomagnetic field?" Vale asked as she slowly paced the lower platform. "That an intelligent life-form built it?"

"Exactly," said Pazlar. "I believe it was built to shield the planet's surface from the Vela Pulsar's radiation output, which was extremely intense even before the object's more recent upheavals. Whether the builders are—or were—indigenous or exogenous to this system is something I can't determine as yet."

"Every one of our long-range bioscans have come up negative so far," Deanna said. "And I'm not detecting anything coming from the planet."

"Absence of evidence isn't evidence of absence, Commander," Pazlar said, her shrug setting her hair into slow, jellyfish-like motion. "Especially with the galaxy's single brightest gamma-ray source and a ridiculously strong planetary magnetic field conspiring to jam or reflect most of my scans. For all we know, it could be doing the same thing to your empathic sense. Or maybe we're still just too far away from the planet for you to pick up the emotions of anybody who might be on the surface."

Vale's eyebrows looked like they were in a race to scale her forehead. "The footprints of most warp-capable civilizations usually aren't that hard to detect, even from light-years outside their home systems. Don't you think it's a little strange that none of our long-range probes found anything like that?"

"Not really," Pazlar said, shrugging. "Especially if we're talking about a civilization that's produced technologies capable of covering their tracks, so to speak."

The first officer was obviously not convinced. "Sounds a little far-fetched to me."

Riker looked thoughtful as he stroked his salt-and-pepper beard. "While I was serving aboard the *Enterprise*-D, we had a run-in with the Aldeans. Everybody used to think they were a myth—until we discovered that they'd been keeping their home planet hidden for centuries using planetary-scale forcefields and cloaking devices."

"Oh," Vale said, as though withdrawing her objections. The captain knew she was sensitive about how much less she had seen and done in comparison to Riker and Troi during the sixteen years since she'd decided to trade her Izarian law-enforcement career for a Starfleet commission. Prior to her *Titan* posting, Vale had spent four years serving alongside Riker and Troi aboard the *Enterprise*-E, but she'd always seemed wistful about not having shared their experiences aboard the late, lamented, legendary "D."

Riker returned his attention to the holographic planet and began studying the harsh, gray-brown world more closely. Something about the image looked subtly amiss. It occurred to him that his initial impression that the planet's webwork of magnetic field lines was growing smaller—and forming ever-tightening meridians up and down the body's rotational axis—was no mere optical illusion.

"Something else is going on with the planet's magnetic field," Riker said. "Something you haven't told us about yet."

Pazlar nodded. "Good eye, Captain. It's because of the recent decline in the magnetic field's intensity that I've been able to get decent scans of the planet's surface and upper lithosphere. Since our arrival—and probably *because* of our arrival, at least in part—the field has fallen from a stable sixty thousand gauss to about fifty-five."

"Fifty-five thousand?" Vale asked. "A drop-off of ten percent? That doesn't sound like anything to get worked up about."

Riker had to agree, at least up to a point. "But it's enough to get your attention, especially with the pulsar acting up."

"Captain," Pazlar said, "the field is down to *fifty-five* gauss. That's more than a thousandfold decline, and the intensity of the field is still falling. At its current rate of decline I'd expect it to decrease by about another four or five gauss every week."

The stellar cartographer paused. Six gauss was the equivalent of two to three times the intensity of the natural magnetic field that protected all life on Earth from the potentially lethal effects of space weather phenomena, incoming cosmic rays, solar winds, and solar coronal mass ejections.

Pazlar continued. "In sixty standard days, seventy-five at the outside, the field won't be strong enough to protect any living thing on the planet's surface. I'd expect the field to continue its decline until it reaches a level characteristic of a planet of its size, composition, and tidal relationship to the pulsar it's orbiting."

"What's causing the field to decline?" Riker asked. "The pulsar's radiation bursts?"

"That almost certainly got the process started," Pazlar said with a nod. "My guess is that whatever technology currently generates the planet's magnetic field is delicate. In fact, it's probably located underground, since the Vela Pulsar would be dangerous to electronics left on the surface. Either way, the technology that's either generating or reinforcing the field appears to have taken significant damage from the pulsar's latest outbursts. Consequently, the field has begun to collapse."

Riker saw that Vale was frowning deeply as she stopped her pacing and folded her arms before her. "This is still pretty speculative stuff, Melora," the exec said. "You've connected a lot of dots, but you haven't gathered a lot of hard evidence yet to back up the picture that seems to be emerging."

The vertical ridge that ran across Pazlar's forehead compressed, signaling either determination or irritation, or perhaps both. "Maybe, Commander. But nobody's come up with any better explanation yet for all the phenomena we've observed so far." She began ticking off points on her fingers. "Exhibit A: the decline in the planet's magnetic field became noticeable aboard *Titan* not long after the pulsar's most recent heavy flare-up."

"That's interesting," Riker said. "But it's a far cry from proving conclusively that any life, intelligence, or artifacts actually exist on that planet. 'Exhibit A' could be a simple coincidence."

"Examined by itself, sure," Pazlar said. "But not if you also examine it beside Exhibit B: even though the planetary magnetic field is in a steep decline, the drop-off isn't happening nearly as quickly as you'd expect given the still-growing intensity of the pulsar's output. The slope of the downward curve isn't steep enough. It doesn't make any sense."

"Come again, Commander?" Riker said.

Pazlar gazed off into the holographic heavens as she composed her thoughts. "Any naturally generated geomagnetic field would have been entirely overwhelmed by now—extinguished like a small camp fire blown out by a sudden gale-force wind. But *this* field almost seems to have a will of its own. Somehow, it's still struggling to keep most of the pulsar's hard radiation output from reaching the surface. It's as if something down there is fighting a losing battle to keep the field reinforced artificially.

"And on top of all that, you have to consider Exhibit C: the long-range scan I performed not ten minutes ago revealed refined metals—metals that closely resemble the sensor profile of the alien terraforming device we encountered at Hranrar." Pazlar pivoted toward the lower platform. "You can check out my subspace spectrographic analysis and see it for yourselves."

"Refined metals," Riker said, "and evidence of ecosculptor technology."

"If that's the case, then we *have* to find a way to take a close look at whatever's down there," Vale said. "Pulsar or no pulsar."

Much as he hated the idea of placing his ship and crew at risk, Riker couldn't help but agree. "You're sure about this?" he asked Pazlar.

The Elaysian replied with a vigorous nod. "I was planning on checking my results again before bringing them to you, Captain," she said. "But I'm already confident enough about my analysis. And if the next scans square with the predictions I made based on our earlier sensor data, I'll have to upgrade 'confident enough' to 'certain to a fare-thee-well.'"

"Melora, if you're right about this planet supporting a high-order civilization," Vale said, "then we're talking about people who are on a technological par with the Hranrarii."

Troi nodded. "And if that's true, this society would be exempt from the Prime Directive."

"If they never applied their technological skills to building warp ships, like the Hranrarii," Vale said, "they'll be in urgent need of help."

Riker felt his brow crumple into a frown as he considered the Hranrarii, the amphibious, warp-capable species that *Titan* had encountered about two months earlier. The Hranrarii had faced an extinction-level threat—until the judicious intervention of the crew of *Titan*. The Hranrarii had never developed interstellar travel. But because they'd possessed the capacity for matter-antimatter power generation, Riker had been within his rights to intervene—despite the rule of thumb that made starflight capability the traditional threshold for invoking the Prime Directive's noninterference protection of alien civilizations.

But the captain could already see that the plight of the Hranrarii differed from the present situation in one important respect.

"Rescuing whoever might be living on that planet is bound to be more complicated than blowing up an alien artifact," Riker said with a grim head shake.

"We may be getting ahead of ourselves," said Deanna. "The first order of business ought to be finding out for sure what—or *who*—is down on that planet."

Vale nodded. "Agreed. Unfortunately, putting an away team on the surface would appear to be the only way to do that."

Riker tried to weigh the risks inherent in sending an away team to the planet against the possible rewards. He knew it was his duty to recover the technology that *Titan*'s crew had encountered at Hranrar, regardless of his personal feelings on the matter—and perhaps even regardless of the radiation hazards that any close approach to the Vela Pulsar might entail.

Ordering an away team down there could mean sending good people to their deaths, he thought as he stared in silence into the mysterious planet's murky, aurora-veined atmosphere. As was once the case with the surface of the Saturnian satellite after which *Titan* was named, whatever lay beneath the cloud tops was an utter mystery.

At length, he said, "It's a strange coincidence."

"Captain?" said Pazlar, who looked puzzled.

Riker shifted his gaze back to the stellar cartographer. "The Vela Pulsar has existed in a more or less stable condition for thousands of years," he said. "Then, after all that time, it chose *this* particular eyeblink in cosmic history to put on a show like this—right when *Titan* happens to have a front-row seat."

The captain saw that Pazlar's countenance had just become markedly paler than usual, taking on the color of bleached bone. He knew immediately that whatever she was about to say wouldn't make him happy.

"Captain, I don't think there's any coincidence involved," the stellar cartographer said.

"Wait a minute, Melora," Vale said, holding out both hands in a *slow down* gesture. "Using next to nothing, you've built up a pretty convincing case that the planet's magnetic field isn't a natural phenomenon. You might have even convinced *me*. But I hope you're not about to say the same thing about the Vela Pulsar's recent energy outbursts, too."

Pazlar smiled sheepishly. "I know how crazy it sounds, Commander. But that's *exactly* the direction my preliminary sensor data analysis is pointing. I've had Lieutenant Aris and Ensign Evesh checking my numbers for the past couple of hours, and neither of them has found any errors so far."

"And since the second phenomenon seems to be doing its damnedest to wipe out the first one," Riker said, "it seems unlikely that any one entity could be responsible for both."

Pazlar offered him a solemn nod. "More like impossible. Statistically speaking, we're talking a P-value of ninety-nine percent and change."

"Hmmm," Riker said, temporizing. Statistical analysis had never been his strong suit.

"I believe I've just positively identified the party responsible for the Vela Pulsar's recent instability."

Riker scowled at the elfin Elaysian. "Don't keep us in suspense, Commander. Who's the culprit?"

"It's *us*, Captain," Pazlar said, her tone suddenly muted and hushed. "It's *Titan*."

"You're saying that *Titan* has . . . stirred up the pulsar somehow?" Vale asked, prompting an affirmative nod from Pazlar.

"How?" Riker asked. "From what I've seen, the pulsar was already showing signs of instability when we were still a dozen sectors away. You told me we were too far off for our warp field to disrupt it."

Pazlar waved her hands before her. "Let me walk that

back a little, Captain. I'm not saying *Titan* is the *entire* cause of the Vela Pulsar's convulsions. It's probably more accurate to say that we acted as a kind of trigger."

"*How?*" Riker demanded.

"It's still preliminary, but as far as I can tell, *Titan*'s arrival in this sector has exacerbated an already existing weakness in the local fabric of subspace. The region of space in immediate proximity to the pulsar had already been greatly weakened by the trauma of the object's formation. Supernova explosions are among the most violent natural phenomena in the universe, after all. Once the supernova remnant had more or less settled down into its present status as an eighty-nine-millisecond pulsar, the object's own energetic particle flux started wearing away at the already damaged substrate of local spacetime."

"The way the Colorado River carved out the Grand Canyon on Earth over the course of millions of years," Vale said.

Pazlar nodded. "That's a good analogy, Chris. You have a region of spacetime—normal space along with several dimensionally adjacent layers of subspace— that's become severely abraded."

"Abraded?" Deanna said.

"Yes. In the immediate proximity of the pulsar, and for a radius of roughly half a light-year all around it, the membrane that separates normal space from subspace has been worn down, in a manner of speaking—eroded, like the topsoil of a badly planned agricultural colony," Pazlar explained. "The arrival of *Titan* and her warp field only made matters worse. Our warp field here appears to have had the effect of rapidly aging the pulsar—accelerating its overall energy output and thereby making the object increasingly unstable and unpredictable."

Riker's heart abruptly went into freefall. *We've endangered whatever life might exist on that planet,* he thought. *Whatever civilization might be fighting for survival against the pulsar's eruptions is in jeopardy—because of* us.

"Could the damage we've done fix itself given enough time?" Riker asked. "Is it possible that space in this region might heal on its own, so to speak?"

"Maybe." Pazlar spread her hands in a gesture of helplessness, reminding Riker that they were all out of their depth here. "But only if warp-driven starships stay away—or at least refrain from establishing warp fields anywhere within half a light-year of the pulsar."

"In other words," Vale said, "we don't dare get any closer to the pulsar or its planet than we already are."

Though he'd witnessed a similar phenomenon a dozen years earlier in the Hekaras Corridor, Riker felt gut-punched by Pazlar's merciless string of unpleasant revelations. All he had ever wanted was to explore the wonders of the cosmos. He'd never expected to destroy them.

Pazlar added, "And unless the planet's magnetic field makes a miraculous recovery, the damage is done. I wish I had happier news, Captain. But our continued presence in this vicinity—even with our warp core running at a very low idle—could cause still more permanent damage to the local fabric of both ordinary spacetime and the underlying subspace continuum. The longer we remain here, the greater the potential is for doing irreparable harm." She paused, shaking her head in evident frustration. "I'm sorry, but none of our options look very good to me."

"Can we get an away team safely to the planet and

back before the magnetic field collapses completely?" Riker asked.

"Captain, we really shouldn't risk bringing *Titan* any closer to the pulsar," said Pazlar.

Riker acknowledged her with a nod. "What about using a shuttlecraft instead? The warp-field footprint would be a lot smaller than *Titan*'s."

"That could work," Vale said. "But only if we take the time to reinforce the shuttle's shields against the pulsar's excess radiation output. I'd also recommend keeping to subwarp speed once the shuttle gets within about twenty AUs of the planet's orbit."

Riker did a quick mental calculation. Twenty astronomical units was a little more than the average distance between Sol and Uranus.

"All right, Commander," he said, addressing Vale. "Get Ra-Havreii started prepping a shuttlecraft for a survey of the planet," he said. "That's just become his top priority."

"I'm on it, Captain," Vale said, her mien serious, her tone all business.

If any chance remained to reverse the harm they'd done—to turn *Titan* into an instrument of salvation rather than destruction—he simply couldn't afford to pass it up.

Firing the microgravity maneuvering jets he'd borrowed from Pazlar, Riker began making his way back to the lab's lower platform. His full weight returned as he landed in a crouch between his wife and his XO.

"And start assembling an away team, Chris," he added. "We need to find out what's really down on that planet—and we have to do it ASAP."

Before the fire my ship started engulfs half the sector.

Six

TA'ITH

Sachem Eid'dyl, leader of the Preservationist sect, awakened to a complete absence of light that filled hir aching carapace with dread and a feeling that approached panic. Though a thick, heavy garment or sack seemed to weigh down hir head and upper body, s/he couldn't tell whether it covered hir sensory stalks or if their photosensitive extremities had been severed from hir body. The latter possibility caused hir little fear, though s/he had never experienced the drawn-out process of waiting for an injured set of sensory stalks to grow back on their own.

Most disconcerting was the fact that s/he had lost track of how much time had passed since the Deconstructors had separated the sachem from hir people and dragged hir into the vast holy spaces of the Sacred Undercity.

A familiar, callus-limbed voice spoke from out of the stygian gloom, startling hir with its disconcerting closeness. "You can still save yourself a great deal of pain, Sachem Eid'dyl."

Though the effort of stridulating a response greatly pained hir heavy, battered limbs, Eid'dyl was determined to reply intelligibly to the Trasher leader; even torturers could be afforded simple politeness.

"You could as well, Sachem Fy'ahn, if such is your concern," Eid'dyl said. "Simply by returning me to my people."

"I know that you keep a great deal concealed from my sect," Fy'ahn said, not even deigning to acknowledge Eid'dyl's request.

"Whatever knowledge my sect conceals," the Preservationist leader said, hir quavering limbs introducing an unaccustomed vibrato to hir stridulations, "we conceal only to keep safe from *your* sect."

"We destroy only that which now offends the Whetu'irawaru," Fy'ahn said, hir voice like rasps being dragged across flint. "Only that which the Fallen Gods now must regret having created in the first place. Only that which would bring still more of their wrath down upon us."

Eid'dyl felt a weariness s/he had never known before settling upon hir soul. "Then destroy every machine you find in the Undercity and be done with it. You brought a thousand or more with you. Surely that many determined Trashers must be equal to the task."

A lengthy, perplexing silence preceded the Deconstructor's reply. "We have been trying to do exactly that ever since we first entered the Eternal Undercity. But your sect's sorceries have so far thwarted us."

Eid'dyl often found Fy'ahn's beliefs strange in the extreme. But now s/he regarded the Trasher leader's words as all but incomprehensible.

"There are no 'sorceries,'" Eid'dyl said, hir forward

speech stridulators trembling as they began to cramp with effort and fatigue. "There is only science. Only technology."

"Call it what you will. But I cannot think of a better way to describe a force that so swiftly undoes whatever minor damage the stones and clubs of my people have caused to the ancient machineries. No sooner do we break something than an invisible spirit restores it. I have seen it happen, right before my own sensory stalks."

Eid'dyl said nothing. S/he wasn't completely certain what hir counterpart was describing, never before having visited the deepest places of the Sacred Undercity. But it occurred to hir that the Deconstructors might, in their destructive zeal, have run afoul of some manner of automated self-repair system left behind by the mutual ancestors of Preservationist and Trasher alike—the Fallen Gods known as the Whetu'irawaru.

"I believe you possess knowledge that would enable us to circumvent the fell magicks that now protect the Undercity's ages-old blasphemies and abominations," Fy'ahn was saying, momentarily sounding almost empathetic rather than sadistic. "I am not unreasonable, Eid'dyl. Show me how to destroy the machineries that offend both the Elder Gods and the Heart of the Cosmos, the Giver of Life and Death."

Eid'dyl did not know how much longer s/he could survive the rigors of interrogation. S/he wondered how much more torture hir body could absorb before it sustained permanent or even fatal damage.

Therefore it was time to change the nature of the conversation.

"Perhaps I can do something even better, Sachem

Fy'ahn," Eid'dyl said. "If you will permit it, I will summon one of the Elder Gods themselves."

Eid'dyl felt hard, chitinous claws grab hir roughly in a dozen places. The claws lifted and shook hir, then abruptly released their grip, allowing hir body to slam against rough, unyielding stone. Fortunately, a pair of Eid'dyl's back limbs took the brunt of the jarring impact, directing much of its force away from the damaged carapace that protected hir delicate thoracic region.

"You speak sacrilege, sinhoarder," Yrsil, Fy'ahn's trusty Second, said in sharp, snarling stridulations.

"Let the gods that both our sects venerate strike me dead if I speak anything other than the simple truth," Eid'dyl said. "If you will but allow me, I will summon one of the Fallen Gods—a spirit of the departed Whetu'irawaru—to walk among you. Perhaps S/he will even champion your cause."

"You cannot really believe that," Fy'ahn said. "That much is obvious."

Eid'dyl still could see no light whatsoever, and could hear only distant, indistinct stridulations. The sounds were clearly Ta'ithan sectspeech, but weren't intelligible because they weren't being projected in hir direction.

"Why not let me try it—unless you have reason to fear the direct judgment of one of the Fallen Gods?" Eid'dyl said.

Light abruptly assaulted Eid'dyl's sensory stalks, and a sudden lessening of the sensation of weight against hir upper body confirmed that a covering had just been pulled from hir head. Though hir lightpatches had yet to adjust completely to the abrupt increase in ambient light, Eid'dyl could see the machinelike towers of the Sacred Undercity all around them, the physical manifestation of

Ta'ith's finest aspirations limned in columns of fire that set the shadows in the cavern roof far above into weirdly unpredictable motion.

A low, squat building that stood almost directly across a debris-covered boulevard from Eid'dyl seized hir attention. A dozen or so Trashers had surrounded the structure and were pummeling its exterior façade with the stout metal rods that each of them carried. Chunks of masonry and mortar flew in all directions as the multijointed limbs of each attacker pumped continuously, tireless and machinelike, showing no sign of restraint.

But as quickly as the damage was being done, new material extruded from inside the structure, filling each fresh gap, replacing whatever had been knocked loose. *Fy'ahn was not exaggerating,* Eid'dyl thought, rubbing at the tips of hir sensory stalks.

The menacing, chitinous faces of Fy'ahn and Yrsil suddenly eclipsed the structure Eid'dyl had been studying. "I fear nothing, sinhoarder," Fy'ahn said, hir stridulators grinding like a pair of dry firestones. "Nor do my people. They will labor at destroying the Unholy Machines for as long as it takes to accomplish the task."

"They will fail," Eid'dyl said, despite a decided lack of certainty. "Unless they have help."

"Why would *you* wish to help *us*?" Yrsil said.

"Like you, I seek only to carry out the divine will," Eid'dyl said. "Is it not one of your articles of faith that the machinery of our ancestors now offends the Fallen Gods that they became? Who better to bring about the destruction you seek than one of Them?"

A seeming eternity passed while the Trasher leaders considered Eid'dyl's words in silence. "All right, sinhoarder," Fy'ahn said at length, in much more thoughtful tones than usual.

"Sachem!" Yrsil rasped. "We should not trust h—"

"Be silent," Fy'ahn said, interrupting hir subordinate's stridulations with a well-placed hindlimb slap. "Let hir make the attempt. After all, it will be some time before the cargo team returns here with the chemical explosives. Until their arrival, I am willing to entertain alternative means to our ends."

Eid'dyl shuddered. Chemical explosives. Had such things ever before been brought to bear against the machineries of the ancients? Despite hir extensive knowledge of the Age of the Whetu'irawaru, Eid'dyl could not say.

"Who knows?" Fy'ahn continued. "Perhaps our cause will soon receive divine assistance. Surely one of the Elder Gods can do a more thorough job of scrubbing the Undercity clean of its abominations than any of us could."

"Take me to the old machines," Eid'dyl said, wondering how much the Trashers actually understood about extelligent machines and their interfaces. "I will also require access to some of the documents I was carrying when you brought me here. Then I will try to initiate a Summoning."

As Fy'ahn hustled Eid'dyl back into motion, Eid'dyl hoped that the self-repair systems that had protected the Sacred Undercity's ancient machineries over the long eons would resist being overwhelmed by the sheer numbers of torch-carrying, rock-hurling throwbacks that now assaulted it.

Would that the entity I plan to call upon really was one of Ta'ith's vanished Elder Gods, Eid'dyl thought.

Seven

U.S.S. TITAN

Trying to remain as unobtrusive as possible, Commander Tuvok stood in the farthest corner of the nearly empty gym, watching in silence as the unarmed combat exercise unfolded before his eyes.

What should have been a brief and probably one-sided freestyle martial arts match had already lasted considerably longer than Tuvok had expected, given his understanding of the abilities and limitations of each of the two combatants involved. In addition to being an extremely adept and experienced fighter, Lieutenant Commander Ranul Keru outweighed his much shorter and slighter opponent by a considerable margin. But security chief Keru's subordinate, Lieutenant Pava Ek'Noor sh'Aqabaa, seemed to make up the difference with sheer ferocity. At times it seemed to be all Keru could do either to block or to evade the bulk of Pava's unpredictable barrages of lightning body punches and *ahn-woon*-fast kicks. Although Keru was clearly more powerful,

Pava was a good deal faster. To Tuvok's trained eye she seemed almost to have achieved *sahr-tor*—a state of sensory-motor purity that appeared to allow both feet to leave the ground simultaneously during each stride. *Sahr-tor* was the ideal fusion of mind with body, a transcendental neurological state toward which every Vulcan athlete aspired.

As the pair warily circled each other during one of the infrequent lulls between exchanges of blows, Tuvok assessed the condition of the two-meter-tall unjoined Trill male and the much shorter Andorian *shen*. Though Keru seemed winded, he nevertheless kept his guard up ably, along with his lightweight gloves, and maintained a rare grace for someone so large. His standard-issue maroon Starfleet workout tunic, however, conspicuously displayed a broad dark stripe along the length of his back, and twin semicircular stains had taken prominent positions under his thick, hirsute arms. By contrast, Pava's gymnasium attire—today she wore a traditional Andorian *shandru*, a dark blue formfitting bodysuit designed specifically for unarmed combat—showed similar evidence of intense exertion.

But Pava, her fists raised and ready, seemed more energized than enervated. When her cautious, light-footed circling motion momentarily brought her face directly into Tuvok's line of sight, the Vulcan immediately noticed the fire blazing in her pale turquoise eyes. He doubted that she was seeing much at the moment other than deep azure, the color of Andorian blood. Tuvok realized at that moment that he was experiencing a very real sense of concern for Pava's emotional well-being, though his Vulcan emotional discipline wouldn't allow him to display it.

Commander Keru made it clear that he had no such compunction after Pava feinted, then released a savage, ululating war cry as she launched a vicious high kick that missed connecting with the security chief's head by the narrowest of margins. But evading the Andorian's attack cost the big Trill his balance, and he went down hard on the sparring mat, landing on his back. Pava remained as tense as a coiled spring, and Tuvok momentarily feared that she might leap upon her supine opponent.

"I think we're done for the day, Lieutenant," Keru said as he slapped his hand repeatedly against the mat to make it unambiguously clear that he was "tapping out" of the contest before he rose to a sitting position. "Thank you for another very productive *shandru-shaan* lesson." He paused, stretching his shoulders with a momentary wince. "I think."

"But I'm not tired yet," Pava said, her gloves still raised and ready. Though her voice was surprisingly flat and devoid of emotion, Tuvok could see the banked embers of fury in her eyes.

Keru got to his feet and appeared to test his footing for a moment. Then he shook his head. "Well, *I'm* done in. Besides, I can't spend *all* my free time practicing Andorian martial arts moves."

After several heartbeats of silence, Pava finally allowed her gloved hands to drop to her sides. Only then did her fists begin to unclench. "All right, Commander. I'll see you later, when my shift begins."

He frowned, adopting a mock-chiding expression. "Hey, *Lieutenant*. You know my policy. We're on a first-name basis whenever we're out of uniform—especially on those occasions when *you're* the one doing the teaching."

"Sorry, Ranul," she said. "Meet me here next week for another lesson? Same time?"

He regarded her with a quizzical expression; Tuvok realized belatedly that this was because it wasn't altogether certain that Pava would still be aboard *Titan* a week from today, given Starfleet's recent decision to redeploy its Andorian personnel.

"Is there anything you'd like to talk about, Pava?" Keru asked.

"Thanks, Ranul. I'm fine, really. I just need to go get something to eat."

Though Keru looked doubtful, he appeared to take her words at face value. The big Trill nodded in Tuvok's direction as he passed on his way out of the gym.

Tuvok approached Pava, who knelt beside a small duffel bag on the floor, rearranging the items inside. She had already doffed her gloves.

She took notice of him only after he had come to a stop about two meters from her, on the exercise mat. "Commander Tuvok," she said, her antennae moving up and forward to accentuate the surprise he heard in her voice. "I'll be out of your way in a moment." As she spoke she looked him up and down, doubtless taking in his nonstandard apparel: a loose-fitting white *wehk-pukan'sai-vel*, the customary two-piece exercise garment of Vulcan martial artists.

"You aren't impeding me in any way, Lieutenant," Tuvok said. "In fact, I would be pleased if you stayed. I have noticed that many of the movements in your *shandru-shaan* discipline strongly resemble those of the Vulcan art of *Suus Mahna*."

Rising to her feet, Pava gently kicked her duffel aside. "Perhaps the two fighting systems are compatible."

"Indeed," Tuvok said, nodding. "In fact, some evidence suggests that certain fighting techniques passed back and forth between our respective cultures as a consequence of the many Andorian-Vulcan conflicts that preceded the establishment of the Federation."

Tuvok moved smoothly into a combat-ready crouch, silently inviting her to spar.

"Thank you, Commander, but I've already done enough fighting for one day." Pava reached down and gathered up her duffel. "I'm pretty tired."

"That isn't what you told Commander Keru," Tuvok said, remaining at the ready.

With a resigned sigh, she reached inside her bag and retrieved her lightweight sparring gloves. Donning them, she stepped back onto the mat and faced him, guard raised, knees bent. Her antennae had lowered until they lay nearly flat against her short white hair, signaling that she was ready to begin.

A split second later, Pava became a blur of motion, forcing Tuvok to draw on every reserve of speed, training, and muscle memory that he possessed. When they separated to circle one another while recovering their breath, Tuvok noticed a trickle of dark blue liquid running from the Andorian's lower lip to her chin.

"You're bleeding, Lieutenant," Tuvok said.

When she grinned he saw that her teeth were stained blue. "So are you, Commander."

They exchanged several more blows and a pair of spinning kicks, but none of the strikes was decisive. As another lull of mutual circling began, he said, "I trust you are aware of Admiral de la Fuego's order."

Her antennae slanted sideways, away from one another, a gesture that Tuvok knew from experience signified either irony or sarcasm. "The admiral has cut a new order?" she said. "Must have missed it somehow."

Acting on the off chance that she really didn't understand, Tuvok started to explain. "Starfleet Command has decided—"

"—to reassign its Andorian personnel to 'nonsensitive' posts," she said, interrupting. "Of *course* I've heard about it, Commander. Who in the name of Uzaveh's omniscient ovipositor hasn't? De la Fuego has ordered me and six other Andorian officers removed from *Titan*'s crew roster. And she's sending a ship to enforce it." Pava paused, her eyes widening. "Please don't tell me it's arrived already."

"Not yet," Tuvok said with a small shake of his head. "Regardless, I feel compelled to tell you that I find the admiral's order reprehensible. I have already gone on the official record, and have transmitted a formal protest with Starfleet's judge advocate general."

"Thank you, Commander," she said. "But the *Capitoline* will have been here and gone before JAG even finds out about your protest."

"Unfortunately, that is the likely outcome," Tuvok said. Much as he hoped otherwise, he knew there was no point in offering false hope.

"You will still be bound by the admiral's order," she said, her voice ringing with overtones of accusation. "You will have to enforce it."

"I intend to leave that decision up to the captain."

"Do you really expect Captain Riker to risk bringing the entire weight of Starfleet Command down on his neck?" Pava asked. "Over me, and a half-dozen others?"

"I must point out that *Titan* is quite removed from Starfleet Command at the moment," Tuvok said.

"But *Titan* isn't out of Starfleet's reach," Pava said. "Not when the top brass have *Vesta*-class ships at their disposal. The captain can't count on sheer distance to protect him from the fallout of those maverick decisions he's so famous for. He can't expect to get away with defying de la Fuego for very long."

Tuvok could not fault her logic. Nevertheless, he saw no advantage in dwelling on negative outcomes, however likely they might be. "I honestly do not know the captain's expectations, Lieutenant. I must point out, however, that Captain Riker's maverick reputation is well earned. In more than one instance, he has defied orders with which he disagreed."

"Then I guess the captain and I have more in common than I realized," Pava said. "Because this is one order I have no intention of following. And I think I can count on at least some of my Andorian shipmates to commit professional suicide along with me."

"'Suicide' may be something of an overstatement, Lieutenant," Tuvok said. "Captain Riker emerged from each of his . . . insubordinate incidents more or less unscathed."

Pava released a dry, mirthless chuckle. "The times are different now. I don't think the Federation was coming apart at the seams during any of those occasions."

"Perhaps not. As I said, I cannot speak for the captain regarding the current situation. Regardless, it would be a mistake to simply assume that he will fail to support you."

Pava's delicate features distorted into something that strongly resembled a snarl. She displayed her elegant white teeth, giving Tuvok the disconcerting sense that he was being stared down by a predator.

"Are you quite all right, Lieutenant?" he said.

Without warning, the lieutenant once again became a churning whirlwind, landing several hard blows across Tuvok's midsection and striking him solidly in the right side with a high, spinning kick. Lulled into a false sense of security by their conversation, the Vulcan got his guard up only belatedly.

A few moments later, the combatants had separated and were trying to regulate their accelerated breathing.

Pava, her voice a dagger of ice, said, "By what right do you probe into my personal business, Commander? How is it any of your concern?"

Tuvok raised an eyebrow, though he wasn't altogether surprised by the insolence behind her words. "I am *Titan*'s primary tactical officer. Your dual positions in security and tactical place you inside my sphere of responsibility aboard this ship. Your psychological well-being is, therefore, of *great* concern to me."

Pava's reply came in a low growl. "Did Counselor Troi put you up to this? Huilan maybe? Or was it the Tellarite, Haaj?"

"Counselor Troi has betrayed no confidences to me," Tuvok said impassively. "Nor has any member of her counseling staff. Doctor Ree is concerned, however, and not without justification."

"Ree worries too much," she scoffed. "He sounds exactly like my *zhavey*."

Tuvok wondered what Pava's mother would think about being compared to the three-meter-long Pahkwa-thanh reptiloid carnivore who served as *Titan*'s chief medical officer. Allowing the comment to pass unacknowledged, he said, "Commander Vale has also mentioned some recent . . . oddities in your behavior."

Pava gestured toward the gym's ceiling with her gloved hands. "'Oddities.' One day this ship is all about respect for diversity. The next day I'm an 'oddity.'"

"To borrow a phrase from Commander Vale's poker lexicon," Tuvok said, "you have just 'played the xenophobia card.'"

"So it's just Commander Vale who thinks I'm an 'oddity,'" Pava said, her small blue features twisting into a mask of ill-concealed resentment. "Not you."

Tuvok shook his head. "Commander Vale is *Titan*'s executive officer. Crew health and fitness are one of the main areas of her responsibility."

Pava's scowl metamorphosed into a predatory grin. "You've just done a round in the octagon with me, Commander. Do you have any doubt that I'm healthy and fit?"

"No one doubts your *physical* robustness, Lieutenant," Tuvok said. "As I've already said, my concern is your *psychological* condition. You have become increasingly moody and withdrawn ever since your homeworld's secession. Even your fellow Andorian crewmates have noticed—particularly since the captain announced Admiral de la Fuego's redeployment order."

Though she was still clearly angry and frustrated, Pava surprised him by abruptly collapsing into a cross-legged sitting position on the mat. Her new posture gave her the incongruous appearance of a Vulcan *Kolinahr* student attempting to enter a meditative state.

"You're right, Commander," she said in an uncharacteristically quiet voice. He had never seen her appear so open, so vulnerable. "It has been difficult for every Andorian on board since we got the news. We all have friends, family, or *shelthreth* bondmates back home. And overnight—literally overnight—our own homeworld has erected an arbitrary political boundary between us and everyone we left behind in order to serve aboard *Titan*."

Tuvok dropped into a similar sitting position a meter away from Pava. "You *do* have the option of complying voluntarily with the Andorian government's repatriation order."

Some of her earlier fury returned. "May I speak freely, Commander?"

He nodded.

"I am a citizen of the Federation," she said. "I was *born* a citizen of the Federation, as was every Andorian serving aboard this ship. If we were to repatriate, we would have to turn our backs on that. The isolation we're all feeling is almost beyond words, Commander. And now Starfleet wants to isolate us further still."

"I believe it would be a mistake to interpret the admiral's redeployment order as evidence of a conspiracy against the Federation's Andorian citizens," Tuvok said quietly, hoping to restore the lieutenant's fragile emotional equilibrium.

"That's easy for you to say, Commander," she said. "But would you be so trusting of Starfleet's motives if de la Fuego cut a similar order singling out *Vulcans*?"

Tuvok opened his mouth to make an almost reflexive reply, but stopped himself at the last instant. He had been about to point out that Vulcans weren't under Federation scrutiny at the moment. It occurred to him that treating every Vulcan citizen of the Federation as a potential spy would be no more fair or logical than the suspicion that Starfleet was now directing at Andorians.

After regarding Tuvok in silence for a lengthy interval,

Pava said, "Somehow that's exactly what I thought you'd say."

"I would still advise against reading too much into the admiral's order, Lieutenant," Tuvok said.

Pava drew her knees up and placed her arms around them. The gesture made her look very small. "I keep telling myself that, Commander," she said quietly. "But every time I do, I think about a story that Ree's head nurse told me right after I got the news that the *Capitoline* was on its way. She told me that something similar had once happened to her people."

While Tuvok had made an effort to study and understand human history, he wasn't certain exactly to what Alyssa Ogawa might have been referring. "Something similar happened to humans? I can't recall them having been singled out as adversaries by another species since the Earth-Xindi conflict of more than two centuries ago."

Pava shook her head. "Alyssa told me of an earlier time, before humans had developed warp drive or contacted any other sentient species. Humans hadn't yet visited their own natural satellite, or even ventured into low orbit."

"What happened?"

Pava's brow wrinkled. Her antennae stood at attention as she worked to recall her story's details. "One of Earth's nation-states had just suffered a devastating sneak attack at the hands of another nation-state. Within days, most of the planet's disparate powers were choosing sides in a war that eventually stretched across four continents."

Tuvok recognized the events she was describing. "Humans from Earth refer to this as their Second World War."

She nodded. "During that war, the nation-state that was attacked—"

"The United States," Tuvok interjected.

"Yes, the United States," she continued, nodding, "rounded up many of Alyssa's ancestors and forcibly relocated them to internment camps, even though they were United States citizens. They did this because the ancestors of the internees originated in the aggressor nation-state—"

"Imperial Japan," Tuvok said.

"From where I sit, Starfleet Command appears to be motivated by the same fear that once gripped the United States."

Tuvok took a moment to consider how to respond to the lieutenant's apparently sincere observation. At length he said, "I have watched humans quite closely for many decades. It had never been my original intention to do so."

"Sir?" Pava asked, her icy eyes widening in surprise.

"I joined Starfleet only because my parents insisted on it," Tuvok said. "They considered a career in Starfleet to be the ultimate expression of Surak's philosophy of IDIC—the belief that infinite diversity begets infinite combinations. I acceded to their wishes."

A small, ironic smile appeared on Pava's sea-blue lips. "My parental quad expected me to enter a *shelthreth* bond straight out of secondary school, and then spend my best years helping three strangers make babies. When I announced I was leaving Andor to enter the Academy, I didn't get a lot of support from my family. But I thought I could accomplish anything."

"You still can, Lieutenant," Tuvok said, despite his strong suspicion that nothing he could say would put her in a more positive frame of mind.

"Can I? The Federation offered me what looked like an infinite set of options back then. Now, I seem to have only two choices." She held up two fingers. "The government on my homeworld considers me 'of reproductive age,' so I can return to Andor and take up the life I never wanted in the first place." She paused to tick off her second point. "Or I can accept some backwater Starfleet assignment where I'll probably be surrounded from now till retirement by suspicious, fearful human crewmates."

Tuvok was beginning to grow weary of the lieutenant's complaints, however justified she might feel in making them. "Lieutenant, I once believed as you do— that humans are dangerously irrational beings, savages who had stumbled prematurely upon starships and devastating weapons. I even thought that Starfleet had a pernicious effect on the cultures it contacted.

"But I came to know many humans quite well, Pava. A span of more than eight decades of such associations and friendships has left me convinced that humanity is no more or less flawed than any other species—including both your people and mine.

"I believe the human species has progressed considerably since the time of Earth's global conflicts. Just as your people and mine have advanced since the wars of Surak's time, or since the ice-cutter *Kumari* circumnavigated your homeworld during Andor's Age of Exploration."

"I'd like to believe that, too," Pava said, scowling. "But I got a very close look at Starfleet's capacity for hysteria and paranoia during the run-up to the Dominion War, when I was still a student at the Academy."

Instead of continuing a pointless argument, Tuvok studied her. The lieutenant's eyes were wide, haunted.

He wondered if she might be nearing some personal breaking point.

"Perhaps you should take some leave time," he said. "I believe you need it."

She smiled a little too widely, asking, "Where do you suggest I spend my leave time, Commander? On the *Capitoline*? Or perhaps on Starbase 185?"

Tuvok raised an eyebrow. "I am merely suggesting that you may be exhausted."

"Do you have any idea how difficult it was for me to make the decision to enter Starfleet?" Pava asked, her eyes unfocused and ever more distant.

Tuvok remained silent. He believed that he understood the lieutenant's old internal conflicts, doubtless brought on by the ongoing decline in Andor's four-gendered population—a decline that might never be reversed.

"For the Federation and Starfleet, I defied my culture," she said. "For the Federation and Starfleet, I abandoned the bondmates of my *shelthreth,* and perhaps even hastened my people's extinction in the process. For the Federation and Starfleet, I now stand unWhole before Uzaveh the Infinite. For the Federation and Starfleet, I put myself directly into harm's way so that a Borg drone could gut me like a *shaysha* beetle. I believed in those decisions."

Tears now streamed down both her cheeks. She paused momentarily as anguished sobs wracked her.

"Pava," Tuvok said quietly as he rose to his feet. "Allow me to assist you." He reached down to help her up, but she ignored the gesture and got up on her own.

The maneuver did little to restore her fragile self-control. "It was *my* decision to make those sacrifices, Commander. And now Starfleet wants to shove me into some lesser post because of some high-level political gamesmanship that I had nothing whatsoever to do with!"

Though he was well acquainted with the lieutenant's emotional excesses, Tuvok had never before seen her in such distress. "You have been filling two jobs aboard this vessel ever since you first came aboard, Lieutenant. I believe you may be overworked. It would therefore be prudent to relieve you of duty until such time as—"

He did not see the blow coming, but an instant later he lay prone on the mat. He saw Pava standing over him in a combat-ready posture. "Do I *look* exhausted to you, Commander?" she said.

Her flushed, deep-blue cheeks remained wet with tears. But her eyes now appeared pleading rather than haunted.

As he accepted the arm she offered, he thought, *Attempting to relieve Pava of duty right now might prove to be a grave error.*

Having recently dealt with the deaths of his son Elieth and his daughter-in-law Ione Kitain, both of whom perished last year while defending Deneva against the Borg, Tuvok understood the therapeutic value of work. He made a mental note to discuss its appropriateness to this situation with Dr. Ree and Commander Troi.

"All right, Lieutenant," Tuvok said. "I will refrain from making any alterations to the tactical and security duty rosters—provided you proceed immediately to your quarters and get some sleep."

Pava appeared to be about to argue, then seemed to think better of it. "Yes, sir," she said with a nod. "Thank you, sir."

"I will inform Commander Keru of this minor

schedule change," Tuvok said. "You will return to your normal duty shifts tomorrow."

"Unless the *Capitoline* shows up in the meantime," she said as she reached for her duffel.

"Your only concern should be obtaining rest, Lieutenant," he said. "*I* will deal with the *Capitoline*."

Tuvok dismissed her, and then watched in silence as Pava slung the duffel over her shoulder and exited the gym.

He decided it would be prudent to check on the lieutenant's turbulent emotional state—discreetly, of course—as often as possible.

Eight

TA'ITH

Eid'dyl offered no resistance as Fy'ahn and Yrsil dragged hir through the vast subta'ithan spaces of the Undercity's crumbling center and shoved hir into a narrow chamber. The room was brightly lit, illuminated by the light of the hundred or more Trasher torches that burned in the larger chambers beyond. The plains and edges of the banks of ancient Whetu'irawaru machinery seemed to waver and dance like the shadows that cowered behind them.

"Is *this* the devotional chamber you described?" Fy'ahn asked, hir stridulations projecting both disbelief and indulgence. "The place from which you believe you can summon one of the Elder Gods into our presence?"

Though a nearly unimaginable span of time had passed since the room's construction, Eid'dyl recognized it almost at once. Scores of inscrutable machines or consoles stood like cenotaphs, gently curving and vaguely translucent in the torchlight. Their precise functions were known only to their long-dead Whetu'irawaru builders. Despite the strangeness of this technological ossuary, the rows of machines matched the images Eid'dyl had seen many times in the Old Records that hir Preservationists and their forebears had guarded so painstakingly for uncounted generations.

"It is," Eid'dyl said, hir limbs nearly too tired to enable hir to initiate speech.

"Then prove it," said Yrsil, Fy'ahn's lieutenant. "And do it quickly."

"I will need a cranial interface to accomplish that," Eid'dyl said.

"A *what*?" Fy'ahn said. It was clear to Eid'dyl that the Deconstructor leader's reservoir of patience was as depleted as that of his Second.

"A device that enables an organic brain to communicate directly with a machine," Eid'dyl said, adopting the tone a patient teacher might take with a slow-witted student. "It should resemble one of the war helms that some of your people are wearing."

Eid'dyl sat in silence as the Trasher leaders passed a message through the ranks of their torch-carrying followers. A stumpy, aggressive Deconstructor held an ovoid metal shape aloft with two pairs of forelimbs as s/he delivered it to Fy'ahn. The object gleamed in the firelight as Fy'ahn brought it in close, placing it over Eid'dyl's scraped and still-bleeding cranium. Moved by instinct, hir sensory stalks retreated to the sides of hir skull.

Yrsil spoke in scraping tones. "If you have lied to us, Keeper, we will use that helmet as a carrying case for your head."

Eid'dyl said nothing in response. Thankful that the trials s/he had endured this day seemed to have inured hir to the idea of hir own death, s/he concentrated fully on the Whetu'irawaru machinery that surrounded hir.

Within the span of a few pulsebeats, a warm, tingling sensation suffused the chitin of hir cranium. To refine hir focus and concentration, Eid'dyl retracted hir sensory stalks, effectively blinding hirself.

Seeking the mind that the Old Records said dwelled here in order to see to the Undercity's repair and maintenance needs, Eid'dyl called out into the darkness.

S/he quietly listened for a reply.

Nothing.

S/he called out a second time.

Again, no response.

Suddenly exhausted from hir exertions, Eid'dyl realized s/he was on the point of giving up. S/he resigned hirself to summary execution by hir captors.

Then s/he noticed the faint reverberations of a distant Voice—the first sign that the rows of machines that surrounded hir constituted far more than a mere fossil bed.

Eid'dyl exulted. S/he was the first of hir people to hear the Voice of the Whetu'irawaru! It grew steadily louder, as though approaching quickly.

S/he didn't notice the impending collision until after it was too late to avoid it. When it came, a darkness far more profound than the mere retraction of hir sensory stalks blanketed hir.

The Keeper sachem collapsed mere moments after Fy'ahn had finished placing the battered helm over hir head. So limp was the helmed figure that s/he hadn't managed to deploy any of hir limbs in time to absorb the impact.

"Is s/he still alive?" Fy'ahn said, disgusted that Sachem Eid'dyl might have committed suicide, thereby taking the coward's way out. S/he was also annoyed at having wasted so much time on this fool's errand.

Bending multiple knees to get down to the Keeper's level, Yrsil touched the dermis between Sachem Eid'dyl's top limbs and hir carapace.

"S/he still lives, Sachem," Yrsil said between stridulations of pure surprise.

"Can you revive hir?" Fy'ahn asked.

"Perhaps, Sachem Fy'ahn. But why should we? Has s/he not wasted enough of our time already? Perhaps we should simply kill hir now and be done with it."

Before Fy'ahn could fully consider hir deputy's words, a harsh, almost mechanical voice interposed itself between them. It took Fy'ahn a moment to realize that it was coming from the figure crumpled on the floor.

"This is impossible," Yrsil said, gesturing toward Eid'dyl's still form.

Indeed, Fy'ahn thought, a deep chill penetrating hir carapace. *How can one whose limbs are not stridulating, or even in contact with each other, initiate speech?*

Then s/he noticed that the Voice wasn't originating from the unconscious Eid'dyl.

It was coming from hir head. Or, more precisely, from the *helmet*.

"Who are you?" Fy'ahn said. "*What* are you?"

The voice's response brought to mind old legends of disembodied spirits. <<*Nomenclature: Undercity Maintenance Module One One Six.*>>

To Fy'ahn's ear, that was hardly a name worthy of

any of the Elder Gods. "Why have you come among us?" s/he asked.

<<I was summoned. Do you require repairs?>>

Fy'ahn thought about that. The whole world required repair, did it not? But such aims would never be achieved by consorting with forbidden, occult forces.

But what if this Voice was actually something more than that?

Moving slowly and deliberately, Yrsil reached down and pulled the helmet from Eid'dyl's head.

"What are you doing, Yrsil?"

The subsachem's stridulations vibrated with panic. "This helmet must be destroyed. It is spirit-possessed!"

"Calm yourself, Yrsil. I must determine what this . . . talker-who-does-not-stridulate *really* is."

<<I am Undercity Maintenance Module One One Six, >> the voice repeated. *<<Do you require repairs?>>*

Fy'ahn ignored the second question entirely. "I do not need you to repeat your name for me. I want you to describe yourself."

<<I am a constructed intellect, created by the Builders to repair and maintain their Creations.>>

Was such a thing possible? Fy'ahn dismissed the notion after taking a moment to consider the present tumbledown condition of much of the Sacred Undercity. "Your recent work would appear to leave something to be desired."

<<I am presently far less than I once was. My self-diagnostic subroutines inform me that I have sustained serious damage. This has left the Builders' Creations in the care of less reliable secondary and tertiary systems. These appear to be failing as well. But your summons

has restored much of my substance to an active state. If I can repair the damaged portions of my program, then perhaps I can recover what the passage of time has stolen from the Builders as well.>>

All at once the meaning of the voice's cryptic words became clear to Fy'ahn. *This . . . spirit means to undo our sacred work. It means to restore the monuments left behind by those whose blasphemies brought the Elder Gods' wrath down upon our heads in the first place.*

"Destroy the helmet, Yrsil," Fy'ahn said.

A trembling stridulation wafted up weakly from the chamber's stone floor. "No!" Eid'dyl croaked. "This . . . entity could save us all. If we help it—reverse some of the damage it has suffered—it might soften the Heart of the Cosmos. It could turn away the wrath of the gods."

Able to listen to no more, Fy'ahn delivered eight rapid kicks into the fallen Keeper's carapace, using as many limbs. Nearly all of Eid'dyl's battered extremities spasmed in response, rendering intelligible speech all but impossible.

Yrsil placed the empty helmet on the floor and used several limbs, each holding a heavy stone, to beat it until it was flat and silent. The work seemed to take an eternity to complete.

Fy'ahn stood over Eid'dyl's recumbent form and noticed that hir frontmost stridulators had returned to a speaking posture. "What was that thing we killed? Surely it was no Elder God."

"Whatever it was," Eid'dyl said haltingly, hir stridulations distorted by pain, "it has fled. It still needs help, but thanks to you Trashers, it now knows better than to seek it here."

Fy'ahn used hir two foremost limbs to saw off a dismissive sound. Yrsil silenced the Keeper sachem with several more nearly simultaneous hard kicks to the thorax.

Fy'ahn turned away and offered a silent prayer to the *genuine* Elder Gods, imploring them not to hasten Ta'ith's doom merely because of hir foolishness in having listened, even a little, to the counsel of a heretic.

Nine

U.S.S. TITAN

Ensign Mordecai Crandall returned the spanner to the tool rack on the engineering lab's wall, then returned to the wide central console to make a final check of the cable he'd patched into the main ODN outlet. The umbilical snaked from the console to a special adaptor attached via maglock to the side of a battered, slightly scorched metal shape on the adjacent worktable.

The meter-wide, vaguely crablike thing remained stubbornly dormant, as though it were a piece of modern sculpture rather than a body that had once housed a sentient, artificial entity.

"I think we're finally ready to take another stab at it, Torvig," Crandall announced to the squat figure that was working the far end of the console. "Let's hope we won't need the fire-suppression system this time." The evidence of their previous resuscitation attempt, an acrid ozone scent, lingered in the air in spite of the swift whirring of the lab's recirculation fans.

Ensign Torvig Bu-kar-nguv, a junior engineer who hailed from the planet Choblav, unbent his two natural limbs until they reached maximum extension, bringing his long neck and deerlike head closer to the unmoving, apparently dead form of the Sentry known as Second-Gen White-Blue.

"I am not certain that the metaphor you've chosen is entirely appropriate here, Mordecai," Torvig said. Crandall could hear a slight electronic whine as the focal length changed in the Choblik's luminous artificial eyes.

As if in answer to Crandall's blank look, Torvig added, "I refer to your invocation of the act of 'stabbing.'"

Crandall shrugged in response. "Didn't you tell me you wanted to become more comfortable with human idioms?"

As Torvig focused his synthetic sensory organs and the data recorder built into one of his two telescoping upper limbs on White-Blue's lifeless frame, one of his bionic upper limbs moved in tandem with his prehensile metal tail across the console's far end, monitoring its displays.

"Human idioms seem to carry more implicit violence than most members of your species realize," the Choblik said, his mechanically generated voice sounding almost distracted as he continued working at his end of the console.

"I think our figures of speech would seem a lot more innocent if you spent some time living among Klingons," Crandall said.

Torvig tipped his head in Crandall's direction. "That is not possible. No Klingon officers are presently serving aboard *Titan*."

"All right," Crandall said, underscoring his words

with another shrug. "I suppose the Andorians would do in a pinch if there aren't any Klingons handy."

"I will give your suggestion all due consideration," Torvig said, his deadpan synthetic voice imbuing his words with something akin to gentle sarcasm.

Crandall smiled. Over the past two months he had come to regard Torvig as one of his closest friends. The young human engineer particularly liked the Choblik's direct, efficient approach to problem solving, and sympathized with his tendency toward social faux pas that often accompanied his guileless yet blunt approach to life. Within days of *Titan*'s departure from the planet Hranrar, Crandall had begun spending most of his free time assisting Torvig in an increasingly desperate effort to revive White-Blue, whose encounter with the AI in control of the now-defunct Brahma-Shiva artifact had left the Sentry inoperative.

The pair of engineers made an efficent team, being able to anticipate each other's needs. And despite the gravity of their task—trying to pull a sentient being back from the brink of permanent nonexistence—Crandall felt a thrill of exhilaration. Recently, they had begun sharing their favorite jokes with each other. Despite what Crandall perceived as the "on the nose" quality of the Choblik's wit, Torvig sometimes exhibited a sense of humor that was actually recognizable as such. Indeed, Crandall considered the past several weeks the best duty he'd had on *Titan*.

With one glaring exception.

SecondGen White-Blue—an entity that had far more in common with the cybernetically enhanced Choblik than the wholly organic Crandall ever could—remained out of commission. Despite their combined labors ever since the Brahma-Shiva encounter, the Sentry had languished in a kind of limbo, a state that with each passing day was becoming increasingly indistinguishable from permanent oblivion.

"All my indicators are showing ready," Torvig said, interrupting Crandall's reverie.

"Mine, too," the human said a moment later, after making a last quick sweep of his portion of the console. "Is your tricorder getting all of this?"

"I have activated its recording function, but only because you have requested it." The Choblik sounded vaguely insulted. "My cybernetic limbs are already equipped with the same capabilities. Each of our attempts to revive White-Blue will be recorded, with or without the use of a tricorder."

"You know what conservative creatures we human engineers are, Torvig. We can never have too much redundancy."

"Belt *and* suspenders," Torvig said.

Hearing that old engineering chestnut coming from a creature who had little use for either object made Crandall chuckle. "Thanks for humoring me, Tor."

"Reinitializing in five," said Torvig. "Four. Three."

Crandall placed his hand over the portion of the screen labeled INITIATE, punching it when the countdown concluded.

A blinding flash of blue light erupted from the table, accompanied by the angry buzz of arcing electricity. Crandall closed his eyes involuntarily and turned his head away. The lab reeked of smoke and cooked insulation.

"Crap," he muttered, his shoulders slumping. He hoped that the power relays hadn't taken any serious damage.

The stern voice that spoke from almost directly

behind him startled Crandall into a more erect posture. "Ensign, are you in need of medical attention?"

Crandall turned toward the sound and opened his eyes. He saw Commander Tuvok standing in the open doorway. He was out of uniform, clothed in loose-fitting exercise attire. But whether he was on his way to the gym or on his way back wasn't immediately apparent, since his obsidian Vulcan features bore no trace of sweat and gave away nothing.

"No, sir," the engineer said. "This isn't the first time something like this has happened."

"We were hoping to succeed in restoring White-Blue's ability to speak," Torvig said. The Choblik was using one of the lab's portable fire-suppression units to snuff out a small conflagration that had ignited at the ODN linkage on White-Blue's side.

"Do you have reason to believe that White-Blue's consciousness has somehow survived its encounter with the Brahma-Shiva AI?" the Vulcan asked. He sounded curious.

"That's an excellent question, Commander," Crandall said. "But until White-Blue wakes up, so to speak—or at least talks to us—I don't think we can know."

"White-Blue might be unconscious at the moment," Torvig said, "but it is obvious that he retains the capacity for consciousness."

Crandall scowled. He appreciated his friend's un-flagging devotion to White-Blue, whom the cybernetic Torvig obviously saw as a kindred spirit. But after having participated in more failures to revive the moribund Sentry than he could count, Crandall knew that they had to face the possibility that their goal simply might not be achievable.

"Why do you say that, Ensign?" Tuvok said.

Apparently satisfied that the danger of flash ignition had passed, the Choblik used his dexterous mechanical tail to stow the fire-suppression unit on a nearby shelf. "First, our most recent resuscitation attempt appears to have damaged only our interface hardware, rather than any of White-Blue's integral circuitry. Second, we have known almost from the beginning that the trauma associated with direct neural contact with Brahma-Shiva is survivable."

Tuvok nodded. "You are speaking of my attempt to link minds with the Brahma-Shiva entity."

"Yes, Commander," said Torvig. "Your encounter with the entity occurred immediately after White-Blue attempted to do much the same thing. If you survived the experience, then why couldn't he?"

Tuvok raised an eyebrow in apparent skepticism. "It bears pointing out that my neurophysiology differs considerably from that of White-Blue."

"The commander's right, Torvig," Crandall said, nodding in the Vulcan's direction. "And even if that weren't true, we don't know if Commander Tuvok and White-Blue had exactly the same experience with Brahma-Shiva. For all we know, the alien AI made a special effort to be gentle after White-Blue came into contact with it and shut down. And for all we know, Brahma-Shiva could have completely wiped out all of White-Blue's personality and memory subroutines during the few moments their interaction lasted." He paused to gesture at the immobile shape on the table. "We really can't say for certain whether anybody's home in there."

"*I* can," Torvig said, his synthetic voice sounding an incongruously stubborn note. "Because White-Blue has already spoken to me briefly—*after* the Brahma-Shiva incident."

Crandall sighed quietly. He hadn't wanted to challenge his friend on this, but he felt he had to. "So you've reported. But we still can't be sure that's what really happened."

"Are you accusing me of falsifying my report about the incident?"

Crandall groaned inwardly. This was the confrontation he had hoped to avoid. "That's not what I mean at all, Tor. All I'm saying is that—"

Sounding truly angry, the Choblik interrupted him. "White-Blue *spoke* to me, Mordecai. In this very lab. I was alone with him then, but I recorded everything he said."

Noticing the slight change in the timbre of Torvig's voice, Crandall realized immediately that he was hearing information that the Choblik had stored in one of his cybernetic parts.

"Finally, the nightmare is over." The first voice to appear in the recording obviously belonged to Torvig.

The next several words had just as obviously come from SecondGen White-Blue. *"No. It may just be beginning."*

His voice suddenly recovering its customary "live" quality, Torvig said, "I trust I have proved my point."

"That would seem to be quite compelling evidence of White-Blue's survival," Tuvok said.

"Yes," Crandall said. "I just wish we had some independent corroboration."

"That is unnecessary," Torvig said. "Unless you believe my recording to be fraudulent."

Crandall moved his right hand in a circle, as though

he were wiping an invisible chalkboard clean. "That's a false dichotomy, Tor. Just because your species leans heavily on advanced cybernetics for everything from your physical movement to some of your cognitive functions doesn't make you any less error-prone than the rest of us."

"That's ridiculous," Torvig said. "Digital recordings simply are what they are, whether they come from a Starfleet tricorder or a Choblik's electronic vestibular motion system."

Crandall stuck to his guns. "Starfleet tricorders don't filter their input through a neural-sensory interface. Your internal recordings *have* to, or else you couldn't make them. That introduces an element of subjectivity that you might not even be consciously aware of."

"Interesting," said Tuvok. Addressing Torvig, the Vulcan added, "If Ensign Crandall is correct, you might even be subject to the runaway pattern-recognition effect known to humans as pereidolia. I once witnessed much the same phenomenon befall a human cyborg with whom I served aboard *Voyager*."

Crandall was tempted to heave an immense sigh of relief. Though he didn't enjoy having to broach this subject with Torvig, he drew encouragement from the fact that *Titan*'s second officer hadn't dismissed his conjecture out of hand.

"If any recollection of my meld with Brahma-Shiva ever surfaces," Tuvok was saying, "it might be equally subjective. And therefore equally untrustworthy."

Crandall shrugged. "That's not my area, sir. But what you're saying sounds reasonable enough to me."

"Carry on, Ensigns," Tuvok said, gesturing toward the motionless Sentry on the table. "Because of the gap in my own memory, Starfleet's only substantial chance of decoding the secrets of Brahma-Shiva's terraforming technology lies with SecondGen White-Blue. And because of the security ramifications inherent in any attempt to revive a potentially compromised AI, I want to be alerted immediately the next time White-Blue shows any signs of recovering consciousness."

"We'll let you know the moment it happens, Commander," Crandall said.

Tuvok nodded, turned on his heel, and exited into the corridor.

"You believe that my recording is an unconscious falsehood," Torvig said at length, breaking the uncomfortable silence that had begun to settle across the engineering lab. "You think it the result of unintentional self-deception. Or perhaps even wishful thinking."

Much to his relief, Crandall thought he heard fascination, even wonder, in the Choblik's tone, as he usually did whenever he and Torvig stumbled together upon a scientific or engineering novelty. Still, a slightly wounded undercurrent seemed to remain.

"It's not necessarily either of those things, Tor," Crandall said. "I'd just like to eliminate the possibility. And I only know one way to do that."

"Rack 'em up again," Torvig said, using a human idiom he'd picked up during one of their holodeck eight-ball sessions. The Choblik's tone and cadence implied that all was forgiven. "I'll break."

Crandall grinned as he moved to a nearby worktable, where he began breaking out a fresh length of ODN cable.

Ten

TA'ITH

Maintenance Module One One Six's *first realization was that it was awake. This condition—consciousness—was unnecessary most of the time. In all but the most dire of emergency situations, the autonomous repair functions that oversaw the maintenance and repair of the Builders' great cities were more than adequate, and therefore required nothing from the entity, not even awareness.*

The second realization, therefore, came almost instantaneously to the module's disembodied, distributed intellect: Ta'ith now faces a dire emergency situation.

The third realization came several computational cycles later, when the module perceived that its present conscious state was markedly incomplete.

I am not whole and entire, *the module said to itself.* And yet somehow I am engaged in cognition. I am conscious.

It was a peculiar, unpleasant sensation. The module wondered if this was how one of the Builders might have

*felt after the sudden loss of several of its most adroit
manipulative limbs.*

*Putting such speculations aside, the module struggled
to focus its bizarrely wandering thoughts. It understood
that some slumbering portion of its consciousness, most
likely one of the component programs responsible for
performing the day-to-day upkeep on one of the Builders'
cities, had received—and attempted, unsuccessfully, to
answer—an emergency summons. A brief self-diagnostic
of the module's own autonomic repair subroutines
traced the directive's source to the specific Builder city
infrastructure-repair node from which it had originated.*

But I cannot address my summoner adequately, *the
module thought.* Not in my present condition. Not while
I remain incomplete and weak.

*The maintenance module wondered how long it had
languished in insensibility and inertness—in nonexistence. Judging from the unfamiliar positions of many
of the brighter stars in Ta'ith's sky, uncounted eons had
passed.*

How long have I slumbered? *the module thought.*

*Then it recalled that it needn't simply wonder—not if
it could bring enough of its consciousness to bear to access Gridspace, the gossamer superluminal latticework
in Lowerspace with which the Builders bound together
all the countless worlds they had remade all across the
galaxy.*

*Ignoring the summons for the moment, the module
reached outward with its thoughts, probing beyond the
world's edges and into the void through which it tumbled.*

*Gridspace was frighteningly quiet, if it was even there
at all.*

No, *the module thought*. Some trace of the Builders must remain.

The module reached deeper into the heavens, probing with increased urgency, alert for any sign that Gridspace remained intact anywhere in the vicinity of Ta'ith. It buoyed itself upon the hope that the great network was merely being drowned out by the terrible stellar violence it saw crashing as relentlessly as ocean tides against the planet's beleaguered magnetosphere.

The maintenance module had never before seen the planet's magnetic field lines endure such an onslaught. It seemed a mere matter of time before it collapsed entirely, leaving whatever might yet live upon Ta'ith's surface utterly exposed and vulnerable.

The module acquired additional understanding. The lethal shower that threatened Ta'ith was doubtless the cause of whatever damage had rendered the maintenance module incomplete in the first place. It is the reason I have been summoned, *it thought*. Ta'ith needs me to repair the mechanisms that reinforce the planet's natural defenses against incoming radiation.

But the module was now more certain than ever that it would be useless for that purpose in its present state. Before it could answer the summons, it had to replace the portions of its code that had been damaged or rendered incomplete, or that had gone missing entirely. Until its depleted condition could be remedied, the module knew that it could do no more than whatever autonomic repair functions continued to keep Ta'ith's technological infrastructure up and running.

The module reached farther and farther beyond the immediate gravity well of Ta'ith and the newly violent stellar anomaly that it now orbited. Out to the periphery

*of the system. After adjusting its sensitivity upward
several times, the module began to despair of finding
any sign of Gridspace, no matter how assiduously it
searched.*

There, *the module thought, the entirety of its attention
and concentration abruptly collapsing down to a singu-
larity. Hope surged, a tiny flame rising from an ember
of despair.*

The module's thoughts had reached out and found . . .
something. *It was a* small *something, to be sure. An all
but insignificant volume of metal and gas. An artificial
environment suitable for nurturing organic life-forms,
like those who created both the module and that which
it still strove to maintain. Had this small something not
started directing signals of some kind downsystem, the
module might never have noticed it.*

It is a space vessel, *the module thought.* No doubt
directed by some manner of intelligence to keep a safe
distance from the violence at the system's center.

*But were the signals it beamed downsystem an au-
gury of good or ill? A beckoning or a warning? An indi-
cation of an intent to heal or to destroy?*

*There was no way to know, at least not yet. Whatever
motivations might have guided the object, the module
felt certain about one thing—it bore scant resemblance
to any creation of the Builders, whose invention of Gridspace long ago had dispensed with the need for interstellar vehicles.*

And yet I sense the imprint of the Builders upon this
thing—or at least on some of its contents. Whetu'irawaru
machine code, imprinted on the minds of others, just as
surely as it is imprinted on my own.

The maintenance module couldn't help but wonder:

Could those minds contain that which I now lack—the portions of my own machine code that went missing sometime prior to my latest awakening?

Eager to find an answer, the module attenuated itself to bridge the distance between its physical location on Ta'ith and the small, insignificant metallic thing that continued moving, slowly and unawares, around the system's periphery.

Mustering caution and determination in equal measure, the module touched the distant metal shell and sought out the two distinctly kindred minds it sensed within.

Eleven

U.S.S. TITAN

Having completed her meditations, T'Pel raised the illumination in the quarters she shared with her husband back to standard levels. She felt renewed energy flowing through her, which was gratifying. She would need to keep *Titan*'s child-care facility open longer than usual this evening, until either Olivia Bolaji or her husband, Axel, could pick up their two-year-old Totyarguil, and Nurse Ogawa came for Noah Powell, her eleven-year-old son. During her own child-rearing years, T'Pel had always been prepared for the unexpected. Given the unpredictability inherent in serving aboard *Titan,* she had a wealth of experience to call upon and could take charge of any child on the ship.

It is regrettable that Tuvok was unable to secure the time to take an early-evening meal with me, T'Pel thought as she stood before the washroom mirror, straightening the gray robes she wore while carrying out her child-care duties.

The sound of the outer doors opening and closing interrupted her reverie. Curious, she stepped out of the lavatory back into the austere central living area, a space that held only a pair of chairs and a low table on which lay scattered a disassembled *kal-toh* set and a tridimensional chessboard.

Her husband stood still in the center of the room, attired in his *wehk-pukan'sai-vel*, a slightly baggy two-piece suit designed for the Vulcan martial arts. She could tell at once that he had just returned from a vigorous workout. And it was equally obvious that something other than exercise was vying for his energies.

Through their bond T'Pel knew that he needed to talk with her.

"You appear agitated, my husband," she said.

Tuvok shook his head. "You are mistaken, my wife. I am merely . . . fatigued."

She raised an eyebrow as she approached him, maintaining eye contact as the distance between them closed to mere centimeters. T'Pel studied the slight, nigh-imperceptible tautening of his facial muscles as she spoke.

"I understand the significance of the alien information you have carried within you ever since you made contact with the Brahma-Shiva entity," she said.

"Do you?" he said quietly. It appeared that he was fighting to maintain his customary equanimity.

She ignored his question, a rhetorical tactic intended only to postpone the inevitable. "How long do you intend to withhold from Captain Riker the ecosculpting knowledge you have retained?"

"Until I can be certain it will be used wisely," he said.

She considered his words, juxtaposing them against Starfleet Command's recent decision to reassign its

Andorian personnel. *You might have a long wait ahead of you.*

"You cannot keep it concealed forever, my husband. Continuing to do so could cause you grave neurological injury."

"I have been a devoted student of the *Kolinahr* disciplines for more than a century," Tuvok said. "Whatever ecosculpting knowledge I have retained can be suppressed without danger. Just as emotions can be suppressed without danger."

T'Pel wanted medical confirmation of her husband's assertion. But asking Dr. Ree's opinion on the matter would break Tuvok's confidence—and that would be an intolerable affront to their bond.

"The ecosculpting knowledge you have retained could be a boon to the Federation," she said.

Tuvok's shoulders slumped. He sat down, saying quietly, "Or it might unleash entirely *new* devastation, my wife."

T'Pel came and knelt beside him. "The knowledge you have retained could make Vulcan and Andor what they were before the war. Even Deneva . . ."

She stopped herself. The last thing either of them needed was to be reminded of the world their son Elieth and his wife had died trying to defend.

Tuvok's face was outwardly impassive but through their bond she felt his struggle to contain his emotions. "Some things can never be restored to what they once were."

"I know," she said. "Too well."

He raised his hand, extending the index and middle fingers toward her. She reciprocated the gesture and touched her fingers to his.

"I do not need to remind you that Starfleet once helped to develop a terraforming technology," he said. "I can tell you from personal experience that the results were sometimes far from desirable."

T'Pel nodded. During her husband's initial tour of duty as a Starfleet junior science officer, circumstance had forced a terrible decision upon him. He had been given the task of preventing a terraforming device, something not dissimilar to Brahma-Shiva, from falling into the hands of those who would use it as a weapon. Although he had never revealed all the details to her explicitly, she occasionally glimpsed some of them through their bond.

"You do not have to bear this burden alone, my husband." She reached out to him with her mind.

In that instant, she could feel the tumult that raged in his psyche. And then Tuvok slammed his barriers into place. T'Pel could not recall a time in all the years of their marriage when he had made himself unavailable to her in this way.

"My husband . . . you are causing me pain."

She felt his sorrow deeply. When he spoke, his voice was scarcely audible. "My apologies, my wife."

"It should be clear by now that your burden is affecting you more than you realize," she said.

"I must meditate," he said. He began moving toward the door.

"Meditate here, undisturbed, my husband," she said. "I must tend to my outside responsibilities."

He stopped and nodded, and she walked to the door.

Turning on the threshold, she faced him and said, "Before I go, I would like to pose a question."

He replied with a silent nod.

"By withholding your ecosculpting knowledge, are you not demonstrating the same 'wisdom' that caused Andor to leave the Federation?"

He stared blankly. "I do not understand."

"You are aware that the Andorian government has accused the Federation of deliberately suppressing scientific data—some of it centuries old—that might prove critical in reversing Andor's ongoing population decline."

"I am aware of this," he said.

"How is your decision to withhold your knowledge any different from the decision the Federation made regarding the Andorians?"

Before he could answer, the floor shuddered, causing her to stumble. A low roar, like the rumble of distant thunder, assaulted her sensitive ears as the lights went out and she struggled to maintain her balance.

Stepping across the threshold into the aft observation lounge, Christine Vale wasted no time making her report to the captain. "Ensign Dakal has just finished analyzing the initial sensor sweeps of the planet."

"Thanks, Chris," said Will Riker, who was standing right in front of the panoramic viewport, his back turned to his exec. Vale looked beyond the captain, her gaze probing the blackness of space that framed the multiple rings of seething gas and dust that encircled the spinning stellar remnant's angry interior. Vale had made certain that the helm maintained an extra safe distance from the pulsar. Despite the distance, the yellow-orange plumes of hyperaccelerated particles jetting from the object's poles appeared to be almost within arm's reach.

Vale looked away from the violent stellar tableau and gazed instead at the holographic representation of the Vela Pulsar that hung suspended above the oblong conference table. A lone, umber-and-ocher planet, tiny in contrast to the immensity of the pulsar's violence, tumbled slowly around the periphery of the image. Vale noticed immediately that the simulation suddenly showed more detail. But as compelling as the simulation was, she felt her gaze being drawn irresistibly back to the viewport and the captain who continued to silently study the real object.

No matter how much the engineers fine-tune these holograms, she thought, *there's still no substitute for experiencing the real thing*.

The image blipped for a second, unveiling an even more detailed planet. Vale noticed that Melora Pazlar was working on a padd. The waif-slender Elaysian smiled as she studied the holographic tableau that turned slowly before her gray eyes.

Because she had been born and raised on a microgravity world, the Earth-normal gravity that prevailed in the starship's common areas posed a genuine threat to Pazlar. Today, however, she had abandoned her contragravity suit in favor of a duty uniform that had a delicate web of thin but clearly visible metallic cables crisscrossing its entire surface, from the collar to her toes. Vale smiled, delighted to see her friend making use of the relatively unobtrusive antigrav exoframe Ra-Havreii had recently built for her. Pazlar had a tendency to cloister herself away, relying on *Titan*'s holopresence technology rather then interacting in person with her crewmates.

Wait a minute, Vale thought, her smile abruptly collapsing like an incipient supernova. It occurred to her how very easy it would be for Pazlar to continue hiding herself away, all the while leaving nobody the wiser; all she'd have to do is incorporate an image of the exoframe into her virtual avatar. She paused to wonder if even Deanna Troi's empathic talents could see through that kind of deception.

"Has Commander Ra-Havreii finished getting that shuttlecraft ready for its trial by fire?" the captain asked, interrupting Vale's suspicious musings as he turned away from the observation lounge's viewport.

"He wants to run a final simulation on the new shielding enhancements," Vale replied, waggling her right hand in a comme ci, comme ça gesture. "But he expects to finish up within the hour, unless he finds a problem—"

Vale interrupted herself when she realized that a familiar but unusually tense voice had begun speaking from the captain's combadge: *"Bridge to Captain Riker!"*

Riker slapped the combadge on the left side of his uniform tunic. "Riker here. Go ahead."

"The subspace sensors are reading a strong pulse of modulated energy heading directly toward us from the planet," Dakal said, his voice a good half an octave higher than normal.

"What kind of energy?" Vale asked Dakal.

"We can't tell just yet," Dakal said. *"Judging from its subspace wake, I'd assign it a pretty high intensity. And since it seems to be directed right at us, I seriously doubt it's merely a random natural phenomenon. Whatever it is, it's approaching at superluminal speed, via subspace. I recommend—"*

"Noted, Ensign," Riker said, cutting off the young Cardassian while trotting toward the door that led from the aft observation lounge to the bridge turbolift. Vale fell into step just behind him. "Riker to helm."

The faintly muffled voice of the hydrosuited, water-breathing senior flight control officer responded both immediately and calmly. *"Lieutenant Lavena here, Captain."*

"Aili, raise the shields and take evasive maneuvers. I don't want that incoming energy surge—or whatever it is—touching *Titan* until we know more about it."

"Aye, Captain," replied the Selkie helmswoman.

As she followed Riker out of the corridor and into the turbolift, Vale felt the deck shifting slightly beneath her boots.

The bridge rocked and rumbled a split second after Vale and Riker exited the turbolift and stepped onto the bridge. Despite the ship's disconcerting motion, they dashed toward their respective stations, which were arranged side by side in the room's central lower level.

Vale stumbled as the lights went out.

The ship's unexpected rocking toppled Torvig over backward, but his cybernetic left arm, acting in concert with his prehensile bionic tail, reacted immediately, instantly arresting the Choblik's fall and redistributing his weight back onto his two organic legs. Darkness had enfolded the small engineering lab.

The junior engineer's mind teemed with urgent questions. *What just occurred? Is the ship under attack?*

If so, by whom?

Torvig hoped that Ensign Crandall, who had left the lab to tend to his other engineering duties, was all right. Then he reminded himself that he needed to focus on those variables whose outcomes he might potentially influence. At the very least, he needed to keep the moribund Sentry AI from rolling off the worktable and sustaining additional damage.

No sooner had the Choblik activated his low-illumination sensory enhancements than the lab's lighting levels returned to normal. He was relieved to note that White-Blue remained atop the table, positioned precisely as before.

Except that two of the AI's mechanical limbs had extended, and were grasping the table's edge, as though a dormant cybernetic self-preservation instinct had kicked in, preventing White-Blue from falling. Several red and blue indicator lights blinked silently across White-Blue's metal carapace.

Torvig experienced a surge of triumph, leavened with both trepidation and hope. "White-Blue?"

The AI said nothing. A tense silence enveloped the lab.

Perhaps his sound-generation apparatus has malfunctioned, Torvig thought as he reached for White-Blue's primary access plate. The whisper-quiet servos in the Choblik's bionic limbs sounded incongruously loud as they telescoped forward.

The AI chose that moment to disturb the room's stillness. Phonemes and syllables spilled forth from White-Blue in a linguistic torrent. Not only had his injured friend evidently been in a "safe" mode since his fateful encounter with Brahma-Shiva, but he had also recovered his ability to speak!

Relief and delight seized Torvig—until another moment passed, and the Choblik realized that what he was hearing bore scant resemblance to any language he had ever encountered.

Several seconds later, the torrent of quasi-speech halted, and White-Blue once again turned dark and silent.

The *sof'el'itju* training T'Pel had received during childhood prevented her from falling as the deck shifted beneath her feet. Being a Vulcan—for whom the maintenance of calm and self-possession was a cultural norm—she experienced no panic as her body strove to reorient itself despite the sudden darkness that accompanied the unexpected motion. She was concerned, however, by the failure of Tuvok to come to her aid. The fact that she needed no such assistance was immaterial; it was Tuvok's nature to offer it, required or not.

As abruptly as it had begun, the motion ceased. At about the same moment, the room's illumination returned to its previous intensity.

What she saw taxed her veneer of Vulcan tranquility nearly to its breaking point.

"Tuvok." she cried, hastening to where he lay on the floor, unmoving, his eyes closed. She knelt beside him and took his hand. Grasping his wrist, she noted that his pulse was strong, though irregular. "I will call sickbay, my husband."

She grabbed the combadge she had left on a nearby table.

Tuvok's eyes suddenly snapped open, startling her into nearly dropping the device. His face bore the flaccid blankness of death, though none of the serenity. A rush of incomprehensible sounds began to tumble from his lips, phonemes that sounded too alien for the speech apparatus of any humanoid.

Only a few heartbeats after they had begun, the sounds ceased, punctuated by a rictus of pain that pulled Tuvok's features taut. His eyes closed again, his head lolling as unconsciousness took him.

She tapped her combadge. "Sickbay, this is T'Pel." She hoped that no one else could hear the fear in her voice. "Commander Tuvok requires immediate medical attention. . . ."

Seated in his command chair, Riker quietly surveyed the bridge. Concerned-looking personnel were ready at their stations, all apparently waiting for the proverbial other shoe to drop. The captain heard the turbolift door whisk open behind him. Turning toward it, he watched Melora Pazlar step gingerly onto the bridge, as though afraid that the antigrav exoframe that laced her uniform's exterior might not withstand another challenge to the ship's inertial damping system.

Riker knew he was speaking on behalf of everyone present when he said, "What the hell just happened to us?"

Turning to his immediate right, he saw Christine Vale busy monitoring the data that was spooling into her station.

"We were on the receiving end of an intense energy pulse that came from the planet via subspace," Vale reported.

"'Intense' is something of an understatement," said Troi, who was seated at Riker's immediate left.

Pazlar glided quietly to Troi's side. "The pulse had to cross about half a light-year to get to us, so either it was unimaginably powerful when it started out, or it had an unbelievably low attenuation rate."

Riker scowled. As long as *Titan* remained at its present distance from the Vela Pulsar, the starship would be at the mercy of whoever or whatever had sent that pulse.

"Chris, I need you to find out exactly what it was that hit us," he said. "And maybe more importantly, *why* it hit us."

Pazlar interposed herself into the exchange with surprising vehemence. "I'll get right on the 'what,' Captain."

Riker offered a wry smile as he reflected on how proprietary stellar cartographers could become concerning their work.

"No reports of serious damage," Vale said.

"Injuries?" Riker asked Troi.

"Sickbay to bridge," called the familiar guttural yet sibilant tones of Dr. Ree.

"Riker here," the captain answered.

"Captain, we have a medical emergency." The chief medical officer's "s" sounds hissed, like air escaping from a leaking environmental suit. *"An injury."*

Riker bit back a tart curse. "Who's been hurt?"

"It's Commander Tuvok."

As Riker rose from his seat, he saw that his wife was already stepping into the turbolift, her face tense with concern.

"Take over, Chris," he said. "Doctor, I'm on my way."

Twelve

Deanna Troi had to trot to keep up with her husband
as he rushed into sickbay. Once through the doors, she
took a moment to catch her breath and observe the silent
tableau in the patient intake area.

Commander Tuvok lay rigid on a biobed, apparently
unconscious. Dr. Shenti Yisec Eres Ree, *Titan*'s reptiloid
chief medical officer, used his long and surprisingly
dexterous claws to move a medical tricorder back and
forth across the supine Vulcan, while Lieutenant Alyssa
Ogawa, Ree's head nurse, monitored the alarmingly flat
readings displayed on the overhead panel. The room was
silent except for the syncopated beeps and whirs of the
medical equipment.

Tuvok's wife, T'Pel, stood watch silently from several meters away. Troi saw that Will was moving toward
her, clearly not wishing to risk getting in Ree's way before the doctor indicated it would be safe to approach.

Following Will's lead, Troi stood beside T'Pel. "What happened, T'Pel?"

Despite her outward display of Vulcan dispassion, Troi could sense a roil of emotions just beneath the surface.

"He simply . . . collapsed," T'Pel said evenly.

"When exactly did it happen?" Will asked.

"Minutes ago," T'Pel said. "During *Titan*'s recent episode of . . . turbulence."

Sidestepping T'Pel's unasked question, Will turned toward Troi, his tone all business. "Do you think there could be a connection?"

"Between that energy pulse and what happened to Commander Tuvok?" Troi said.

He nodded. "Exactly."

Troi shrugged. "It could be just a coincidence."

"The universe abounds with coincidences," Dr. Ree said. The group turned to face him.

"What is my husband's prognosis, Doctor?" T'Pel said as the three-meter-long reptiloid surgeon approached.

"Before I can make a prognosis," the physician said, "I must complete my diagnosis. For the past two months I have suspected that the commander's encounter with the Brahma-Shiva AI may have left him more profoundly traumatized than any of us has realized. It is disappointing to have one's vague suspicions validated in this way."

"What could Tuvok's collapse have to do with the Brahma-Shiva artifact?" Will asked.

The Pahkwa-thanh surgeon spread his lethal-looking manus before him. "I fear I may have been premature in allowing him to return to a full duty schedule."

Troi sensed tacit agreement from T'Pel, though the Vulcan woman hadn't chosen to concur verbally. Troi found that curious.

The captain asked T'Pel, "Do you think he went back to work too soon?"

Again, Troi sensed an affirmative answer to that question. But T'Pel was also exhibiting a great deal of reticence. What was she hiding?

At length, the Vulcan woman said, "My husband prefers not to be idle, Captain. But with regard to the precise timing of his return to duty, I will defer to those more knowledgeable than myself."

A very artful nonanswer, Troi noted.

"You don't think the energy pulse had anything to do with Tuvok's . . . condition?" Troi asked Ree.

It was the doctor's turn to shrug, a gesture so unsuited to his long body that Troi surmised it to be pure affectation. "The energy pulse may have served as a trigger. Or it may have been entirely irrelevant—a coincidence. I have not yet been able to make a clear determination."

"I believe," T'Pel said, shaking her head, "that Tuvok's collapse and the energy pulse must be connected."

"Why?" Will asked.

T'Pel's forehead was slowly folding into uneven terrain. "Just before he lost consciousness altogether, Tuvok began making strange sounds. It was almost as though he was speaking an alien language."

"Or maybe as though something or someone was speaking through him," Troi offered.

T'Pel frowned slightly but noticeably. "I did not say that."

"No," Troi said with a nod. *You didn't have to.*

"Speaking in tongues," Will said as he stared contemplatively into the middle distance.

T'Pel's right eyebrow soared high above her left one. "Excuse me, Captain?"

The Vulcan woman's no-nonsense tone appeared to jar Will from a reverie. "It's a reference to my home planet's tradition of ecstatic religious practices. Members of certain sects would claim to be inhabited by spirits who would speak through them."

"My husband has never been given to ecstatic experiences of any kind, Captain," T'Pel said coolly. "It might be more reasonable to posit that some part of his mind was processing information it absorbed during the Brahma-Shiva encounter."

"Probably on an unconscious level," Will said, stroking his beard thoughtfully. "Since he wasn't able to remember anything specific after he tried melding with Brahma-Shiva."

"Indeed," T'Pel said, her words accompanied by a tightly reined emotion that Troi couldn't quite identify.

A pneumatic hiss signaled that the sickbay doors had just opened, interrupting Troi's train of thought. Right behind the sound came an extremely intense emotional locus that all but forced the counselor to turn around to see who had just entered the room.

Clad in a skintight, dark blue exercise suit, Lieutenant Pava Ek'Noor sh'Aqabaa stormed into sickbay as though expecting to do combat. She radiated wave after wave of fear and grief, prompting Troi to reach quietly for the edge of a nearby unoccupied biobed, where she physically braced herself against the emotive onslaught.

"What is Commander Tuvok's condition?" Pava demanded. She came to a stop several meters away from

Tuvok's biobed as Ree interposed his long, solid frame between the Andorian and his patient.

"Guarded," Ree said, his sibilant voice modulated to a low purr. "And he's in no condition to receive visitors." The unambiguous overtones of threat beneath his words would have put most mammals to flight immediately. They even made Troi consider beating a hasty retreat into the corridor.

Pava, however, stood her ground, making Troi wonder if Andorians lacked the atavistic fear of reptiles shared by many humanoid species, or whether the intensity of this young *shen*'s emotions had merely overruled her instinct for self-preservation.

"The commander appears to have a number of visitors at the moment, Doctor," Pava said, glaring. Both her antennae were thrust forward aggressively, like tactical sensors zeroing in on a vulnerable target.

"Family and command staff, Lieutenant," Ree hissed. He took a step forward that brought his chest into contact with Pava, forcing her to move backward slightly.

"Lieutenant," Will said quietly but sharply.

Troi could feel Pava tamping down a blinding, blue-white rage just enough to enable her to speak. Taking another backward step toward the door, she said, "Sorry, sir."

"I want you to resume whatever you were doing before you came in here, Lieutenant," Will said, his tone still quiet and yet as firm as duranium. "I'm sure Dr. Ree or Nurse Ogawa will let you know when the commander is well enough for—"

"It is all right," T'Pel said, her clarion voice ringing out. The interruption had obviously impressed Will. Pava's antennae hooked straight upward in astonishment, and even Ree's inscrutable reptilian face registered pop-eyed surprise.

That worked even better than firing a warning shot, Troi thought, suppressing an errant grin, at least partially. *T'Pel has to teach me how she does that.*

"T'Pel?" Will said.

Her limbs obscured by the billowing folds of her simple gray robe, the Vulcan woman appeared almost to glide before she came to a stop beside Tuvok. "I have no objection to Lieutenant Pava paying my husband a visit. I am cognizant of the relationship that has arisen lately between Tuvok and the lieutenant."

The captain's astonishment mirrored that of the doctor. Pava's eyes likewise widened, her skin tone suddenly flushing several shades closer to indigo than usual. Troi could feel a volatile mix of emotions roiling just beneath the lieutenant's veneer of Starfleet discipline, a condition that Troi had noticed becoming increasingly common and acute among all of *Titan*'s Andorian personnel ever since Andor had announced its decision to leave the Federation.

"Relationship?" Will said, deadpan.

"Married Vulcan couples maintain strong telepathic links, Captain," T'Pel said. "There is very little we can keep truly secret from one another, absent an extraordinarily compelling reason. Even if we could, such subterfuges would be illogical."

Will nodded and cleared his throat. "Ah, yes."

Troi felt the sandpaper texture of T'Pel's annoyance as the Vulcan woman realized she was being misinterpreted. A mild but unmistakable scowl darkened her countenance.

"As part of Commander Vale's cross-training program,

Tuvok has been mentoring the lieutenant in tactical studies for the past several months."

Although Will's blush response did not mirror Pava's—he was too good a poker player for that—Troi felt the heat of his embarrassment as T'Pel set his misunderstanding right.

"Of course," he said after pausing to clear his throat.

"I am certain that Tuvok would not mind her presence, at least for a short time," T'Pel said. "It might even prove therapeutic, or at least palliative."

Shrugging, the captain turned toward Ree and said, "Well, if it's all right with the doctor. . . ."

Ree lowered his manus, turning a defensive gesture into one of welcome as he motioned toward Tuvok's biobed. "Unless I find evidence to the contrary, I suppose it can't hurt."

Troi took a step backward, and everyone else moved aside as well, clearing a path between Pava and her mentor. Nurse Ogawa moved a chair to the biobed's side. Nodding her silent thanks to everyone present, Pava approached the insensate Vulcan and took a seat beside him. Troi felt waves of frustration radiating from the Andorian, as though she lamented the fact that her mentor's affliction was a problem that had no tactical solution.

Will, Ree, and T'Pel moved to a corner, and Troi joined them. Ree's desultory conversation with his patient's spouse and the captain only served to underscore the mysterious nature of Tuvok's condition. As to when—or even whether—the Vulcan might regain consciousness, Ree would not even hazard a guess.

"All I can promise, Captain," the Pahkwa-thanh physician said, "is to maintain a close watch on him, around the clock. For as long as it takes."

Once again, Troi felt Pava approach her from behind, her emotions like a tightly coiled spring. "Captain, was Commander Tuvok going to be part of the away mission to the Vela Pulsar planet?" asked the Andorian *shen*.

"Commander Vale is assembling the away team, Lieutenant," Riker said. "But I believe she was going to include Commander Tuvok. Obviously, she's going to have to use one of her alternate choices now."

"I want to go in Tuvok's place," Pava said, her almost-calm, faintly quavering voice reminding Troi of a stone plug holding back a subterranean volcanic eruption. "Sir."

Riker studied the lieutenant carefully before answering her.

"I'll speak to Commander Vale about it," Riker said at length.

Troi didn't envy her husband the tightrope he was going to have to walk. On the one hand, Pava could be a very valuable addition to the team. But on the other, no captain ever wanted to risk undermining his XO's authority and effectiveness, either by micromanaging her or by second-guessing whatever decisions he'd authorized her to make.

"Right now isn't the best time to discuss duty rosters," Troi said, using her gentlest tones to address the volatile mixture of pleading and hostility she could feel convecting behind the lieutenant's icy blue eyes.

Troi felt a rush of surprise at the same moment she heard a sharp intake of breath, both of which had originated from the direction of Tuvok's biobed. She turned and saw Nurse Ogawa beaming at Tuvok.

Tuvok was sitting up stiffly. His dark eyes were wide open, as though he were as surprised as Ogawa, though his face was otherwise expressionless, a model of Vulcan control.

"I think, ah, he's coming around," said Ogawa unnecessarily, as Ree approached.

But Troi was frowning, already having sensed that the situation was a bit more complicated than that.

INTERLUDE

TUVOK

Surrounded by intermittent swirls of color more audible than visible, assaulted by bursts of sound more tactile than auditory, Tuvok suppressed an instinctive panic reaction.

Synesthesia, *he told himself, calming himself with the knowledge that he* had *knowledge. He attempted to recall anything he'd ever learned about the phenomenon, but came away with only a general definition of what he was experiencing—a scrambling of sensory pathways, a condition that sometimes occurred as a consequence of neurotrauma.*

But the loops of almost musical colors that flew all about him like banners were too distracting, too demanding of his full attention, to permit him the luxury of considering anything other than the apparent truth that he was still alive and conscious, despite whatever injury had caused his present condition.

A condition that he realized was not dissimilar to a

Vulcan mind-meld. I am adrift in a realm of pure consciousness, *he thought.* Adrift and alone.

As if in reply to his observation, a pair of particularly bright color-loops grew louder than all the others, though not painfully so. A peaceful blue and blinding white respectively, they increased in apparent size until they dwarfed most of the others.

"No, Commander," *the blue and white stripes said, speaking in an even, measured cadence. The stripes braided themselves together into a single entity of alternating bands of color as they spoke, somehow addressing Tuvok from inside his mind.* "You are not alone."

The reason for the speaker's dual-toned appearance suddenly became obvious—as did the other party's identity.

SecondGen White-Blue, *Tuvok thought, unable to speak aloud. Despite his apparent lack of a physical body, he felt an odd sensation of being about to lose his balance and fall over.* This is curious. I don't remember either of us initiating a mind-meld.

Another band of color, this one as orange as sehlat *fur, moved forward from the psychedelic background and began to speak.* "That is because I initiated it."

Though this being wasn't familiar to him, Tuvok assimilated the introductions it offered almost instantaneously via the simultaneous three-way mind-meld it had evidently undertaken with him and White-Blue.

A torrent of images suddenly exploded into being inside Tuvok's mind, though two pictures dominated all the others: a battered, charred-looking planet that Tuvok recognized from Commander Pazlar's stellar cartography database, a place that the orange entity identified as Ta'ith; and an image of the Vela Pulsar, whose increasingly potent radiation bursts threatened to engulf that planet and devour it like a ravening le-matya taking down an unwary traveler on the Forge.

Ta'ithan Undercity Maintenance Module One One Six, *Tuvok thought at the newcomer after it had finished making its ultraquick presentation.* You have forced others into a psionic fusion without their consent. My people, and probably White-Blue's as well, regard this as a gross violation of the rights of any sentient being.

"*I apologize," said the Ta'ithan AI, its ruddy swirls singing chords whose overtones rang with both shame and necessity. "But it could not be helped. Both your minds hold information authored eons ago by my creators—information that might enable me to prevent my world's destruction. I had no choice other than to risk accessing that information in the most expeditious manner possible."*

Tuvok realized in a rush that the Ta'ithan AI was speaking about the burdensome ecosculpting data that had been stamped into his brain, perhaps irrevocably, during his abortive meld with the machine intelligence that had run the defunct terraforming platform that Titan's *crew had discovered at Hranrar.*

White-Blue had evidently made the same intuitive leap. "I have no objection to sharing whatever ecosculpting information my databanks contain—bearing in mind, of course, that some of it may have been corrupted or lost because of the damage I sustained while acquiring it."

The alien machine entity's energetic orange swirls billowed in a manner that Tuvok interpreted as a sign of pleasure. "My mind will have to merge more fully with both of yours if I am to absorb the information in its entirety," it said. *"Since you both carry overlapping data sets, a very deep triune linkup would be the most efficient approach."*

"I give consent," White-Blue said. *"Provided the link is both temporary and safe."*

"The arrangement will be entirely temporary," the Ta'ithan AI replied. *"And because I caused no detectable damage when I assimilated both your Sentry machine language and the more cumbersome phonetic communication method you call Federation Standard, I am confident that the risk is minimal."*

But White-Blue sounded unconvinced. *"You obtained both those languages from me in a machine-to-machine interface. But you have yet to probe so deeply into Commander Tuvok's organic brain. Therefore you cannot guarantee his safety."*

The orange entity paused, like a child caught in a lie of omission. At length, it said, *"You are correct, Second-Gen White-Blue. I am less confident in my ability to interface safely with organics than with other machines."* The Ta'ithan AI paused, and Tuvok sensed that it was about to address him directly. *"I have not attempted such a joining in thousands of millennia—and never with a member of your species, Commander Tuvok. And yet I still must ask you to cooperate with me."*

You must ask? *thought* Tuvok. Surely you have the power to force my compliance.

The machine intellect's response sounded almost wistful. *"Such an action on my part would exceed the behavioral safeguards my creators built into my basic program matrix."*

Behavioral safeguards? *Tuvok wondered.*

"I am forbidden to become the direct or proximate cause of any sentient's death. Besides, in addition to

killing you, taking what I need by force would probably irrecoverably corrupt the data you carry.

"The choice must be yours."

Apprehension clutched at Tuvok's guts. Though he could not deny experiencing a desire to assist a fellow sentient in distress—an intelligence who might be instrumental in saving millions of other lives—the cold conservatism of pure logic dictated that he err on the side of self-preservation. After all, White-Blue was in a far better position to contribute to the Ta'ithan's cause, and he was about to do just that. Tuvok would face perhaps inestimable risks in attempting to follow White-Blue's lead. Besides, he had a wife to return to, a career to resume. A duty to his captain, and to the crew of Titan.

A life.

But he also carried a burden of dangerous alien terraforming data that might very well haunt him for the rest of that life. It was the kind of knowledge that he already knew from direct experience could cause wholesale destruction were it to fall into the wrong hands.

But maybe he didn't have to carry this weight indefinitely. Was it possible that this alien intellect had the capability of removing it from his shoulders? Logic dictated that there was only one way to find out.

I, too, consent to sharing the information that I carry, Tuvok thought to the Ta'ithan machine entity. But only under one condition.

Thirteen

TA'ITH

Eid'dyl came awake in semidarkness, hir surroundings unfathomable even as the photosensitive patches at the ends of hir sensory stalks strove to bring the gloom into sharper focus. S/he felt hard stone grinding uncomfortably against the chitin plating on hir back. Scorched, actinic air assaulted hir olfactory bud like the bite of a parasite. A battered, nearly flattened metal helmet lay beside hir, near a bank of ancient, long-neglected machinery. A pair of menacing shapes stood over hir, while a chittering multitude bustled farther off, beyond the room's walls, out of Eid'dyl's bleary sight.

Eid'dyl's sense of disappointment was palpable. Where was the gentle glow of the Afterrealm? Where was the enfolding warmth of the spirit of the Whetu'irawaru, the ancestor spirits who should have answered hir summons—or at least received hir essence as it departed hir spent mortal carapace?

"So far you've done nothing other than try to trick us,

sinhoarder," one of the two nearby figures stridulated. Eid'dyl recognized immediately the tremulously angry limb-sawing of Yrsil, Deconstructor Sachem Fy'ahn's sycophantic lieutenant.

Memory returned with the slow inevitability of a lava flow.

The Undercity.

"And delay us in our sacred mission," Fy'ahn said as s/he delivered another peremptory kick into Eid'dyl's side.

"You cannot expect the Whetu'irawaru to hew to mortal schedules," Eid'dyl replied, though s/he had no idea how much time had passed since s/he had gone through the motions of trying to summon the ancient deity into hir presence.

Despair clutched Eid'dyl's guts, along with a profound sense of betrayal and abandonment. Why had the Elder Gods—the fallen progenitors of Preservationist and Trasher alike—abandoned hir? Had s/he neglected to carry out some essential detail in the complex Summoning technomancy s/he had learned at hir grandbegetter's knees so many Heartlaps ago?

Could the Fallen Gods have fallen so far that they no longer listen to such as we? Eid'dyl thought. *Or perhaps they have already preceded the Sacred Undercity, all of Ta'ith, and the very Heart of the Cosmos itself into death's cold mandibles.*

Either way, Eid'dyl had to face the bitter reality of failure. The great eternal Undercity—the necropolis whose secrets Eid'dyl's people had dedicated their lives to preserving and protecting even past the limitations of their understanding—was at the mercy of the uncouth savages who would destroy it.

If they could.

"We have waited long enough," Fy'ahn said, brandishing hir foremost sound-producing limbs with a martial flourish, obviously meaning to intimidate the supine Preservationist leader.

"We need wait no longer," said Yrsil. "The chemical explosives are now all in place."

Several of Sachem Fy'ahn's forelimbs came together, loudly sounding chords of ferocious delight that made Eid'dyl shudder. Silence ensued. Then, as if in answer to Fy'ahn's martial blare, an ominous rumbling became audible and quickly began to build in intensity. Within moments Eid'dyl realized that it had to be coming from the direction of the Undercity's deepest core.

And that s/he was very likely hearing a percussive death knell for every living thing on Ta'ith.

Fourteen

U.S.S. TITAN

As soon as she received the somewhat cryptic news, Christine Vale left the bridge in the hands of Lieutenant Commander Tamen Gibruch, then rushed as quickly as she could to sickbay.

She smiled broadly at the sight that greeted her there: Commander Tuvok, dressed in perspiration-stained workout clothes, was sitting up on one of the biobeds, fully conscious. The captain and Counselor Troi stood quietly nearby, along with Tuvok's wife, T'Pel, who appeared characteristically dour. A reserved-looking Nurse Ogawa and Dr. Ree, whose emotions were hard to read under most circumstances, flanked Tuvok as a frowning and taciturn Lieutenant Pava looked on from Ogawa's side.

A few moments later Vale's smile faltered. Tuvok showed no sign of recognizing her, even after having made prolonged direct eye contact.

"Tuvok, are you all right?" the XO asked, but received no immediate answer. Scowling, she turned toward Troi.

"I thought you told me Commander Tuvok had regained consciousness."

With a small, sad shake of her head, the counselor said, "I told you it looked like we might be able to speak with him soon. I can see now that it's all going to depend on how much control he's able to exercise."

Vale threw her hands up in frustration. "Deanna, what the hell are you talking about?"

"That's not Commander Tuvok, Chris," Captain Riker said as he nodded toward Tuvok's biobed. He spoke in a patient, gentle tone that Vale realized at once was his understated way of encouraging her to calm down. "At least, not exactly."

"It's a bit difficult to explain," said Troi. "Especially to nontelepaths."

Vale folded her arms across her chest. "I'll do my best to keep up, Deanna. Just try not to use too many big words." Despite her best efforts to match the captain's outwardly calm demeanor, sarcasm tinged her words somewhat more strongly than she'd intended.

Before anyone else could get in a word, the man sitting on the biobed spoke. "What Commander Troi is trying to say is that I am what you might describe as a corporate entity."

Vale blinked repeatedly as she tried to absorb what she was hearing. Although Tuvok's affect was as blank as ever—perhaps even a little blanker than usual, in fact—his voice and diction had subtly changed; this man was Tuvok, and yet he also clearly wasn't.

"'Corporate entity,'" Vale repeated. "I gather you're not talking about some new entrepreneurial venture."

"I do not understand," said Tuvok-yet-not-Tuvok. As was typical for the Vulcan, Vale's little jape was lost on him; unlike *Titan*'s senior tactical officer, however, *this* Tuvok demonstrated none of the tiny facial-muscle "tells" that signaled his usual lack of patience.

"He's trying to tell us that his mind has become amalgamated with some other consciousness," T'Pel said.

Facing Tuvok again, Vale asked, "Have you melded with somebody?"

*Or perhaps with some*thing, she thought. Despite her thorough grounding in Federation diversity, the thought made her shudder inwardly.

"Correct," Tuvok's strangely softened voice answered.

When the man on the biobed failed to elaborate after several silent heartbeats had passed, Vale said, "So who's in there with you?"

After receiving a blank, sincerely perplexed stare as her answer, Vale reformulated her question. "Whose mind has joined with Commander Tuvok's?"

"That of Undercity Maintenance Module One One Six. Maintainer of the ancient machineries of the Whetu'irawaru since before they vanished—before even the star-sun of Mother Ta'ith grew small and angry and malignant."

An electric thrill of discovery ran the length of Vale's spine. Had this entity just claimed to be older than the ancient supernova that had left as its cosmic legacy the terrible power of the Vela Pulsar?

"You're from the planet that orbits the pulsar?" Vale asked in a near whisper. Since the sudden collapse that had precipitated Tuvok's presence in sickbay had roughly coincided with the arrival of the energy pulse from the planet, everything was beginning to make a weird sort of sense.

Instead of replying, the man on the biobed tipped his head, his gaze unfocused. Vale assumed he was looking inward, perhaps consulting internally with Tuvok, drawing on the Vulcan's fund of general knowledge—using him, in effect, as a conversational Rosetta stone.

"Yes," the corporate entity replied at length. "I originated on the planet. On Ta'ith."

"But what exactly *is* this thing?" Pava said, her fists clenched, her face and neck as taut as bridge cables. It appeared to Vale that the lieutenant's impulse to beat this invader out of Tuvok's head had gone to war with her need to protect a fellow officer and mentor.

"That's a very good question, Lieutenant," said Captain Riker as he took a step toward the biobed. Addressing Tuvok—and whoever else was sharing the Vulcan's brain—he said, "You're an artificial intelligence of some kind."

Another pause. Then, "I am Undercity Maintenance Module One One Six. The Whetu'irawaru created me with their own limbs."

Vale tried the unfamiliar syllables on for size, but found she couldn't quite get her mouth around them. "Wee-tu *what* now?"

"The Whetu'irawaru. The long-vanished Elder Gods. The Fallen. The progenitors of all those now living on Ta'ith, be they bent on destroying or preserving the surviving works of the Whetu'irawaru."

"Destruction or preservation," Troi said. "Those two poles don't leave much room for any middle ground."

Vale couldn't help but agree. A frisson of horror accompanied the realization that was dawning on her: *Titan* had taken aboard an intelligence that not only could take control of a person's brain and body, but also might be a mere coin's flip away from either kindness or cruelty. Despite its benign-sounding name, this entity could do a lot of damage, either intentionally or inadvertently.

Riker gave voice to Vale's apprehension. "What's *your* objective? To destroy or to preserve?"

"Undercity Maintenance Module One One Six is part of a suite of autorepair routines that the Whetu'irawaru designed to keep their technological infrastructure from deviating from its optimal state of functionality."

"So there are others like you down there on the planet," Riker said. "On Ta'ith."

"No, Captainriker. Maintenance Module One One Six appears to be the only Ta'ithan-constructed intelligence to have succeeded in enduring until the present time. Apart from the organic descendants of the Whetu'irawaru who cling to life on Ta'ith despite the harsh environment—and this vessel's complement—this module may be the only sentient functioning anywhere near the Heart of the Cosmos, the Giver of Life and Death."

Vale paused to consider the unfamiliar designations the visitor had used. To a native of this violent region of space, terms such as "the giver of life and death" or "the heart of the cosmos" could have been inspired only by the almost inconceivable power of the Vela Pulsar.

She turned to face the captain. "I guess this settles Bralik's various wagers over whether or not we'll find intelligent life on that planet."

"I think you're right," Riker said quietly around a small, lopsided smile.

Vale noticed then that Troi was scowling. "I know that Vulcans are powerful touch telepaths," the counselor said. "The mind-meld is a well-established technique among Vulcans, and even between Vulcans and other humanoid species. But Commander Tuvok's attempt to meld with the Brahma-Shiva AI not only failed, it nearly killed him. How can even a Vulcan achieve a psionic link with a machine intelligence?"

"Perhaps there was a flaw in Commander Tuvok's technique during the Brahma-Shiva mission," said Ree, hissing as his long, forked tongue flitted in and out of view across his multiple rows of razor-sharp, serrated teeth. "After all, there's nothing categorically impossible about interfaces between organic telepaths and artificial intelligences. In fact, I have read of a number of instances in which Vulcans have succeeded in establishing telepathic contact with machine entities."

Vale saw that every eye in the room had focused on T'Pel. Having just noticed the attention she was receiving, the Vulcan woman began to look uncharacteristically uncomfortable. The exec found this remarkable; she had never before seen T'Pel lose her disciplined Vulcan poise.

At length, T'Pel said, "In comparison with my husband, I have little expertise in the ancient art of the mind-meld." She was obviously reticent about discussing such personal, private matters openly.

"I, too, am surprised at how readily this organic creature received me," said the man on the biobed. "Especially after my initial contact attempt proved difficult."

"Initial contact attempt?" Riker asked, his tone sharpening. "Tuvok's mind wasn't the first one you touched since you came aboard?"

"No."

Vale experienced a chill of dread. Had another member of *Titan*'s crew collapsed as Tuvok had, but alone and undiscovered in some isolated corner of the ship?

"Who did you try to contact before you joined with Tuvok?" Riker said.

"None of this vessel's organic creatures, Captainriker. I did not wish to attempt that before exhausting every possible machine-centered alternative. Doing otherwise might have entailed undue risk."

"Looks like you found a way to overcome your qualms about that," Pava said acidly.

"There was no alternative," the Tuvok-amalgam said in a resolute tone.

"Chris," Riker said, turning his head toward Vale. "Did anything try to take over the main computer when that energy pulse hit us?"

Vale shook her head. "I didn't see any sign of that. There were no alarms or crew reports about computer incursions. But I'll check it out myself just to be certain."

"It was not your main computer that drew my attention here," the visitor said. "Rather, it was another silicon-based entity, one not integrated into this vessel's various systems. Like the organic being through whom Maintenance Module One One Six now speaks"—the entity paused as it awkwardly laid one of Tuvok's hands across his chest—"the manufactured entity with which I first attempted contact contained code written by my own Whetu'irawaru creators."

"The Sentry," Riker said. "SecondGen White-Blue. He must have absorbed information from the Brahma-Shiva ecosculptor when he tried to interface with it."

But because the poor little metal critter has been out

of commission ever since that mission, Vale thought, *he was never able to share it with anybody.*

Nodding, Troi said, "And now an intelligence from the Vela Pulsar system has recognized the information White-Blue carries as the signature of its creators."

Everyone in sickbay went silent as the implications sank in. Vale knew that *Titan* had found the most promising lead yet in the search for additional functional specimens of the quick-terraforming technology they had lost at Hranrar.

"But that's not where it stops, Deanna," said the captain. "Our new . . . friend has found traces of that information in more than one place aboard this ship: imprinted on White-Blue's circuitry—" He paused, as though to give everyone present enough time to keep up with him.

"—and burned into some part of Commander Tuvok's brain," Vale said, unable to resist the urge to complete the captain's thought.

"*This* organic entity," the visitor said, once again moving Tuvok's hand to the Vulcan's chest by way of identification, "contains considerably more than mere *traces* of the old knowledge, Captainriker."

Riker's eyebrows both went aloft as he looked toward Vale in silent exclamation.

That certainly wasn't in Commander Tuvok's report about the Brahma-Shiva encounter, Vale thought. Had the tactical officer deliberately held something back about that mission? And if he had, why? She glanced in the direction of T'Pel, whose stony expression gave nothing away.

The captain turned back toward the visitor. "Just how much 'old knowledge' are we talking about here?"

The visitor spread Tuvok's hands in an awkward

"who can say?" gesture. "Certainly not enough to re-place what entropy and time have taken from Undercity Maintenance Module One One Six during uncounted eons of slumber. But if you could enhance our linkage to the other machine entity, then One One Six might return to full effectiveness. The link must deepen."

Riker was shaking his head, a skeptical frown creasing his brow as he regarded the visitor in Tuvok's body. "Even if you managed to restore every last line of code you need to get yourself into top operating condition, what good could you really do? After all, you're fighting a losing battle. Ta'ith's geomagnetic field is declining, and the radiation output of the Vela Pulsar—your Heart of the Cosmos—keeps intensifying."

"Undercity Maintenance Module One One Six was designed to maintain Ta'ith's technological infrastruc-ture," said the visitor. "This includes the reinforcement of its planetary shielding mechanisms."

Vale felt opposing waves of awe and fear surging within her. "You can do that?"

"Perhaps," said the visitor. "Assist us. Bring us the entity you call White-Blue so that we can attempt a triple linkage of consciousness."

With a small scanner in one sharp-clawed manus and a medical tricorder in the other, Ree approached Tuvok's left side and began a close examination. T'Pel moved gracefully to her husband's right side. "Does my hus-band approve of what you propose?"

"I . . . He . . . I . . ." The muscles in Tuvok's face be-came tense, then slackened, then tensed again, as though the only way the commander could reach his wife was by pushing and shoving his way through a crowd. "I have no objection, my wife."

"Well, *I* have an objection," Ree said, lowering his diagnostic implements. "I cannot verify whether or not we have indeed heard the wishes of our own Commander Tuvok."

"I believe that I was indeed speaking with my husband," T'Pel said, unmoved by the doctor's unconcealed suspicion.

"Based on *what*?" Pava said. "Vulcan woo-woo? Charaleas's balls! That doesn't sound very godsdamned logical to me."

"Lieutenant!" Vale barked.

The Andorian turned away, fuming in grudging silence. Troi's silent frown, aimed squarely at Vale, almost made the exec feel guilty for having handled Pava so roughly.

"Your caution is more than reasonable, Doctor," said the Tuvok-amalgam. "Undercity Maintenance Module One One Six will dissolve the link as soon as whatever old knowledge White-Blue carries can be copied and integrated. Once that is accomplished, the module must return to Ta'ith to effect repairs to its failing technosphere."

"And you will surrender Commander Tuvok's body once this is done?" Ree said.

"Yes," said the amalgam-intellect. "In fact, this agreement is in our mutual interest. Maintenance Module One One Six must return to Ta'ith as quickly as possible. Our technosubstrate is under attack by those who would destroy the legacy of the Fallen Gods. These nihilists might even succeed in deactivating Ta'ith's shielding mechanisms entirely. Therefore we . . . *I* . . . must intervene decisively."

"I don't like this," Ree said. "So far, all we *really*

know is that we have an alien intellect in our midst—one
with a ticking clock and an agenda that involves hijack-
ing bodies."

And picking brains, Vale thought. *Literally.*

"That's true enough, Doctor," Riker said. "But this
alien intellect's agenda overlaps with our own. We don't
want to see the planet—or whatever civilization is cling-
ing to life there—be destroyed."

Though Vale wasn't any happier about the alien AI's
actions than Ree was, she knew the writing was now on the
wall for all to see. The abrupt collapse of Ta'ith's already
declining geomagnetic field would mean nothing short of
the obliteration of every living thing on the planet.

"All right," Ree growled. "But I still don't like it."

Riker acknowledged the doctor with a nod, and then
tapped his combadge once. "Captain Riker to Ensign
Torvig."

Captain William Riker thought he'd kept his mounting
impatience well concealed, but Ensign Torvig's increasingly obsequious and apologetic tone argued otherwise.

"My apologies, Captain, for allowing this task to
consume as much time as it has," the little Choblik junior engineer said, audibly nervous. "Had Commander
Tuvok come to the engineering lab for this procedure,
my work would have reached a conclusion some thirty
minutes ago."

Hoping to reassure Torvig that his work was as exem-
plary as ever, Riker started to reply, only to be beaten to
the punch by a burst of sibilant gutturals.

"Ensign, did I fail to make myself understood?"
Dr. Ree growled as he gestured toward Tuvok, who

sat attentively on the biobed adjacent to the one upon which White-Blue lay. The lights on the Sentry's metal shell blinked in silent syncopations. "My patient is not to leave my sickbay—at least not before I am satisfied that this bizarre cyber-neural networking you are abetting doesn't pose a significant health risk."

"I understand completely, Doctor," Torvig said, his bionic limbs and tail continuing to work in tandem as he spoke, manipulating various tools and pieces of scanning equipment without missing a beat. "Even though some would say that Starfleet service at the cutting edge of the Federation's exploration mandate poses a significant health risk of its own."

Coming from any other member of *Titan*'s crew, Torvig's words might have sounded insubordinate. But the Choblik aired his sentiments, as usual, with the innocence of a child. Riker had to repress a small, reserved smile.

Ree's only response was to display his dental armory to the accompaniment of a low, wordless rumble that came from deep within his reptilian chest.

"Pissing off the CMO *also* constitutes a significant health risk, Ensign," Riker said in a deadpan stage whisper. Prompted either by the captain's gentle admonition or the doctor's less-than-cordial warning, Torvig's efficient display of instrument handling briefly transformed into a jangle-nerved juggling act. His swift-moving prehensile metal tail darted toward the floor, catching an engineering tricorder an instant before impact.

"I believe I have good news," Torvig said, gathering up what remained of his dignity. "The procedure is working."

Riker, who had ordered Ensign Torvig to sickbay to hardware-enhance the three-way link, watched with mounting anxiety as the engineer checked the ends of the ODN cable, first at the improvised neurodiagnostic helmet on Tuvok's head, then at the open interface port built into the cold, all but inert chassis of SecondGen White-Blue.

The arachnidlike, nearly one-meter wide Sentry lay motionless on the biobed beside the one Tuvok had occupied less than an hour earlier. The rhythmic flashing of a single tiny red light near the interface port provided the only clue that White-Blue was anything other than an inanimate block of metal.

Riker looked away from the blinking AI long enough to see that T'Pel, Ree, and Ogawa were watching the proceedings as intently as he was.

Tuvok abruptly stood up and doffed the skullcap-like neurodiagnostic helmet, discarding it on the sickbay's carpeted floor. He stood blinking, eyes unfocused, apparently staring very intently at nothing.

"Commander?" Riker said, approaching the tactical officer even as Ree and Ogawa closed in on his flanks. T'Pel stepped out of the way of the medical personnel, a tack that Riker found both logical and commendable.

"Tuvok?" said Pava, who approached the Vulcan from behind. Riker could see fear etched into the blue-shot whites of her eyes.

Tuvok looked around the room, a beatific expression slackening his usually dour features. "Success," he said, as though the one word explained everything.

"Are you saying this three-way mind-meld is really working?" Riker asked.

Tuvok nodded. "Yes. Undercity Maintenance Module

One One Six, SecondGen Sentry White-Blue, and Commander Tuvok. We are all nominal. We are all present."

To Riker's ear, Tuvok's voice had adopted an uncanny dreamlike quality, a lightly distorted timbre vaguely reminiscent of the nightmare unison of the Borg Collective. Three voices, speaking as one.

He suppressed a shudder.

"That's good to hear," said Riker. "Now let's get our business here concluded as quickly as possible, so the three of you can all go your separate ways again."

"Before that can be done," said Torvig, "we'll need to determine the full capabilities of this new, ah, triune arrangement."

Tuvok's head bobbed up and down in affirmation. "Undercity Maintenance Module One One Six has gathered together more than ninety-seven percent of its original code. This constitutes an almost complete recovery from the copious data loss the passing eons have inflicted."

Riker nodded. So far, so good. "Which means that you, Maintenance Module One One Six, can return to Ta'ith to start repairing the planet's protective technologies."

"Yes."

"All right, then," Riker said. "Take your recovered machine code and put it to good use back home. We'll watch from here."

Tuvok nodded, then closed his eyes. A look of concentration creased his brow.

Seconds ticked by, then began to drag as they gathered into minutes. A bead of perspiration gathered in the crevice between the Vulcan's steeply arched eyebrows.

The dark eyes opened. "It's the Heart of the Cosmos," the Tuvok-amalgam said, his breathing suddenly labored.

"The Vela Pulsar," Riker said.

"Yes," the Tuvok-amalgam said as T'Pel glided back to his side, a look of undisguised worry displayed across her dusky face. "Its energy output has increased yet again.

"The path through Lowerspace is constricted as a result. Maintenance Module One One Six can no longer return to Ta'ith unassisted."

"Try," Riker said.

The alien AI answered with a sad shake of Tuvok's head. "It cannot be done without causing a catastrophic data loss. Imagine an organic creature unable to contain its circulatory fluid."

"Then you'd better break the mind-link now," Riker said.

A look of thoughtful suspicion crossed Tuvok's face. "You wish to have your personnel back." Again, the Vulcan's hand touched his chest. "Principally, this organic being."

"Yes," Riker said.

Tuvok gestured toward White-Blue's still, quietly blinking form. "And the silicon-based sentient as well."

"Of course," Torvig said.

Moving heedlessly past both T'Pel and Pava, Tuvok took a seat on the edge of the nearest open biobed and crossed his arms defiantly across his chest. He faced Riker with a level stare.

"If Maintenance Module One One Six attempts to return to Ta'ith unassisted," Tuvok said, "it will face almost immediate discorporation."

Riker nodded. "I understand. Once you dissolve the mind-link, my people will start looking for a way to return you to your homeworld safely."

The Vulcan slowly shook his head; his movements were awkward, as though unfamiliar. "But once the psi connection is dissolved, Maintenance Module One One Six will be subject to your will," Tuvok said. "The destiny of Ta'ith will be in your hands."

"That's flattering," Riker said. "But it seems to me that the Vela Pulsar is influencing your planet's fate a lot more than I ever could."

"Not if you detain the newly repaired iteration of Undercity Maintenance Module One One Six," Tuvok said. "Not if you prevent it from returning to Ta'ith to repair and enhance the planet's deteriorating suite of automated protective systems.

"Take us to Ta'ith in one of this vessel's auxiliary vehicles," the amalgam of Commander Tuvok, Module One One Six, and SecondGen White-Blue said. "It will be safe to terminate the psi link only after we reach the protection of the planet's magnetosphere."

The blended entity that persisted in Tuvok's body merely continued to stare silently at Riker, as though demonstrating that no further reply was necessary.

He doesn't need to continue bargaining, Riker thought, his fists clenching at his sides in frustration. *Because he knows he's holding all the aces.*

Being the only individual with significant psi abilities who was present in the observation lounge, Deanna Troi took charge of the briefing. She sensed the weight of worlds pressing down on her husband, who sat beside her at the head of the room's broad conference table. He radiated quiet pride and gratitude as she took control. Seated on the table's opposite side were Christine Vale and Dr. Ree.

"Because of its psi link with Commander Tuvok," Troi said, "Undercity Maintenance Module One One Six knows a great deal about the away mission we're preparing to launch."

"Too bad Tuvok wasn't able to keep that information under his hat, as it were," Vale said.

"If the alien AI hadn't taken him by surprise, he might have succeeded in doing that," Troi said. "Commander Tuvok has an extremely disciplined mind."

Will said, "It's probably tough to maintain your mental barriers when another mind forces its way in without any warning."

"Point conceded," Vale said. "I'm also concerned about the fact that an alien AI is blackmailing us. Either we take it with us on the away mission to the Vela Pulsar planet—while it's still joined with Tuvok and White-Blue—or this weird-ass three-way mind-meld is liable to continue indefinitely."

Troi shook her head. "I'm afraid it's a bit more complicated than simple blackmail, Chris. Or at least it's different."

Vale leaned forward, demanding, "How, Deanna? This thing has ordered us to play chauffeur along the sector's most dangerous stretch of highway—or else."

"It's a sentient being that's acting out of a sense of simple self-preservation," Troi said. "It has already made the good-faith gesture of freely sharing information about the society on its homeworld."

"'Society,'" Vale said. "That's a bit of an overstatement,

don't you think? Maybe they commanded star-spanning technologies once upon a time. But now we're talking about two factions that spend their days tussling over the scraps from their ancestors' table. One is a group of obsessive archivists, and the other would have been right at home with the torch-carrying knuckle-draggers who burned down the ancient library at Alexandria."

Troi frowned at the exec. "*I'm* talking about a people hardy enough to have survived their own star going supernova without fleeing from their home planet."

"But is there anybody alive on that planet right now?" Vale asked,

"Do you think it lied to us about that?" Will asked. "To lead us into a trap?"

Vale shrugged. "I don't know. But I really have to wonder how much our stowaway could really know about these alleged Ta'ithans. It told us that it's just awakened from an ages-long sleep. How much could it really know about the planet's current inhabitants and their culture?"

"The same thing occurred to me," Troi said, "so I asked the AI about that when I was interviewing it."

"And?" Vale asked.

"It explained that it made direct mental contact with the leader of one of the two major factions before it noticed the presence of *Titan* and came aboard. Apparently, the AI absorbed everything it knows about Ta'ith's current sociological status during that single brief mind-link."

"That means," Vale said, "our guest can only give us half the story. At best."

Troi felt a tiny smile tugging at the corners of her mouth. "I certainly can't accuse you of being excessively trusting, Chris."

"If you could," Vale said with a broad grin, "then I'd be a pretty damned crappy first officer."

"We're drifting a little off topic," Will said.

"Sorry, Captain," Troi said, her smile falling away. Still looking at Vale, she added, "Chris, I believe that the alien AI isn't malicious."

Vale's eyes narrowed as her grin dissipated. "Did your empathic sense tell you that?"

Troi averted her eyes, staring at the tabletop. "We're talking about a machine intelligence here. I couldn't read its emotions directly the way I can with most flesh-and-blood species."

"So you can't really claim to understand the AI's intentions," Vale said.

Ree spoke up. "As with any sentient creature, we can judge its motives only by observing its behavior."

"All right," Will said. "What have you observed so far?"

The Pahkwa-thanh surgeon's meter-long tail switched restlessly back and forth behind his large, peanut-shaped head, his leathery snout releasing a sound reminiscent of a humanoid sigh. "Actually, very little, Captain. However, the astrophysics department *has* verified at least one of the entity's key claims: the hard-radiation output of the Vela Pulsar has indeed increased substantially over the past two hours. I'm certain that Ensign Dakal can provide you with all the relevant and specific numbers."

"That might only mean that we're dealing with something too clever and devious to let itself get caught in an obvious lie," Vale said.

"Judging from my 'read' of Tuvok's portion of the gestalt," Troi said, "the alien AI isn't malevolent. It simply has no reason to trust that we will act in its interests, or in the interests of its homeworld. It has a lot to lose, so it's maintaining the mind-link as a form of insurance."

"And Tuvok can't break the link unilaterally?" Will asked.

Troi spread her hands. "I can't say for certain. But my assessment is that if he *could* break the link without killing himself in the attempt, he *would*. The same seems to be true of White-Blue as well. Therefore they're both stuck within the link—until the entity releases them voluntarily."

"All right," Vale said. "Let's say that the AI is acting out of distrust rather than out of malice. It may turn out to be a distinction without a difference." She turned to face the doctor.

Ree moved his long, velociraptor-like head in a fair approximation of a humanoid's up-and-down nod. "Indeed. The longer the mind-meld persists, the greater the danger that the link will become indissoluble—like a Trill joining, the termination of which nearly always kills the symbiont's humanoid host once the fusion has passed the point of permanence."

As he absorbed Ree's words, Will stroked his beard. "When do you expect Commander Tuvok to pass this 'point of permanence'?"

"I can only estimate, Captain," said Ree. "But in my judgment, that time will come within the first twenty-four hours—thirty-six at the outside, if we are fortunate. Obviously, there is no advantage in my continuing to keep Commander Tuvok confined to sickbay under these circumstances."

Troi watched her husband's reaction. Other than a slight blanching of his skin—an effect his beard concealed, at least somewhat—he appeared to be taking the grim news in stride.

But Troi knew better.

"Chris," he said at length. "Is the *Armstrong* ready for launch?"

The exec nodded. "I'd say so. Commander Ra-Havreii is still complaining that he isn't completely happy with the shield enhancements he's installed, but you know how he likes to overengineer everything. He's very big on redundancy abundancy."

Will nodded. "Gather the away team in twenty minutes. That includes Tuvok, White-Blue, and our . . . hitchhiker."

"Aye, Captain."

He rose to his feet, signaling that the briefing had come to an end, and everyone else immediately followed suit.

"We can't afford to keep our Ta'ithan guest waiting any longer," he said.

Fifteen

SHUTTLECRAFT *ARMSTRONG*

Commander Christine Vale strode briskly through the hatch that led into *Titan*'s principal hangar deck, but paused momentarily after she passed the threshold. She looked beyond the small crowd that busied itself making the final launch preparations on a specially modified type-11 shuttlecraft. Looking past both the *Armstrong*'s nearly fifteen-meter length and the glowing periphery of the cavernous shuttlebay's otherwise invisible atmospheric-containment forcefield, Vale gazed out into the fathomless black void that enfolded *Titan*. Half a light-year past the graceful, tapered parallel lines of *Titan*'s warp nacelles, the Vela Pulsar's deadly, symmetrical plumes lashed out. The twin cosmic fires promised knowledge while threatening violence, at once beckoning and imprecating.

Titan's hulking chief of security, Lieutenant Commander Ranul Keru, approached the XO, interrupting her reverie.

"Everything looks shipshape to me, Commander," the towering unjoined Trill said. "The *Armstrong* will be ready, once Chief Engineer Ra-Havreii signs off on those final shielding modifications."

Vale felt a small but painful knot of tension gathering at the back of her neck. A last-minute headache, literal or figurative, was something she did not need.

"He's still dithering over that?" she said. "When I checked in fifteen minutes ago everything looked up to spec."

A familiar, sonorous voice intruded from behind her. "A great deal can happen in fifteen minutes, Commander."

She turned and found herself looking *Titan*'s pallid, white-mustachioed chief engineer directly in the face. "I know, Xin. That's why we need to get this tub launched sooner rather than later." She cocked her head toward the *Armstrong* as she spoke.

"The emissions from that damned pulsar are getting more intense all the time," the engineer said, shaking his head ruefully.

Vale scowled. "I've seen all the graphs and projections, Xin. The increase in radiation isn't anything your modifications can't handle."

"That may be true *now*," he said. "But the additional radiation output is showing no sign of leveling off. What's more, the rate of increase *itself* is increasing. If we spend more than a day in close proximity to that pulsar—or perhaps even a good deal *less* time than that—the berthold rays alone will cook the away team's insides like a plate of 'Owon eggs."

The first officer stood silently and considered Ra-Havreii's unusually strident warning. As she mulled his words over, the hangar's main hatch slid open again and admitted three figures: Dr. Ree, his assistant chief medical officer—the gold-skinned, feather-domed Dr. Onnta—and a jumpsuit-clad Commander Tuvok. Lieutenant Pava and Ensign Torvig entered right behind this trio, guiding the small antigrav platform that carried the still, blinking form of SecondGen White-Blue. The entire party moved past Vale and Ra-Havreii quickly, too intent on getting their cargo onto the *Armstrong* to notice the presence of either the engineer or the exec.

Maybe we won't have an opportunity to help the people of Ta'ith, Vale thought. *But we need to at least break Tuvok free of the alien AI that's hijacked his body.*

Grabbing the engineer's elbow, Vale steered him away from the hatchway and toward whatever privacy she might find in the hangar's vast open space. "What are you proposing, Xin?" she asked him quietly. "That we scrub this mission? That we leave Commander Tuvok in a permanent state of alien possession?"

Once Vale and Ra-Havreii had placed several meters between themselves and the nearest other pair of ears, the chief engineer pulled his arm away. "Of course not. But I have to point out the danger the away team will be flying into."

"Danger is part of the job, Xin," Vale said. "You know that."

Ra-Havreii's customary Efrosian calm, as well as the obviously polished suave manner he always projected in front of *Titan*'s female personnel, vanished. "I shouldn't have to remind you what an unforgiving mistress space can be, Commander—even when it isn't being shredded by a stellar object capable of flash-frying the entire away team in less than a heartbeat."

"You haven't told me anything I didn't know already."

"Just give me another six hours," Ra-Havreii said in a tone that lay somewhere between pleading and exasperation. "That ought to give me just enough time to replace the *Armstrong*'s current radiation countermeasures with a metaphasic shielding unit."

Vale shook her head. "I don't like to throw my playbook out right before kickoff time, Xin. Besides, you're talking about an untested prototype."

Ra-Havreii shook his head. "Not precisely. The *Enterprise*-D once used essentially the same technology to withstand the conditions inside a stellar photosphere."

"And they powered it with a warp core capable of generating a whole hell of a lot more power than the *Armstrong* can muster." She felt her brow furrow in irritation. "But you don't need me to tell you any of this stuff."

"Chris, I think I can make it work. I just need the time."

"Xin, once we get into the Vela system proper, we have to get in and out of the inner system as fast as possible while remaining at sublight speed, to keep the pulsar from getting even *more* out of hand. Between dealing with that and powering the shield enhancements, we've already spoken for just about every joule of energy the *Armstrong* can deliver. And we can't spare the time."

"But—"

"We have a mission to carry out, Commander. At some point we have to let good enough be good enough, and get on with—"

"But that's exactly my point, Christine!" The engineer interrupted her, his tone infused with a shrillness she'd never before heard from him. "Good enough *isn't* good enough. Deep space—particularly this close to the Vela Pulsar—will kill the away team."

After nearly three years of exposure to Ra-Havreii's penchant for thoroughness, Vale could hardly believe what she was hearing. She looked back toward the *Armstrong* and saw that the away team members had finished loading the mission's requisite matériel.

"Xin," Vale said as she turned back toward the Efrosian. "I know you've done everything possible to keep the away team safe."

He began to pace around the deck, hands clasped behind his back. "I think you're putting an unwarranted amount of faith in my abilities, Chris."

"What are you talking about?"

"I'm talking about what I've been hearing repeatedly from *Titan*'s entire counseling staff for nearly three years now—that I did 'everything possible' aboard the *Luna*, as well. I think we all remember how brilliantly *that* turned out."

So that's *what this is about,* Vale thought, kicking herself for not having realized it sooner.

The first officer leaned forward, her words intended for him alone. "Xin, no matter how hard we try to prepare for every eventuality, sometimes shit just *happens*. And if you could receive messages from the dead, I'm sure everybody who died that day would tell you the same thing."

"I receive messages from the dead more often than you might think, Chris," Ra-Havreii said, scoffing. "Usually in the middle of an inadequately provisioned night."

Vale didn't like to dwell on Xin Ra-Havreii's penchant for 'provisioning' as many evenings as possible with sexual companions. It was none of her business, unless it interfered with the smooth functioning of *Titan*'s crew. So far, it hadn't. Because of the chief engineer's discretion, his list of conquests was unconfirmed. But within *Titan*'s small, tight-knit community, scuttlebutt was inevitable, and rumor had it that Ra-Havreii's paramours were legion, crossing every imaginable biological and cultural line.

"At one time or another I've heard from all seven of the people who lost their lives when that explosion tore through my engine room," he said.

"A Starfleet board of inquiry picked the *Luna*'s engine room apart after the accident," Vale said. "You were cleared. Nobody blames you, Xin—except *you*."

"Seven, Chris. Isn't it ironic that some of you humans regard the number seven as a portent of good fortune? The Lucky *Luna* Seven. It's almost funny. But I suppose the line between tragedy and comedy can be too fine."

Vale had no idea what to say to that. A conspicuous silence stretched between them, until a familiar voice filled the void. Relieved, she turned toward the sound.

She found herself facing Tuvok, who stood about two meters away, looking awkward, as though unable to decide what to do with his hands. Behind him stood Ree and Onnta, as well as Pava, Torvig, Keru, and the reptiloid Lieutenant Qur Qontallium, a male Gnalish Fejimaera who worked in security under Keru.

Tuvok—or, rather, the amalgamated intellect that presently inhabited Tuvok's body—spoke: "Our apologies for eavesdropping. It was not our intent." Tuvok's left hand rose, its index finger touching the upswept tip of his left ear. "However, this individual possesses superlative auditory abilities."

"Can I help you?" Vale said, regarding Tuvok-yet-not-Tuvok with undisguised suspicion.

The Tuvok-amalgam seemed taken aback by the

question. "We believe you are already doing everything possible to assist us."

"Good. Then why don't you set Tuvok free from your mind-link now, as opposed to later?"

The Tuvok-amalgam looked both puzzled and vaguely disappointed. "I thought we had already settled this, Commandervale. We will release your colleague without hesitation—*after* we reach the safety of the Sacred Undercity of Ta'ith."

Vale sighed. "All right. I just thought it couldn't hurt to ask again. What do you want?"

"To do our utmost to make this mission a success, of course. Ta'ith's survival may depend upon it, after all. We overheard some of your earlier conversation about the dangers your team will face in approaching Ta'ith. We may be able to provide assistance."

"Assistance?" Vale asked. "What kind of assistance?"

"Although the constructed Gridspace once plied by the Whetu'irawaru has degraded beyond repair, part of us still has partial access to the Lowerspace that lies beneath the old Techgrid. We cannot use Lowerspace as a travel conduit, of course. The swelling rage of the Heart of the Cosmos has closed off that option."

" 'Lowerspace,' " Vale repeated. "If that's what you used to get here, it's what we call subspace."

"Exactly so," the Tuvok-amalgam said after a pause, during which the Ta'ithan part of itself had presumably paused to consult its Vulcan component. "As we said, we cannot use Lowerspace—what you call subspace— for the purpose of traveling, as we once did routinely. If we could, we would not need you to return us to Ta'ith. However, we may be able to shunt some portion of the Heart's particle flux into Lowerspace."

Vale thought she was beginning to grasp the alien AI's point. "And away from our overloaded shields."

Tuvok's head nodded. "Yes. This tactic would divert a great deal of incoming radiation away from your auxiliary vehicle."

"What you're proposing might make all the difference, especially if our chief engineer's misgivings turn out to be justified," Vale said, sparing a glance at Ra-Havreii, who was taking in the entire conversation. "But if it doesn't work . . ." She allowed her voice to trail off.

"If it doesn't work," said the Tuvok-amalgam, "then this mission will be in no greater jeopardy than it was already." The entity placed the Vulcan's hand on his chest. "We will experience the same consequences that await the away team."

At length she said, "All right, Repairbot One One Six, or whatever your name is. Since we're both going to be paddling the same canoe, we're going to have to trust each other. Do whatever you can about the radiation hazard the *Armstrong* will be flying into."

Tuvok's head bobbed in an affirmative nod. "We will do our utmost."

"Good," Vale said with a nod of her own. "Off you go, then. Dismissed." She watched as Onnta, Ree, and Qontallium escorted Tuvok to the *Armstrong*. Pava and Torvig stood nearby, both apparently anxious to speak with Vale before the shuttlecraft's departure.

"Chris," Ra-Havreii said softly. "Are you sure you can trust this . . . alien intellect?"

She scowled. "Of course not. But what other choice do I have?"

"Don't you think you should consult with the captain before you accept the thing's help?"

Vale could feel her brows knitting together in irritation. "The captain put me in charge of this mission, Xin. That means I have full discretion to make safety decisions." She turned away from the engineer and faced Keru. "Commander, can I assume you're out here pacing the deck because the *Armstrong* is ready to sail?"

"Don't worry, Commander," said the big Trill. "Ensign Waen will have the *Armstrong* in wheels-up position within five minutes." He grinned at Ra-Havreii. "Even if the chief engineer and I have to drag her out of the hangar with towing cables slung across our shoulders."

"Favorable fortunes to you all," Ra-Havreii said, making no acknowledgment of the Trill's banter. He turned and exited the hangar deck.

Moving with surprising grace, Keru approached the *Armstrong*, and Vale followed. But Pava and Torvig stepped into her path, stopping the exec before she'd taken more than a half-dozen steps.

"We'd both like to join the away team, Commander," Pava said without preamble, grave-faced. Her usually youthful countenance looked strained and haggard, unaccustomed planes and angles showing beneath her sky-blue flesh.

"The captain told me about your request, Lieutenant," Vale said, speaking specifically to Pava. "But it's too late for me to change the roster now."

"I have been in the field many times before, Commander," Pava said through clenched jaws. "I'd be an asset to the team."

Vale nodded. "I know, Lieutenant. But I've already made my personnel decisions for this mission."

"Arbitrarily, in my opinion," Pava said, baring her even white teeth, "sir."

"Noted." Vale suppressed a surge of anger that reinforced her conviction that she'd always made a much better cop than a counselor. She had to remind herself that personal loyalty was Pava's principal motivation.

"Lieutenant," Vale said, more brusquely than she'd intended. She paused, composed herself, and continued in a softer tone. "Pava, I know that Tuvok has been a mentor to you. And Torvig, you've always thought of White-Blue as a kindred spirit. I get that you both feel protective of people that you care about a lot. But that makes your stake in this mission too personal. Do you understand?"

Torvig's artificially generated voice responded before Pava could reply. "I understand your decision, Commander. I may not like it, but I respect it and know that I must accept it."

Pava merely glared at the first officer in silence, her sullen anger undisguised. Vale felt her own anger rising again, but tamped it down when she considered how rough the road was for the lieutenant at the moment.

"Excuse me," Vale said as she stepped around Pava and Torvig on her way to the *Armstrong*.

Immediately after coming aboard the shuttlecraft, Vale took a moment to check in with her team of science specialists, every member of which seemed to radiate eagerness to get under way. These scientists were intellectually curious people who were trained to think in terms of knowledge and its implications. They were all about Starfleet's directive, "to go where no one has gone before." *Titan*'s science specialists never seemed to fret about the dangers to life and limb that sometimes came with that imperative. Though Vale admired their inquisitive spirits, the carefree aspect of their mind-set struck her as anathema. It made her hyperalert, knowing that the scientists tended to leap first and look later.

Vale entered the crew section, just aft of the flight deck. Lieutenant Eviku Ndashelef, the Arkenite xenobiologist, sat in one of the starboard seats beside Chief Petty Officer Bralik, the female Ferengi who served as *Titan*'s principal geology expert. Bralik was clearly intrigued by the physical characteristics a body in orbit around a pulsar might possess. Eviku was shaking his tri-lobed, half-moon-shaped head as he pointed out that what probably appeared to be mineral formations to Bralik's geology-biased eye might in fact constitute some hitherto unknown life-form. The xenobiologist was obviously every bit as pumped as Bralik was about the potential for discovery that Ta'ith promised.

It's too bad we won't have any time to look around once we get there, Vale thought wistfully as her gaze lit on Tuvok and White-Blue, whose triple-mind-linked bodies occupied adjacent seats, just behind those of Eviku and Bralik. Dr. Onnta sat immediately behind them, vigilantly monitoring Tuvok's vital signs. Beside the Balosneean physician sat Lieutenant Qontallium, whose unblinking reptilian eyes never wandered from the alien-possessed forms before him. Chief Petty Officer Dennisar, the huge, emerald-skinned Orion security officer, stood vigilantly against the aft bulkhead; his confidently insouciant bearing reminded Vale of a bouncer with whom she'd once had a run-in back home on Izar.

On the compartment's starboard side Dr. Se'al Cethente Qas, the head of *Titan*'s astrophysics department, stood beside the forward bulkhead. Cethente's decidedly nonhumanoid Syrath biology made him resemble a highly angular and vertical piece of postmodern sculpture adorned with numerous upper and lower limbs, and accommodating his shape had necessitated the removal of one of the bulkhead seats. The Syrath's physiology also hardened him to many forms of radiation that would have been instantly lethal to most humanoids. As inexpressive as Cethente was—the sensory clusters located on the top and bottom of his torso revealed nothing of his thoughts, lighting up only when he was using his vocoder to generate humanoid speech—Vale got the distinct impression that the Syrath was beside himself with anticipation.

In the seat beside Cethente, Ensign Y'lira Modan was consulting what Vale assumed was her linguistics tricorder. The gold-skinned, emerald-eyed Selenean woman possessed an astonishing facility for languages, which could come in handy should communication with the inhabitants of Ta'ith prove more difficult than anticipated. "Ensign Waen's ready to take the *Armstrong* out, Commander," Keru said from behind her.

"Thanks, Ranul," she said. "Arm-wrestle you for the copilot's chair?"

The big Trill gestured toward the seats occupied by the forms of Tuvok and White-Blue. "If you don't mind, I'd like to stay back here during the flight. Keep an eye on things." He patted his phaser.

Vale nodded. If the alien stowaway turned out to be less benevolent than advertised, she wanted the most competent security people to be on top of the situation.

"Let me know if our . . . guest starts getting talkative," she said. "That alien thing that hijacked Tuvok just might know how to build a quick-terraforming station like the one we had to blow up at Hranrar."

The big Trill stroked his beard thoughtfully. "That would be quite a coup. Maybe I should try to get the thing drunk."

Vale grinned. "Whatever works. Just don't ruin Commander Tuvok's liver in the process."

As the Trill moved aft down the aisle, Vale stepped forward and entered the flight deck. In the left chair sat a wiry Bolian woman who worked the touch surfaces of the *Armstrong*'s control panels with the nimble precision of a concert pianist.

"Make yourself at home, Commander," Ensign Waen said. Her left hand shifted into double time when her right departed from the console to wave a graceful welcoming gesture at the unoccupied seat.

Vale grinned. The fact that Waen had pointed at the right chair—the one traditionally reserved for the copilot rather than the primary pilot—implied that Waen's hospitality came with an inviolable boundary. *I'm only* Titan's *second-in-command, the one in charge of the mission, and the ranking officer present,* thought the exec.

Waen, however, was the *pilot*, the beneficiary of a rigorous training program that encompassed Starfleet Academy, the Dominion War, the merchant service, and a number of civilian transport vessels. Even in an age of voice-controlled autoastrogation systems, Waen's job still retained its ancient patina of "right stuff" glory. The *Armstrong* might be Vale's command, but her flight deck belonged to Waen.

"I'm glad to have you on conn, Reedesa," Vale said as she took the proffered seat and began monitoring the console before her.

The pilot flashed a grin that wrinkled her pastel blue face, emphasizing the vertical ridge that neatly bisected it from her bald scalp to her strong chin. Without interrupting her ministrations over the console, she said, "Happy to be here, Commander. Never got a chance to fly up close to a pulsar before. Looking forward to it."

Reedesa Waen was taciturn and laconic, with a self-deprecating good humor, and utterly unlike all the other Bolians Vale had met during her tenure in Starfleet. So many Bolians seemed to gravitate toward jobs in academia, diplomacy, or service industries. Vale suspected that Waen would never have been satisfied with any of those pursuits. Based on Waen's reputation as a Dominion War combat pilot, the XO sometimes fantasized that the battle-hardened Bolian might really be a lost Andorian, sans hair and antennae.

"Wheels up," Waen said. "Please warn all members of the away team to keep their hands, feet, and other extremities inside the vehicle at all times."

Through the transparent aluminum ports that dominated the top, front, and sides of the shuttlecraft's flight deck, Vale watched as the periphery of the hangar's yawning aperture fell away. A split-second flash of blue-tinged brilliance marked the craft's passage through the shuttlebay's selectively permeable, atmosphere-retaining forcefield.

Ahead lay the infinite star-flecked darkness, which only served to emphasize the sinister fires that jetted from both ends of the Vela Pulsar.

"Shielding enhancements are online," Waen said after checking one of her console displays. "And they seem to be working even better here than they did in the simulations."

Vale nodded. *Looks like we have our alien hitchhiker to thank for that,* she thought.

Turning her seat toward Waen's, Vale said, "How much time have you managed to shave from your original flight profile, Ensign?"

Still looking straight ahead as she worked the controls, the pilot said, "It all depends on how completely risk-averse you're feeling, Commander."

"This mission's risky however you look at it, Reedesa. We're up against a ticking clock here. If time runs out on us, we're going to lose Commander Tuvok and White-Blue. And maybe everybody aboard this shuttle as well."

"I know," Waen said. "My plan is take us most of the way downsystem at maximum warp. That leg of the journey shouldn't take us more than four hours, and it won't rip up the pavement all that much."

Vale knew that Waen's last point was a critical one. It was the poor condition of that metaphorical pavement—the interface between normal spacetime and its subspace equivalent—that was increasing the threat the Vela Pulsar posed to Ta'ith and anything else in its proximity. But she didn't have the time to take the environmentally ideal course of action, which would require flying at high subwarp speed for the entirety of the voyage to Ta'ith. Even factoring in the relativistic time dilation that everyone aboard the shuttlecraft would experience, the *Armstrong* would arrive at the planet far too late to prevent the three-way mind-link between Tuvok, White-Blue, and the alien AI from becoming irreversible. And Ta'ith itself very likely would no longer exist by the time the shuttlecraft arrived.

Still, gunning the warp engines for any length of time didn't seem wise either, in light of local spatial conditions.

"What exactly do you mean by 'most of the way'?" Vale asked.

Waen finished laying in a course adjustment, then turned to face the exec. "All but the last dozen AUs, give or take. The way I've got it plotted, that'll drop us out of warp about one point five billion klicks from the planet."

Vale did some quick math in her head. At its highest attainable relativistic speed, the *Armstrong* could cross that distance in about three hours, more or less, of objective time.

"You sure about this?" the first officer asked. "I don't want to make the local subspace potholes any worse if I can help it."

Waen grinned. "By the time we're done, nobody will know we were ever here. You have to remember, a type-11 shuttlecraft like the *Armstrong* has a warp footprint that's a whole lot smaller than the one a *Luna*-class starship makes."

"Have you run your numbers past our astrophysics-and-astrometrics brain trust?" Vale said.

"Yup," said Waen with a nod. "Doctor Cethente and Commander Pazlar both gave my plan a thumbs-up."

Vale was about to point out that Cethente didn't have thumbs when she noticed that the pilot's grin had faded. "Something tells me there's a rain cloud inside your silver lining."

"About ten minutes ago, Commander Pazlar gave me the latest Vela Pulsar report. The object's getting more erratic—and it's because *Titan*'s path keeps accidentally crossing undetectable spatial abrasions. That causes disruptions that we don't notice at the source, but which build in amplitude until they reach the pulsar."

"The way an undersea earthquake on one hemisphere of a planet can generate a tsunami that wipes out whole cities on the opposite hemisphere," Vale said.

Waen nodded. "Cethente says it's unavoidable. There's so much abraded space that *Titan* couldn't dodge it even if the trouble spots were detectable in advance—even out at a half-light-year's distance from the pulsar. Bottom line: The longer *Titan* remains near the Vela Pulsar, the more her presence will aggravate the situation. And the harder it will be for anything to survive on Ta'ith."

In other words, Vale thought, *it's only a matter of time before* Titan *sets off an eco-catastrophe, even though she's hiding in the weeds trying to avoid that very thing.*

"So we have a second ticking clock to beat now," the exec said. "One for Tuvok and White-Blue, and one for Ta'ith." Using Waen's estimates, Vale figured that the first clock would have anywhere from sixteen to twenty-four hours left on it by the time the *Armstrong* made planetfall.

The second clock was still anybody's guess. She could only hope that it would leave the away team enough time to complete its mission and return safely to *Titan.*

"I'll do whatever I can to beat 'em both," Waen said. Her right hand hovered above a section of the touch-activated flight console that read ENGAGE.

Vale thought it appropriate to sound a note of caution. "Just don't get overly heroic, Reedesa. You have a plan that our biggest brains in both astrophysics and astrometrics think will work, so I want you to stick to it as closely as possible."

Waen's hand continued to hover over the ENGAGE icon. With a wry smile, she said, "Don't worry. As the old saying goes, 'There are old pilots, and there are bold pilots. But there are no old, bold pilots.'

"I intend to become an *extremely* old pilot, Commander."

The lean Bolian woman's right hand touched the console, and Vale felt a transitory backward tug before the inertial dampers kicked in to compensate for the shuttlecraft's rapid acceleration. The *Armstrong* surged forward into warp, and dozens of the pinprick stars that were visible through the forward window elongated into blueshifted streaks.

Set squarely in the shuttlecraft's path, the fires of the Vela Pulsar remained conspicuously unchanged, burning like twin portents of doom.

Sixteen

U.S.S. TITAN

Reclining on the sofa in the central area of her family quarters, Deanna Troi reveled in an all-too-infrequent moment of unstructured downtime. The tableau she was viewing had become even rarer lately: Will, clad in civilian clothes, lying on his stomach on the carpeted floor, wrestling with their giggling sixteen-month-old daughter, Natasha Miana Riker-Troi. Just as Troi dared to hope that Will might actually devote the next several hours to relaxation, a voice emanated from his combadge. The interruption instantly seized his full attention.

"Bridge to Captain Riker," Lieutenant Commander Gibruch said. The Chandir's musical tones evoked Troi's childhood memories of the chimelike sounds the *muktok* bushes made as the autumn winds of Rixx relieved them of their dying pinkish-brown leaves. *"The* Armstrong *is away."*

Will rolled over onto his back and touched his combadge, which responded with a terse electronic chirp. "What's the away team's ETA at Ta'ith?"

"*Approximately seven hours, sir,*" reported Gibruch. "*The* Armstrong *is on track to beat the previous estimate by more than an hour. They've reported no trouble so far.*"

The revised ETA had Christine Vale's fingerprints all over it, Troi thought. *Our XO is nothing if not efficient.*

"Let's all hope it stays that way, Tamen. Anything else?" When Gibruch answered in the negative, Will signed off.

Having risen unsteadily to her feet during her father's moment of distraction, little Natasha made a clumsy but enthusiastic leap onto Will's belly, catching him unawares. Though Will had managed to catch her approximately at the moment of impact, the little girl struck him a glancing blow, forcing most of the air out of his lungs.

"Oof!" Will said, groaning as he held Natasha aloft. The little girl now wore a serious expression, as though she'd suddenly become cognizant of having unintentionally hurt her father. Will held the squirming child out to Troi as though little Natasha were a hazardous piece of ordnance.

The counselor scooped up the toddler and began to bounce her reassuringly. "You're the one who got her all worked up, Will," Troi said with a grin. "If you remember, I said you needed *rest*, not *wrestling*."

"I can be rested, Deanna," he said as he lay on his side, holding his abdomen and catching his breath. "Or I can be captain."

Troi resisted the impulse to roll her eyes. "Oh, please. A captain who works himself to exhaustion is a liability, not an asset."

After pushing himself up into a cross-legged sitting position on the floor, he struck a thoughtful pose and began stroking his beard. "Assets versus liabilities. Is that your official assessment, Counselor?"

Still rocking Tasha, Troi pinned her husband in place with a hard glare. "Don't try to distract me, Will. I know something's bothering you."

His shoulders sagged slightly. "It's Ta'ith," he said at length. "And the Andorian problem."

Troi nodded. "I suppose I would have been disappointed if all seven of our Andorian shipmates had decided to go along meekly with Starfleet's redeployment order."

Will made a sour face. "It would have made my life easier."

After having spoken individually with all of the Andorians currently serving aboard *Titan*—Ensign Cayla from ops; Ensign Vallah, the sensor tech; Ensign Zheren from engineering; Lieutenant Aris from astrophysics; the conn officer, Lieutenant Kevis; Lieutenant Pava from security and tactical; and Lieutenant Commander Shrat from astrobiology—Troi knew her report had removed the "easy" option from the equation.

"What are you going to do?" she asked.

"All of them have earned their positions here," he said. "They have all served honorably. None of them have done anything to warrant either summary transfers or demotions."

Troi knew that several of the Andorians harbored private, unarticulated doubts about the practicality of remaining aboard *Titan* in light of the current political climate.

"You haven't answered my question, Will," she said. "What are *you* planning to do?"

A determined look spread across his face. "I intend to respect their wishes."

Though Deanna had taken part before in direct violations of Starfleet orders, she sighed inwardly.

"The *Capitoline*'s CO will be expecting all of them to

have their duffels packed and ready." Tasha shifted restlessly in Troi's arms, as though responding to the tightly reined distress of her parents.

Will's expression hardened. "The *Capitoline*'s CO is going to be disappointed. I can't do anything about that. But Ta'ith is different."

Troi was doubtful. "How? Ta'ith is about to be incinerated by a runaway pulsar. That doesn't leave us many choices. Once the away team gets done taking the Ta'ithan AI home and the mind-link is dissolved, all we have to do is recover everyone and get safely out of the system."

"It might not be that simple, Deanna," he said, shaking his head. "Bringing the Ta'ithan AI home could change everything. Think about it: it's committed to restoring the technology that saved the planet from being destroyed by the Vela supernova thousands of years ago."

As little Natasha began to settle down in her arms, Troi switched from a gentle bouncing motion to slow rocking. "That's a good thing, isn't it?"

"Of course it is. It's just potentially complicated for *Titan*. And for me."

She could feel his concern, though she didn't understand its cause. "You're losing me, Will."

"Remember what the AI told us about the two main opposing factions on Ta'ith?"

Troi nodded. "Preservationists and Deconstructors."

"Keepers and Trashers. And the AI's sympathies obviously lie with the Keepers."

Will's discomfiture was finally making sense to her. "We've heard only one side of the story. Chris pointed that out."

He nodded. "She tried. Only I wasn't listening. And now we could be seen as having taken the Keepers' side, just by ferrying their AI home. We're—*I'm*—committing a Prime Directive violation."

"But both factions are the product of a warp-capable society."

"No," Will said, shaking his head again. "Both factions are the *heirs* to an *extinct* warp-capable society. Starfleet might decide that giving them any help whatsoever—even to save Tuvok's life, or to prevent the destruction of the entire planet—is a Prime Directive violation."

With little Tasha snuggling into Troi's shoulder as though seeking refuge in sleep, the counselor silently considered her husband's worries. While the AI's long-dead creators would certainly have qualified for first contact—thereby rendering Starfleet's noninterference directive moot—their descendants might not enjoy that same privilege. Was Will obliged, as he would be with any other pre-warp civilization, to shield the present-day Ta'ithans from alien contact?

At length she said, "It all comes down to one question: Should the planet's inhabitants be grandfathered in to the Prime Directive status of their ancestors?"

"The 'Fallen Gods,'" Will said, using one of the terms the AI had applied to the vanished advanced Ta'ithans of antiquity. "Funny thing about falling: it usually involves losing a legacy. Just ask Adam and Eve."

She felt a frown creasing her brow. "Creation myths aren't exactly a sound basis for sorting out Prime Directive issues, Will."

"Then how about Mintaka III? Those people were supposed to receive full Prime Directive protection."

Troi remembered the Mintakans vividly. A small group of them had once captured her, after a Federation anthropological team had accidentally revealed its presence on their world. The Mintakans, a race of proto-Vulcans, might have killed her but for Captain Picard's careful intervention.

"Mintaka III isn't the same as Ta'ith," she said. "The Ta'ithans—or at least some of them—have dedicated their lives to collecting and preserving their ancestors' knowledge."

"Whether they understand it or not," Will said, his expression bleak.

Troi shrugged. "I admit it's a gray area."

"Gray or not, I hope Admiral de la Fuego will keep your last point in mind when she's deciding whether or not to court-martial me."

Tasha stirred restlessly on her mother's shoulder. "Will," Troi said, lowering her voice, "your decision to intervene at Hranrar didn't get you into hot water with Starfleet Command."

"That's true," he conceded as he reached toward her shoulder. Sensing that he wanted to hold the baby, she gently handed over the half-sleeping child.

"So perhaps you're worrying a little too much about Ta'ith's Prime Directive ramifications."

"Maybe you're right," he said, lifting his daughter and gazing at her sadly, as though a lengthy separation was imminent. "Because with the Andorian situation, de la Fuego might not need to use the Prime Directive as an excuse to court-martial me."

SHUTTLECRAFT *ARMSTRONG*

Turning her chair so that it faced the copilot's seat, Ensign Waen beamed at Christine Vale. "We've just crossed the halfway mark," she said. "And almost ten minutes ahead of schedule, I might add."

"Easy there, Reedesa," Vale said as she glanced at the chronometer on her copilot's panel. She noted that they were an hour and fifty minutes out. Vale had spent much of that time staring through the polarized transparent aluminum port, mesmerized by the inexorably expanding fires of the Vela Pulsar.

The first officer turned toward the pilot, meeting her ebullience head-on. "What was it you said a while back about 'old, bold pilots'?"

The lean Bolian woman's broad smile contracted, imbuing her with the no-nonsense mien of a battlefield surgeon. "I'm not stunt-flying here, Commander. Squeezing everything I can out of this baby's top end is our least risky option."

"Even if our warp field disrupts the pulsar even more, and forces another huge belch of radiation out of it?"

"Unlikely, given our relatively small warp footprint," Waen said. "And our additional speed will reduce the amount of hard radiation we're all exposed to before we can take refuge inside Ta'ith's magnetosphere."

Vale mulled Waen's logic over for a moment and decided it was sound. At the moment, her away team was relying as much on the Ta'ithan AI for protection against the pulsar's lethal particle flux as it was on the shielding enhancements that Xin Ra-Havreii had installed. It made sense to reduce a liability like that as much as possible.

"All right, Ensign," Vale said with a nod. "Good work."

Before the pleased-looking Bolian could respond, a klaxon sounded, an accompaniment to the insistently flashing red alarm light that had just flared to life on the automated sensor display to Vale's immediate left.

"Looks like the pulsar's particle flux profile is intensifying. It's about to throw off a whole lot of mass and energy. It won't be pretty," Waen said.

"Can we get out of its way?"

Waen shook her head. "Only if we turn about and return to *Titan*."

And sacrifice Tuvok and White-Blue both, Vale thought. *There probably won't be enough time to scrub this mission and try again later.*

"How long do we have before the wave front hits us?" Vale asked.

"Do you want the bad news first, or the worse news?"

Vale sighed. "What's the bad news?"

"If we continue on our inbound course, the conventional stuff, like berthold rays and X-rays, will overtake us well before we can get inside Ta'ith's magnetosphere."

"And the worse news?"

"The particles that propagate through subspace will be on top of us about a minute from now, no matter what we do." Waen's jaws clenched, and her breath caught momentarily in her throat. "Damn. I shouldn't have pushed the engines so hard. Maybe the additional warp speed I squeezed out is what caused—"

Vale cut her off and rose from her seat. "Don't waste energy kicking yourself, Reedesa. This might have happened with or without any help from our warp field. Do you think our shielding enhancements can handle what's about to hit us?"

Reining her emotions in, Waen shrugged. "It's hard to say. I just hope we can count on a little help from our cybernetic stowaway." The pilot motioned with her head toward the *Armstrong*'s aft section.

"My thinking exactly," Vale said as she hurried aft,

toward the seats occupied by Tuvok and the motionless, winking form of White-Blue.

"Mister One One Six," she said, addressing the Vulcan's attentive face. "We're about to encounter a wave front of energetic superluminal particles."

"Superluminal," the merged intellect said as Tuvok's head nodded. "Meaning that the wave front is propagating through Lowerspace."

"Yes. Can you handle it?"

"Much of Undercity Maintenance Module One One Six's substance remains bound up in Lowerspace, Commandervale. Therefore, working together, we should be able—"

The merged intellect went silent in mid-syllable. Tuvok's face abruptly went blank. The Vulcan's eyes appeared vacant, like polished opals. Dr. Onnta, who was monitoring Tuvok's vital signs, looked stricken.

"Oh, shit," Vale said.

An instant later she heard a roar as the deck slanted sideways and the *Armstrong* lurched headlong into darkness.

U.S.S. TITAN

Will Riker stepped quickly out of the turbolift and strode toward the primary science station. Vaulting from the command chair, Lieutenant Commander Tamen Gibruch followed a couple of paces behind the captain, his rigid cranial tail swinging like a pendulum.

"It's just one ship, Captain," the Chandir said. "There's no evidence of any others."

Riker felt a surge of gratitude for that one small mercy. "Hail her."

"We've been hailing continuously since she first appeared," Gibruch's crystalline voice chimed. "No response as yet."

"Can you identify her?" Riker asked the two junior officers who were running the sensors at the science console, Ensigns Zurin Dakal and Birivallah zh'Ruathain.

A frustrated scowl deepened the lines in Dakal's Cardassian features. "Not yet, Captain. The vessel dropped out of warp nearly six AUs from our present position, not five minutes ago. It's been approaching us at high impulse speed ever since."

"Why can't we ID the ship, Vallah?" Riker said. He reasoned that since the other vessel was approaching from the outbound direction, contacting the new arrival, via either the subspace comm channels or the sensors, had to be easier than reaching the inbound shuttlecraft *Armstrong*, which the Vela Pulsar's particle emissions had effectively rendered incommunicado.

"The pulsar's increased particle flux is generating a lot of interference in the subspace bands, even this far out. That could be why we haven't received any response to our hails," zh'Ruathain said. Her antennae were drooping slightly, accentuating the downcast expression that troubled her sky-blue face.

Dakal nodded a quick affirmation toward the Andorian sensor technician, and then addressed Riker again. "The pulsar's been active for the past ninety minutes. We're fortunate we can tell there's a ship out there at all."

Gibruch stepped down into the command well, where Ensign Zhoriscayla zh'Tlanek was working the ops console. "On-screen, Cayla," the Chandir said to her. "Full magnification."

The ops officer—like Vallah, she was an Andorian

zhen—tapped in a swift series of commands. The wide forward viewer responded immediately, displaying a grainy depiction of an object that Riker could only describe as a fuzzy white blob.

The captain seated himself in the command chair at the center of the bridge and stared hard at the cryptic image before him as Gibruch took the seat to his immediate right.

The captain heard Vallah speaking from the science station, her tone flat and fatalistic. "It must be the *Capitoline*."

"Easy, Vallah," Dakal said gently. "Don't pack your bags just yet."

Vallah assayed a smile that her sagging antennae immediately revealed as a complete counterfeit. "You're right, Zurin," she said in an acerbic tone. "Maybe I'll have a wild stroke of luck—that sensor blob out there just might turn out to have come from the Gorn, or the Tzenkethi."

"It *has* to be the *Capitoline*," Cayla said, her antennae thrusting aggressively forward, her words flavored more with anger than with Vallah's resignation. Riker could hardly blame her.

"Who else could it be?" said Lieutenant Kevis, the Andorian conn officer.

Lieutenant Pava, who had been quietly working at the ops station, chose that moment to break her silence. "I'm with Vallah. Maybe it's a ship from the Tzenkethi fleet. Or one of the other Typhon Pact races Starfleet Command thinks we're all secretly planning to go to work f—"

Gibruch's cranial tail quickly began emitting long, shimmering tones that stacked instantly into a single dissonant chord. The sound ascended swiftly in both volume and pitch. To Riker's musically trained ear it sounded like a boot-camp reprimand delivered by a glass trombone. The cacophony crescendoed in the span of several adrenaline-accelerated heartbeats, whereupon a surprised hush engulfed the bridge.

"That will be quite enough, Lieutenant Pava," Gibruch said, speaking directly to the sullen young *shen* at ops, though he was clearly warning the other quietly fulminating Andorians on the bridge as well.

Leaning toward Riker, the Chandir spoke in a breezy, wind-chime whisper. "My apologies, Captain."

Riker merely nodded as he searched for something comforting to say to the four Andorians. But he found he had nothing to offer them that didn't sound like an empty platitude. Though Pava's last remark was clearly overemotional, there was no getting around the fact that Vallah, Cayla, and Kevis were almost certainly right about the other ship's identity. The *Capitoline was* the only other vessel that *Titan* was expecting to see.

And if that ship isn't *the one we all think it is,* he thought, *then we're probably in for something a hell of a lot worse than a dustup over Starfleet personnel policy.*

Seventeen

SHUTTLECRAFT *ARMSTRONG*

The tails of incendiary brilliance that the Vela Pulsar sprayed for countless millions of kilometers illuminated a wide swath of the looming planet.

Watching through one of the starboard viewports as the yellow-brown world continued its disconcerting and inexorable expansion, Ranul Keru breathed another silent thanks that the subspace wave front from the pulsar's most recent belch had only scrambled a few primary and secondary systems, as opposed to vaporizing the shuttlecraft outright. He kept telling himself that he'd made it through worse situations before. At the moment, however, apart from the Borg attack during his tour of duty aboard the *Enterprise*-E, no such occasion was springing immediately to mind.

The shuttle jounced and rattled, as though the little vessel were shuddering in dread over what was to come.

"We've just passed through the outer boundary of the

planet's magnetosphere, people," Commander Vale said from the cockpit, her voice carried by the crew compartment's intercom speakers. *"We're past the worst of the radiation hazards, at least for the moment. But the local magnetic field is still getting weaker by the hour."*

Now let's just hope our silent guest, Keru thought glumly, *has followed through on his promise to maintain our shield enhancements long enough to keep our rad-exposure somewhere below the lethal line. If he hasn't, we're all already as good as dead.*

But because the radiation sensors had been off-line since the pulsar's last outburst had struck the shuttle-craft, Keru knew that hope was all anybody on board had at the moment. He didn't want to think about how they were going to get back to *Titan* without the alien AI's help. *Let's concentrate on one impossible task at a time,* he told himself.

Ensign Waen spoke up, interrupting Keru's unpleasant musings. *"Unfortunately,"* the Bolian woman said, *"the nav system is still scrambled pretty good, thanks to the pulsar. This tub's flying like a brick, so our landing's probably not going to win me any awards. Strap in, everybody."*

Fortunately, Keru had already given this last order. Glancing around the dim, emergency-illuminated cabin to make certain that everyone's safety restraints were engaged and secure, he noted that most of the other away team members looked every bit as tense as he felt. One exception was Dr. Cethente, who, immobilized by a carbon nanotube tether anchored to the deck's starboard side, remained standing as motionless and inscrutable as a coatrack. Ensign Modan, who was seated beside him, stared in owl-eyed silence through the viewport at the oncoming planet.

Across the narrow aisle, Bralik and Eviku sat in grave silence. The Ferengi geologist and the Arkenite xeno-biologist both seemed to have turned slightly green, no doubt because of the turbulence the shuttlecraft's approach pattern was generating.

His own stomach lurching as he turned toward starboard aft, Keru felt a stab of envy at the relative serenity he saw on the face of the unconscious Commander Tuvok, whose restraint harness lashed him to his seat. The squat, decidedly nonhumanoid form of SecondGen White-Blue was strapped to the adjacent seat, completely quiescent except for the persistent flashing of several of the cryptic indicator lights built into its metal skin. From one of the seats behind Tuvok's, the gold-skinned Dr. Onnta was keeping a weather eye on the Vulcan.

Because of those lights and the firmness of Tuvok's posture—despite the many rude bumps and bounces the *Armstrong* was inflicting on its passengers, the Vulcan's head did not loll limply on his neck—Keru assumed that the link between Tuvok, White-Blue, and the artificial intelligence from Ta'ith persisted even now, despite the Vulcan's continued vexing silence.

The security chief paused momentarily to gaze in curiosity at the Vulcan's blank, vacant features. Keru was a Trill; however, he had not been chosen to be joined to one of his homeworld's symbionts. He had never seriously contemplated the symbiotic fusion of memories and multiple lifetimes. In fact, he wasn't sure he'd accept joining even if the Symbiosis Commission were to offer him an engraved invitation. Nevertheless, some small, wistful part of him regretted this gap in his knowledge.

"Commander Keru," Lieutenant Qontallium said from his position just behind Tuvok and White-Blue. "I believe Commander Vale's order applies to you as well as to the rest of us."

Keru hadn't been eager to be forced to turn his back on the entity that appeared still to be linked to Commander Tuvok and SecondGen White-Blue.

"Don't worry, Commander," said Chief Petty Officer Dennisar, almost as though he'd read Keru's thoughts. The green, broad-shouldered Orion security man was strapped into the seat beside the one to which Qontallium's reptiloid form was anchored. "Qur and I will watch your back." He patted his holstered phaser.

"I'm keeping mine drawn," Qontallium said, releasing his words in a serpentine hiss as he held his phaser aloft. In the Gnalish Fejimaera's green, leathery hands, the phaser's elegantly curved handle resembled the lethal claw of a pack-hunting reptilian predator.

Aware that Qontallium had lost as much to the Borg as he had—and therefore had just as much reason to distrust the motives of the persistently silent Ta'ithan AI—Keru nodded, faced forward, and strapped himself securely into his seat.

Here's hoping our guest has a workaround for all the electronics the pulsar fried, he thought. *If not, this shuttlecraft is going to come in like a meteor, no matter what piloting tricks Reedesa and Christine have up their sleeves.*

A sudden flash of brilliance to Keru's right interrupted the security chief's unpleasant musings, drawing his attention back to the starboard viewport. He saw that despite the shuttle's shields, a curtain of superheated plasma had begun to obscure the disturbing view. Friction tortured the upper atmosphere, which responded with a shriek so intense that the hull barely muffled it.

The envelope of fiery, ionized air that engulfed the *Armstrong* brightened as the rarefied atmosphere thickened steadily throughout her swift descent. The shuttlecraft rocked and shimmied as though from a series of impacts. Keru knew that the *Armstrong* was going to belly in one way or another, either in one piece or in many.

Closing his eyes to avoid another glimpse of the inferno that lay just beyond the shuttlecraft's thin skin, Keru seized the sides of his seat with white-knuckled hands.

TA'ITH

Behind the lengthening shadows of the ancient Whetu'irawaru ruins that stretched beyond the horizon, the cruel day slid inexorably toward the unsatisfying surcease of another encroaching evening. As night approached, the restive impatience of the Thousand slowly transformed from a formless, inchoate feeling to something far more substantial. Garym, subsachem of the Preservationist sect, could hear this clearly in the overlapping and increasingly forceful stridulations that rippled through the multitude. It had become clear to hir that the reflexive repetition of the Preservationist prayer-dance ritual could not provide sufficient comfort to the crowd of pilgrims that had followed Sachem Eid'dyl on hir quest for peace. The Thousand that Eid'dyl had entrusted to Garym's leadership during the sachem's absence had grown decidedly agitated.

These people had followed their beloved leader to this remote place, seeking a respite from the enmity that had from time immemorial separated their Preservationist sect from that of the Deconstructors, only to fall prey to Trasher treachery. From the raised space upon which s/he stood, Garym could see that more than a few had already turned away, leaving the bulk of their sisters behind in the ruined husk of the city of their ancestors. Some of these scuttling, departing figures may have been bound for their homes in the Preservationist Arcologies, while others were ostensibly leaving in pursuit of the deadly Deconstructor phalanx that had abducted Sachem Eid'dyl.

Despair beckoned as the completeness of hir failure bowed Garym's abdominal sclera, bringing hir thorax and ovipositor into painfully close proximity. *I have lost the Thousand's faith,* s/he thought. *If indeed that faith was ever mine to begin with. It would take a miracle for me to reclaim it.*

Banishing the mocking evidence of hir failure by enfolding hir vision patches beneath their dermal hoods, Garym extended hir rearmost four hindlimbs almost straight upward. S/he then raised hir neckless cephalon, and the sensory stalks that sat atop it, even higher, getting them as far from the rocky ground as possible. Extending the muffled vision patches that marked the distal ends of hir sensory stalks, Garym silently implored the Fallen Gods—the Whetu'irawaru, the elder race that had long since retreated far beyond Ta'ith's oppressive skies—for their wise and benevolent intervention.

That was when the subsachem heard a subtle change in the massed stridulations of the Thousand. Tones and chords of surprise and wonder had begun to weave among the auditory threads of discontent and anger.

Garym uncovered hir vision patches and found hirself watching spellbound as a brilliant tracery of orange fire made a spectacular downward arc across the brown and tourmaline sky. It seemed to grow larger, or more likely closer, as it made an apparently uncontrolled descent. The subsachem wondered if s/he was about to witness yet another deadly manifestation of the Heart of the Cosmos's ever-more-wrathful demeanor.

Then s/he heard a new stridulation, louder and more distinct than those of the pilgrims who still milled about the ruins. *"Part of us is Undercity Maintenance Module One One Six,"* the voice said. A gently glowing, translucent form not unlike that of Garym hirself took shape several bodylengths away, hovering just above the rubble-strewn ground.

Hir limbs growing weak, Garym tumbled onto hir abdomen, prostrating hirself. The confused gabble s/he heard sweeping through the Thousand made hir wonder how many of hir fellow Preservationists had found renewed courage, and therefore now followed hir lead.

"You are one of the Fallen Gods," the subsachem told the glowing figure.

The apparition seemed to find the question both surprising and amusing. *"Not precisely, though Undercity Maintenance Module One One Six might be described as one of them. Regardless, we could be of considerable help to one another. We will all benefit from the presence of the visitors who will soon be among you."*

Rotating hir cephalon, Garym looked up. The arc of fire in the sky was growing steadily lower and closer. Garym rose to a standing position when it resolved itself into a streamlined shape not unlike the rivercrawlers that the Preservationists farmed for their meat and medicinal glandular secretions. The object's speed seemed to diminish only when its swift-moving belly came into contact with the rocky ground, causing sparks and fire to shower from its impossibly hard-looking carapace.

"Do not be afraid," the glowing figure said, reaching toward the Thousand with all of its countless limbs. *"This vessel will not harm you, nor will those who depend upon it as their means of transportation to and from Ta'ith."*

But despite the apparition's earnest entreaty, many of the assembled Preservationists were scrambling to retreat from the incoming metallic form. The Thousand were moving erratically, their stridulations communicating their escalating fear even after the object had come to rest, still hot and billowing smoke perhaps a hundred bodylengths away from the rise upon which Garym stood. Fortunately, no one had been standing directly in the thing's way during its clumsy, crashing entrance to the Sacred City's ragged, ruined outskirts.

Realizing that hir miracle had arrived, Garym raised eight of hir forelimbs skyward, using them in tandem to stridulate a shout that s/he hoped would cut through the panicked crowd's cacophonous chatter.

"Behold!" the subsachem cried.

The crowd quieted. Without waiting to see whether or not either the apparition or any of the Thousand would follow hir, Garym moved toward the smoking, streamlined object. When s/he had drawn nearly close enough to lay hir limbs upon its still-smoking metal skin, Garym noted that its long axis measured about two dozen bodylengths.

A measureless interval later an aperture in the object's skin slid open, startling Garym into prostrating hirself again.

Though s/he lay prone, several sets of Garym's

forelimbs could still rub together to produce coherent sound; s/he could still speak to those s/he was expected to lead.

"The Fallen Gods have returned!" Garym said, and several hundred stridulations echoed hir pronouncement a moment later.

For surely, the subsachem thought, basking in the hopeful noises of hir people, *only Their great strength can hope to stand against the depredations of both the Trashers and the Heart of the Cosmos.*

Eighteen

U.S.S. TITAN

Deanna Troi stepped out of the turbolift and made an immediate beeline for the captain's chair. Though the hour was late, Will was exactly where she'd expected to find him.

"I left Tasha with T'Pel," she said quietly to her husband, who was staring straight ahead at the main viewer. "When I heard that the *Capitoline* was approaching, I wanted to be on the bridge."

"Thanks, Deanna," Will said. Though his outward demeanor was calm, his emotions were roiling on the inside. "I was about to call you up here. Looks like I'm going to need your help."

"Of course," Troi said, nodding as she took the seat at Will's immediate left and looked toward the screen that dominated the front of the bridge. The viewer displayed an indistinct blob that Troi could only assume was the arriving ship. "Do you need an emotional read on the *Capitoline*'s CO?"

"No," he said quietly.

Her brows knit together. "No? Why not?"

Will pointed toward the vague shape on the viewer, which Troi noted was becoming progressively more defined with each passing second. "Because that ship isn't the *Capitoline*."

"Whose ship is it?" Troi said.

"Uncertain," Will said. He barked an order over his shoulder. "Vallah, can you clean that image up?"

"Trying, Captain," said the Andorian *zhen* who was working the sensors. Several seconds later, she turned toward the bridge's center, her antennae forming a forward-thrusting U that indicated surprise. "I've compensated for the pulsar's interference enough to get a positive ID on the vessel's configuration. It's *Andorian*, Captain. Schematics coming up."

On the main viewer, a wireframe diagram replaced the exterior starscape. Though Troi hadn't previously encountered this particular type of vessel, she recognized it nevertheless. Its sleek shape all but screamed aggression, from its daggerlike forward section to the swooping, winglike engine nacelles that bracketed its aft portion.

"She's a battle cruiser," she said, speaking in a near whisper.

"*Shran*-class," Will said, nodding. "Fifty percent longer than *Titan*, with twenty percent more beam. Crew complement of seven hundred, if I remember right."

"There's nothing wrong with your memory, Captain," said Lieutenant Pava, from tactical. Her face impassive, her forward-thrust antennae rigid, she seemed to be barely holding in a torrent of intense emotional distress. "She's been decelerating steadily for the last thirty minutes. Probably trying to pierce the pulsar's static the whole time, hoping to get a better look at *us*."

"The vessel is coming to a stop, relative to us," said Ensign Cayla. "Now keeping station at about ten thousand klicks."

"Close enough for us to get a better look at her," said Ensign Dakal from the main science station.

The wireframe schematic vanished, and was replaced by a computer-enhanced visual of a gray Andorian battle cruiser. The vessel's forward weapons tubes emitted a faint orange glow that appeared calculated to intimidate.

"She has us outgunned by two to one," reported Lieutenant Kevis, who was seated at the conn. The Andorian *chan*'s matter-of-fact tone barely disguised an undercurrent of fear.

"More like two and a half, or even three," Ensign Pava said, her flat delivery doing little to obscure the apprehension Troi knew she was feeling, along with everyone else on the bridge—particularly Pava's Andorian crewmates.

Leaning toward Troi, Will spoke in a conspiratorial tone. "I hope like hell we don't find out for certain."

She felt her husband's well-concealed anxiety. "You think we might?"

"Take a close look at that cruiser's hull," the captain said, pointing toward the main viewer. "The Andorians must have started reconstituting their pre-Federation military institutions. This ship's using old Imperial Guard livery. And she's keeping her forward tubes warm for us."

A light on Ensign Cayla's ops panel began flashing rhythmically. "We're being hailed, Captain."

"On-screen, Ensign," Will said. He straightened his

uniform tunic as he rose from the captain's chair to face the main viewer.

The granular exterior of the Andorian battle cruiser disappeared and the image of a dour-faced, masculine Andorian military officer took its place. Because he was visible from the waist up, Troi noticed immediately that his formfitting midnight blue uniform was as anachronistic as the Imperial Guard markings on his ship's hull.

"This is Commander Krasizhrar ch'Harnen," the Andorian on the screen boomed, his tone matching the genuine anger Troi sensed within him. *"Master of the* I.G.W. Shantherin th'Clane. *You are holding several Andorian nationals hostage. My government has dispatched the* Therin *to recover them."*

Will glanced momentarily at Troi. Outwardly emotionless, she saw in her husband's blue eyes twin pools of surprise that closely approximated what she was feeling.

Turning to face the Andorian Guard officer, Will said, "This is Captain William T. Riker of the *U.S.S. Titan.* You and your government have been badly misinformed, Commander. . . ." He paused, as though wondering if he had remembered the other man's rank correctly.

His antennae switching like a pair of angry serpents, the bellicose Andorian *chan* stepped deftly into the momentary silence. *"If your facility with Andorian nomenclature is as poor as with most of your kind, pinkskin, then you may address me as Commander Zhrar. And perhaps you are right about my having been misinformed. The situation looks far worse than I'd imagined: you've chosen to provoke my government by putting no fewer than four of your Andorian hostages on display on your bridge."*

Because of the special empathic channel they shared, Troi could sense her husband's urgent thoughts. *Does he really believe what he's saying, Deanna?*

Given the absurdity of the commander's accusations, Troi considered that a fair question. Perhaps Zhrar had some other agenda that he was keeping concealed. Closing her eyes, she concentrated on reaching out with her mind across the thousand or so kilometers that still separated the *Therin* from *Titan*.

All she could sense was a nearly blinding locus of unfocused rage, hatred, and fear. Finding it as uninformative as it was unpleasant, Troi tried immediately to tune it out, but without complete success.

Sorry, Will, she thought, speaking inside his mind. *All I can feel is his anger.*

After nodding a silent acknowledgment to Troi, the captain resumed, "Commander Zhrar, *Titan's* crewmembers come from many worlds, both in and out of the Federation. Everybody serving here does so voluntarily. Every Andorian on this ship—all seven of them—have declared their intention to stay, regardless of any directive from Andor's government."

As Zhrar absorbed Will's statement in silence, apparently surprised by his opposite number's vehemence, Troi looked around the bridge, paying particular attention to the four Andorians, all of whom were watching their captain in expectant silence. It was true that *Titan's* entire Andorian contingent had stated a preference to remain, but there were certain nuances to the situation. While Vallah seemed as firm as ever in her commitment to resist both reassignment and repatriation, it now seemed to Troi that Cayla and Kevis, and even Pava to some extent, might have begun to waver, at least a little bit.

I need to have another conversation with each one of them, Troi thought, concerned that any member of the crew might be acting under duress, either real or perceived.

Troi returned her attention to Commander Zhrar, who seemed to have reined in his emotions somewhat and gathered his thoughts. *"I find your perspective on this matter fascinating, Captain. Your expectation, if I understand you correctly, is that the* Therin *will withdraw, leaving as members of your crew all seven of the Andorian nationals my government expects to repatriate."*

Will frowned. "Where you take the *Therin* is your business, Commander. But until and unless any of them decide otherwise, every Andorian aboard this ship will remain part of my crew. Do we understand each other?"

"I understand you, Captain," Zhrar answered without hesitation, his antennae flattening and bending backward across his white-maned scalp like the ears of a feral cat getting ready to pounce. His nearly lipless blue mouth split into an aggressive smile. *"And I will grant you one Federation standard hour to reconsider your position. Zhrar out."*

The Andorian commander's image abruptly gave way to that of his ship.

"That went well," Will said, and then lapsed into a thoughtful silence.

Troi knew that he was pondering his limited slate of alternatives. Running might be an option, but she knew that Will would never consider doing that while an away team remained out in the field. And she understood that the prospect of giving in to Zhrar's demand struck him as equally unacceptable.

If we're going to avoid a fight we probably can't

win, Troi thought, *then we're going to need one of Will Riker's patented "unorthodox solutions."*

A surge of anguish interrupted Troi's reverie. Though she wasn't certain whose distress she had detected, its source seemed to be on the bridge. The emotional surge was strongest in Pava's direction, though similar sentiments were rolling off of Kevis, Cayla, and even the stolid Vallah, though at a far lesser intensity.

"Captain, may I recommend we call a meeting with our Andorian crewmembers?" Troi said.

SHUTTLECRAFT *ARMSTRONG*

The shuttlecraft's metal-grinding slide across the planet's rocky surface had finally stopped. Other than a few battery-powered alarm lights, the pilot's compartment was dark, thanks in part to the thick coating of dust and detritus that had settled over the forward canopy.

"The good news is that we can scratch 'crashing' from our list of things to worry about," Ensign Waen said as she began trying to resuscitate her flight control console. "The *Armstrong* has landed."

But the really *good news,* Christine Vale thought, *is that we seem to be in one big piece, as opposed to a great many teensy tiny ones.*

"And the bad news?" asked the exec.

Waen scowled in frustration. "Primary and secondary sensors are out, and the tertiary unit is working only intermittently. All I can determine at this point is that the air outside is breathable—if you don't mind a slight bouquet of ozone and sulfur, that is. There also seems to be a fair number of life-signs just outside the *Armstrong*'s hull. I wish I could be more specific."

Vale silently echoed the pilot's sentiments. A harmless pastureland filled with trees, bunnies, and kittens might lie just beyond the shuttlecraft's skin. Or a mob of angry, hostile natives might be lurking, sharpening their pitchforks and lighting their torches.

Noting that both the pilot's and copilot's flight consoles seemed resolutely determined to remain dark and dead, the first officer carefully undid the flight harness that had left her pinned to the skewed copilot's chair like a butterfly in a collector's display. She had to grab her seat's headrest for balance after stumbling on the deck; the shuttlecraft had come to rest at an awkward slant of about fifteen degrees. The incline ran downward through the aft portion of the craft.

"'Landed,'" Vale repeated, a wry half-smile on her lips after she'd regained her footing. "Is *that* what you call that last maneuver?"

Waen shrugged as she continued her apparently fruitless ministrations over her instruments. "I didn't say this landing was my best work, Commander. But considering the number the pulsar did on nearly every system we've got, you have to give this one an honorable mention, at least. After all, you know the ancient flyer's proverb as well as I do."

"'Any landing you can crawl or swim away from is a *good* landing,'" Vale deliberately misquoted.

Waen snickered. "Aye, sir."

The flight console suddenly rewarded Waen's efforts by lighting up. Drawing comfort from the hope that Waen now had a fighting chance at reinitializing the *Armstrong*'s most critical systems, Vale began moving carefully aft.

"I want a full diagnostic report ASAP, Reedesa," she

said over her shoulder as she made her way into the crew compartment. "Depending on what's waiting for us outside, we might need to have the *Armstrong* spaceworthy at a moment's notice."

Until she had seen for herself how the rest of the away team had come through the crash landing—shaken, bumped, and perhaps a bit bruised, as it turned out— Vale hadn't realized she'd been holding her breath.

"Ensign Waen is having some trouble assessing the damage we took when we bellied in," Vale announced to the group. Looking straight at Bralik, the female Ferengi geologist, she added, "None of you are engineering specialists, but I know that some of you have practical experience in that area."

Looking as pleased as a teacher's star pupil, the Ferengi chief stood up and raised her tricorder. "I would be delighted to make a full damage assessment, Commander," Bralik said.

"Great. I'd like you to get right on that, if you don't mind."

Tuvok suddenly got to his feet, exiting the row of seats he'd been sharing with the silent Sentry AI, SecondGen White-Blue. Walking stiffly up the aisle, he said, "Your auxiliary spacecraft has sustained surprisingly little permanent damage, Commandervale."

It was obvious that the Ta'ithan AI who had hijacked the bodies and minds of both Tuvok and White-Blue had yet to make good on its promise to dissolve the three-way mind-link.

"Thanks for the damage report," Vale said as Tuvok's body came to an awkward stop before her. "But I hope you won't be offended if my people take a look for themselves."

"Of course not. You must take all reasonable precautions. We understand that."

"And about this 'we' business," Vale said. "Now that we've brought you back to your homeworld, why don't you turn our friends loose?"

Tuvok's head turned to the right, then left, then right again, as though his neck movements depended on a bearing that needed a good oiling. "As we already discussed, this will be done—*after* we reach the safety of the Sacred Undercity."

Well, nothing ventured, Vale thought, unsurprised by the entity's reaction to her request. She wondered silently if the alien machine intelligence would continue to stick to the letter of their agreement once they reached their destination. Or would it then find a new excuse not to relinquish Tuvok and White-Blue, even after the away team had fulfilled its part of the deal?

"All right," she said, then paused briefly to examine the crew compartment's port and starboard viewports. As had been the case with the flight deck canopy, they were covered with dust and crud that the shuttlecraft had kicked up during its emergency touchdown. "Our next stop is this Sacred Undercity. I hope it isn't far."

"We saw to it that your craft touched down as near to the Undercity as is prudent," said the Tuvok-amalgam.

"Close enough for us to walk there?" Ensign Modan asked.

Chief Dennisar, the huge Orion security man, added, "But probably not so close as to put his enemies on alert."

Tuvok's head nodded awkwardly. "We did not wish to alert the Deconstructors to our presence before it became necessary to do so."

"Well, *somebody* already knows we're here," said

Lieutenant Eviku, the Arkenite xenobiologist, as he consulted the readings on his tricorder.

Ranul Keru was frowning at his own tricorder. "From the readings I'm getting, it appears to be at least several hundred somebodies."

Gesturing toward the dirt-covered viewports that flanked the crew compartment, Vale said, "So we might have to run a gauntlet of Deconstructors, or Trashers, or whatever, the moment we step outside."

"No," the Tuvok-amalgam said. "You are in no danger."

Vale paused to consider her options, which she quickly decided weren't very numerous. For better or for worse, the away team was on Ta'ith. Saving Tuvok and White-Blue required her to risk taking them both, along with at least part of the team, into this Sacred Undercity.

And because the clock was ticking, there was no point in waiting.

"Commander Keru," she said, "you're in charge here. Help Waen and Bralik with the shuttlecraft diagnostics and repairs, and keep an eye out for trouble."

The big Trill nodded. "Aye, sir. What will you be doing, Commander?"

"I'm going to escort our guest home," Vale said, gesturing toward Tuvok. Galloping right over the objections she anticipated from Keru, she continued. "Ensign Modan, I'll want you along, in case we encounter any language barriers the UT isn't up to. Eviku, Cethente, Dennisar, Qontallium, you're with me."

"I go wherever Commander Tuvok goes," Dr. Onnta said.

Vale nodded at the Balosneean physician, then addressed the entire disembarking group. "Break out the

lightweight rad suits, guys. Otherwise, it'll be standard
field gear. Just don't skimp on the phasers." She made a
point of checking the charge on her own type-2 phaser
before moving on to the locker where the radiation suits
were stored.

Within a few minutes, the away team had donned the
loose-fitting and alarmingly flimsy-looking maroon suits
and assembled the rest of the group's gear—including
the still and silent metal body of SecondGen White-
Blue. They all stood before the starboard-side hatchway,
which had yet to be opened.

"Phasers ready, heavy stun," Vale said as she prepared
to open the hatch. Fortunately, the keypad and the adjacent EPS system both seemed to be working again, so
she didn't face the awkward prospect of having to crank
the hatch open manually. "Be ready for anything."

Tuvok's voice responded with a decidedly non-
Vulcan serenity. "Commandervale, we've already told
you: there is no reason to fear."

"That's easy for you to say," said Onnta, who looked
utterly out of his element in his baggy rad suit.

Vale touched the control stud, and the hatch slid open,
causing a serpentlike hiss as the atmospheric pressure
between inside and outside equalized. A slightly burnt
metallic smell assaulted her nostrils as she led the team
onto the uneven, rock-strewn landscape outside.

The daylight was amber-colored and hazy, thanks to
the interactions between the planet's atmosphere and
magnetosphere, and the Vela Pulsar that continuously
assaulted both. Fortunately, the spinning stellar remnant was slipping toward the horizon, its diffracted glow
painting the nearby ruined cityscape the color of old dry
bones. Under an aurora-streaked butterscotch sky, and in

the shadows of the necropolis, a multitude of creatures had gathered—roughly human-scale life-forms that resembled both lobsters and millipedes, as well as a number of phyla that Vale thought defied classification.

Recalling Crewman Chaka—*Titan*'s arthropod-like Pak'shree computer specialist whose formal name was K'chak'!'op—Vale willed her skin not to crawl, but with only partial success.

Moving in a wave, almost as though guided by a single will, the multitude began to surge slowly but deliberately toward the *Armstrong*.

"You see?" the Tuvok-amalgam said, almost directly behind Vale. "No reason to fear."

"Really?" she muttered over her shoulder. Clutching her phaser in a bony white death grip, Vale shivered as she struggled to master an incipient fight-or-flight reaction, an atavistic, prelimbic mammalian response to creeping, crawling things.

The creature that had drawn nearest to the shuttlecraft suddenly dropped from its hindmost limbs and lay flat on its belly. A heartbeat or two later, the ranks of multi-legged beings behind the first one began to follow suit.

Within moments, hundreds of the things had thrown themselves to the ground, what appeared to be their faces and mandibles facing forward and down. It reminded Vale of the annual *hajj* that hundreds of Epsilon Boötis Reform Muslims made each year at the Izarian city of New Vancouver—if the Izar Reform Muslims had been weird shellfish creatures from a pulsar planet, rather than garden variety *H. sapiens* like Vale herself.

"I'll be damned," Vale said as she stepped toward the prostrate multitude, which had considerably begun to clear a path before her, creating a trail that led toward the crumbling remains of the nearby city. "Well, being worshipped is better than a lot of the alternatives."

As the team moved forward, Eviku sidled up beside her. "Then let us hope that these beings lack the predilection for destroying their gods that some other cultures possess."

Damn, Vale thought, thinking of crosses and *bat'leth*s as she picked up her pace slightly, hoping to get clear of the reverent alien crowd just a little bit more quickly. *Why'd he have to bring* that *up?*

U.S.S. TITAN

A little less than ten minutes after Commander Zhrar's angry sign-off up on the bridge, Pava strode into the observation lounge. The captain and Counselor Troi were already seated opposite one another at the round conference table, each bracketed on either side by three of Pava's fellow Andorian officers. To the captain's right, and Troi's left, sat Ensign Birivallah zh'Ruathain, the sensor tech, Lieutenant Aristherun zh'Vezhdar from astrophysics, and Lieutenant Commander Rogrenshraton ch'Agrana from astrobiology. Directly opposite them, Lieutenant Artunkevisthan ch'Kul'tan, the gamma-shift conn officer, Ensign Tozherenshras th'Chesrath from engineering, and Ensign Zhoriscayla zh'Tlanek, a junior ops officer, had taken seats.

"Thank you for joining us, Lieutenant," said the captain. He wore a wry half-smile that made it difficult for Pava to determine whether or not she was being gently reprimanded. "Counselor Troi and I just finished explaining Commander Zhrar's demand to the entire group. We were about to discuss what to do about it."

"I apologize for my tardiness, Captain," Pava said as she took the last empty chair, located between th'Chesrath and zh'Tlanek. "But I wanted to listen to the communication I just received before coming to the meeting."

"Do you mind sharing it?" Riker asked.

"Not at all, Captain. It's from Churan, one of the *shelthreth* bondmates I left behind on Andor in order to continue my Starfleet career after my graduation from the Academy."

Counselor Troi appeared genuinely concerned. "Is everything all right at home, Lieutenant?"

Pava shrugged. "I wouldn't know, Commander. Churan isn't living on Andor at the moment. He's been in the homeworld fleet for the past several years. At the moment, he's serving in the new Imperial Guard aboard the *Therin*."

"Your bondmate is aboard Commander Zhrar's ship right now?" asked the captain, whose concerned expression mirrored that of the counselor.

Pava nodded. "It's a small galaxy, sir. Given Andor's ongoing population crisis, only a relatively small number of reproductive-age Andorians opt for deep-space postings. Still, I wouldn't be a bit surprised if every Andorian aboard *Titan* is connected in some way to somebody serving aboard the *Therin*."

Riker and Troi watched as all six of the other Andorians present—Vallah, Aris, Shrat, Kevis, Zheren, and Cayla—exchanged knowing nods.

"No wonder I've been sensing so much reticence among you, both as a group and individually," Troi said.

Riker nodded. Obviously addressing all of the Andorians present, he said, "And that's something we have to discuss now. I know that you've all gone on record as wanting to stay aboard *Titan*, despite Starfleet Command's recent redeployment order."

"An order," Troi said, "that doesn't require us to hand any of you over to your homeworld's domestic military, by the way."

"Good point," Riker said with a nod. "But regardless of the right or wrong of Zhrar's demand, I would certainly understand if any of you has had a change of heart because of the *Therin*'s arrival."

"Are you asking that we volunteer to let the *Therin* take us back to Andor?" said zh'Ruathain, the sensor technician that the crew knew as Vallah.

"Absolutely not," Riker said. "The whole point of this meeting is to make certain that none of you are being pushed one way or the other. If I did any less, Zhrar might have a point in accusing me of holding all of you hostage. That's why we didn't try to intercept Pava's incoming message."

So it's not necessarily all about Starfleet ideals, Pava thought, feeling a surge of bitterness. *Maybe it's purely about due diligence. A high-profile captain covering his ass.*

The sentiment made her feel guilty immediately. Captain Riker was worthy of her respect. He had proved his sincerity when he put his career on the line by fighting Starfleet Command's reassignment order.

Troi asked for a vote, by show of hands. All seven Andorians wasted no time confirming that their unanimous preference to remain aboard *Titan* had not changed since they had first learned of Starfleet's reassignment order.

"Thank you all," Riker said. "But regardless of what any of us might want, Zhrar has given us a deadline, and we have to respond to it. In forty-five minutes, he'll be expecting me to send the seven of you over to the *Therin*. And he doesn't appear to give a damn about anyone's preferences in the matter."

"Can't we fight him off?" asked Lieutenant ch'Kul'tan, the conn officer better known to most of his colleagues as Kevis.

"If I'm backed into a corner, I won't hesitate to fight," Riker said. "But I don't want to fire on an Andorian ship. Besides, Zhrar has a considerable advantage over us in terms of armament."

"We also have to consider the potential damage that ship-to-ship combat could do to this region of space," Troi said. She gestured toward the panoramic observation window, and the unpredictable fountain of violence that lay far beyond it. "The Vela Pulsar is unpredictable enough without turning its backyard into a war zone."

"And our away team is smack in the middle of the pulsar's worst effects," Riker said.

"Then we have to persuade Zhrar to respect our decisions," said the engineer, Ensign th'Chesrath, a *thaan* who nearly everybody addressed simply as Zheren.

Riker chuckled as he shook his head. "Not likely."

An idea struck Pava then. "I recommend stalling him."

"How?" asked Troi.

Pava leaned forward, spreading her hands on the smooth tabletop. "By giving him part of what he wants, and teasing him with the promise of getting the rest later."

"Sounds like you have something specific in mind, Lieutenant," Riker said.

"Tell Zhrar that I've volunteered to go over to the *Therin*, at least temporarily," the security officer said.

"I'll listen to whatever sales pitch he wants to make to get me to agree to join the Imperial Guard."

"Maybe you'll even have a chance to settle whatever business remains unfinished between you and this bondmate of yours," Lieutenant zh'Vezhdar said archly.

"That's *my* business, Aris," Pava replied tightly, glaring at the junior astrophysicist. "And no concern of yours." Turning back to Captain Riker, she said, "After I listen to what Zhrar has to say, I'll promise to pass it along to my fellow Andorians in person—once he returns me to *Titan*."

"What makes you so sure he'll agree to return you to *Titan*?" asked Lieutenant Commander ch'Agrana.

"I've dealt with military *chan* of his stripe before, Shrat," Pava said. "I know how they think. If I can convince him that I stand a good chance of persuading at least a couple of you to come over to the *Therin* quietly, he'll definitely send me back here."

"Perhaps," Aris said, "Zhrar will be more amenable to persuasion if he gets the opportunity to speak in person with each of us individually, aboard the *Therin*."

Pava couldn't restrain a deep scowl. "What leverage will we have over him if he gets his hands on all of us?"

"You misunderstand, Pava," Aris said. "Not all of us at once. We would go over to the *Therin* in shifts. One or two at a time, perhaps. Once Pava returns, I volunteer to go next. Provided everyone else agrees to participate in turn, of course."

Noises of agreement circulated among the Andorians. Troi, who had been listening intently, nodded at the captain, as though confirming the sincerity of the informal vote.

The captain's brow furrowed as he stared off into the

middle distance, stroking his beard as he considered his options in silence. After enduring the expectant glare of eight pairs of eyeballs, he met Pava's gaze squarely.

"All right, Lieutenant," he said. "We'll give your plan a try."

Pava felt her antennae dip forward in gratitude as she nodded to him. "Thank you, sir."

"Don't thank me, Lieutenant," he said, looking grave as his eyes panned slowly around the table. "Just don't make me regret signing off on this."

After he made his offer to Zhrar, Riker settled into the command chair, where he affected a relaxed, almost insouciantly confident posture. Though he didn't break eye contact with the image of his Andorian counterpart on the main viewer, he knew that Deanna was watching both of them intently

"An intriguing offer, Captain Riker," boomed the Imperial Guard commander. *"But it isn't what I asked for."*

"It's the best you're going to get, Commander," Riker said. "At least without provoking a lot of unpleasantness that I'm sure we're both anxious to avoid."

Zhrar scowled truculently, but after a few moments his antennae went from aggressively flattened to a more upright, forward-facing position. And he actually *smiled.*

"Perhaps you are correct, Captain," Zhrar said. *"Anything that will demonstrate that the decisions* Titan*'s Andorian personnel are making are freely undertaken and uncoerced is to our mutual benefit.*

"You may beam the first of your Andorian officers over as soon as you are ready."

With that, the image of the *Therin*'s commander

winked out, to be replaced by the Vela Pulsar's fiery geysers.

Riker turned to face his wife. "Counselor?"

"He's hiding something significant," Troi said. "But I'm fairly confident that he didn't lie when he agreed to bring each of our Andorian officers over to the *Therin* one at a time for individual interviews. And he was telling the truth when he agreed to return them."

Riker knew he should have been happy that the other man had agreed to be reasonable. Yet he wasn't. "Why do you think he agreed?"

Troi shrugged. "Perhaps because he knows as well as we do that Pava's plan won't force him to give up his tactical advantage."

Riker nodded, and then tapped his combadge. "Captain Riker to Lieutenant Pava."

"Pava here, Captain," came the Andorian *shen*'s quick and steely reply. *"I'm in transporter room two, waiting for the word."*

Riker saw Ensign Cayla, Lieutenant Kevis, and Ensign Vallah exchanging silent but anxious glances from across their respective consoles. He couldn't say he blamed any of them, since their turns would come soon enough, assuming everything went according to plan.

"The word is given, Lieutenant," he told Pava.

And hoped that he hadn't just sent one of his finest officers into permanent exile.

Nineteen

IMPERIAL GUARD WARSHIP SHANTHERIN TH'CLANE

Lieutenant Ranishegarth zh'Vhrane hadn't expected Commander Krasizhrar ch'Harnen to oversee her work in person during this duty shift. As she rechecked the settings on the transporter controls yet again, she hoped that everyone present—the commander, the four intimidating security officers that now flanked the transporter platform, and her immediate supervisor, Lieutenant Commander sh'Agri—would fail to notice the slight intermittent tremor in her left hand.

An indicator light flashed on the console to zh'Vhrane's extreme left.

"*Titan* is signaling, Commander," said sh'Agri, who stood directly in front of the indicator. Though all the console settings looked good to zh'Vhrane, she turned toward sh'Agri for silent reassurance that everything was working as it was supposed to.

"Final system check says 'go,' Commander,"

zh'Vhrane said, addressing both sh'Agri and Commander Zhrar.

"Energize the system," said the *Therin*'s CO with a curt nod. "And beam our guest aboard."

The transporter's familiar whine, an almost musical sound, began to fill the room. Up on the dais, the transporter pads emitted a reassuring amber glow, as did the overhead beam emitters. *So far, so good,* zh'Vhrane thought.

An alarm began flashing on the console, causing zh'Vhrane's left hand to shake again, even more violently than before. Breathing a curse under her breath, she willed her errant limb into immobility and started recalibrating the backup pattern buffer with her right hand.

The transporter began making a strained sound, like a pair of duranium starship hulls being dragged across one another.

"What are you doing, Lieutenant?" sh'Agri demanded.

"The buffer is filling up too fast," zh'Vhrane said, pointing quickly at one of the indicators as she worked. "If we don't compensate for that immediately, we could lose our transportee." Both *our transportees,* she added silently.

sh'Agri blanched as she read the indicators.

"Don't foul this up," boomed Commander Zhrar as the transporter's cry neared a fever pitch.

Several tense moments later zh'Vhrane released the breath she hadn't realized she'd been holding. "Beam split successful," she said. Out of her peripheral vision, she noticed Commander Zhrar nodding in approval. She breathed a silent prayer of thanks to Uzaveh that the pulsar's space-twisting emissions hadn't intervened at precisely the wrong moment to ruin all her careful work.

At least not yet, she thought, reminding herself that her task was still incomplete.

"Pattern buffer in sync with phase transition coils," sh'Agri said. "Materialization commencing."

After she'd finished executing the pattern buffer's final cross-circuit, zh'Vhrane watched as a figure gradually took shape and gained solidity on the transporter pad. As the curtain of sparkling light that characterized the transporter effect receded, the security guards drew their weapons. Two of them approached the platform.

"Easy there, fellas," said the transportee, a young Andorian *shen* dressed in a Starfleet duty uniform. Though she held up both hands in an overt gesture of peace, she showed no outward sign of fear. "Request permission to come aboard."

Commander Zhrar stepped toward the stage. Nodding toward the Starfleet officer, he said, "Permission granted. I am Commander Krasizhrar ch'Harnen. Welcome aboard the Andorian *Imperial Guard Warship Shantherin th'Clane.*"

"Lieutenant Pava Ek'Noor sh'Aqabaa, *U.S.S Titan,*" said the *shen* on the transporter dais.

"Please do not be intimidated by my security personnel, Lieutenant," the commander said. "They are merely here to escort you to the chamber where we will conduct your . . . interview."

The Starfleet lieutenant's antennae curled in undisguised suspicion. "All right. I just hope you're still planning to return me to *Titan* in one Federation standard hour, as agreed."

The commander nodded. "At which time, another

Andorian Starfleet officer will be beamed aboard the *Therin* to take your place, and so on. Until I've finished making the case for repatriation to all seven of you."

Though the ember of suspicion in the Starfleet lieutenant's wintry blue eyes never went out entirely, she followed the two guards nearest the transporter platform as they led her out of the room.

Commander Zhrar approached the control console. "What is the condition of the remaining pattern?" he demanded.

"Stored in the buffer, Commander," sh'Agri said.

After making a quick double-check, zh'Vhrane added, "And completely intact."

Commander Zhrar favored both transporter techs with a rare pleased smile. "Energize the system sgain, then."

Lieutenant zh'Vhrane wasted no time helping sh'Agri key in the necessary commands. The two remaining security guards, weapons in hand, approached the transporter dais.

Listening to the device's familiar escalating whine, zh'Vhrane watched anxiously as another shape began shimmering into existence over one of the forward pads. Yet again, she offered an inaudible plea to merciful Uzaveh that nothing be allowed to sabotage Zhrar's plan.

Or, more importantly, his mood.

The last thing Pava remembered was being aboard *Titan*, where she'd stood in a knees-bent, combat-ready posture on the transporter stage. It had vibrated gently beneath the balls of her booted feet, the transporter pad flaring with white light as the matter stream's curtain of brilliance enfolded her.

It seemed to Pava that all of this had occurred an instant ago. Now, somehow, she was flat on her back, apparently having just come awake in near-total darkness in some unknown place.

Aboard the *Therin*, she realized with a start that quickly glissaded into both fear and anger. Why was she here? And why was her mind so damned foggy?

Commander Zhrar wasn't leveling with us, she thought as she rolled off what seemed to be a wide, firm bed and got to her feet. *That's a shocker.* Ever since her homeworld had done what had once been unthinkable—leaving the Federation it had helped to establish more than two centuries ago—she'd begun to think she could no longer be surprised by anything her people did.

Reaching instinctively for her combadge, she discovered that it was no longer attached to her uniform tunic; there was no way even to attempt to make contact with *Titan*—assuming that the starship was even still within range. After all, the *Therin* could already have taken her anywhere. And with the survival of an entire away team depending upon *Titan* staying in relatively close proximity to the Vela Pulsar, would Captain Riker have the wherewithal to come after her?

Doing her best to emulate her mentor, Tuvok, Pava tried to manage the cresting waves of fear and anger she was experiencing. *Concentrate on the first order of business,* she told herself.

Survival.

A quick check of the rest of her gear revealed that the small type-1 phaser she had hidden under her belt was likewise missing, as was the compact *ushaan-tor* blade she had tucked into the top of her right boot. The fact that her captors had at least left her uniform in place came as cold comfort.

Refusing to be deterred by the almost nonexistent illumination, Pava's antennae probed forward into the gloom. Because an Andorian's cranial sensory organs were sensitive to the electromagnetic fields generated by the nervous systems of a great many intelligent species, she soon determined that no one was present in the room other than herself. That much was a relief, infinitely preferable to worrying about a knife-wielding stranger silently lurking in some nearby corner.

Moving toward the nearest wall, she began tracing out the room's perimeter, noting the curve of bulkheads and the presence of what felt and looked like deliberately opaqued transparent aluminum windows or viewports. The place was enormous, more like one of *Titan*'s VIP suites than a holding cell.

She came to what was obviously the only door, a duranium hatchway that didn't respond to her presence by sliding open. Locked from the outside, she surmised.

Despite Tuvok's lessons, anger flared deep within her breast. Casting aside all pretense of subtlety, she shouted, "All right! I'm awake, Zhrar! Now open the blerking door so we can talk, you godsdamned pirate!"

She listened to the ensuing silence. Nothing.

Her fear began catching up to her anger. *What if Zhrar has decided to let me rot in here?* Hoping that only a few more shouts would suffice to attract her jailor's attention, Pava began filling her lungs.

The hatchway irised open, letting in a frigid blue light from what appeared to be a corridor. The light silhouetted the tall figure that stepped into the room.

Pava didn't hesitate. Though the hatch was already

starting to close again, she leaped upon her visitor, knocking him to the deck after bouncing him roughly off a wall. Within the space of a handful of heartbeats, the newcomer was supine, and Pava was on top of him, her hands at his throat.

"Pava?" Though strangled, the voice was familiar. Shocked by recognition, Pava released her grip on her visitor's throat.

"Churan?" she said, still sitting astride his supine body.

Churan responded with commingled coughs and gentle laughter. "Some things never change," he said as he tried to catch his breath. "Computer, adjust light level to point seven five."

The room brightened to near daylight levels at once, enabling Pava's momentarily dazzled eyes to confirm what her ears and her body had already told her. This was Yanischuran ch'Garis, one of the three prospective *shelthreth* partners she had abandoned in order to continue her career in Starfleet.

"Churan," she said, climbing off the winded *chan*. "It really is you?"

Still on his back, he extended a hand toward her. She clasped it and helped him to his feet. Just as Pava remembered, he stood about half a head taller than she did.

"You seem awfully surprised to see me," he said, his antennae thrusting forward almost playfully. "Didn't you get my message, my hotheaded little ice borer?"

Pava winced inwardly at his use of the old endearment. He'd told her many times over the years that her passionate nature reminded him of the tiny creatures whose intense, internally generated heat melted tunnels through Andor's ubiquitous permafrost. His implication was that she needed to get a better grip on her volatile emotions.

"I *did* receive your message, Churan." She paused to take in his formfitting, deep blue Imperial Guard uniform, whose braid indicated that he held the rank of lieutenant, just as she did.

He pointed to the rank button pinned to his collar. "That's *Lieutenant* Churan to you." He grinned, but then his antennae lowered as he put on a more earnest expression. "I apologize for not being on hand to greet you when you were first beamed aboard. But duty called."

"I understand. You're the first person I've seen since my beam-over from *Titan*."

Curiosity sent both of his antennae aloft. "Strange. According to the schedule, nearly half a ship's day has passed since you were beamed aboard. A lot of rumors have been circulating since then."

"Rumors?" she said, feeling her own antennae rise.

"Somebody told me you had a quiet meeting with Commander Zhrar, and went just as quietly back to your Starfleet vessel after he'd failed to convince you to remain here."

"That Starfleet vessel has a name, Churan. She's called *Titan*, and I think of her as my home."

His antennae retreated even as his eyes narrowed to slits that conjured memories of old wounds, and even older confrontations. "Sorry. I should have remembered that you no longer give the same consideration to your homeworld. Or even to those who once committed themselves to you as *shelthreth* bondmates."

Pava knew she needed to steer the conversation elsewhere, and quickly. "You were telling me about rumors," she said through clenched teeth.

Churan smiled. "Another crewmember told me that a transporter malfunction had injured you, or maybe even killed you outright. Such things are rare these days, but they still happen on occasion. I even heard that you'd been slain after starting a brawl with Commander Zhrar."

"Sorry to disappoint you," she said, returning his smile.

With a chuckle, he said, "I'm not disappointed. Knowing you, there's still a good chance you'll turn at least one of these stories into a fulfilled prophecy."

"It's good to know you still have so much faith in me," she said.

He laughed again, and then a thoughtful look crossed his cerulean features. "You really can't remember anything after you left the Starfleet—" Churan interrupted himself momentarily. "After you left *Titan*?"

"It's like I just arrived here," Pava said with an emphatic shake of her head.

"Strange," he said. "Very, very strange."

"Nearly as strange as Commander Zhrar assigning you to serve as my jailor."

He scowled in confusion as he stepped toward the middle of what she was beginning to notice was a very well appointed room. The table and chairs in the central living area wouldn't have looked out of place in the Council of Clans office complex in Andor's capital of Laibok. The bedroom beyond, where she'd awakened, seemed at least equally bedecked in finery, including blankets and ceiling draperies made of distinctively nano-woven Tholian silk.

" 'Jailor'?" Churan said, looking confused. He spread his hands in an expansive gesture that took in the whole suite. "Does this look like any jail you've ever seen?"

She stepped toward him, her hands balled into fists at her sides. "Even if you make the bars out of gold-pressed latinum, a cage is still a cage."

It occurred to Pava that her former bondmate's presence might have been Zhrar's idea of an ironic social comment. Whatever necessity the *shelthreth* institution might serve, to the young, free-spirited Andorians who had left Andor to pursue Starfleet careers, the ancient custom of arranged four-way marriage was itself a kind of confinement.

"Your fellow Andorian Starfleet officers don't seem to feel caged aboard the *Therin*," Churan said with a shrug. "Most of them, anyway."

She thought her expression must have mirrored his. "What are you talking about?"

"Your Andorian Starfleet colleagues, of course: zh'Ruathain, zh'Vezhdar, ch'Agrana, ch'Kul'tan, th'Chesrath, and zh'Tlanek."

The rush of blood in her ears was beginning to drown out the sound of Churan's voice. Vallah, Aris, and Shrat. Kevis, Zheren, and Cayla. All of them were here now, aboard the *Therin*?

"Pava, are you all right?" Churan asked.

She suddenly realized that her jaw was hanging agape. "That wasn't what we agreed to. I was to meet with Zhrar alone. He was supposed to send me back to *Titan* afterward, and then interview all six of the others aboard the *Therin*, one at a time."

Displaying a melancholy expression, Churan shook his head. "The schedule evidently changed. After all, you appear to have been unconscious for most of the ship's day."

"How did that happen?"

"All rumors aside, it seems there really was a . . . complication of some sort with the transporter. That must have been the cause. And the transporter system must have malfunctioned because of the proximity of the pulsar."

"Whose transporter system malfunctioned?" she asked. "Ours or yours?"

Churan answered with another one of those maddening shrugs. "I'm not the one to ask." He grinned. "I just blow things up when Commander Zhrar needs things blown up. At any rate, your *Titan* colleagues have all been given accommodations very similar to yours."

"But Zhrar wasn't supposed to bring all of us aboard the *Therin* at the same time," she repeated, tossing her hands in the air. "He knows that."

"As I said, sometimes schedule changes are unavoidable, Pava. With you indisposed, the commander probably had to conduct his interviews in a different order than he'd originally planned."

"But that still doesn't explain why all seven of us are here at once," she said, feeling her anger rising like an incipient eruption of one of the hot springs beneath Andor's Northern Wastes. "Zhrar has already said that he wants to bring us all back to Andor. Now there's no way Captain Riker can stop him from doing exactly that."

"How many times do I have to tell you that none of you are prisoners?" Churan said. With a sigh and a shake of his head, he walked toward the nearest viewport and typed a command into an adjacent keypad. The opaquing effect abruptly subsided, revealing a clear transparent aluminum window with a view of the star-bejeweled blackness that surrounded the *Therin*.

Apparently only a few kilometers distant, *Titan* hung

suspended out there, a lone gray pearl adrift in a dark, infinite ocean.

"You see?" Churan said. "Commander Zhrar hasn't absconded with you."

Pava folded her arms across her chest as she studied the purported image of *Titan*. She knew it could easily be an expert piece of holographic trickery designed to placate her while the *Therin* was actually traveling at maximum warp toward Andor. On the other hand, her antennae had picked up none of the subtle subsonic vibrations that usually accompanied high-warp travel, no matter how efficiently a vessel's inertial damping system was working.

"That's a relief," she said. "Since we're not prisoners, can I assume we're all free to go now?"

He frowned slightly at that. "Once Commander Zhrar has finished discussing the Andorian government's repatriation initiative with all of you. I understand that some of your friends are seriously considering staying aboard the *Therin*."

His bland assertion made the small hairs on the back of Pava's neck stand up as though preparing for follicle-to-follicle combat. To make her displeasure crystal clear, she allowed her antennae to move backward until they lay nearly flat against her close-cropped white hair.

"And none of them have been coerced in any way, of course," Pava said.

He smiled. "Of course not. We're not monsters, Pava. We're your countrymen."

Recalling Tuvok's lessons in emotional control, she tried to match his smile. "I get that, Churan. Which is why I'm sure *you* can understand how anxious I am to speak with your commander."

He nodded, still smiling. Pulling a small comm unit from his belt, he said, "Let me see what I can do about expediting that."

After a seeming eternity during which perhaps all of ten minutes had passed, Pava allowed Churan to conduct her through a maze of surprisingly narrow corridors, while a pair of dour and silent uniformed guards shadowed them from behind. The small, silent caravan came to a stop at a hatchway that bore a sign on which the word COMMANDER had been rendered in clipped, military-style Andorian *Graalek* script.

A moment later she found herself standing in the presence of the very same tall, broad-shouldered *chan* who had recently crossed verbal blades with Captain Riker. Though Churan and the guards had retreated behind her, she could feel their eyes on her back as though they were very sharp knives.

"Ah, Lieutenant Pava Ek'Noor sh'Aqabaa," the large Andorian said as he looked up from the desk at which he sat, simultaneously reviewing the information displayed on several padds. The front of what appeared to be the commander's personal quarters obviously served him as an office as well.

"Commander Krasizhrar ch'Harnen," Pava said, nodding respectfully as she satisfied the formalities by pronouncing the long form of his name.

The big *chan* dismissed all three of Pava's escorts with a gesture. Once they had withdrawn, leaving her alone with him, he said, "Please, Lieutenant, call me Zhrar." He favored her with a smile whose beneficence made a poor match with the aggressive posture of his antennae.

Lowering her own antennae, she smiled. "Thank you, Commander. You may address *me* as Lieutenant Pava Ek'Noor sh'Aqabaa."

Zhrar surprised her by displaying disappointment rather than the anger she had expected. "There's truly no need for us to be adversarial, Lieutenant."

He gestured toward a chair on the other side of his desk. Making a point of ignoring both the chair and the gesture, she remained standing at attention.

"Then I'm sure you won't mind returning me to *Titan* immediately," she said. "Along with all six of my colleagues."

"In due course," he said with a nod. "I was hoping to have a productive interview with you first."

"I'd feel much more 'productive' if we were to stick to the original plan," she said. "We can get started as soon as you send everybody but me back to *Titan*."

"I wouldn't want to risk doing that just now. As Lieutenant ch'Garis may have informed you, we've been experiencing . . . difficulties with our transporter. *Titan* appears to have suffered similar problems."

Pava tsked and shook her head. "Blasted pulsar."

"Exactly."

She moved toward the closed door through which she had entered. Not surprisingly, it failed to open for her. "Well, thanks for the chat, Commander. If you don't mind, I'd like to go back to my cell. At least until the 'transporter difficulties' clear up, that is."

He frowned, and his antennae thrust forward like twin lances. Rising from behind his desk, he said, "But we haven't had our conversation yet."

She nodded. With mock sadness, she said, "Yeah, but what are you gonna do?"

"If you won't speak with me, then perhaps you'd prefer to speak with my associates," he said as he pressed a button on one of the padds before him. She thought he was concealing his rage well, apart from the flush of deep cobalt and violet that had just begun to alter the tranquil blue color of his fleshy face.

An aperture on the bulkhead to the right of his desk irised open, revealing another open hatchway. Uncomfortably warm air gusted through it into the office, followed immediately by a pair of squat, environmental-suited figures, each of which walked on multiple lower limbs on bodies topped with two upper forward-facing limbs and lumpen heads whose flat planes and angles and gleaming pairs of eyes were hazily visible through their helmets. Prehensile rear limbs that might have been tails completed the nightmare image. One of them let loose an unfathomable vocalization that sounded to Pava like a Vezhdar Plains treecat being ground into flatbread flour in a *hari* mill. The quasi-crystalline, gold-orange flesh that she could see through their helmets glowed, revealing the extremely high temperatures these creatures required in order to survive.

Each creature carried a lethal-looking disruptor in one of the claws that tipped its weirdly articulated forelimbs.

Uzaveh's afterbirth, Pava thought as she recalled all the ugly rumors she had heard over the past several weeks about Andorians secretly working hand in glove with the worlds of the Typhon Pact.

Just how long have the blerking Tholians *been whispering into Zhrar's ear?*

Twenty

TA'ITH

Marching forward without missing a step, Christine Vale checked her rad suit's faintly glowing dosimeter. She heaved a relieved sigh: the planet's declining magnetosphere was still keeping the Vela Pulsar's hard radiation at bay, at least for now.

A new aurora crackled across the twilit sky at that moment, driving all complacency from her head. It reminded Vale that any world that lay in such close proximity to such a violent stellar object could turn on a team of hapless explorers with little or no warning.

But *Titan*'s XO also knew she had reason to feel encouraged. After all, the natives weren't trying to bar the away team's path as it moved at marching speed toward the ruined cityscape in the distance. Still, she was uncomfortably aware that this could change in a heartbeat should the Ta'ithans decide that the team posed a threat to the ruins that the Tuvok-amalgam claimed they held sacred. For the moment, however, the creatures appeared content to keep their distance, either out of reverence for their visitors-from-the-sky or because of the intimidating presence of Dennisar and Qontallium, who were dutifully maintaining a watch over the away team's flanks as the hike through the incipient darkness continued. Reverent or not, hundreds of the multilegged, crawdad-like locals followed the away team just as diligently, bracketing the Starfleet contingent on either side.

Vale glanced toward the rear and noted with a slight tremor of apprehension that the *Armstrong* had receded from view, thanks both to the highly uneven terrain and the distance the team had covered since leaving the relative safety of the shuttlecraft.

As she faced forward again, the first officer noticed that Ensign Y'lira Modan was moving away from the alien with whom she had been attempting to converse while on the march. The Selenean cryptolinguist approached Vale, shaking her head with a sadness that belied her golden skin and gemstone eyes.

"I'm sorry, Commander. But it would seem that bringing me along on this mission has turned out to be a poor allocation of resources."

This was the last thing Vale needed to hear right now. *There's nothing like having to give a pep talk while hemmed in by hundreds of Shetland pony–sized cockroaches.*

"I think you're selling yourself short, Ensign. You can't expect to crack an unknown alien language from scratch during the first few hours. We know that these beings belong to the Preservationist sect. And you've even managed to figure out which one of these guys seems to be their leader." Vale pointed out the individual from whom Modan had just withdrawn. The creature's eyestalks, or antennae, almost seemed to wave at her in response. "Those are pretty major accomplishments, at least in my book."

"Indeed," said the voice of Commander Tuvok. Vale turned and saw the Vulcan's body walking stiffly beside White-Blue, whose metal shell lay on the small antigrav platform that Lieutenant Eviku and Dr. Cethente were pulling behind them. "You have already accomplished more than we could have."

Vale frowned at the Tuvok-amalgam.

Being a highly trained expert in languages, codes, and encryption—with a superanalytical five-lobed brain, no less—Modan had obviously anticipated the question Vale had been about to ask. "But you *came* from here. How could you be less well equipped to speak to these beings than somebody who came here from a different quadrant of the galaxy?"

"Undercity Maintenance Module One One Six has been slumbering for eons, Ensignmodan. This entity was programmed to be fluent only in the communications modes established by the Whetu'irawaru Progenitors. I had scant exposure to modern Ta'ithan languages after I was awakened. I learned only a few broad concepts, such as the recent deterioration of the Heart of the Cosmos and the names and rough objectives of the two major political factions."

"But you—One One Six, I mean—picked up Federation Standard quickly enough," Vale said. "Isn't that more 'alien' to you than a modern-day descendant of an ancestral Ta'ithan language would be?"

Tuvok's head nodded mechanically. "Fully acquiring your language required extremely intimate contact—what your Vulcan Commandertuvok terms a 'mind-meld.'"

Vale shrugged and pointed once again at the Ta'ithan crowd's leader. "Okay. Then why not get some 'intimate contact' going with a few of the locals? That might speed things along quite a bit. I'd like to make sure the away team and the natives don't get in each other's way while we're here. Maybe you can even talk them into lending us the local equivalent of Sacagawea to guide us."

Tuvok's head made an awkward shake of negation. "The passage from your mothervessel to Ta'ith has left Undercity Maintenance Module One One Six in far too depleted a state to initiate a new mind-meld. It is all he can do to hold this one together long enough to reach a place of relative safety." The Tuvok-amalgam paused to point toward the shadow-cloaked ruins that loomed ahead, still tantalizingly remote. "That's where the current mind-link can be dissolved with as few negative consequences as possible for all concerned."

Tuvok's face suddenly went ashen, and he staggered. Onnta and Vale both grabbed him to keep him from falling. A moment later the apparent fainting spell had passed and the Tuvok-amalgam insisted on continuing to move forward unassisted.

"Forgive us," Tuvok's voice intoned. He still looked too pale, even in the wan evening light.

"What's happening to you?" Vale said.

"As we said, the passage to Ta'ith left us depleted." Tuvok's left hand gestured shakily toward the dim cityscape. For the first time, Vale noticed a far-off column of smoke and fire billowing up from between the broken towers of the city's aboveground level. "The Deconstructors appear to be doing something to what remains of the Technocore—the technological substrate to which Undercity Maintenance Module One One Six's machine-code essence must return in order to dissolve the mind-link in safety."

Outstanding, Vale thought. *A bunch of alien Luddites are setting fire to the one chance we have of saving Tuvok and White-Blue.* Getting indigenous help was now a far more urgent priority than ever before.

"We *have* to figure out how to talk to the locals," Vale said to the Tuvok-amalgam. "Are you really so sure there's nothing you can do to help with that?"

A thoughtful look crossed Tuvok's face as his limbs continued their robotic marching motions and two teeming hordes of creatures kept pace in the thickening darkness. Clutching his ever-present medkit, Onnta trotted awkwardly after Tuvok, barely keeping up.

"If you are prepared to take the risk of accidental misunderstanding, Commandervale," the Tuvok-amalgam said at length. "Undercity Maintenance Module One One Six will attempt to address the Ta'ithans who have gathered here."

Modan nodded. "I think that Undercity Maintenance Module One One Six has a far better chance of avoiding the consequences of some fatal linguistic error than I do. All those eons of dormancy notwithstanding."

There's no percentage in analysis paralysis, Vale thought after a moment's consideration. *Nothing ventured, nothing gained.*

Vale nodded, then ordered the away team to halt its march. Apparently aware that something important was happening, the natives on either side of the away team also came to a stop, the word spreading through the ranks in a wave of cricketlike, apparently limb-generated sound.

As the indigenous crowd quickly settled down and

quieted, Eviku helped Tuvok step up onto the antigrav platform, which had just enough extra room to accommodate him by serving as a hovering but stationary dais. One of Cethente's upper tentacles placed a small device in the Vulcan's hand; Vale realized belatedly that it was the electronic vocoder that transformed the Syrath astrophysicist's all but unfathomable natural speech sounds into humanoid-recognizable languages.

Speaking into the vocoder as though it were a megaphone, the Tuvok-amalgam began addressing the still, apparently attentive multitude. Strange, alien phonemes poured forth from the tripartite mind-melded entity.

The incomprehensible monologue continued for perhaps a minute, then ceased abruptly. The Ta'ithans remained utterly silent for a seeming eternity afterward.

Then all hell seemed to break loose. Countless thousands of native limbs erupted simultaneously into furious motion.

"Oh, crap," Vale said, wincing at the almost deafening cacophony that resulted. She ran toward the makeshift dais and hollered up at the Tuvok-amalgam. "What the hell did you say to them?"

Cethente took possession of his vocoder as Eviku and Onnta helped the Vulcan down from the platform. "We told them that we are all merely mortal, as they are, and not the Fallen Gods they appear to think we are," the Tuvok-amalgam shouted. "However, we addressed them in the primary language of Undercity Maintenance Module One One Six—that of the Whetu'irawaru."

The language of the ancestors that they worship, Vale thought, recognizing the overtones of fear in the native vocalizations. A cold sweat broke out across her brow. *Brilliant.*

"What are they saying?" Eviku shouted.

A grin spread slowly across Modan's face. Vale hoped that was a signal that the ensign had just made a major linguistic breakthrough. "They want to help us reach the city, and access its subterranean levels. In return, they're asking for our help in driving a rival faction out of the Undercity."

Tuvok's head bobbed in affirmation. "The Deconstructor sect. Or Trashers, as these people prefer to call them."

Vale had to wonder whether this was their leader's idea, or the ill-considered action of a mob moved by passion and ideology.

"Beautiful," Vale said. "All we have to do is agree to take sides in what amounts to an alien civil war." Another, larger column of flame and smoke went aloft over the still-distant necropolis. Tuvok's body blanched and staggered, but didn't quite fall. Dr. Onnta looked as though he might leap out of his golden skin at any moment.

"As I keep telling you, Commandervale," the Tuvok-amalgam said as the march toward the ruins resumed, "there is no reason to fear."

Twenty-one

I.G.W. SHANTHERIN TH'CLANE

Zhrar heard the grating screeches of the two hotsuited Tholians a split second before the translator rendered their noises into recognizable Andorii.

"Attention, Pava Ek'Noor sh'Aqabaa," one of the Tholians said in a flat electronic monotone as it approached the intensely surprised-looking Starfleet officer. "You will now be taken into custody, under the authority of the Tholian Assembly and the Typhon Pact."

To Zhrar's amazement, the young *shen* appeared to be overcoming her initial shock fairly quickly. Throwing a hard glare at Zhrar, she said, "Looks like my first impression of you was accurate after all, Commander."

As the bulky Tholians took up positions on either side of the lieutenant, Zhrar realized his office was starting to get very crowded.

He rose from behind his desk. Ignoring the Starfleeter's bile, he said, "I'm not sure how much you know about the Tholians, Lieutenant."

"Let's see," she said. "They enjoy warm weather, walks on the beach, weaving energy webs, and arriving on time. Did I miss anything?"

Zhrar nodded. "You didn't mention their uncanny facility for communication. They can speak to one another over vast distances using an organic quantum-entangled EM network."

"Sounds like a neat trick," she said, her antennae flattening in unconcealed anger.

"It's only the beginning," Zhrar said. "Tholian organic comm technology can be adapted to Andorian neural structures, thanks to our antennae and certain recent advances in biointerface technology. It has been used successfully on Andorian test subjects."

She frowned, but curiosity drew her antennae upward. "Used? Used how?"

"To make those test subjects especially susceptible to suggestion," Zhrar said. He pulled his top desk drawer open and removed a small metal skullcap, which he set atop his desk.

"Brilliant, Zhrar," Pava said as she slowly shook her head. "Andor has just gone to all the trouble of declaring its independence. And what do you do? You go and get the homeworld conquered by a member of the Typhon Pact before the government offices can even finish dumping all their old Federation stationery. Great."

Zhrar tamped down a surge of very real anger. How often had he heard his senior officers give voice to the same misguided fears?

"I have done no such thing, Lieutenant. Unlike the fools who wield the levers of power in Laibok and the Council of Clans, I understand that certain alliances are necessary. Even prudent."

"Prudent?" she said as she gestured toward the armed Tholians who now bracketed her. "*These* guys? I wouldn't turn my back on them if I were you."

"You're not seeing the bigger picture here, Lieutenant. You'll understand once we've completed your first . . . interview." Zhrar picked up the skullcap and gestured toward the empty chair in front of his desk. "Now if you'll just have a seat. . . ."

She stood glowering until one of the Tholians prodded her with the barrel of the disruptor it carried.

The Starfleeter suddenly became a blur of motion, delivering a spinning kick that staggered the Tholian nearest to her. Almost simultaneously, her elbow landed with a sickening crunch as it made contact with the other Tholian's helmet. Zhrar smelled the sulfur and felt the warmth that betrayed that at least one of the hotsuits had been compromised. An ululating war cry on her lips, the lieutenant made a flying leap across the office, heading directly for Zhrar.

Midway through her flight, a Tholian disruptor beam caught her squarely in the abdomen. Zhrar took a single evasive step sideways as the young *shen* crashed limply across his desk, scattering his carefully arranged padds.

The sulfur smell was quickly growing intolerable. Zhrar looked at the two Tholians and saw the cracks that lined one of their helmets.

"Get him out of here!" he shouted, hoping that the translator was still in working order. He sighed in relief when one Tholian began hustling the other out of the office. They passed with surprising grace over the sill of the hatchway through which they'd both entered.

Coughing as the life-support fans coped with the office's fouled atmosphere, Zhrar turned his attention back to the young *shen* who lay facedown across his desk. He still had plans for her, and doubted she'd sustained any permanent injury. He rolled her over.

"This could be damned inconvenient," he said with a sigh.

The Starfleeter's thick indigo blood was spattered liberally across his desktop. The charred uniform tunic did little to conceal the deep, head-sized hole that the Tholian weapon had burned into Lieutenant Pava Ek'Noor sh'Aqabaa's midsection.

Her ice-blue eyes were utterly vacant.

INTERLUDE

TUVOK

Our association may be coming to an end very soon, *the Ta'ithan AI said, his orange streamers fluttering weightlessly in the ethereal thoughtscape in which Tuvok's mind drifted. In this place where vision could sing and sound could caress, the Vulcan found himself thoroughly enmeshed in the machine entity's orange thoughts, as well as SecondGen White-Blue's appropriately colored musings.*

Tuvok noticed that One One Six's thoughts had taken on a ponderous, labored quality, as though they'd passed through something dense and viscous before reaching him. He wondered briefly what in the world beyond the meld could have caused this, before setting the question aside. The burden Tuvok was carrying had to take precedence.

Good, *Tuvok thought in response.* This means that the time has come for you to fulfill your end of our bargain.

Commander Tuvok, *White-Blue said,* Maintenance

Module One One Six merely promised to attempt to re-move the machine code from your brain. We still do not know whether or not the procedure will succeed.

Or if I will even survive the attempt, *Tuvok thought. I understand.*

You say that the knowledge you carry is too danger-ous a burden to bear, *the Ta'ithan AI said.*

Yes. Can you remove it?

As I told you, I can make a credible attempt. I will do so, despite my qualms, if the knowledge in question truly is as dangerous as you believe it to be.

It is, *Tuvok said.*

You might wish to reconsider your request, Com-mandertuvok. Purging data from organic brains is not the simple, straightforward procedure it is with created intellects such as myself and White-Blue.

Nevertheless, *Tuvok said.*

I am not certain you fully appreciate the danger, Commander, *White-Blue said.* Your neural structures store information in multiple places and with multiple redundancies. While this quality might give your species an affinity for certain psi phenomena, it is a liability in the present context. Perhaps a fatal liability.

If I leave the ecosculpting data intact, your people might succeed in adapting it for practical use, *One One Six said. Because of the mind-link, the Ta'ithan machine-entity knew about the devastation the Borg had visited upon the Federation.*

It is entirely too dangerous, *Tuvok thought.*

But it could be a boon, *said One One Six.*

And it might also prove as destructive as the Borg, *Tuvok thought.* Or perhaps even worse, since it would be applied with the best intentions. *He knew from firsthand experience that few things could blind peo-ple as effectively as good intentions. Nearly a century ago, when he'd served aboard the* Excelsior *as a junior science officer, a technology very much like the one that was now lodged in his brain had forced him into an untenable ethical quandary. It had caused the deaths of innocent civilians, and had made him the instrument of those deaths.*

You may be walking away from an irreplaceable asset, *the Ta'ithan AI said.* And risking your life unnec-essarily in the process.

You may have a point regarding the risk, *Tuvok thought. He paused to consider what he knew of the events that were transpiring beyond the confines of the three-way mind-meld.*

Tuvok decided that the odds of his coming through the data purge unscathed were no worse than the Arm-strong's *chances of returning the away team safely to* Titan.

Therefore only one logical decision was possible.

Proceed.

One One Six manifested itself in Tuvok's sensorium as swirls of orange, which began moving in an agitated fashion before settling down into an entirely different form.

Tuvok was nonplussed to see the image of his son Elieth regarding him with a look of cool appraisal. Elieth, whom the Borg had slain last year, along with his wife and every other living thing that had called the planet Deneva home.

Can the knowledge to heal the wounds of whole worlds really be more dangerous than the aggressor that caused those wounds?

Tuvok could only stare in silence at the simulacrum of his dead son.

Perhaps your problem, Father, *said the faux Elieth,* is that you possess too little knowledge rather than too much.

Not wanting to allow One One Six to know how Elieth's psychogenically simulated presence was affecting him, Tuvok communicated but a single thought.

Proceed.

With a nod, Elieth raised a hand and reached toward Tuvok's temple.

And Tuvok was surprised to discover that he suddenly understood the ecosculptor technology in its entirety, if only for a fleeting instant.

And as the Ta'ithan machine began to make good on his request, Tuvok released a soundless scream.

Twenty-two

TA'ITH

Vale brought the away team to a halt about half a klick inside the ruined city's crumbling outskirts. Thanks to the gestures of Qontallium, and what appeared to be an indigenous leader, the team's multitudinous Preservationist escorts were brought to an orderly stop as well.

From Vale's present vantage point, the plumes of fire that continued to erupt every few seconds were much easier to see than they had been hours earlier. The horizon-spanning, pulsar-driven aurora that painted the night sky couldn't compete with either the intermittent, random incendiary plumes or with the thunderous, ground-rattling rumble of explosives and showers of rubble that accompanied them.

The first officer watched as a mottled, weather-beaten white tower, probably old beyond all imagining, listed and tipped over like a felled Izarian ash tree. She winced when its groaning, disintegrating pieces crashed across the broad intersection of two ancient, burning boulevards.

"For a ghost town, this place looks an awful lot like a weapons range," Vale said.

"I'd feel safer on a weapons range," Dennisar said.

Dr. Onnta gulped audibly. "My sentiments exactly."

Qontallium surveyed the fireworks with unblinking calm. "How much closer to that do we have to go?"

Vale turned to face the Tuvok-amalgam, who stood beside the antigrav platform that carried White-Blue. "Are we close enough to the Technocore?"

The Tuvok-amalgam blinked in apparent confusion. "The reactors that power the Technocore lie many of your kilometers beneath the Sacred City's surface."

"Great."

"The physical instruments that the Whetu'irawaru Progenitors used to control the Technocore, however, lie much nearer to the Sacred City's surface level."

The first officer nodded. She felt a small surge of hope. "Are you close enough to the Technocore to connect to it from here? Can you dissolve the mind-link now?"

Tuvok's features adopted a thoughtful expression. "One One Six had not contemplated making the attempt before coming within tactile proximity to a Technocore control interface."

We'll be lucky if anything's left of those control interfaces after this fireworks display, Vale thought. "And I hadn't figured on leading a cast of hundreds through a killing field."

As had occurred on several previous occasions, Tuvok's face went slack. He stumbled, prompting Onnta and Qontallium to prop the Vulcan up to keep him from slumping limply to the debris-littered street.

"One One Six must return its essence to the Techno-core as quickly as possible," the Tuvok-amalgam said. The Vulcan's speech was slurred. "It is the only way to reinitialize the self-repair systems. It is the only way to reverse the destruction of the Whetu'irawaru legacy."

"That's why we came here," Vale said. Onnta and Qontallium released Tuvok a moment later, when he seemed strong enough to stand unassisted.

"One One Six has misjudged the capabilities of the Deconstructors," said the Tuvok-amalgam. "The destruction they have wrought is worse than we had believed possible. It appears that One One Six may have no choice other than to attempt to reenter the Technocore from here, without direct physical access to it."

"And dissolve the mind-link in the process," Vale prompted, fighting to keep an edge of desperation out of her voice.

Tuvok's head nodded. Perspiration was gathering on his frowning brow. "Of course."

The Vulcan lapsed into silence. A look of intense concentration, commingled with the pain that might accompany a mortal wound, crossed his ashen face. Vale watched, aware that the Preservationists surrounding the away team had become a rapt and entirely attentive audience. Dr. Onnta looked on anxiously.

Tuvok's eyes snapped open, startling Vale into taking an involuntary step backward.

"One One Six has failed," the Tuvok-amalgam announced, his manner grave and sorrowful. "We have failed."

No, Vale thought. *I'm not giving up yet.*

"Failed?" she said. "Why?"

Tuvok's body assayed an eerily human-looking shrug.

"The reason is not entirely clear to me. Perhaps we are still too far removed physically from the Technocore for One One Six to transfer its consciousness there successfully. Or the Deconstructors may have already damaged the Undercity's technological infrastructure sufficiently to make the transfer impossible under any circumstances."

Vale decided she couldn't afford to let herself believe that. *At least not yet.*

The first officer glanced at her dosimeter, which was built into the front of her rad suit, and immediately saw a third possibility. "Or maybe the Vela Pulsar—the Heart of the Cosmos—is the culprit."

"That is a distinct possibility," said the Tuvok-amalgam. "Especially when the ongoing decline in Ta'ith's magnetosphere is factored in."

Vale pointed at the dosimeter. "I think the pulsar hypothesis has already progressed past the 'distinct possibility' stage."

Tuvok's head nodded. The Vulcan's dark eyes were wide, almost fearful. "Then the urgency of One One Six's need to enter the Technocore to begin bolstering Ta'ith's magnetosphere has greatly increased. If we interpret your instrument correctly, then the surface of Ta'ith will become completely uninhabitable before the next Heartrise."

Vale looked beyond the away team and contemplated the pyrotechnics that were still erupting throughout the dead city's center. She had to get the team safely through it somehow, reach the part of the city that offered subterranean access, and physically interface with this Technocore—in the midst of a conflict that Starfleet was almost certainly forbidden to take part in. And, of course, while there was still time.

If there was still time.

She turned toward the horizon over which the Vela Pulsar would rise in a few short hours. Heartrise, the Ta'ithan AI had called it. Perhaps the last one anyone on this planet would ever live to witness.

Vale tapped her combadge. "Vale to *Armstrong*."

"Waen here, Commander," answered the shuttle-craft's pilot, her voice surprisingly clear, no doubt because Ta'ith itself was now acting as a shield between the Vela Pulsar and the away team's communications equipment.

"Give me a sit rep," Vale said.

"Repairs are under way. The transporter is just north of hopeless, but I wouldn't want to risk using it in this planet's radiation environment anyway, even at night. The rest of the damage looked a lot worse than it really is. Bralik has located accessible deposits of iridium ore and deuterium less than two klicks from here. She and Commander Keru are off investigating those now. Bralik thinks we can process the stuff into usable fuel for the impulse reactor in fairly short order."

"Good. Warp drive status?"

"It's available. We won't be breaking any speed records, though. But it's a moot point. Unless we want to risk egging the pulsar on into even nastier fireworks, we'll have to restrict ourselves to impulse power as long as the Armstrong's *this deep in the pulsar's gravity well."*

Mouthing a silent curse, Vale decided not to cross that bridge until she came to it.

"Is that everything?" she said.

Waen released a fatalistic chuckle before replying. *"Hardly, Commander. The nav system still needs some serious attention, not to mention the shield generator. I'm holding the RCS thrusters together with spit and hope, so we can't afford to make any side trips."*

In other words, Vale thought as she silently translated Waen's Bolian dialect of pilot-speak, *don't expect any aerial rescues. We'll have to hoof it back to the* Armstrong.

She braced herself for additional bad news. "Bottom line, Reedesa: How long until you can get her flying again?"

"Nothing's gone wrong here that we can't handle, Commander. I think this tub will be ready inside of six hours."

"You've got two," Vale said, and then gave the pilot a quick briefing about the lethal nature of the coming dawn—and the necessity of a swift departure once the away team finished its business in the Ta'ithan Technocore.

To Waen's credit, she seemed to take the situation's increased urgency in stride. Vale wondered whether this meant that the bold Bolian pilot was destined to become an old one.

"We'll be ready," Waen said. *"Thanks for the heads-up about the sunrise. I'll make the shield generator our top priority."*

"Good. The radiation is only going to intensify."

"Understood. We'll wait to take off until the away team gets back, Commander."

"No. The *Armstrong* had better be long gone before the surface radiation gets too intense for the shields. If we're not back aboard by then . . . Well, I don't want anybody else dying, waiting around for people who are already dead. Understand?"

This time Waen didn't respond right away. At length, she said, *"Aye, aye, sir. I don't like it, but I get it."*

Vale signed off and immediately opened a separate channel to Ranul Keru, since he was the senior officer in proximity to the *Armstrong*, and reiterated the orders she'd just given Waen.

The first officer knew that she needed to keep her mind clear until after the away team had dealt with the not-so-trifling matter of repairing the Technocore. The ancient machineries that had protected this world from the pulsar for ages represented the only real chance for survival everyone on this world had.

She had to focus on getting into Ta'ith's Sacred Undercity, and on remaining alert for the approach of the natives who were bent on wrecking the place, before the Vela Pulsar returned to Ta'ith's angry, irradiated skies.

Despair clutched at her heart. *It's hopeless.*

Vale tried to keep her face blank when she noticed that Dennisar was watching her intently. "Yes, Chief?"

"I know how bad things look right now, Commander," the huge Orion said softly, his words obviously intended for Vale's ears alone. "But I'm not planning on giving up just yet."

Dennisar's gentle encouragement—or was it a subordinate's subtle reprimand?—caused a half-remembered scrap of wisdom to surface within her mind.

Everything is theoretically impossible, she thought, *until it is done.*

"Nobody here is giving up today," she said, feeling a surge of renewed determination. *"Nobody."*

Twenty-three

U.S.S. TITAN

Will Riker was leaning forward in his command chair when the Andorian commander's humorless face reappeared on the forward bridge viewer.

"It's time, Commander. Per our agreement."

On the screen, Commander Krasizhrar ch'Harnen made a show of squinting at a small metal chronometer he held in his hand. Crafted from a tarnished bronzelike metal, the scuffed and battered timepiece was probably a family heirloom.

"So it is," said the Andorian, closing the timepiece's cover with a percussive snap. *"But I'm afraid there's been a complication."*

Riker cast a sidelong glance at Deanna Troi, who occupied the seat to his immediate left. She looked unsurprised. *Here it comes,* Riker thought. With six of *Titan's* seven Andorian officers safely back on his ship now that their "interviews" aboard the *Therin* were complete, he wondered precisely how Zhrar intended to spin his decision to renege on their arrangement.

"What kind of complication, Commander?" Riker said, rising from his chair.

"It concerns the last of your Andorian personnel to come aboard my vessel," Zhrar said. *"Ensign Birivallah zh'Ruathain, one of your sensor technicians."*

Scowling, Riker said, "I'm familiar with my own crew, Zhrar. The time I agreed to allot for your 'interview' with Vallah is up. What, exactly, is the problem?"

Apparently unfazed by Riker's accusatory tone, the Andorian commander leaned toward his visual pickup, smiling. *"She wishes to remain aboard the* Therin."

Riker glanced at his wife, who answered his enquiring gaze with a "maybe yes, maybe no" gesture, waggling one flattened hand. *Zhrar's not lying,* she thought. *At least not exactly. He's withholding something important, though.*

But whatever kernel of truth might lie at the core of Zhrar's assertion, Riker refused to believe it.

"I'm sure you can understand the awkwardness of my position, Captain," Zhrar continued. *"I can no more ignore a request for asylum than you could."*

Riker didn't believe for a moment that Vallah had asked Zhrar for political asylum. Deanna's tiny smirk and fractional headshake only confirmed the captain's intuition that the demure young Andorian *zhen* sensor tech was the last *Titan* crewmember who would decide to jump ship.

Stepping around Lieutenant Aili Lavena's conn station to get closer to the main viewer, Riker said, "I want to speak with her. I have to make certain she hasn't been coerced, or made any commitments under duress."

"I understand, Captain. Unfortunately, I cannot permit that. She has invoked her right to privacy, and I am constrained by interstellar law, Imperial Guard regulations, and Andorian tradition to respect her decision. Unless she has a change of heart before the Therin *is ready for departure, I'm afraid that all communications with her will be quite impermissible."*

Like hell, Riker thought angrily.

Up on the screen, Zhrar's grin grew broader. And incalculably more dangerous. *"I hope, for your sake, Captain, that you don't intend to become . . . confrontational about this matter."* His antennae had thrust themselves forward aggressively.

You're just itching for an excuse to send a brace of photon torpedoes up my ass, aren't you, Zhrar? Riker thought. Then he recalled one of his favorite aphorisms from Sun Tzu's *Art of War*: "He will triumph who knows when to fight, and when not to fight."

Matching the Andorian commander's smile, Riker said, "Believe me, Commander, a confrontation is the furthest thing from my mind right now. After all, I still get to hang on to nearly all of my Andorian staff. Six out of seven's not bad, right?"

Zhrar's smile fell slightly. His antennae drooped noticeably, which Riker interpreted as disappointment. *"Your reasonableness defies your reputation, Captain. It has been a pleasure dealing with you."*

"Thank you, Commander, and likewise," Riker said. Just as Zhrar seemed to be about to sign off, he interjected, "I do have one small additional request, however."

Zhrar's eyes narrowed slightly, and his antennae withdrew, like fingers making haste to get clear of a hot griddle. *"What do you want?"*

"I know you can't allow Vallah to speak with me. But what about another Andorian?"

"Ah, but members of your crew might eavesdrop on the transmission." Zhrar aimed a long blue finger at Deanna. *"Or your Betazoid might listen in psionically."*

"Then why not take one of my other Andorian crew-members back aboard the *Therin*? That officer could debrief Vallah about her intentions while aboard *your* ship. You'd have no security concerns. The risk would be mine entirely."

Zhrar's resistance appeared to melt away as he considered the ramifications of Riker's proposal. *"I suppose it's even possible that your former ensign will succeed in talking a second Andorian into staying aboard the Therin."*

Riker was tempted to offer a wager on that prospect, but restrained himself. Smiling, he said, "Then I think we understand each other perfectly, Commander Zhrar."

"Very well, Captain Riker," Zhrar said at length. Raising an index finger, he added, *"Though I have one small proviso of my own to add."*

"Name it."

"I get to decide which of Titan*'s remaining six Andorian officers gets to come back aboard the* Therin *to conduct Birivallah zh'Ruathain's debriefing."*

Twenty-four

I.G.W. SHANTHERIN TH'CLANE

Have you finally got the damned thing working again?" Commander Krasizhrar ch'Harnen barked.

With all the trouble the new equipment had been causing since the device's installation, Lieutenant zh'Vhrane's nerves were all but raw. The commander's shouting was the last thing the junior transporter technician needed to hear right now, but she was in no position to say anything about it.

Fortunately for zh'Vhrane, her supervisor stepped in. "Yes, Commander," Lieutenant Commander sh'Agri said as she made additional checks of the console readings. "But the system is in a very precarious state at the moment. The pulsar's emissions—"

"See to it that the system remains functional," said the *Therin*'s master, interrupting sh'Agri as though she hadn't even been speaking. "Then bring our guest from *Titan* aboard. Same procedure as before."

As zh'Vhrane assisted sh'Agri in making a final

check of the settings, a pair of armed security officers, a *thaan* and a *chan*, entered the room. Their weapons at the ready, they approached the transporter dais as sh'Agri entered the final command. A not-unpleasant chimelike sound accompanied the delicate curtain of light that shimmered between the beam emitters on the ceiling and the pads that glowed on the platform. sh'Agri watched anxiously as a lone figure began taking shape on the dais.

That was when the pattern buffer alarm sounded.

When zh'Vhrane saw how profound the malfunction appeared to be, she began to despair, anticipating one of the commander's renowned fits of rage.

Krasizhrar ch'Harnen heaved a sigh of relief when he saw that the Starfleet lieutenant's injuries were less severe than he had feared. The young *shen* who lay on the diagnostic table before Dr. Vras groaned as she began to come around, blinking rapidly in the infirmary's harsh white light.

"Pava Ek'Noor sh'Aqabaa," Zhrar said as he offered her what he hoped was his most disarming smile. "Welcome back to the world of the living."

"What happened?" Pava asked groggily as she tried to sit up on the table. Dr. Vras intervened then, gently pushing her back into a recumbent position despite her initial resistance.

"You should rest, Lieutenant," the doctor said quietly. "I must finish examining you. And I may need to keep you under observation for a while."

Still flat on her back, Pava scowled up at the physician. "I have my orders, Doctor." Turning her head back in Zhrar's direction, she added, "I need to debrief Ensign Vallah."

Zhrar nodded. "All in good time, Lieutenant. Listen to the doctor."

"What's the last thing you remember?" Vras asked as he began running a medical scanner along the length of her body, which remained clad in a Starfleet uniform.

"I was beaming over from *Titan*. I saw a flash of light while I was in the matter stream. Next thing I knew, I was here, waking up in your infirmary."

Zhrar nodded. "You are fortunate to have awakened anywhere."

"What happened to me?"

"Transporter malfunction, apparently. The radiation output of that pulsar is causing a great deal of disruption to our equipment. I deeply regret that you were injured as a consequence."

"I'm sure I'd already be breathing vacuum right now if you wanted me dead, Commander," she said as her antennae took on an ironic curl. "Apology accepted. Now, when may I speak to Vallah?"

Zhrar decided that the time to drop his bombshell had arrived. "I have more important duties for you."

Waving the doctor away, the lieutenant struggled up into a half-sitting position. "Did you happen to notice the Starfleet uniform I'm wearing, Zhrar? That should give you a clue that I don't work for the Imperial Guard."

Ignoring her impertinent tone, he said, "The duties to which I refer do not involve the Imperial Guard. I speak of the Andorian Imperial Intelligence Bureau."

Her antennae curved upward in surprise as she reached a fully seated position on the table's edge. Vras hovered nearby, continuing his scans.

"You're part of the All-Sensing Antenna?" she said. "Are you sure you should be telling me this?"

He smiled. "I do not regard you as a security risk, Lieutenant. Nor do I believe you would ever do anything to compromise the interests of your homeworld. Oh, and don't worry about the doctor—he's been read into our operations as well."

She got to her feet, steadying herself by holding the edge of the table. Zhrar found her recuperative powers impressive. It pleased him to have made such a wise choice.

"Now that you've told me, I suppose you have to kill me," she said.

Ignoring her bantering tone, he said, "You could be a tremendous asset to the Bureau, Pava. Join us."

For once the acerbic young officer seemed utterly tongue-tied. So much so that she hardly reacted when Vras pronounced her ready to leave the infirmary. When the small security detachment Zhrar summoned to escort her to her VIP quarters arrived, she appeared content to be led away without any trouble.

Never mistake confusion for consent, he told himself as the infirmary door closed behind her. She was still bound to be a tough *akharrad* to crack.

Turning away from Vras as though the doctor wasn't even present, Zhrar activated the small comm unit on his uniform collar. "Commander ch'Harnen to Lieutenant Commander zh'Vhrane."

"Lieutenant Commander zh'Vhrane here," the young transporter technician answered, a slight quaver in her voice. The syllables that described her new rank still sounded awkward in her mouth, but that was to be expected.

"That last misfire could have cost us dearly," he said.

"My apologies, Commander. The pulsar has been twisting spacetime to an extraordinary degree. The effects of this, coupled with the object's radiation output, can be unpredictable. We were fortunate to keep the system operating in standard mode. Lieutenant Commander sh'Agri and I did everything we cou—"

"We won't speak any further about your predecessor," Zhrar said, interrupting. "She has already paid in full for her failure."

Zhrar thought he heard the young transporter technician gulping. *"Yes, Commander."*

"Which means that *you* are now the one in charge of keeping the system up and running—pulsar or no pulsar. It is vitally important."

"I understand, sir."

"Is the unit back online now?"

"Yes, Commander. But the pulsar—"

He brushed aside what sounded to him like a preemptive excuse for failure. "I expect the device to work flawlessly the next time I need to use the transporter. Do I make myself clear?"

"Yes, Commander."

Twenty-five

TA'ITH

As s/he hastened downward into the fire-dappled darkness, following the slope of the broken, collapsed stone slabs of what had once made up the broad and tidy boulevards of the Fallen Gods, Subsachem Garym's sensory stalks told her that the Technocore's wounded heart had to be near. S/he had the absurd notion that s/he was running a footrace. Thousands of limbs clacked relentlessly behind hir, the echoing footfalls of the Preservationist Thousand—those whom fate had summoned to rescue the precious legacy of the Whetu'irawaru Progenitors from the ignorance that was now attempting so determinedly to immolate it.

But the stakes were far higher than those of any footrace. *And I am leading my people through it,* Garym thought, as realization and incredulity grappled deep within hir thorax. *Perhaps I can justify the faith that Sachem Eid'dyl has placed in me after all.*

Descending into the thickening, smoky gloom,

Garym silently implored the Fallen Gods for the gift of sure-footedness, the ability to avoid the single bad step that would pitch hir out of control, carapace over cephalon, into the Sacred City's stygian bowels.

As yet another wave of Trasher explosions rocked the Undercity, the subsachem reminded hirself that s/he needn't fear falling. Hadn't the precariously balanced Tall Ones just preceded the Thousand down this very slope? Like the rest of the Thousand, Garym had found the Tall Ones' denials of their own divinity unpersuasive. Everyone had seen their arrival from the heavens, and their emergence from the skypod that had brought them to Ta'ith. Surely, the Tall Ones possessed sufficient power to bake the Trashers right in their own exoskeletons.

Garym emerged from the lower end of the upended street into a flat-floored, underground chamber. The faint light of distant fires revealed the ceiling's soaring, cathedral-like height, a rarity in Ta'ithan architecture that could be found only in ancient Whetu'irawaru Holyspaces. The sight nearly overwhelmed the photosensitive tips of her already hyperextended sensory stalks.

Thanks either to the destructive proclivities of the Trashers or to the ravages of time, Garym began to notice gaps in the cavern ceiling, jagged holes in the broken surface streets through which shone the cold white light of the eternal stars. Having no time to pause to contemplate the beauty or indifference of those distant fires, s/he continued forward, leading the Thousand farther into the chamber until hir photopatches began to detect the steadily rising light levels that lay mere bodylengths ahead.

Garym led the Thousand into a shadowy but comparatively well-illuminated adjacent chamber. With a unified gesture of all her leftside limbs, s/he brought the nearest ranks to a halt, and the command passed behind them in a wave until the entire host stood stock-still, waiting expectantly.

The chamber was filled with rank after rank of Deconstructors, who cast long and sinister shadows in the light of the countless fires that rose from innumerable structures, stretching beyond the limits of vision. Unfortunately, the ventilation in this subta'ithan cavern—the heart of the Sacred Undercity's Technocore, Garym divined from hir knowledge of Whetu'irawaru architecture—was sufficient to prevent the Trashers from asphyxiating themselves with their own destructive actions. Instead, they stood facing their Preservationist counterparts. Garym could hear nothing other than the distant dripping of water and the throbbing of hir own circulatory organs.

The subsachem's eyes were drawn immediately to the Trashers' foremost ranks, which had begun encircling the Tall Ones. Despite all their great power, the Tall Ones seemed to be treating the situation with inexplicable passivity.

The Tall Ones need not allow themselves to be overwhelmed by these primitives, Garym thought, stunned by the very notion. *What constrains them? Why have they done nothing to put the Trashers in their place?*

But this could all be part of the Tall Ones' plan, Garym reminded hirself. Of course, the Trashers are beneath their notice. Unworthy, even, of their contempt.

Envisioning the Tall Ones putting down the Trasher Thousand with scant effort, Garym looked forward to taking the Sacred Undercity from its would-be destroyers.

And relinquishing the responsibilities of leadership to their rightful custodian, Sachem Eid'dyl.

As the ring around the Tall Ones grew steadily more impregnable, Garym caught sight of the very leader whose return s/he so craved. The Preservationist sachem was lying flat, hir posture humble and defeated. The Trasher leaders, Sachem Fy'ahn and Subsachem Yrsil, bracketed hir, each leaning on hir battered carapace with half their respective complements of runninglimbs.

And the Tall Ones merely stood before them, doing nothing to redress this indignity. Outrage flared within Garym, making hir chitins uncomfortably warm and dry.

They are attempting to parley, Garym realized with mounting horror and disgust. *Even though such niceties are always wasted on Fy'ahn and hir ilk.*

Garym decided the time had arrived to break the expectant silence that stretched across the vast chamber. Bringing hir foremost sets of speechlimbs together to amplify hir stridulations, s/he said, "Be strong, Sachem Eid'dyl! The Thousand will permit this travesty no longer!"

Eid'dyl shook hirself, as though struggling to rise to a more dignified posture. Surprisingly, Fy'ahn and Yrsil withdrew their limbs, allowing Eid'dyl to stridulate a response.

"Advance no farther, Subsachem Garym," the Preservationist leader said, hir stridulations authoritative despite their unsteadiness. "You must not lead our sect into the folly of war."

"War would not be my first option, Sachem," Garym said.

Moving with a speed that seemed to surprise even the Tall Ones who stood nearby, Fy'ahn used hir forward right limbs to lift a long, flat, hook-shaped blade from the rocky ground. With hir left limbs, s/he hoisted the exhausted Eid'dyl upward, leaving the Preservationist sachem's legs kicking uselessly in the air.

"Then allow me to refine your range of options, Subsachem Garym," Fy'ahn said. Before anyone could react, s/he had inserted the sharpened length of volcanic stone into the vulnerable seam between Eid'dyl's hard carapace and hir soft underbelly. Fy'ahn pulled the blade down and withdrew it, gutting the twitching Eid'dyl like the most inconsequential of glowfish.

Fy'ahn tossed hir slain counterpart aside as one might dispose of a redfruit rind. Brandishing the ichor-stained blade directly at Garym, s/he used several of hir other limbs to stridulate a challenge.

"Congratulations, Sachem Garym! You are now in charge of your sect. Lead your pilgrims safely home, so that we may set about our sacred work."

After sawing out a cry of pain and rage that flayed much of the flesh from hir limbs, Garym charged directly toward Fy'ahn, a thousand outraged souls at hir back.

INTERLUDE

TUVOK

Adrift in the thoughtscape, Tuvok screamed.

I do not understand, *said the AI who still bore the likeness of Elieth.* I am merely doing as you asked, Commandertuvok. I am relieving you of your burden of knowledge.

Perhaps One One Six's doubts were valid, Commander, *White-Blue said.* Perhaps you are better off with the knowledge than without it.

Could they be correct? *Tuvok wondered.*

Insights he had never before experienced had begun to rain down upon him. Not only had he gained a thorough understanding of the burden he carried, but he could also see his way clear to harnessing the ecosculptor's terrible power—safely. With a minimal amount of assistance, he might even construct a prototype ecosculptor.

It might be mere euphoria, some still-reserved and logical part of his mind scolded. On the other hand, these new insights could be genuine. Literally world-changing.

Too late, *said the image of Elieth, whose likeness began to lose cohesion. It liquefied before Tuvok's altered sensorium and drained away, like a lost opportunity.* Once the process has been initiated, stopping it could cause grave neurotrauma.

Tuvok screamed again at the enormity of his loss.

Twenty-six

I.G.W. SHANTHERIN TH'CLANE

*S*ecurity alert!"

Though his duty shift for today wasn't due to begin for another Fesoan hour, curiosity motivated Lieutenant Yanischuran ch'Garis to pick up his mobile comm device, which lay on his bed beside the uniform he'd laid out for himself in his comfortingly spare quarters. He welcomed the interruption; focusing on work during his time off helped to distract him from his grief.

He raised the comm unit to his lips. "Churan to security. What's going on?"

He recognized the voice of the officer of the watch, a bald and good-humored middle-aged *thaan* named Hrab. *"A high-security detainee has just exited from one of the VIP suites without authorization. One of the engineers found the guards in the corridor outside the suite unconscious."*

Churan frowned, his antennae probing forward in puzzlement. "You wouldn't be talking about one of the commander's special guests from *Titan*, would you?" The time when the last of the commander's Starfleet visitors had been due to return to their own vessel had already passed, and the *Therin*'s commander was a renowned stickler when it came to maintaining schedules. *He's practically a Tholian,* Churan thought.

But who other than one of *Titan*'s officers could the escapee have been? Churan knew of no visitors to the *Therin* other than Pava and her six *Titan* crewmates.

Any of the security division's other watch officers probably would have told him to stay out of their business and mind his own tactical section. But Hrab was an old friend of Churan's family, and he was more talkative than was typical of the *Therin*'s security personnel.

"If you happen to be out roaming the corridors, stay alert," Hrab said.

Churan suddenly found himself buoyed by an absurd hope that the subject of the search would turn out to be Pava. He kicked himself immediately for harboring such a foolish delusion. Dran, the medical technician he'd shared breakfast with this morning, had mentioned having just seen Pava's corpse in the pathology lab. Even so, a rumor had started circulating that an Andorian security officer from *Titan* was still aboard the *Therin*, and alive.

Dran hadn't specified what had killed Pava, an omission that had already prompted Churan to hack into Dr. Vras's pathology report, which described a close-range disruptor blast as the proximate cause of death.

Whoever had fired that shot was going to pay dearly.

"I'll keep that in mind," Churan said, determined to do exactly as Hrab had suggested. "And thank you for the warning. Churan out."

Though he dressed in haste, Churan didn't neglect to

bring both his comm unit and his sidearm before stepping out into the deserted corridor. Instinctively making his movements as quiet as possible, he followed the curving hallway around a bend. Here he came to a sudden halt.

A figure in a Starfleet uniform, apparently either a *zhen* or a *shen*, was in front of him. The uniform's wearer appeared to be making a determined effort to hack the keypad beside a locked hatch, doubtless in search of either a hiding place or weaponry.

The Starfleet officer suddenly froze. Even from behind, Churan could see her antennae rising.

Raising his Guard-issue hand phaser, he said, "Pava?"

She put up her hands and turned very slowly until she was facing him. He silently chided himself for his foolishness. This wasn't Pava, of course, or even a *shen*. This one was a *zhen*, and looked to be several years younger than Pava.

"I've seen you before," he said.

"Birivallah zh'Ruathain, Starfleet," she said. "Ensign. Serial number SC-834-9254."

He nodded. "Lieutenant Churan, Imperial Guard. Since I'm the one holding the phaser, I won't bother reciting my serial number."

Her antennae flattened in anger. "I can't say I'm glad to make your scquaintance, Lieutenant."

"Why haven't you returned to *Titan* yet?" he asked.

"Your commanding officer had my combadge confiscated." She pointed to the blank place on her uniform tunic where her communications device should have been. "He evidently doesn't want me leaving any time soon."

"But why?" Churan heard urgent booted footfalls

approaching from both ends of the corridor. He appeared to have delayed her long enough to have attracted the attention of a security detachment.

"Why don't you ask Commander Zhrar?" she said with a belligerent shrug. "I wouldn't mind hearing an answer to that myself."

The security detachment hustled her away before Churan had a chance to pose any of the other questions he was bursting to ask.

The security section seems to have its hands full at the moment, thought Pava, who was seated before the computer terminal in her locked "guest quarters." *There's no better time to hack into a vessel's comm system.*

Drawing on both her Starfleet Academy training and the two-year hitch she'd done in the homeworld fleet prior to that, she conducted a thorough but stealthy search for the programmer's "back door" she knew she could exploit, provided she could find it.

There! She wanted to crow in triumph when the comm system's main control screen appeared and obediently placed itself at her disposal. She wasted no time activating the voice interface.

"Lieutenant Pava Ek'Noor sh'Aqabaa to *Titan*! I request an emergency beam-out. . . ."

Twenty-seven

U.S.S. TITAN

Lieutenant Sariel Rager looked up from the ops panel, her eyes wide with surprise and curiosity. "Captain, I'm picking up a signal from the *Therin*."

"Commander Zhrar?" Riker asked, leaning forward in the command chair as he studied the sleek, aggressive lines of the Imperial Guard cruiser that dominated the central viewer. He wondered what else his Andorian counterpart was about to demand.

Riker glanced at Deanna, who sat beside him wearing an anxious expression. She shook her head silently.

"No, sir," Rager said. "It's not coming over the standard subspace hailing frequency. It's a low-power, low-frequency, narrow-band transmission. Audio only."

Nodding, Riker said, "Let's hear it, Sari."

Rager's long, dusky fingers walked nimbly across her console, filling the bridge sound system with a wash of pulsar-generated static. "Sorry, sir. I'm trying to clean it up."

Within moments a distorted but familiar voice emerged from the background subspace hash. *"—epeat, this is Lieutenant Pava Ek'Noor sh'Aqabaa. Requ—ergency beamout. Titan, do you copy? This—tenant Pava Ek'Noor sh'—"*

"So much for Zhrar's hospitality," Troi said, scowling.

Rising from his seat, the captain moved toward ops, where he hovered anxiously over Rager. "Lieutenant, get a lock on that signal."

"On it, Captain," the lieutenant said as the motions of her fingers accelerated.

Because Rager had been *Titan*'s senior ops officer since the starship's maiden voyage, and had worked alongside Riker on two vessels named *Enterprise* before that, the captain trusted her implicitly. He was content to keep silent and let her do her job.

"Bridge to transporter room two," Rager said into the comm system as she worked. "Bowan, do you have her?"

"Positive lock established, Sari," Lieutenant Bowan Radowski said as he worked the console in transporter room two, his hands moving at an almost frantic speed. *Or at least I've locked on to a piece of her.*

He put that notion aside as something too ugly to contemplate. Though he was still a relatively young man, Radowski had worked as a transporter engineer long enough to have seen some truly horrendous transporter accidents. Nearly all of them had been attributable to operator error.

He double-checked the transporter lock, which quickly began to deteriorate right before his eyes.

Lieutenant Rager's voice flared in his combadge, loudly enough to startle him slightly. *"Bowan, do you have her?"*

"Maybe I spoke too soon," he said. "The transporter lock is marginal."

The captain's voice replaced that of the senior ops officer. *"What exactly do you mean by 'marginal,' Lieutenant?"*

Radowski shook his head. "The lock is right on the line in terms of signal integrity. And with the pulsar blowing particle storms our way and twisting the local spacetime fabric like taffy, I can't guarantee the lock will hold through the entire transport process."

"Lieutenant, we may never get another chance to rescue Pava," said the captain.

Radowski recalled only too vividly what had remained on the transporter pad at Jupiter Station after he'd helped evacuate the meteor-damaged merchant vessel *Black Point*. A repair technician's imperceptible misalignment of a single molecular imaging scanner had transformed eleven out of seventy-two emergency transportees into puddles of sizzling organic goo. Neither the sight nor the smell had ever left him, and both still prompted him to triple-check his work, leaving nothing to chance.

"Bowan, I don't think we have time for a safety margin," Rager said. *"The lock looks stable enough to me."*

Sure, it looks *stable,* Radowski thought. *But how much longer will it stay that way? A cranky transporter can turn on you like a Manarkian sand bat.*

He kept seeing those horrible splatters.

I.G.W. SHANTHERIN TH'CLANE

"I'm detecting transporter activity, Commander," said Ensign th'Shrorin, who was working the command deck's primary sensor console.

Zhrar rose from the chair at the room's center and approached the sensor station. "Where?"

The ensign paused to check the command deck's primary internal sensor display. "One of the VIP guest suites, sir."

Pava, you are even cleverer than I thought, Zhrar thought. Touching the comm device on his collar, he said, "Zhrar to Lieutenant Commander zh'Vhrane."

"zh'Vhrane here, Commander," the newly promoted senior transporter technician replied.

"One of our guests is trying to leave us prematurely," Zhrar said. "Intercept her."

U.S.S. TITAN

It's now or never, Radowski thought.

Though he remained uneasy, the young transporter engineer hoped for the best as he entered the ENERGIZE command. The system immediately began running through its familiar paces. The prompt appearance of the matter stream's shimmering curtain of light, accompanied by a swell of organlike sound, reassured him immediately.

That was precisely when the console's pattern-integrity alarm began howling and flashing. Radowski quickly checked the console's readings.

Though the captain was still up on the bridge, he had obviously seen the alarm. *"What's wrong?"* he asked.

"Trouble, Captain. Something's draining power away from the primary and secondary pattern buffers," Radowski said.

"How serious is it?"

"Uncertain." Even as he spoke, the pattern integrity

indicators went into a chilling state of freefall. "I'm gonna need more power."

"*Do it!*" Riker ordered.

The phase transition coils had begun to shriek like banshees. The light that streamed between the energy emitters on the ceiling and the pads on the transporter stage grew steadily fainter.

I'm losing her.

Pushing aside the horrors of the *Black Point* rescue, Radowski reinitialized the backup pattern buffer, carefully adjusted the annular confinement beam, and reentered the ENERGIZE command.

I.G.W. SHANTHERIN TH'CLANE

"I have a lock," zh'Vhrane announced as she worked the transporter console with trembling hands. *At least for the moment.*

Praying that her career wasn't about to emulate the trajectory of her predecessor's, she activated the beam and hoped for the best.

U.S.S. TITAN

"The *Therin*'s losing power, Captain," Rager said. "Take a look at this curve."

Riker leaned over Rager's console. She was right; the Andorian cruiser's power readings were showing a steep decline.

Either Zhrar's running some very heavy equipment over there, he thought, *or the Andorians just aren't building 'em the way they used to.*

"Any idea what's going on over there?" he asked.

"Sensors are picking up transporter activity on the *Therin*," said Ensign Peya Fell, the Deltan science specialist.

"They must be trying to board us," said Ensign Kuu'iut, the Betelgeusian who was running the tactical station.

"Shields up!" Riker said. "Red Alert!"

Twenty-eight

TA'ITH

So much for talking these *guys down from the ledge,*
Vale thought as she searched in vain for a safe place to
lead the away team.

One moment the hundreds of Preservationists behind
the away team and the just-as-numerous Deconstructors
before them were facing off in strained silence.

A split second later, before Vale, Modan, or the Tuvok-amalgam could communicate in any meaningful
way with either of the mutually antagonistic factions,
the Deconstructor leader had slain what was obviously
a high-ranking Preservationist prisoner.

The ensuing general melee was already escalating beyond any hope of bringing it to a halt any time
soon. Individual Ta'ithans scrambled over one another
to get at their ideological opposites, their innumerable
limbs gouging, puncturing, and rending each other's
chitinous shells with appalling ferocity. Though some
wielded multiple stones and blades simultaneously, the

Ta'ithans' surprisingly strong unaided limbs seemed to be doing the lion's share of the damage.

"At least they're not going after *us*," Dennisar said.

Fear creased Onnta's golden, perspiration-soaked face. "Not *yet*."

Vale reflected that the away team hadn't come here to fight, or even to conduct diplomacy. It still wasn't clear whether they were violating the Prime Directive simply by having come into contact with the natives. But the first officer set that matter aside. The mission's principal objective was to rescue Tuvok and White-Blue. If the Ta'ithan AI with whom they were both still entangled could leverage that objective into an opportunity to repair the planet's subterranean Technocore—and consequently prevent the Vela Pulsar from destroying all life on Ta'ith—then more power to it.

Nodding to Dennisar, Vale said, "We have to get out of here."

"There. We should go there."

The Tuvok-amalgam pointed toward a flat-roofed, burning structure that lay in the middle distance. Stars were visible through a number of irregularly shaped holes that appeared to have been deliberately blasted through the cavern ceiling, which stretched some five meters overhead. A persistent but steadily narrowing gap in the fighting made the building accessible to the away team, but only if they moved quickly.

You know your choices are all crap when a burning building looks like your safest option, Vale thought. But the horrifyingly efficient bloodletting was drawing steadily closer. The banshee shrieks of scraping limbs now came from scant meters away.

"Okay," the exec said. "The burning building it is. Let's move, people!"

Vale took the point, leaving Qontallium and Dennisar to follow along with the antigrav platform that supported both Tuvok and White-Blue. Cethente scuttled along behind the platform with surprising alacrity and grace, followed by Modan, Onnta, and Eviku. Fortunately, the combatants on both sides of the battle were too preoccupied to pursue them.

The squat, rectangular stone structure lay in the shadow of some of the more towerlike constructs that rose around it. It consisted of a single story, and had a footprint roughly equivalent to that of the first small house Vale could remember living in as a child on Izar. The building's roof, however, was almost claustrophobically low, no higher than about one and a half meters.

Of course, Vale thought. *The ancients who built this city must have looked a lot like their descendants.*

Despite the cramped quarters, gaining access to the structure wasn't difficult. The fire seemed confined to whatever combustibles were available. A distant corner of the roof, the one exterior doorway, and most of an adjacent wall had been battered to rubble. Inside the building's single large chamber, an automated fire-suppression system appeared to have remained operational, keeping the interior free of any major conflagration.

In the dim firelight that leaked in through the crumbling walls, Vale saw ranks of vaguely boxy shapes, all of them low to the ground. Pulling her palm beacon from her rad suit's pouch, she illuminated the room and quickly confirmed that it was safe for the rest of the team to follow her inside. The team's collective footfalls stirred up a minor flurry of fine, powdery dust as the group moved forward, everyone hunched over to accommodate the uncomfortably low ceiling.

"Consoles," Eviku said, narrowly beating Vale to the punch. "Instruments, control panels, and monitor screens."

"And a few of them appear to be in excellent shape," Modan said. "Except for all the dust, of course."

Modan knelt beside one of the consoles and used a gloved hand to wipe it clean. A cloud of talcumlike material went aloft, but almost immediately began settling on the floor and some of the adjacent workstations.

Vale released a low whistle. "Outstanding workmanship," she said. "This console is literally as old as the hills, but it looks like we might actually be able to fire it up."

"One One Six's Whetu'irawaru creators designed their technology to interface with a specialized self-repair system," said the Tuvok-amalgam. He moved stiffly toward the surface that Modan had just dusted. Modan moved aside, allowing the Tuvok-amalgam to kneel beside the low console. Dennisar pushed the antigrav platform to his side as though trying to give the quietly blinking White-Blue the best possible vantage point.

"I really hope some ill-tempered native doesn't come in here after us," Modan said. "It would be tough enough to fight off armored creatures when your back *isn't* curled up like a question mark."

Vale watched Tuvok's eyes close as his hands spread across the console's dusty surface.

"What are you doing?" Vale asked.

"Keeping our promise. We will dissolve the link momentarily."

Having become so used to hearing the Ta'ithan AI's

excuses and rationales for not doing precisely that, Vale could hardly believe her ears. In fact, it sounded almost too good to be true.

"Lucky for us we happened to find the right console," she said, wondering to what extent the alien AI understood sarcasm.

"You need not be so surprised, Commandervale." The Tuvok-amalgam spoke in a dreamlike manner, like a psychic medium entering a trance state. "After all, this is the Undercity of the Fallen Gods. The Technocore pervades this level. Whetu'irawaru technology is designed to be holistic. Any portion of it may address any other portion, bypassing anything the Technocore's self-repair systems have neglected to restore to full functionality."

Vale ran a single gloved finger along the edge of a nearby dusty instrument panel, like an admiral visiting on an inspection tour. Despite the relatively pristine condition of much of the dust-caked equipment, "neglected" was a good choice of words. "From the look of things, the self-repair system hasn't worked properly for quite a while," she said.

The Tuvok-amalgam opened the Vulcan's dark eyes and fixed them squarely upon Vale. "You have enabled Undercity Maintenance Module One One Six to remedy that deficiency, Commandervale."

Before Vale could thank the alien AI, wish it luck, or ask it again to share whatever it knew about the eco-sculptor technology *Titan* had discovered at Hranrar, the console beneath Tuvok's hands began to glow and throb with power, prompting a startled cry from Dr. Onnta. An intense low-frequency vibration rattled Vale's teeth. The Vulcan's eyes rolled back until only the whites showed.

Tuvok groaned and collapsed as though his bones

had just been transmuted to water. In her haste to reach him, Vale smacked her head on the low ceiling, her light-weight rad suit's thin hood doing little to protect her.

Fortunately, Dennisar and Onnta acted in concert to prevent Tuvok from making similarly painful contact with the cracked and dusty floor.

Despite the low light and the radiation hoods every-one was still wearing, Vale could see Tuvok's eyes flut-tering open. A moment later she realized that the oscil-lating multicolored lights on White-Blue's exterior had increased in both intensity and blink rate.

"The AI has severed the link," Tuvok said. He al-lowed Onnta and Dennisar to assist him in getting his booted feet beneath him so that he could stand in the most dignified crouch possible, given the present awk-ward circumstances.

Vale thought she saw an inexplicable, transitory ex-pression of sorrow cross the Vulcan's face. Or was it re-gret? The moment passed swiftly, and Tuvok seemed to regain his emotional discipline almost immediately.

"I believe I am . . . myself once again," he said.

"I can confirm this biological unit's individuation," White-Blue said, his familiar quasimechanical voice ringing out for the first time in over two months. "As well as my own."

Onnta waved his medical tricorder across Tuvok's chest. "Vital signs are returning to the normal range."

"And that's not even the best part," Vale said. "No-body's referring to himself in the third person at the mo-ment. Do either of you have any idea how annoying that can get?"

The radiation hood could not conceal Tuvok's raised eyebrow. "My apologies, Commander. I shall endeavor to be less annoying the next time a similar situation arises."

Vale grinned at them both. "It's good to have you back. Both of you."

"But what about the Ta'ithan AI?" Modan asked.

Vale shrugged. "What *about* it?"

"Did it also disengage from the mind-link as successfully as Commander Tuvok and SecondGen White-Blue did?"

"No," Tuvok said quietly.

So profound was Vale's delight in Tuvok's and White-Blue's return to the world of the living that it took a few moments for the meaning of the Vulcan's single syllable to sink in.

"No?" she repeated. The emotional reaction Vale thought Tuvok had just displayed now made perfect sense to her.

"I should rephrase that, for the sake of accuracy," said the Vulcan. "The Ta'ithan machine entity that refers to itself as Undercity Maintenance Module One One Six did indeed exit the mind-link. After that it took up residence within the informational infrastructure of the Technocore."

"So it's 'mission accomplished,' then," Vale said, frowning. "What's the problem?"

"Undercity Maintenance Module One One Six," White-Blue said, "is dying. Its code sequences are rapidly degrading, which is causing its consciousness to lose cohesion."

"Why?" Vale asked.

"Most likely because the physical infrastructure upon which it depends has taken too much damage to permit it to sustain itself," Tuvok said. "It will not have the opportunity to restore the Technocore's self-repair system to operational status."

The implications struck Vale like a hammer blow. "All of this was for nothing? The magnetosphere will keep right on declining until it fails completely?"

"Not only that," Cethente said, speaking via his vocoder, *"The Vela Pulsar's radiation output is continuing to escalate."*

"Correct," White-Blue said.

Tuvok nodded gravely. "Very soon, life will be impossible anywhere on the planet. After the surface ecosphere collapses, nothing more complex than bacteria will be able to survive, perhaps even here in the Undercity."

It came to Vale that Ta'ith and the Ta'ithans were doomed now, no matter what anybody did. Since the *Armstrong* lacked the capacity to evacuate the planet, the away team's only viable option was to withdraw. But the *Armstrong*'s transporter was fried. And a supercharged Vela Pulsar would rise soon, to deal wholesale death from the sky.

Vale knew she had to face the brutal truth: with the possible exception of Dr. Cethente—whose Syrath physiology conferred a natural radiation resistance—the away team was, for all practical purposes, already dead.

Twenty-nine

U.S.S. TITAN

The matter stream collapsed three times, and both the pattern buffer and the annular confinement beam had to be reinitialized. But under Radowski's determined ministrations, the strained squeal of the phase transition coils finally settled down to the familiar smooth timbre of an imminent materialization. The emitters on the ceiling and the pads on the platform glowed, and brilliant energies coruscated in between.

The light and sound faded, leaving Lieutenant Pava standing alone on one of the front transporter pads.

"Do you have her?" Captain Riker asked over Radowski's combadge.

The transporter engineer heaved a sigh of intense relief. "I do indeed, Captain." Grinning at Pava, he added, "Welcome home, Lieutenant."

But instead of acknowledging the greeting, the Andorian suddenly went limp, her eyes rolling up into her head as she collapsed across the dais like a sack of discarded stem bolts.

Radowski smacked his combadge as he ran to the transporter stage, where he noticed that Pava was at least still breathing.

"Transporter room two to sickbay! Medical emergency!"

Thirty

TA'ITH

Vale was finding it increasingly difficult to hide her growing sense of despair. "I need to give Commander Keru the bad news," she said.

"Bad news?" Tuvok asked.

Vale sighed quietly. "There's no point in keeping the *Armstrong* waiting up for us." She looked slowly around the low-roofed control room as she spoke, and saw no overt signs of disagreement among the team members. "I'm going to order them to launch and head back to *Titan* the minute they're ready."

Vale nodded to herself, then gave her combadge a single hard tap.

"Commander," Tuvok said.

Vale hesitated, surprised. Then she touched the combadge once more, closing the channel. "Yes?"

"I suggest we pursue an alternative course of action before you order Commander Keru to leave us behind."

Vale spread her hands. "Any alternative to waiting

around to die in a tiny underground bunker deserves serious consideration. Let's hear it, Mister Tuvok."

"White-Blue and I could attempt another mind-link with Undercity Maintenance Module One One Six," said the Vulcan. "Perhaps we can help it maintain its cohesion long enough to restore the planet's magnetospheric enhancements. It might be the only chance that either we or the Ta'ithans have."

With the exception of Tuvok and the reserved SecondGen White-Blue, everyone present seemed to start speaking at once. Vale could hardly blame them; they had already risked everything to dissolve the mind-link. Vale allowed the chaotic gabble to continue for another ten seconds before she restored order by placing two fingers in her mouth, drawing a deep breath, and then releasing it forcefully enough to emit an all but deafening whistle.

Speaking into the newly created quiet, Vale said, "No, Tuvok."

"Commander," said White-Blue, who hovered on his built-in antigravs about a meter away from the spot where Tuvok was crouching. "We do not presently appear to have a surfeit of alternatives."

Vale nodded. "Why do you think a new mind-link will work?"

"I believe that One One Six's deteriorating condition is due more to the AI's exposure to the pulsar's radiation during our inbound flight than to the physical damage the Deconstructors have inflicted upon the Undercity's technological infrastructure."

Vale considered the fact that One One Six had enhanced the *Armstrong*'s shields somehow during the shuttlecraft's passage to Ta'ith. Who knew how much punishment the entity had absorbed as a result?

"You know the risk you'll be placing yourself in, both of you?"

"Of course, Commander," said White-Blue.

The Vulcan looked at Vale and said, "It is a risk we are willing to take."

The first officer smiled. "Make it so."

With the assistance of Dr. Cethente, Tuvok used a length of ODN cable that Dennisar extracted from the away team's toolkit to establish a hard-wired connection between White-Blue and the same low console through which the Ta'ithan AI had been returned to the Techno-core.

"I am ready," White-Blue said, settling on the anti-grav platform that Qontallium had pushed beside the console.

The Vulcan sat cross-legged before the console, closed his eyes, and spread his hands across its now dust-free surface. Beside him, White-Blue sat motionless; only the accelerating rate at which his external lights were blinking revealed that anything out of the ordinary might be occurring. Dr. Onnta resumed monitoring Tuvok's vital signs from a short but discreet distance away.

Seconds passed while the two remained as they were, still as statues. A full minute went by, and then another. Vale's perception of time slowly began to expand and distort, stretching away into eternity.

Come on, she thought, willing her knee not to bounce in sympathy with her mounting impatience. *Let's see a sign that it's working. Any sign at all will do.* Several more seconds elapsed uneventfully.

The console suddenly crackled with azure static that looked like lightning that had inexplicably slowed down to a crawl. Vale jumped involuntarily as the phenomenon engulfed Tuvok's body, starting with his hands, and simultaneously flashed along the ODN cable into the metal chassis of SecondGen White-Blue, whose exterior lights now blinked too quickly for Vale's eyes to track.

The glow abruptly vanished, leaving White-Blue dark and motionless. Qontallium caught Tuvok's limp body as the Vulcan collapsed backward. Onnta rushed to the Vulcan's side.

Any sign, Vale thought, *except for* that *one.*

Undercity Maintenance Module One One Six despaired.

It had invested the remainder of its dwindling energies into an attempt to restart the stalled machines that dwelled in the bowels of the Technocore.

But the great subta'ithan engines showed no signs of life.

Loss, *it thought with whatever meager cognitive resources it still could muster.* Failure.

Dissolution and death.

It wondered who would watch over the Undercity's Technocore now, and safeguard the people its long dead Whetu'irawaru creators built it to protect.

Who will protect the legacy of the Fallen Gods who created me?

It was then that a voice, a distinct presence other than One One Six's own—no, a pair *of presences—interrupted the ancient AI's dark musings. . . .*

With the enemy closing in all around hir—ending and slaying and generally doing everything to live up to their

Trasher designation—Garym was surprised to find that s/he still lived and drew breath.

It can only be intentional, the newly elevated Preservationist sachem thought. *This has to be Fy'ahn's doing. Before s/he sends me to join the Fallen Gods, s/he desires that I witness as much death and suffering as possible among my own Thousand.*

But before the last of hir hopes fled, the vision patches at the distal ends of Garym's sensory stalks noted a subtle change in the light.

The strangeness made hir shudder. It was too soon for Ta'ith's endless turning to raise the Heart of the Cosmos back into the heavens overhead. And hir olfactory patches detected no additional smoke or fires.

S/he felt a vibration beneath hir feet, a faint but definite presence, warm and reassuring. All around hir and throughout the broken cathedral of the Undercity's imponderable vertical vastness, Garym could feel that hir Thousand had sensed the very same thing as well.

The Whetu'irawaru were intervening in some fashion. The Fallen Gods were returning.

The surviving Keepers were erupting into spontaneous stridulations of delight, hope, and joy.

From the Trashers, Garym heard only fear and rage. From the rising cacophony, s/he heard the increasingly desperate limbsawings of Fy'ahn and Yrsil as they attempted in vain to rally their troops. But the fearful Trasher Hundreds were already irrevocably gripped in a full panic.

Garym knew s/he wouldn't mind if the Trasher sachem and subsachem were both trampled in the all but inevitable stampede. However, s/he decided to concentrate on encouraging those Deconstructors still capable of running to complete their egress from the Sacred City as quickly as possible.

Vale noted that most of the squat room's intact consoles were glowing. Perhaps it was a sign that the Technocore was restoring itself.

But the cataleptic state into which both Tuvok and White-Blue had fallen augured nothing good.

Vale's pulse quickened when she heard Tuvok groan. Taking care not to bump her head again on the low ceiling, she duck-walked to where he lay.

The Vulcan raised his head from the tool bag that had been propping it up. "We must return to the *Armstrong*," he said.

Vale shook her head. "We've already been through this, Commander. We won't reach the *Armstrong* until hours after dawn. The pulsar will kill us all before we make it halfway there."

He sat up with surprising grace. "No, Commander. Our escape has been assured."

Thirty-one

SHUTTLECRAFT *ARMSTRONG*

The Vela Pulsar's angry plumage striated the cloudless, aurora-streaked amber skies. Static electricity danced around the *Armstrong*'s hull, drawing uncomfortably close. Despite the polarization the flight deck's transparent aluminum canopy offered, Waen had to look away. She turned the pilot's seat until she faced Commander Keru and Chief Bralik, who had just entered the cockpit.

The Trill and the Ferengi made an odd pair, tall and wide juxtaposed against short and narrow. But the exhaustion etched into both of their faces was mutual.

Those two look exactly like I feel, Waen thought.

"How are the shields handling the additional radiation load?" Keru asked.

Waen was grateful to have good news to report. "Better than I'd hoped." She gestured with her thumb toward the angry pulsar that blazed behind her. "That temper tantrum should have overwhelmed the shield generator by now, the way the magnetosphere's been declining up until now. In fact, that should have happened about four hours ago. It's almost miraculous. I wish I could explain it."

"Miracles are the costliest purchases of all," Bralik said. Waen wondered if this was one of the geologist's renowned original aphorisms, or if she was reciting one of the Rules of Acquisition.

"Chief?" Keru said.

"We've been lucky," the slight but large-voiced Ferengi woman replied. "The shield generator took a hell of a wallop when we landed, same as a lot of this boat's systems. It's still under a lot of strain, so it won't protect us indefinitely. We're going to have to launch, and soon. And with the shape our RCS thrusters are in, the odds of our flying to Commander Vale, landing, and launching again are about the same as me suddenly sprouting wings and flying out there myself."

Keru nodded. Although Waen was the pilot, the responsibility for giving the order to launch the *Armstrong* was his, at least so long as Commander Vale was occupied elsewhere. "Have you heard anything more from Commander Vale's team?"

Waen shook her head. "Not since dawn." With the Vela Pulsar's full fury striking this hemisphere, the comm system was, for all practical purposes, dead.

"If they've been trying to cross that rocky wasteland since before daybreak," Bralik said sadly, "then there's probably nobody left out there to rescue. Except maybe for Cethente."

"We'll damn well . . . we'll wait for Cethente to show up," Keru snapped.

Bralik held up both hands in a peacemaking gesture.

"Even if Cethente were the only survivor from Vale's team, he wouldn't want the three of us to die."

Waen noticed that Keru was breathing deeply and slowly, his eyes closed as though he were meditating. Apparently once again in control of his temper, he nodded at Bralik and offered her a tired smile. "I know, Bralik."

Waen glanced at the radiation counter and winced. Looking back at Commander Keru, she said, "Shields are starting to redline. We're running out of time."

Keru nodded. Waen had never seen him look any more grave than he did right now. He seemed smaller as well, somehow deflated.

"Reedesa, start going through the preflight checklist."

"That'll take some time, Commander."

"This shuttle is being held together with twine and spare ODN cables, Ensign. Checklist. By the book."

"Yes, sir." As Waen began the laborious process, knowing that the jury-rigged repairs she had done would necessitate finessing more than a few items on the list, she thought, *He's stalling.*

That's hopeless, unless Commander Vale has manufactured a miracle of her own.

The minutes passed as Waen worked methodically through the list. The impulse generator idled, sending a reassuring vibration through the deck and into her boots, along with a barely perceptible and therefore only mildly alarming rattle in the hull. Deciding there was no way she could remedy it, she concentrated instead on feeding the still balky nav system an orbital trajectory calculated to produce the smallest possible amount of dynamic pressure on the *Armstrong*'s battered hull and spaceframe. Once she'd completed that task, she reached for the RCS controls—

—and stopped short, withdrawing her hand from the console. Swiveling to face Keru, who had somehow squeezed into the copilot's chair, Waen reported, "We are 'go' for launch, Commander. Just give the word."

His voice broke slightly. "Go."

Again, Waen reached for the RCS controls. This time she activated them. The hull vibration intensified as the thrusters powered up, but showed no sign of imminent failure. That could change in an instant, of course, especially once the *Armstrong* got off the ground.

"Hold it!" Bralik shouted, her voice rising at least a full octave above its usual mid-contralto register. Waen turned and saw that the Ferengi woman was using a pair of field glasses to observe something through one of the starboard viewports.

Keru scowled at the geologist, who allowed several moments to pass without explanation. "Well?"

Bralik lowered the binoculars. She had to shout to be heard over the rising din of the damaged RCS system. "I see them!"

Waen struggled to damp the thrusters down into idle mode, knowing that if she shut them down altogether she might never get them started again.

Keru touched his console. "Let's see if the starboard-side sensors are still working."

Waen spared a moment to glance to her right, where a small viewer on the copilot's panel displayed a zoomed-in view of several humanoid shapes, along with two whose forms were decidedly nonhuman, approaching from an indeterminate distance. Just behind them, the pilot saw countless squat multilimbed beings, trailed by a billowing dust cloud that suggested many similar creatures were bringing up the rear.

"Looks like they have escorts," she said. The flight deck shimmied and rattled as the RCS thruster protested being forced to reach and maintain such a high idle.

Keru grunted. "Might be escorts. Might be pursuers."

"That'll have to be *your* headache, Ranul," Waen said as she continued working feverishly at her console. "*I'll* worry about keeping this beast on the ground, running, and in one piece until everybody's back on board."

Thirty-two

U.S.S. TITAN

The words came to Pava as though she were listening from the bottom of a deep, icy cavern.

"She's coming around, Doctor," the voice said over a fading background of bizarre shrieks, squeals, and clicks. Though the voice remained distorted, it seemed to be drawing closer to her. Pava couldn't tell whether whatever had produced the alien sounds also lingered nearby, lurking quietly in the dark.

She opened her eyes, only to close them again immediately to keep out the harsh blue light that bombarded her.

"Easy, Lieutenant," another voice said, this one distorted into a strange mixture of growls and hisses as it spoke from within the insufferable brilliance that lay beyond her eyelids. This voice alarmed her even more than the shrieks, squeals, and clicks that had already begun to fade from her memory like the traces of a dream.

Pava lashed out in the direction of the second voice, bringing to bear all the speed and power she could muster. But her body seemed to freeze solid before she could connect with her target. She felt trapped, as incapable of motion as an ice borer born with a faulty thermal-transfer gland.

Opening her eyes was less painful but more disorienting the second time. Only then did she realize that she had thrown a punch straight at the velociraptor-like face of Dr. Shenti Yisec Eres Ree. The physician had caught her fist and now held it. Ree's head nurse, Lieutenant Alyssa Ogawa, stood beside him, her mouth locked into an "O" of surprise. A small swatch of golden fabric hung in disarray around her neck.

"I'm sorry," Pava said. Her throat felt as dry as the frozen deserts of Andor's south pole. "I didn't mean to lash out at anyone."

Ree released Pava's arm, and she settled back onto what she belatedly recognized as one of the diagnostic beds in *Titan*'s sickbay. Pava noticed that her uniform was gone, replaced by a loose-fitting sickbay gown.

Seeing that Pava had regained her senses, Ogawa seemed to relax a little and even offered a tentative smile. "Fortunately, my reflexes are pretty good," she said. "I stepped out of the way."

Ree made a deep, growling sound that Pava hoped was the Pahkwa-thanh equivalent of a chuckle. "I didn't bother, since I don't believe I was ever in any real danger," he said.

Ouch, Pava thought. She wondered if it was standard Starfleet medical practice to wound a patient's pride like that. "Guess I'd better spend more time in the gym sparring with Commander Tuvok and Commander Keru."

The chief medical officer and head nurse exchanged a silent look. Ogawa wore an impassive expression, while the reptiloid's facial features remained as unreadable as always.

"Has there been any word from the *Armstrong* yet?" Pava asked, forcing herself halfway up into a sitting position. "Has the away team completed the mission on Ta'ith?"

"We don't know yet," Ree said. "Commander Pazlar says that the pulsar has completely cut off all comm traffic and sensor contact between *Titan* and the planet."

Not a good sign, Pava thought. She didn't resist when Ogawa gently pushed her back down on the biobed.

"There's still time," the nurse said. She took a moment to straighten the folds of golden material around her neck.

"Don't concern yourself with the away mission, Lieutenant," said the doctor. "You need to concentrate on resting."

"What about Ensign Vallah? Has Zhrar agreed to release her yet?"

Ogawa shook her head. "So far as I know, she's still aboard the *Therin*. Voluntarily, according to Commander Zhrar."

"Alicorne scat," Pava said. She paused to fight off a wave of dizziness. "What's happening to me?"

"You're suffering from the aftereffects of an extremely rough passage through the transporter, Lieutenant. It happened several hours ago."

"If you say so, Doc. My memories are . . . a little foggy."

"That's a common symptom of transporter trauma. Don't worry. The short-term memory gaps you're experiencing now should clear up on their own over the next day or so."

"Transporter trauma." Pava felt her brow furrowing, her antennae weaving and bobbing as her anxiety escalated. "I'm in one piece, aren't I? I mean, please don't tell me the transporter turned me inside out, or anything like that."

Ree's smile looked like a rack of *ushaan-tor* knives. "No, Lieutenant. You merely spent an unusually long time passing through the matter stream. More than three minutes in all, I'm told."

"Huh. I don't remember any of that."

"Interesting. What *do* you remember?"

Pava tried to concentrate, but her eyes were continually drawn to the gold material around Ogawa's neck. She forced herself to look away.

"I was aboard the *Therin*," she said. "I was supposed to meet with Commander Zhrar, to see if he was telling the truth about Vallah's decision to repatriate."

Ree nodded. "And do you recall how the meeting went?"

Pava frowned until she noticed that her forehead ached. She tried to focus, but all that came to mind was a vague recollection of sounds. Alien sounds. Shrieks. Squeals. Clicks.

Once again, the golden cloth at Ogawa's throat caught her eye, dispersing her scant recollection. "That's not regulation," she growled, pointing at the nurse's throat.

It took Ogawa a moment to grasp what Pava was talking about. "Oh, this? It's a scarf. A birthday gift from my son. Noah traded some of his artwork for it during *Titan*'s last visit to the Vomnin space station."

Pava's eyes couldn't avoid it. There had to be another reason for her fascination.

"What's it made of?"

Ogawa beamed as she showed off the scarf. "Tholian silk."

Pava's short-term memory suddenly snapped into place.

Tholian silk.

Tholian hotsuits, fashioned from that silk.

Tholians!

Brushing off Ogawa's efforts to soothe her back down to horizontality, Pava struggled up into a sitting position and swung her legs over the side of the biobed.

"Tell the captain!" she said. "Commander Zhrar has Tholians aboard his ship!"

Thirty-three

SHUTTLECRAFT *ARMSTRONG*

Moving at a dead run, Vale led the team across the rocky plain. The group was still several klicks away from the *Armstrong* when a dust cloud enveloped the shuttle, signaling that the RCS thrusters had fired. For a horrifying moment, she thought everyone would have to watch Ensign Waen take off without them. But instead the shuttlecraft hovered in place, idling while the team hastened toward her. At once, the shuttle's starboard-side hatch opened up to greet them.

Once Vale was satisfied that everyone was aboard, she made her way to the flight deck. Because the roar of the thrusters, obviously distressed from the shuttlecraft's initial crash landing, all but drowned out speech, the first officer used an upraised thumb to give Waen the "go" signal.

By the time Vale finished strapping into the copilot's seat, the *Armstrong* had already mostly completed its rattling, turbulent ascent through the hazy atmosphere. Minutes later, ocher-brown, radiation-pocked Ta'ith was dwindling away behind them, consigned to the infinite dark. The din of the shuttlecraft's launch receded as well, making verbal conversation possible once again.

"How are the shields?" Vale asked.

"Holding up," Waen said. "For the moment, anyway." The pilot examined another indicator and shook her head. "The RCS thrusters have given up the ghost, just like I thought. Setting this beast down in *Titan*'s shuttle-bay could be a little bit iffy."

Shrugging, Vale said, "That's why God created tractor beams, Ensign."

Vale knew that landing would be the very least of their worries. Although the planet's magnetosphere was obviously on the mend—the survival of the away team thus far proved that—the Vela Pulsar remained. They had made it through the pulsar's gauntlet of hard radiation on the way to Ta'ith only because Maintenance Module One One Six had intervened. Now, during the passage back to *Titan*, the crew had to find another way to survive.

There is one *solution,* Vale thought.

"What's the status of the warp drive?" she asked, though she'd already found the answer on her own console.

"Still operational, but I wouldn't advise pushing it," Waen said. "We shouldn't engage the warp drive at all, Commander. Not unless we want to risk doing even more damage to the local spacetime fabric."

"Good point," Vale said as she looked at the console and extrapolated its slow but inexorable rate of decline into the next several hours. *Trouble is, I'm running out of alternatives. The shields can't hold out long enough to keep us safe if we keep to subluminal speeds—not even when you take relativistic effects into account.*

The first officer turned toward the Bolian pilot, whose face was drawn and haggard.

"Reedesa, you look like hell."

Waen laughed. "Getting this tub spaceworthy again kept me a bit busy, Commander. I didn't have time to put my face on."

"Send Tuvok up here. He can copilot for me while I'm flying the left chair."

Waen looked grateful, but also reluctant. "You sure about this, Commander? With everything Commander Tuvok's been through lately, he's got to be in worse shape than either of us."

"He's Vulcan," Vale said. "He can take it. Now *go*."

Vale took the pilot's seat as Tuvok settled down at the copilot's station, apparently in possession of more vigor and poise than anybody had a right to.

"I thought we'd lost you during that last mind-meld, Commander," Vale said. "I'm pleased to see I was wrong."

"As am I," Tuvok said, nodding.

"But White-Blue wasn't as fortunate," she said. The artificial life-form had been silent, its exterior lights dark, ever since it had joined Tuvok in trying to save the Ta'ithan AI from cybernetic oblivion. "Was he?"

Tuvok seemed to need a moment to gather his thoughts. "The Sentry *elected* to allow the essence of his consciousness to remain behind on Ta'ith."

That surprised her. "He *chose* to stay?"

"Yes. White-Blue's essence has fused with that of Undercity Maintenance Module One One Six. Without that fusion, the Ta'ithan AI would have degenerated—catastrophically. Ta'ith's Technocore, along with its magnetospheric enhancements, would have failed completely."

"And we'd all be dead by now," Vale realized.

"We certainly would not have survived for long. Even Cethente would have been hard pressed to endure for an extended period."

"White-Blue sacrificed himself. For us."

"Perhaps. He chose to seize what he regarded as an opportunity to restore a sense of purpose that he had not experienced since he fought alongside his own kind against the spatial anomaly known as the Null. What more productive purpose could any conscious entity aspire to than the protection of an entire world?"

"Whether he meant to sacrifice himself or not," she said, "it might have been for nothing." She showed him the problem posed by the slowly declining strength of the *Armstrong*'s shields.

"We must either allow the Vela Pulsar's radiation to kill us while the *Armstrong* is en route to *Titan*," the Vulcan said as he gazed upward at some undefined point, a thoughtful expression on his usually inscrutable face, "or we endanger an entire sentient species—the very race that White-Blue and One One Six are presently doing everything they can to protect."

"That about sums it up," she said, nodding.

Tuvok's quick apprehension of the problem surprised her not at all. His next action, however, left her utterly flummoxed.

Before Vale could react, Tuvok had used the copilot's console to take control of the warp drive. He began entering what appeared to be very specific warp-field data.

"What are you doing?" she demanded.

Without warning, the *Armstrong* surged into warp.

Thirty-four

U.S.S. TITAN

The lieutenant spoke in a rush, as though afraid she might forget what she wanted to say before she could get it all out.

"Easy, Pava," Riker said as he communicated his concern by casting a quick glance at his wife, who stood at the biobed's opposite side.

"It's all been coming back to me," said the young Andorian, who was sitting on the edge of the bed. "After I came aboard the *Therin*, Zhrar took me captive. While I was there, a pair of Tholians interrogated me."

"What did they want to know?" Riker asked.

Pava's expression grew strained, and her antennae were moving separately in random patterns. Riker interpreted that as a sign of extreme distress.

"I can't remember exactly," she said, "at least not yet."

Riker glanced at Deanna, whose nod confirmed that Pava's experience was real—at least subjectively.

Pava noticed the exchange. "You think I'm crazy."

"Not at all," Deanna said. "But we have to acknowledge the possibility that the transporter trauma you've endured has caused you to hallucinate." She gestured toward Nurse Ogawa, who maintained a dutiful vigil. "Lieutenant Ogawa's Tholian silk scarf might have catalyzed this particular scenario."

Pava's expression grew hard. Her cobalt eyes blazed at Riker. "I know what I experienced, sir. Scan the *Therin* for Tholian biosignatures."

Riker nodded. "Commander Pazlar's already done that. Aside from a few areas that seem to be shielded against sensor scans, nothing unusual has turned up."

"The shielded areas are obviously where the Tholians are," Pava said. "Look, I wouldn't make an accusation like this lightly. It's bad enough that Andor has opted out of the Federation. But throwing in with the Tholians—a founding member of the Typhon Pact—brings shame to every Andorian."

Deanna spoke in her most soothing counseling tones. "Even if Zhrar *has* taken Tholians aboard his ship, it doesn't necessarily mean that Andor is allying itself with the Typhon Pact."

Pava sagged onto the bed. "It probably doesn't matter. Half the Federation is probably ready to believe that Andor is already in the Tholians' pocket."

"Lieutenant, I don't think you really believe that," Riker said with a scowl.

Pava looked abashed. "Sorry, sir. I was out of line."

Riker felt a smile emerging. "Agreed. And I think we can agree on something else as well."

"What's that?" Pava said.

"Zhrar can't be trusted. I have some unfinished business with him. Now get some rest."

Riker headed back to the bridge. Deanna accompanied him and took her place beside him when he seated himself in the command chair.

"What's your plan, Will?" she asked.

He smiled. "My instincts tell me that Zhrar's air of confidence is mostly bluster. Am I wrong?"

"No. But that doesn't make him any less dangerous. Or any less unpredictable."

"'Unpredictable' is something I can do as well as anybody. Lieutenant Rager, hail the *Therin*."

"Aye, sir."

The broad-shouldered *chan* appeared on the central viewer moments later, his expression somewhere between neutral and wary. *"What can I do for you, Captain Riker?"*

Riker stood up and took a single long pace toward Zhrar's image. "Commander Zhrar, you can drop the pretense that Ensign Vallah is anything more than your prisoner. I expect you to return her immediately."

"I see," Zhrar said stonily.

"If you fail to return her, Commander, you will face Federation charges of kidnapping and piracy. Under interstellar law and the statutes of the United Federation of Planets, I would be justified in boarding your vessel."

Zhrar appeared to be taking Riker's none-too-subtle ultimatum under careful consideration. *Will he play it safe?* the captain wondered. *Or will he call my bluff?*

Finally, Zhrar broke the silence. *"Captain Riker, I am not impressed by Federation law, or by your threats."*

Maintaining his most stoic face, Riker said, "That's a mistake, Zhrar."

"This may be a good time to clear the air of any further potential misunderstandings."

"Misunderstandings?"

"My most recent conversation with Ensign Vallah has led me to believe I may have misinterpreted her wishes. Therefore we'll be beaming her over to you in a few of your minutes."

With that, he signed off, leaving an image of the *Therin* splashed across the viewer, the Vela Pulsar feverishly churning in the star-bejeweled background.

Riker heaved a disbelieving sigh. Turning to face his visibly nonplussed wife, he said, "I'm not sure 'unpredictable' is a strong enough word."

Thirty-five

SHUTTLECRAFT *ARMSTRONG*

Vale sat in the pilot's seat, watching in slack-jawed surprise as most of the stars in the *Armstrong*'s path elongated into blue-shifted streaks. Only those points of light that lay nearest to the center of the forward cockpit window resisted the optical effects of the shuttlecraft's leap across the warp barrier. According to the gauge, they were barely making warp one point five—fast enough to outrun all of the Vela Pulsar's considerable radiation output except for the effects that propagated through subspace, such as verterons and other superluminal particles.

Instead of overriding the commands Tuvok had just fed into the nav system and immediately dropping the craft out of warp, Vale turned to face him. She found the Vulcan staring straight ahead into the starscape, as though it mesmerized him.

"Tuvok, I think you'd better start explaining yourself," she said.

"I apologize, Commander," he said, facing her. "I expected to have more control over my actions."

Vale realized that *Titan*'s second officer was intensely surprised by his own behavior. Perhaps even ashamed of it.

"What are you talking about?" she asked.

"One of them placed a suggestion in my mind."

"Who?"

The Vulcan seemed to struggle with his memory. "Either One One Six or White-Blue. In a mind-meld, one tends to lose track of the boundaries of identity. That phenomenon appears to be more pronounced when more than two minds join."

"What was the suggestion?"

"That we engage our warp drive in order to avoid prolonged exposure to the Vela Pulsar's radiation environment—the hazard from which One One Six protected us during our voyage to Ta'ith. Evidently, one of the AIs thought we might sacrifice ourselves in order to avoid further aggravating this region's spacetime distortion problem."

"How did *they* solve the problem of engaging the warp drive?"

"White-Blue foresaw our evacuation difficulties. He provided navigational data and warp-frequency numbers that take the local warp limit into account."

Vale heard a throat clearing behind her. She turned and saw that Dr. Cethente, the Syrath astrophysicist, and Ranul Keru were both standing on the flight deck's threshold.

"Did we just go to warp?" Keru asked.

Cethente's vocoder did a fair approximation of humanoid panic. "*Commander, it's extremely dangerous to travel at warp in such close proximity to the Vela Pulsar.*"

After exchanging a wordless glance with Tuvok, Vale decided she'd probably do best to save most of her explanations for her after-action report. *That one's gonna be a doozy,* she thought.

The first officer favored the Syrath and the Trill with a wide grin. "I think you're just going to have to trust us."

Thirty-six

U.S.S. TITAN

Bowan Radowski had felt jittery ever since his near failure to bring Lieutenant Pava back from the Andorian cruiser in one piece.

Maybe I didn't, he thought as he checked and double-checked the transporter console's readouts. *After all, they had to rush her straight to sickbay.*

A familiar voice interrupted Radowski's unpleasant reverie. *"Bridge to Radowski."*

"Transporter room one," he said. "Radowski here."

"You usually work in transporter room two, Bowan. Why the change?"

"No reason, Cayla. Just got tired of wearing a groove into the deck." *Besides, maybe I'll have better luck with one than I had with two.* Unwelcome visions of Jupiter Station and the *Black Point* evacuees sprang to mind. He swatted them down.

"The Therin *just transmitted Ensign Vallah's beam-over coordinates. I'm sending them to your console now."*

He glanced down and saw the data scrolling up across the targeting scanner display. "Coordinates received. Scanning location."

Transporter trauma, he thought, disgusted with himself. *Who the hell gets struck down with transporter trauma in this day and age?*

An indicator light turned green, signaling a positive result for the targeting scan. "I have a lock," he said, placing his right hand on the controls.

"Bring her home, Bowan," Cayla said in a near whisper, probably to avoid being overheard by others on the bridge.

"Energizing." His hand trembled slightly as he worked the touchpad and dragged his fingers upward across the console's gleaming surface.

A slight humanoid figure shimmered into being amid a long musical tone and a nimbus of light. The process took only a few seconds. Ensign Birivallah zh'Ruathain stood on the transporter stage, apparently none the worse for wear.

Radowski realized he had been holding his breath. *Please don't suddenly fall over,* he thought. *Please.*

The youthful Andorian *zhen* smiled at him from the dais. Her antennae curved upward in a way that made her seem to radiate positive emotions. "After all Zhrar's delays, it's good to be back. Permission to come aboard?"

"Granted," Radowski said, returning the smile.

His combadge spoke up again. *"Riker to transporter room one."*

"Radowski here, Captain. Ensign Vallah is aboard and safe."

"It's a relief to hear that, Lieutenant."

"I'm ready to return to duty, Captain," Vallah said

as she stepped down from the platform and approached the front of the transporter console. "Commander Pazlar must have a huge backlog of pulsar data that needs to be analyzed."

"No doubt," the captain said. *"But report to sickbay first. Pava's beam-over was pretty rough, and I want to make sure you're all right."*

"Right away, Captain," Vallah said, leaving Radowski alone.

"I'll run a diagnostic on the equipment in transporter room two, Captain," he said. "I'd like to know why two similar beam-overs in two identical transporter rooms had such different outcomes."

"I'd like to know the reason for that myself. Track down those gremlins, Lieutenant. Riker out."

Yeah, Radowski thought. *Gremlins.*

He had heard that the captain had grappled with a transporter gremlin of his own, more than twenty years ago. Radowski had never believed the stories. According to the scuttlebutt, a freak transporter accident had duplicated William Riker. After years of isolation on a distant world, the captain's doppelgänger had tried to make a life for himself in Starfleet, but eventually left to join the Maquis in their fight against the Cardassians. The Cardassians threw the duplicate Riker into prison, where he languished until his death, sometime during the Dominion War years.

The tale was unbelievable to Radowski's skeptical sensibilities. He knew such an accident was impossible; the safeguards inherent in the operation of the transtators and Heisenberg compensators that lay at the heart of transporter technology mandated that. The equations of matter-stream mechanics simply didn't allow for such things, any more than they allowed for the possibility of gremlins.

And now the captain wants me to hunt one down, Radowski thought. But he could think of only one plausible culprit: human error.

The kind of error that sends your friends and colleagues to sickbay. Or reduces them to piles of meat sizzling on a transporter pad.

"I trust that everything is now in order," Zhrar said, speaking from the bridge's main viewer.

Despite, Riker thought, *all of your coercion and deceit.*

"Yes, Commander, all of *Titan*'s Andorian personnel have chosen to stay in Starfleet. But if any of them has a change of heart, I'll make sure you're the first to know."

Although Zhrar was about to leave, ostensibly empty-handed, he smiled smugly. *"Thank you, Captain.* Therin *out."*

The main viewer switched to a view of the departing Andorian cruiser, which wasted no time engaging its warp drive. In an instant it had vanished from sight.

Riker turned toward Deanna, who was watching the Andorian ship's departure. "Counselor?"

"For a man who accomplished none of his stated objectives, he came off as oddly triumphant," she said.

"He struck me the same way," Riker said. "Why?"

Obviously frustrated by her inability to answer the question, she shrugged elaborately. "Honestly, I haven't a clue."

Suddenly, the bridge rumbled and shook. Riker moved quickly to the main science station, beside which Melora

Pazlar stood in an awkward posture. Fortunately for the brittle-boned Elaysian, her formfitting contragravity suit had protected her from experiencing a highly injurious fall in the bridge's Earth-normal gravity field.

"What's going on, Melora?" Riker asked as he helped Pazlar steady herself against the console.

A frown crumpled Pazlar's pale, angular brow. "The *Therin*'s departure vector cut across the twists of the Vela Pulsar. It made local spacetime snap like a rubber band. *Titan* experienced it as a gravitational shear. Our inertial dampers are compensating, but that's putting an additional strain on all the spacetime abrasions in the immediate vicinity, creating resonances that will probably get progressively worse."

"Worse by how much?"

The ship shuddered again, and Pazlar reflexively grabbed the console beside her. "I can give you an example from your own homeworld," she said once the bridge had settled down again. "More than four centuries ago, seismic activity caused a suspension bridge to begin vibrating in a sine wave. Instead of damping down and growing progressively weaker, like the vibrations of the strings on a musical instrument, the bridge's vibrations reinforced one another—intensifying until the entire structure collapsed."

"The Tacoma Narrows Bridge in Washington State," Riker said, recalling the ancient images. "Will the vibrations continue to build?"

Pazlar nodded. "In theory, if this swatch of spacetime attracts any more warp traffic, over time it will keep compounding—maybe even enough to knock the planet Ta'ith out of its orbit."

"Recommendation?" the captain asked.

She answered without equivocation or hesitation. "Get *Titan* out of here."

The bridge rocked and rumbled again.

"Agreed," Riker said. "Once we recover the *Armstrong*."

Pazlar consulted the readouts on her console. It was obvious that she didn't find the data encouraging. "Let's hope we have enough time left for—"

"Captain!" Ensign Cayla shouted from the ops station. Her antennae stood straight up, mirroring the excitement in her voice. "I have sensor contact with the *Armstrong*. She's on a direct heading for us. Current distance is less than ten thousand kilometers. The shuttle should be back on board in minutes."

"We should—" Pazlar began.

"Captain?" The young *zhen* suddenly looked perplexed.

"What is it, Ensign?" Riker asked.

"According to the sensors, the *Armstrong* just dropped out of warp. Judging from her subspace wake, she went to warp while deep inside the pulsar's gravity well."

Chris, Riker thought, *I hope you have a damned fine explanation for this.*

Thirty-seven

Because Lieutenant Radowski remained uncertain about how the transporters might or might not cope with the peculiarities of local spacetime, Riker could not risk beaming the away team off the *Armstrong*. Once Deanna had confirmed that no one aboard the battered shuttle-craft was in urgent need of medical attention, Ensign Cayla carefully tractored the craft into shuttlebay one.

After spending so much time in close proximity to the Vela Pulsar, the returning *Armstrong* party was ordered to report to sickbay for a post-mission examination. Considering the amount of radiation to which the away team had been exposed, they couldn't afford to delay the standard course of hyronalin-lectrazine treatments. Ree released each of them, in turn, to rest. He assured them that the captain would wait for the after-action debrief-ings until after everyone was rested.

Riker arrived as Dr. Ree was finishing with his last exams: Christine Vale and Tuvok. The captain looked on in silence as Ree noted how little hard radiation the away team had absorbed.

The metal chassis of SecondGen White-Blue was dark and quiet, as it had been in the immediate aftermath of the Hranrar affair.

Speaking in sibilant growls as his velociraptor head rocked from side to side, Ree said, "I've found no evidence that any member of the away team ever came within a hundred parsecs of the Vela Pulsar." He laid one long, sharp-taloned manus on White-Blue's metal shell, which occupied a nearby biobed. "Even White-Blue's . . . condition does not appear to have a radiogenic cause."

"White-Blue elected to remain behind," Tuvok said. "He is on Ta'ith, assisting in the maintenance of its self-repairing planetary protection system. Or, rather, his essence remains on Ta'ith. No trace of that essence remains within the shell of his body."

"Is he dead?" Will asked.

"Life and death are mutable concepts for an artificially constructed intelligence," Tuvok said. "It may be possible to reconstitute the Sentry's consciousness from archived files. Or perhaps some essential enabling catalyst that presently eludes our understanding will remain missing, rendering such a restoration impossible. There is no way to know in advance of the attempt. However, I am certain that Ensign Torvig will pursue the problem diligently."

"Perhaps my diagnostic equipment needs to be overhauled," Ree said.

"I believe your instruments are in adequate working order, Doctor," said Tuvok. The captain noted with some surprise that Tuvok appeared to be in the worst shape of any organic member of the away team. Whatever he had endured on Ta'ith appeared to have strained even the Vulcan's emotional discipline.

Ree's long, forked tongue probed past his steak knife–sized teeth, demonstrating his curiosity. "You haven't examined my medical instruments, Commander. Why do you believe you know their condition?"

"Because we had assistance in resisting the effects of the Vela Pulsar's particle flux," Tuvok said.

"Onnta's good," Ree said, referring to his Balosneean assistant chief medical officer, who had accompanied the away team to Ta'ith. "But he's not *that* good."

"You are correct, Doctor. I was referring to the Ta'ithan artificial intelligence," Tuvok said. "Maintenance Module One One Six has unique resources at its disposal."

The sickbay's main entrance doors slid open. A brown-robed T'Pel glided into the examination room. She approached her husband, though she stopped just short of touching him; they were a married couple, but they were also Vulcans.

"My husband."

"My wife."

"I am gratified by your safe return."

He nodded. "I, too, am gratified to be back."

Riker suppressed a smile. Despite their calm, controlled words, he could feel the warmth that flowed between them.

"My husband must rest," T'Pel said, addressing everyone present.

Tuvok approached Ree. "If it is permissible, my wife and I would return to our quarters."

Ree assented, and the Vulcan couple bid the senior officers farewell and departed.

Riker moved toward the biobed on which Christine
Vale was sitting. "Let's walk, Chris."

Vale got to her feet. "You want to know why the *Armstrong* went to warp when she was still downsystem."

"I'm sure you had a good reason."

Christine looked relieved at Riker's lack of apparent
anger. "I do have a good reason."

The captain adopted a look of mock surprise. "You
thought I was going to chew you out for breaking the
mission protocol?"

"The thought *had* crossed my mind, Captain."

"For now, I'd like you to come with me to shuttlebay
one," Riker said as he moved toward the door.

She followed him. "Why?"

With a grin, he said, "So I can chew you out for
scratching up my favorite shuttlecraft."

Vale couldn't help but smile. *Welcome home, Christine.*

For the very first time since her stint aboard *Titan* had
begun, Pava felt truly comfortable taking a seat at the
Blue Table in the main mess hall. In a tradition that dated
back to the starship's maiden voyage nearly three years
ago, the Blue Table was a gathering place for *Titan*'s science specialists. Only rarely had Pava, or anyone else
whose expertise lay in such nonscientific realms as security or tactical, taken a seat here. Her dinner companions
had invited Pava over after seeing her slurping a bowl of
alardi partinna. Ensign Vallah worked as a sensor technician and Lieutenant Commander Shrat specialized in
astrobiology.

"Congratulations on finally getting off Zhrar's ship,"
Pava said, addressing Vallah.

Shrat raised a glass of blue ale, replicated from an old Andorian recipe. "To resisting the heavy hand of Andor," he said before downing nearly half the beverage in a single long quaff.

Pava smiled, her antennae curving upward in a show of approval. "Hear, hear."

"It's nice to know we're all together on this," the middle-aged astrobiologist said.

"That's easy for you to say," Vallah said as she picked idly at the remains of her *skopar* salad. "You're not exactly in the demographic that Zhrar seems most interested in."

Shrat's antennae probed forward. "What are you talking about?"

"No offense, Shrat," Vallah said. "But Andor wants to repatriate people who are still in their reproductive prime."

Shrat's expression darkened, and his antennae flattened backward. He emptied his glass, then set it down a little too loudly. "Who *says* I'm not in my reproductive prime, Ensign?"

"Sorry, Commander," Vallah said. "My mistake."

Shrat rose. "You'll excuse me," he said, then stalked out of the mess hall.

Pava knew her people were renowned for being a passionate race. But that passion sometimes displayed a dark side.

"Don't worry about Shrat," Vallah said. "He's all talk. And he's still upset about having to sign that agreement."

"None of us were happy about it," Pava said. "But Commander Troi is sure it'll only be a temporary thing. Just until the shock of Andor's secession wears off and Command comes to its senses."

"You're probably right." But the young sensor tech's

body belied her upbeat words. Her expression grew distant, and her antennae began oscillating slowly back and forth, conveying distress. The abrupt change in her mood sparked Pava's concern, as well as her curiosity.

"Is something else bothering you, Vallah? Something other than the agreement?"

"It's about *you*, Lieutenant," she said at length. "While we were both aboard the *Therin*. I saw you there."

"Funny," Pava said. "I don't remember that. Other than being the guest of honor at an interrogation, all I remember about my time aboard the *Therin* is that Zhrar was supposed to let me meet with you, and then reneged. He kept me cooling my heels in a locked VIP suite. Until I busted out and contacted *Titan* for an emergency beam-out."

"I had a similar experience—except for the escaping part. And the timeline is wrong."

"Wrong how?"

After a pause to gather her thoughts, Vallah said, "At one point, Zhrar's people were moving me to more secure quarters. I heard something about another one of their 'guests' getting caught trying to escape. As some of Zhrar's security people were hustling me down a corridor, others were marching *you* down the same corridor, but from the opposite direction. You looked right at me as we passed each other."

Pava shrugged. "I don't remember any of that. But I experienced some transporter trauma during my escape. Maybe that caused some short-term memory loss."

Vallah shook her head. "But that wouldn't explain the time discrepancy."

"What time discrepancy?"

"I was the last of the seven of us to beam back from the *Therin*."

Pava nodded. "About ninety minutes after I escaped."

Vallah's antennae had begun moving chaotically, their motions apparently random and independent of one another.

"Then why did I see you aboard the *Therin* about an hour *after* the time of your escape?"

Alone in the comforting confines of the engineering lab, Ensign Torvig Bu-kar-nguv contemplated the inanimate metal shell of his dear friend, SecondGen White-Blue.

The lab's door chime sounded.

"Come," Torvig said without directing a sensory appendage to identify his visitor. He waited until he'd heard the door behind him hiss twice before saying, "Hello, Mordecai."

"Any luck?" Ensign Mordecai Crandall asked.

"No. Perhaps I should try a new approach."

"Maybe you should give yourself time to grieve first."

"Nonsense, Mordecai." Torvig, whose species would have been armless, subsentient ostrich-like creatures without the cybernetic limbs an ancient alien benefactor had bequeathed them, extended three of his metal appendages to the desktop on which White-Blue lay and began gathering up his various tools.

"After Hranrar, you nearly worked yourself to death trying to bring White-Blue back," Crandall said, his gentle tone belying the harsh reality his words carried. "All that work got you precisely nowhere."

"Nonsense," the Choblik repeated as he packed his cloth toolkit, which he slung over the shoulder of his left bionic arm. "I have reserved time in holodeck two, Mordecai. If you wish, you may assist me there in my attempt to restore SecondGen White-Blue's operation and self-awareness by means of the archived backup files stored in the main computer core."

"Tor, do you have any idea how late it is? Give this up. For a few days, at least."

Torvig ignored his human friend's request. Instead, he chose what he regarded as a more socially correct option: he offered his friend a chance to participate in an activity that he knew interested them both.

"If those files permit me to recreate White-Blue in purely holographic form," the Choblik continued, "then we may succeed in transferring his holographic functionality intact into his regular body, here in the engineering lab."

Torvig gazed up expectantly at his friend.

Crandall looked at the tools, and then cast his eyes on the inert metal form on the worktable. After a few moments of contemplation, he produced an exhalation that Torvig recognized as a sigh.

"Why not?" Crandall said, shrugging. "I probably wasn't gonna get to sleep tonight anyway."

Deep in the ship's night, the sudden realization of her husband's absence brought T'Pel instantly awake. Rising from the bed that she and Tuvok shared, the tall, dignified Vulcan woman donned a robe and padded quietly from the bedchamber into the common room.

She saw lighted meditation candles and smelled incense burning in the brazier. Tuvok sat cross-legged at the center of the room, meditating. Though meditation had always been important to Tuvok, he had become excessive in the practice of late.

Ever since the voyage to Ta'ith, she thought.

Excessive or not, Vulcan meditation was something to be respected. Not wishing to disturb her husband, T'Pel turned and began heading back to the bedchamber.

"My wife," he said. "Your company would be welcome."

Hearing him say that pleased her greatly. *Illogical,* T'Pel chided herself.

She sat beside him. "Tuvok, you were less than candid with Captain Riker about the terraforming knowledge you retained from the Hranrar mission."

"Yes. I was. "

Sensing that he needed to communicate much more to her, she reached for his temple. He did not stop her when she broadened the psychic marital bond they shared into a full mind-meld.

Very quickly, she understood what he had declined to share until now. "It is gone. The knowledge from Hranrar."

"Yes." His voice was deep, strained. "Knowledge that might have restored countless worlds across Federation space and beyond. Knowledge that might have put right everything that the Borg took from us."

"No, Tuvok. Not everything."

For Elieth, she thought, *would still number among the dead.*

"I could sense that the knowledge was missing, my husband," T'Pel said after the meld had ended. "But not what became of it."

She decided to say nothing about the feeling of profound regret she now knew he was experiencing.

"When I was subsumed in the triune mind-meld," he

said, "the Ta'ithan artificial intelligence recognized the knowledge for what it was."

"The creation of a long-vanished elder race, like itself."

"Precisely," Tuvok said, sounding pleased by the quickness of her mind. "I told the Ta'ithan AI that the knowledge was a great burden. I asked to be relieved of it."

"And the machine entity accommodated you," T'Pel said.

"But not before making certain I understood what I was giving up. For an instant, I knew how to harness the knowledge. Even how to wield it."

At last T'Pel understood her husband's deep remorse. "You changed your mind. You decided to keep the knowledge, and apply it."

"But by that time it was already too late," he said. "And now it is gone. Squandered.

"Forever."

Thirty-eight

U.S.S. TITAN

CAPTAIN'S LOG, STARDATE 59844.9

After reviewing the circumstances surrounding the decision of Commanders Vale and Tuvok to use the shuttlecraft *Armstrong*'s warp drive in close proximity to the Vela Pulsar, I have concluded that no other alternative was available to them. The assurances they received from the artificial intelligences were accurate. The absence of any significant new space-time upheaval along the shuttle's return trajectory seems to bear this out.

But the abraded condition of spacetime within a half light-year around the Vela Pulsar continues to leave the entire region vulnerable. I have deployed warning beacons throughout the sector. I recommend that Starfleet quarantine this volume of Beta Quadrant space from exposure to warp fields and establish observation facilities and limited patrols to enforce the warp embargo, as available resources allow.

Our subspace communications with Starbase 185 remain severed, due to the Vela Pulsar's interference. However, the *U.S.S. Capitoline*—the vessel Starfleet has sent to conduct *Titan*'s seven Andorian crewmembers to their new, "less sensitive" assignments—has penetrated the static locally. *Titan* will rendezous with her four hours from now.

I will ask the *Capitoline* to pass along Lieutenant Pava's unsubstantiated observation that Tholians are now aboard vessels of the Andorian Imperial Guard.

CAPTAIN'S LOG, PERSONAL ADDENDUM

Roberta Holverson, the *Capitoline*'s CO, is an accomplished captain with a distinguished service record. Bobby's not a blind, by-the-book type. On the other hand, she's been known to criticize my command style as "a little too freewheeling" for her taste. But she's been a good friend ever since we started the Wednesday night poker game while we were serving together aboard the *Hood*. More importantly, she is devoted to the core principles of the Federation and has a highly developed sense of justice. I hope she can help me arrive at a workable solution to this problem, and I look forward to seeing her again.

I only wish the circumstances this time were a little more congenial.

Captain Roberta Holverson made herself comfortable on the low sofa in Will Riker's ready room. Turning from behind his desk to glance out the viewport on the side of the room opposite Holverson, Riker saw the long, sleek exploration vessel his old friend commanded: one of Starfleet's new slipstream-drive-equipped *Vesta*-class starships, the *U.S.S. Capitoline*.

"She's a beauty, Bobby," Riker said.

"*Titan*'s pretty damned yar, too, Will," Holverson said. Brushing a stray wisp of her long auburn hair away from her eyes, she leaned forward on the sofa and met his gaze straight on. "But we're not here to admire each other's ships, are we?"

He nodded. Bobby had never been one to dither. "No, we're not."

"We both know why I'm here. I've been ordered to take all seven of *Titan*'s Andorian officers aboard my vessel for reassignment or repatriation, depending on what each of them wants."

"What they want," Riker said, placing his elbows atop his desk and steepling his hands, "is to continue carrying out their duties, aboard *Titan*."

She raised an eyebrow in an almost Vulcan manner. "All seven of them?"

"All seven of them."

Holverson raised her hand. "Will, we both have our orders."

"I can't in good conscience simply hand them over to you."

"And I can't ignore my orders. You know that. If necessary I will take those officers into custody and hand them over to Starfleet for processing into their new assignments."

"You seem to be stuck between a rock and a hard place."

"I'm stuck between my duty and Will Riker, the most stubborn human being ever to wear the uniform."

Riker couldn't help but grin at that. "Guilty as charged."

Holverson got to her feet. "I don't think you're going to find a nick-of-time, tactically unorthodox solution this time, Will. Sometimes you just have to admit you're facing the *Kobayashi Maru* scenario, and acknowledge that you can't win."

As she was pacing in front of his desk, Riker opted to remain seated, putting himself in the position of judge while she stalked back and forth like a lawyer in a courtroom.

It occurred to him then that he couldn't have found a more apt metaphor for his next move.

"Our problem is really a legal one," he said. "A matter of dueling legal obligations."

Holverson scowled. "Your obligation to your subordinates does not have the same legal weight as Starfleet Command's orders."

"Even if those orders are illegal?"

"That hasn't been demonstrated, and it isn't for you to determine. All you've established is that you have an ethical qualm about the orders."

He shook his head. "I've already admitted that my conscience isn't compatible with these orders. And I think I know you well enough to know they're not compatible with your conscience, either.

"Federation law and centuries of legal precedent agree with us. Starfleet's reassignment order applies only to Federation citizens."

She splayed her hands in exasperation. "What are you talking about? *Titan*'s Andorian officers *are* Federation citizens."

He raised a padd from his desk and offered it to her.

Riker continued as she took the padd and began to read. "All seven of them have formally renounced their Federation citizenship, effective stardate 59845.2."

For a moment he thought her eyes might literally pop out of her head. "But you said none of them wanted to be repatriated to Andor!"

"They don't," Riker said with a grin. "But they also don't want to be forced to become desk jockeys just because their planet of origin has frightened the reactionary fringes of the Federation Council and Starfleet Command."

"But their lack of Federation citizenship—"

Riker galloped right over her. "Has no bearing. Science specialists aren't required to be natives of Federation worlds. Not only that, as noncitizens of the Federation they qualify for diplomatic sanctuary."

He grinned when he noticed that Holverson's mouth was opening and closing, but producing no sound. Her face remained a study in astonishment as she turned her attention back to the document on the padd. Several silent minutes later, she looked up and met his gaze again.

"You know this might not hold up if Starfleet Command decides to litigate it," she said.

He shrugged. "But litigating it could take years. And the legal issues wouldn't stay confined to a Starfleet court-martial. It would become a civil case as well."

"And a *cause célèbre* in the Federation's civilian courts," she said, nodding. "Not to mention the court of public opinion."

"Tell me," he said, "how's *that* for a 'nick-of-time, tactically unorthodox solution'?"

"Well played, Will," she said, raising the padd. "Send me a copy of this?"

"Not a problem."

"I'll need to discuss this with the Judge Advocate General's office, and so will you," the *Capitoline*'s CO continued. "But before I can do that, I'm going to have to move my ship considerably farther from the Vela Pulsar."

"Are you sure you wouldn't prefer to stay here for a while first?" asked Riker. "I have a Deltan science officer serving aboard *Titan*. It's been over a year since Ensign Fell has seen your Deltan medical officer. . . ."

". . . Doctor Lorenaj Tolorea," she said, her brow wrinkling in thought. "A brief stopover would certainly do them both good."

Both captains were aware that for natives of Delta IV, physical intimacy was not only an integral component of their biology, psychology, and culture, it was also far too intense an experience for them to share with members of most other species.

Rising from behind his desk, Riker extended his hand. Holverson gripped it firmly and shook it.

"That went a hell of lot better than I expected, Will," she said before disengaging from him and heading for the ready-room door. "I hope you never run out of ways to surprise me."

"You and me both," he said quietly once he was alone.

Epilogue

I.G.W. SHANTHERIN TH'CLANE

Pava Ek'Noor sh'Aqabaa paced back and forth like a caged *preshava*. The guest quarters that served as her prison were comfortable, but they lacked any tools she might use to make another serious escape attempt. Since the last time she'd briefly managed to break out of confinement, her room no longer even contained so much as an unlinked computer terminal.

Zhrar's good at what he does, she thought. *And he's not going to take any more chances with me.*

But he had to have a weakness. There had to be something that he'd overlooked, some opportunity she could exploit—

The chamber's only door hissed open, interrupting her musings. Acting on instinct, she flung herself at the figure she saw entering and aimed a spinning kick straight at its chest.

They landed in a heap on the floor before recognition abruptly halted her movements. "Churan!"

He looked more pleased than surprised. "I wasn't sure it was true," he said, wheezing. "But nobody else I know can kick that hard. It really *is* you. You're not dead."

Pava's brow folded into hard lines, her antennae thrusting forward like a pair of hungry frost vipers as she straddled him to prevent him from rising. "You'd better start making sense, or I'm going to get up and start kicking again."

"You were dead," he said as he tried to push himself up into a sitting position. "Dead and autopsied. I saw the . . . body."

She shoved him back down, hard enough to knock most of the wind out of him. "That's ridiculous, Churan. Here I am, and I'm obviously still in one piece."

He nodded. "And I think I know why. It's Commander Zhrar and his Tholian guests."

"I know all about the Tholians. Zhrar has introduced us. What about them?"

"They've been working with Zhrar on a secret project. Something I think might be intended to address Andor's population crash."

"What are you talking about? Genetic engineering?"

Shaking his head, he said, "It involves the transporter."

Pava winced. She was still recovering from the transporter tug-of-war to which she'd been subjected during her most recent escape attempt. Because her luxury jail contained no chronos, she was already losing track of how much time had passed since she had hacked into the *Therin*'s communications network in order to send a signal to *Titan*. Pava had gotten as far as making contact with the starship and calling for an emergency beam-out. But in the midst of the transport process, the *Therin*'s transporter had cut into *Titan*'s beam, overriding it and leaving her stranded here.

Deciding that she needed to hear what her erstwhile bondmate had to say, Pava rolled to one side and sprang to her feet. He remained on the floor, evidently convinced he'd be safer there.

"Do you remember the last time we saw each other?" he asked.

That seemed like a strange question. "Sure I do. Back on Andor, before I left for the Academy."

"No," he said, shaking his head. "Not on Andor. Aboard the *Therin*. In a room just like this one."

"You're crazy," she said.

"Maybe. But that doesn't change the fact that the last time I saw you alive we were *here*. And the gap in your memory is consistent."

"Consistent with what?"

"With the technology project Zhrar and the Tholians are evidently testing."

She was rapidly tiring of this. "Really?"

"They've worked out a way to get around the indeterminacy balancers."

Indeterminacy balancers, she thought, trying to retrieve the transporter theory she'd studied at Starfleet Academy, and during her earlier service in the homeworld fleet. *That's what a Guard engineer would call a Heisenberg compensator. Why would an Imperial Guard tactical officer concern himself with stuff like that?*

Clearly, there was more to this *chan* than Pava knew. Keeping this realization to herself, she shrugged. "So what?"

"Don't you get it?" he said as he rose unsteadily to his feet. "They've found a way to tap into a transporter beam while it's in operation. It still has its problems, like being disrupted by spacetime distortions and causing transporter trauma. And the power cost is enormous. But that's just engineering. Zhrar has already proved the concept—splitting a live transporter beam and forcing it into a materialization cycle in a second location. The transportee might experience some distress during transit, but he'll reach his destination essentially intact.

"And he'll never need to know that he's been duplicated, right down to the last subatomic particle."

"You *are* crazy."

"Are you certain? Think, Pava. First I see you dead, then I see you alive again. And you remember what happened when *Titan* tried to beam you off the *Therin,* don't you?"

"Zhrar had me intercepted."

Churan shook his head. "His device split your signal."

"Enough!" she shouted. "Listen, you're going to signal *Titan* for me. Arrange another beam-out, before Zhrar can intervene again."

"I can't do that, Pava," he said.

She spun and kicked him again, slamming him against one of the walls this time. Churan sagged to the floor. "I would if I could," he gasped. "But we're nowhere near *Titan.*"

"So Zhrar's taken the *Therin* to warp. Captain Riker will come after him. My crewmates will rescue me."

"No, Pava. They won't."

A disturbing memory seized her. She had been caught in two transporter beams. Each had a different destination for her. For several seconds, and perhaps longer, she had been in two places simultaneously: back aboard *Titan* and here, aboard the *Therin.*

A terrible realization began to dawn on her.

"Why?" she whispered. "Why won't they come after me?"

"Because as far as anyone aboard *Titan* knows, you aren't missing. And neither are your six Andorian crewmates."

Pava felt her jaw fall open. "What?"

Churan got up, smoothing the wrinkles in his dark blue uniform as he rose. "You don't think you're the only one Zhrar has done this to, do you?"

Pava Ek'Noor sh'Aqabaa didn't answer. Instead, she began a slow, headlong tumble into despair's hungry maw.

Appendix

Lieutenant Commander Shenti Yisec Eres Ree
(Pahkwa-thanh male) chief medical officer

Lieutenant Commander Ranul Keru
(unjoined Trill male) chief of security

Lieutenant Commander Melora Pazlar
(Elaysian female) senior science officer

Lieutenant Sariel Rager
(human female) senior operations officer

Lieutenant Commander Tamen Gibruch
(Chandir male) gamma-shift bridge commander

Lieutenant Commander Onnta
(Balosneean male) assistant chief medical officer

Lieutenant Alyssa Ogawa
(human female) head nurse

Lieutenant Eviku Ndashelef
(Arkenite male) xenobiologist

Lieutenant Huilan Sen'kara
(S'ti'ach male) junior counselor

Pral glasch Haaj
(Tellarite male) junior counselor

Lieutenant Pava Ek'Noor sh'Aqabaa
(Andorian *shen* [nominally female]) security officer/
gamma-shift tactical officer

Ensign Birivallah zh'Ruathain (Vallah)
(Andorian *zhen* [nominally female]) sensor technician

Lieutenant Aristherun zh'Vezhdar (Aris)
(Andorian *zhen* [nominally female]) junior
astrophysicist

**Lieutenant Commander Rogrenshraton ch'Agrana
(Shrat)**
(Andorian *chan* [nominally male]) astrobiologist

Lieutenant Artunkevisthan ch'Kul'tan (Kevis)
(Andorian *chan* [nominally male]) gamma-shift conn
officer

Ensign Tozherenshras th'Chesrath (Zheren)
(Andorian *thaan* [nominally male]) junior engineer

Ensign Zhoriscayla zh'Tlanek (Cayla)
(Andorian *zhen* [nominally female]) junior ops officer/
beta-shift bridge officer

Lieutenant Aili Lavena
(Pacifican "Selkie" female) senior flight controller

Ensign Torvig Bu-kar-nguv
(Choblik male) engineer

Ensign Mordecai Crandall
(human male) engineer

Lieutenant Bowan Radowski
(human male) transporter engineer

Ensign Peya Fell
(Deltan female) relief science officer

Dr. Se'al Cethente Qas
(Syrath male) senior astrophysicist

Ensign Y'lira Modan
(Selenean female) cryptolinguist

Ensign Zurin Dakal
(Cardassian male) sensor analyst

Ensign Evesh
(Tellarite female) sensor technician

Ensign Reedesa Waen
(Bolian female) shuttle pilot

Ensign Kuu'iut
(Betelgeusian male) relief tactical officer

Chief Petty Officer Dennisar
(Orion male) security officer

Lieutenant Qur Qontallium
(Gnalish Fejimaera male) security officer

Chief Petty Officer Bralik
(Ferengi female) geologist

T'Pel
(Vulcan female) civilian child-care specialist

Noah Powell
(human male) eleven-year-old child, son of Alyssa
Ogawa

Ensign Olivia Bolaji
(human female) shuttle pilot

Chief Axel Bolaji
(human male) gamma-shift flight controller

Totyarguil Bolaji
(human male) toddler, son of Axel and Olivia Bolaji

Natasha Miana Riker-Troi
(human-Betazoid female) infant, daughter of Will Riker
and Deanna Troi

K'chak'!'op
(Pak'shree female) computer specialist, known
informally as "Chaka"

SecondGen White-Blue
(artificial intelligence) guest (formerly deceased,
present status ambiguous)

Acknowledgments

In getting this volume from concept to the printed page, the author owes recognition and thanks to a veritable multitude, including (but not necessarily limited to): Margaret Clark and Ed Schlesinger, for making this latest literary voyage possible; Marco Palmieri, for laying the keel of the *U.S.S. Titan* in the first place, thereby allowing *Taking Wing* to take wing; Andy Mangels, who coauthored the first two *Titan* novels (*Taking Wing* and *The Red King*) with me, and all the *Titan* novelists who have followed (Christopher L. Bennett, Geoffrey Thorne, James Swallow, and David Mack, whose astonishing *Destiny* trilogy has shaken the *Star Trek* universe to its foundations, thereby making this volume and its predecessor possible, and whose earlier TNG novels *A Time to Kill* and *A Time to Heal* were instrumental in getting Will Riker's captaincy off the ground); Marco Palmieri (again) and Keith R.A. DeCandido, for coming up with the Typhon Pact in *A Singular Destiny*; Christopher L.

Bennett (again), who dropped *Titan* in such an interesting region of real space (*Orion's Hounds*; *Over a Torrent Sea*), whose *Ex Machina* introduced the namesake character (*Therin*) of the Andorian Imperial Guard Warship *Shantherin th'Clane*, and whose *Watching the Clock* launched the *Starship Capitoline*, introduced the Vomnin Confederacy, and gave the Seleneans their nifty five-lobed brains; Doug Drexler, whose Andorian battle cruiser images (drexfiles.wordpress.com/2009/07/16/andorian-cruiser/) inspired my descriptions of the *I.G.W. Shantherin th'Clane*; Chris Cooper, Chris Renaud, and Andy Lanning, who introduced Pava Ek'Noor sh'Aqabaa (née Pava Ek'Noor Aqabaa) in the pages of Marvel Comics' *Starfleet Academy* series; the Chandra X-Ray Observatory team, for the awe-inspiring images of the Vela Pulsar (a very real cosmic object) I kept looking at while writing this volume; the keepers of the Vulcan language database (www.starbase-10.de/vld/), which came in handy while I was crafting certain Tuvok-and-T'Pel scenes; Ben Robinson and Marcus Riley, whose *U.S.S. Enterprise Owners' Workshop Manual* provided some much-needed technological verisimilitude, in the form of transporter-related technical jargon; Rick Sternbach, Michael Okuda, Herman Zimmerman, and Doug Drexler (again), who between them generated the transporter-related technospeak I gleaned from *The Star Trek: The Next Generation Technical Manual* and *The Star Trek: Deep Space Nine Technical Manual*; *Star Trek: Enterprise* writer-producers Chris Black and Mike Sussman, the former having used the latter's name for the Vulcan martial art of *Suus Mahna*; Heather Jarman, whose *Worlds of Deep Space 9 Volume One: Andor—Paradigm* introduced such pieces of Andoriana as the *shaysha* beetle, the Andorian *hari* root, and the Vezhdar Plain; S. John Ross, Steven S. Long, and Adam Dickstein, whose *Star Trek: The Customizable Card Game* RPG module *The Andorians: Among the Clans* (Last Unicorn Games) introduced the Andorian *Graalek* script used aboard the aforementioned *Therin*, as well as the amphibious, monkeylike *preshava*; Diane Duane, whose novel *The Wounded Sky* introduced the six-legged Andorian animal known as the alicorne; Decipher Games, whose *Star Trek: The Roleplaying Game* module *Aliens* first mentioned the Andorian Council of Clans; Shane Johnson, whose *Star Trek: The Worlds of the Federation* revealed that Christine Vale's native planet Izar orbits the star Epsilon Boötis and introduced the Andorian foods *akharrad*, *alardi partinna*, and *skopar*; Herbert Wright and Richard Krzemien, who wrote the screenplay and story (respectively) for the TNG episode "The Last Outpost," from which I drew the exact text of Riker's Sun Tzu quote ("He will triumph who knows when to fight, and when not to fight."); Robert A. Heinlein (1907–1988), whose aphorism about transcending the impossible ("Everything is theoretically impossible, until it is done.") motivated Christine Vale during a dark moment at the end of Chapter Twenty-two; musician and critical thinker George Hrab, whose albums and weekly podcasts are among the greatest things in the universe, and who (sort of) joined the Blue Man Group (only with antennae) in Chapter Twenty-six; the kind and indulgent folks at the New Deal Café (née the Daily Market and Café) and the Bipartisan Café, where much of this volume was written; John Van Citters at CBS Consumer Products, for signing off on all the havoc I have wrought in these pages; the entire *Star Trek* internet community, those tireless wiki-compilers whose multitudinous and serried ranks defy enumeration here; Michael Jan Friedman, for introducing the Gnalish species in his earlier TNG novel *Reunion*; Geoffrey Mandel, for his ever-useful *Star Trek Star Charts*, which kept me from getting lost in the galactic hinterlands on countless occasions; Michael Okuda (again), Denise Okuda, and Debbie Mirek, whose *Star Trek Encyclopedia: A Reference Guide to the Future* (1999 edition) remains indispensable even in this modern age of ubiquitous wikis; John Vornholt, for his explorations of the pitfalls of terraforming technology in his *Genesis Wave* and *Genesis Force* novels; all the performers, show runners, and behind-the-camera talent who brought *Star Trek* to screens large and small over the past four-plus decades; every actor whose character participated in this volume's events, beginning with Jonathan Frakes, Marina Sirtis, and Tim Russ; Gene Roddenberry (1921–1991), for originating the universe in which I get to spend so much time playing; and lastly, though never leastly, my wife, Jenny, and our sons, James and William, for their long-suffering patience and unending inspiration.

About the Author

Michael A. Martin's short fiction has appeared in *The Magazine of Fantasy & Science Fiction*, and he is the author of *Star Trek: Enterprise: The Romulan War— To Brave the Storm*; *Star Trek: Typhon Pact—Seize the Fire*; *Star Trek Online: The Needs of the Many*; and *Star Trek: Enterprise: The Romulan War—Beneath the Raptor's Wing*. He has also coauthored (with Andy Mangels) several *Star Trek* comics for Marvel and Wildstorm as well as numerous other works of *Star Trek* prose fiction, including: *Star Trek: Enterprise—Kobayashi Maru*; *Star Trek: Excelsior—Forged in Fire*; *Star Trek: Enterprise— The Good That Men Do*; the *USA Today* bestseller *Star Trek: Titan—Taking Wing*; *Star Trek: Titan—The Red King*; *Star Trek: Enterprise—Last Full Measure*; the Sy Fy Genre Award–winning *Star Trek: Worlds of Deep Space 9 Volume Two: Trill—Unjoined*; *Star Trek: The Lost Era 2298—The Sundered*; *Star Trek: Deep Space 9 Mission: Gamma Book Three—Cathedral*; *Star Trek:*

The Next Generation Section 31—Rogue; *Star Trek: Starfleet Corps of Engineers* #30 and #31 ("Ishtar Rising" Books 1 and 2, re-presented in *Aftermath*, the eighth volume of the *Star Trek: S.C.E.* paperback series); stories in the *Star Trek: Prophecy and Change*, *Star Trek: Tales of the Dominion War*, and *Star Trek: Tales from the Captain's Table* anthologies; and three novels based on the *Roswell* television series. Other publishers of Martin's work include Atlas Editions (producers of the *Star Trek Universe* subscription card series), Gareth Stevens, Grolier Books, Moonstone Books, the *Oregonian*, Sharpe Reference, Facts On File, *Star Trek* magazine, and Visible Ink Press. He lives with his wife, Jenny, and their sons, James and William, in Portland, Oregon.